"You're at odds with your brothers. The ranch is in debt. The timing couldn't be worse."

"I'm going to kiss you, Reese."

The sparks ignited a shiver. "You say that like I don't have a choice."

"You do. You can tell me no. But I happen to think you'd like me to kiss you, too."

He was obviously skilled at mind reading. Gabe's confidence was annoying. It was also very attractive. Reese felt herself falling for him in a way she hadn't fallen for a man before and, she admitted, was a little scared.

"No," she said, in an attempt to regain control.

He lowered his head. Their mouths were almost, nearly and then barely touching. "I don't believe you."

"What do you want from me?" she whispered.

"Surrender."

ARIZONA
✦ COUNTRY LEGACY ✦

A COWBOY FOR CHRISTMAS

New York Times Bestselling Author
Cathy McDavid

Marin Thomas

Previously published as *Her Holiday Rancher* and
Twins Under the Christmas Tree

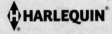

ISBN-13: 978-1-335-20956-6

Recycling programs
for this product may
not exist in your area.

Arizona Country Legacy:
A Cowboy for Christmas
Copyright © 2020 by Harlequin Books S.A.

Her Holiday Rancher
First published in 2015. This edition published in 2020.
Copyright © 2015 by Cathy McDavid

Twins Under the Christmas Tree
First published in 2013. This edition published in 2020.
Copyright © 2013 by Brenda Smith-Beagley

This edition published by arrangement with Harlequin Books S.A.

For questions and comments about the quality of this book,
please contact us at CustomerService@Harlequin.com.

Harlequin Enterprises ULC
22 Adelaide St. West, 40th Floor
Toronto, Ontario M5H 4E3, Canada
www.Harlequin.com

Printed in U.S.A.

Since 2006, *New York Times* bestselling author **Cathy McDavid** has been happily penning contemporary Westerns for Harlequin. Every day, she gets to write about handsome cowboys riding the range or busting a bronc. It's a tough job, but she's willing to make the sacrifice. Cathy shares her Arizona home with her own real-life sweetheart and a trio of odd pets. Her grown twins have left to embark on lives of their own, and she couldn't be prouder of their accomplishments.

Books by Cathy McDavid

Harlequin Western Romance

Mustang Valley

Cowboy for Keeps
Her Holiday Rancher
Come Home, Cowboy
Having the Rancher's Baby
Rescuing the Cowboy
A Baby for the Deputy
The Cowboy's Twin Surprise
The Bull Rider's Valentine

Harlequin Heartwarming

The Sweetheart Ranch

A Cowboy's Christmas Proposal
The Cowboy's Perfect Match

Visit the Author Profile page at Harlequin.com for more titles.

HER HOLIDAY RANCHER

Cathy McDavid

To the two groups who have made me a better writer, given me guidance and unconditional support, and opened up a whole new world for me: my critique group (twelve years strong, can you believe it?) and Valley of the Sun Romance Writers. You are more than my friends, you are pieces of my heart.

Chapter 1

What the small brown mare lacked in size, she more than made up for in muscle and determination. Lowering her head, she put all her weight into her forequarters and plowed up the mountainside. With each powerful step, dirt and small rocks exploded from beneath her hooves, tumbling downward like a miniature landslide.

Gabriel Dempsey rode the mare hard to the top of the rise. Once there, they stopped to rest, both of them breathing hard, their legs trembling. Despite her exertion, the mare would keep going if he asked. She wasn't just young and strong. The blood from generations of wild mustangs ran in her veins, infusing her with a spirit and unbreakable will unmatched by any other breed of horse.

No, it was Gabe who couldn't go on. He was spent. Utterly and completely exhausted. Not from the trail ride, but from the emotional events of the past four days.

Exactly seventeen months and twenty-three days after the doctor's initial prognosis, cancer had taken his father's life.

Today, the family had memorialized him in a service that had brought out half the town of Mustang Valley, along with a hundred other mourners from all over Arizona. Tomorrow Gabe and his family would spread August Dempsey's ashes in the flower garden behind the house.

His father would spend eternity where he, Gabe's grandfather and great-grandfather had lived and toiled their entire lives, on the three-thousand-acre Dos Estrellas Ranch.

Shading his eyes against the glaring afternoon sun, Gabe stared at the ranch nestled in the valley below. From this distance, the house, barns and outbuildings appeared deceptively small, like a painting hanging on a wall. Adding to the illusion were horses in the back pastures and sixteen hundred head of cattle dotting the extensive grazing lands beyond the pastures.

Grief suddenly gripped Gabe's chest like a giant metal vise, colder than the November wind ripping across the rise from the slopes of the nearby McDowell Mountains.

He sat straight in the saddle, refusing to succumb to emotion or show the slightest sign of weakness. Even out here, where there wasn't another living soul for two miles in any direction. The battle facing him at home promised to be a difficult one. This was only the beginning.

Among all the mourners gathered at the ranch to pay their final respects to one of Mustang Valley's greatest citizens were two strangers. Gabe's half brothers. August Dempsey's *legitimate* sons. Rumor had it, they'd come to claim their share of the Dos Estrellas Ranch, left to them by the father they barely knew. Gabe would know for sure tomorrow afternoon at the reading of the will.

If they did inherit, he intended to fight them tooth and nail, regardless if he had a legal right to the ranch or not. He was the son who'd worked side by side with their father for over two decades. The son who was proud of his heritage and treasured it. Who loved the ranch with the same fervor and devotion as any Dempsey before him. He hadn't left as a kid and never returned.

Giving the mare a nudge, Gabe followed the narrow deer trail south as it alternately dipped, climbed and snaked. Not far below him, a line of barbed wire fencing ran parallel to the trail.

The fence separated Dos Estrellas from its nearest neighbor and longtime cattle-ranching rival, the Small Change, though *small* was a misnomer. The ranch was twice the size of Dos Estrellas and these days, owner Theo McGraw ran close to thirty-five hundred head of fat, sassy cattle.

Cancer was a greedy disease and had taken more than Gabe's father. Astronomical medical bills continued to pour in daily, many of which weren't covered by health insurance. With no choice, Gabe and his mother had sold off what they could, depleting Dos Estrellas's resources. It wasn't enough, and the wolves continued to prowl outside their door. Gabe and his half brothers might well wind up fighting over a pile of scraps.

The trail abruptly veered west. Gabe and the mare dropped down into the mouth of a ravine thick with creosote, sage and cacti. Last month's heavy rains had resulted in abundant desert foliage that had survived the recent cold snap and remained a vibrant green.

At the bottom of the ravine, the mare halted. Lifting her head, she smelled the air, her ears pricked forward.

"What do you see, Bonita?"

Gabe had been raised around horses and trusted their instincts, especially those of a mustang born in the wild. Something was amiss.

He sat still and listened, his eyes scanning the uneven horizon. Coyotes and bobcats regularly traveled this ravine, along with the occasional mountain lion. None were an immediate threat. Desert predators usually avoided humans. The mare's survival instincts, however, were powerful, and she might attempt to flee.

She didn't, which Gabe found interesting. Whatever lurked in the bush clearly wasn't a predator. What, then—

A sharp, shrill screech pierced the air followed by a faint cry of distress. Pausing long enough to choose the best course, he set off in the direction of the sounds, taking the steep trail at a brisk trot, the fastest he dare go without endangering himself or Bonita.

At the top of the rise, his heart stopped cold. The entire back half of a horse was submerged in a sinkhole, nearly up to the saddle horn. The horse's head and front legs stuck out of the narrow opening at a painful and impossible angle, almost as if he were standing up. Covered with mud and wide-eyed with fright, the horse flailed helplessly.

On the ground in front of the horse, beyond the reach of the sinkhole, a woman attempted to free him by jerking on the reins and calling out encouragements. Both woman and horse were clearly done in from the struggle. Without help, the horse would eventually die. Every moment counted.

Gabe dug his boot heels into Bonita's sides. The mare didn't hesitate and carried them down the steep slope. More than once she nearly lost her footing, slipping and sliding over the rocky terrain. At the bottom, Gabe tugged hard on the reins, slowing Bonita and bringing her under control.

"Are you okay?" he called to the woman, covering the remaining distance at a lope.

"I need help." She spared him the briefest of glances, paused for a fraction of a second, then went right back to pulling on the reins.

Gabe's brain registered two things simultaneously. First, there was no way in hell she was ever going to save that horse by herself. Maybe no one could. Second, he'd seen the woman a mere four hours earlier at the funeral. She'd sat in the rear pew of the crowded church next to her father, Theo McGraw, Gabe's father's rival.

"Hang on." Gabe jumped off Bonita and, leading the mare, approached Reese McGraw. "Got yourself in a fix here."

"I missed the hole. It was covered with twigs and dead leaves."

Sinkholes weren't uncommon in the desert, especially after heavy rains, though they were generally larger. This particular hazard was deceptively small, measuring three and a half feet at its widest point, and easy to miss.

"It happens," he said matter-of-factly.

"Can you help me get him out?"

"I'll try."

She swallowed, and Gabe noticed the dried streaks on her cheeks. Had she been crying or was the cold wind responsible for her tears?

"Are you hurt?"

"No." She shook her head, and a hank of shoulder-length strawberry blond hair loosened from its clip. As if sensing his gaze, she said, "I lost my hat when I bailed off."

"We'll find it later." The hat didn't matter. He was simply trying to calm her. She'd need all her strength for the ordeal ahead, along with her concentration.

She continued tugging on the reins, which the confused horse fought, jerking his big head to the side rather than using the added momentum to hoist himself out of the hole.

"Take it easy," Gabe said.

"I can't. If I do, he'll sink deeper."

"No, he won't. Trust me." Gabe put up a restraining hand. "Hold steady, but don't pull. Not yet. Wait until I tell you to."

"What are you going to do?" Worry filled her eyes.

Gabe hadn't noticed their vibrant green color before. Then again, he generally avoided Reese. "Well, if we can't drag him out, I'll ride for help."

Neither of them voiced aloud what they were doubtless thinking; there may not be time for that. Who knew the depth of the hole? One wrong move, and the horse's own weight could drag him under the mud.

Gabe decided he'd seen enough death for one week. If it was at all humanly possible, he would save this horse.

"Focus on keeping his head up," he told Reese.

Gabe lined up Bonita next to her. The mare obediently stood quiet. Next, he removed the coil of rope from his saddlebag and fastened one end to a metal ring on the right side of his saddle. Letting out rope a foot at a time, he neared the panicked horse.

"Easy now, partner," he cooed. "That's right."

Sides heaving and nostrils flaring, the big paint stared at Gabe. Perhaps his imagination was working overtime, but he swore the horse understood he was trying to help.

He continued talking to the paint as he pondered how best to fasten the rope. Simply around the head wouldn't provide enough leverage. They'd strangle the horse before they rescued him. No way could he feed the rope beneath the horse's chest and behind his front legs, which would be ideal. He'd likely injure his hand in the process.

Gabe decided to run the rope through the girth on either side of the saddle. A tricky operation. One miscalculation and the results could end in disaster. For the horse and Gabe.

"Here goes nothing."

Thankfully, the horse remained quiet while Gabe circled him and attached the rope to both sides, looping it behind the saddle horn for added resistance. It was the best he could do under the circumstances. By the time he finished, sweat had gathered on his forehead and soaked the inside of his shirt.

He removed his cowboy hat and combed his fingers through his damp hair.

"You holding up?" he asked Reese.

"I'm fine."

Right. She looked ready to drop. He gave her credit, though. She wasn't a quitter.

"Then, let's get this horse out."

He patted Bonita's rump. She'd done well so far. What came next would be the real test.

Glancing over his shoulder, he inspected his handiwork one last time. The big paint cooperated by not moving. That, or he was past the point of fighting.

Gabe stood at Bonita's head and gripped the side of

her bridle above the bit. The rope stretched taut from both sides of her saddle to both sides of the paint's.

"Good girl." He rubbed her soft nose. "You can do it."

Bonita nuzzled his hands, not the least bit concerned.

He peered over her back at Reese. "You ready?"

"Yes." She didn't look it. Her hands shook and her face was alarmingly pale.

"Your job is to keep that horse's head up. Bonita and I will do the rest. You understand?"

"Got it."

"Any sign of trouble, you let go. I mean it. Don't put any of us in danger."

She nodded.

"All right then. On the count of three. One, two, three." He clucked to Bonita and yanked on her bridle.

Muscles straining, hide quivering, the mare took one step forward, then a second.

Gabe glanced back at the paint. He'd yet to move, other than stretching his head and neck out as far as they would go.

"Come on, boy. Now or never."

They could only do so much. It was entirely up to the horse. If he didn't haul himself out of the sinkhole and onto solid ground, he would die right where he was.

Bonita didn't quit and, once again, Gabe admired the little mare he'd handpicked from his friend Cara's herd of rehabilitated wild mustangs.

"He's doing it!" Reese hollered.

Gabe looked. True enough, the horse had found the will to save itself. With tremendous effort, he dug his front hooves into the ground and, with the aid of the primitive pulley, climbed out of the deep mud.

"Don't quit on us now." Gabe wasn't sure who he

was talking to. The horse or Bonita or Reese. Did it really matter?

With a final mighty groan, the horse heaved himself out, landing with a grunt on his belly. Gabe let go of Bonita and rushed to the paint, afraid the unsteady horse would slide back into the hole.

One rope in each hand, he pulled with every ounce of his strength. It wasn't enough.

"Help me," he said to Reese.

In a flash, she was there.

"Grab the saddle."

She did, and by some miracle, they dragged the horse two feet before they gave out. The ground beneath the heavy horse held. He lay there, his back legs suspended over the hole and dripping mud, his breathing coming in great gusts.

"Give him a few minutes," Gabe said, flexing his cramped and aching fingers. "Then we'll get him up."

"Okay." Reese stood bent at the waist, her hands braced on her knees.

Gabe, too, rested. How long had this taken? Thirty minutes? An hour? He wasn't sure. Except that, for whatever time it took, he hadn't once thought of his father's death.

"My God, Gabe, you did it! You saved him."

The next instant, Reese slammed into him, her arms circling his neck. He automatically steadied them both by holding on to her.

"Thank you," she said, clinging to him, her face buried in his coat.

He stared at the top of her head, momentarily stunned. He'd touched Reese just one other time in their entire lives. They'd been in high school, at their senior prom.

He'd cradled her while she cried and begged him not to tell anyone she was pregnant.

"You should call the vet right away."

Reese didn't need Gabe to tell her that. Of course she'd call the vet. The second she and General arrived home. But, seeing as Gabe had rescued her father's favorite horse, and she was eternally grateful, she bit her tongue.

"I will."

They'd finally managed to coax General to his feet after a ten-minute respite. The poor gelding was utterly depleted and stood with his head hanging low and his nose to the ground. If it were at all possible to drive a truck and trailer into these rugged hills, she'd do it. Unfortunately, she and General would have to travel by foot.

"Come on." Gabe grabbed hold of his mare's reins and mounted with the grace and ease of someone who rode daily. Once seated, he stared at her expectantly.

"What?" she asked.

He patted the mare's hindquarters. "Climb aboard. Daylight's wasting."

Reese blinked in astonishment. "You're suggesting we ride double?"

"Your horse won't make it thirty feet carrying you."

Did he believe her a nitwit? Just because she'd been away from Mustang Valley for a long time didn't mean she'd forgotten everything she'd ever learned.

"I was planning on walking." She picked her hat off the ground from where it had fallen. "At least to the road."

"I'll take you," he said, as if it were already decided. He removed his left foot from the stirrup.

"You don't have to do this."

"You're tuckered out. And it'll be dark soon."

He was right. The sun had started dropping, along with the temperature. General was wet and starting to shake. If she didn't get him moving soon, he'd catch a chill. Her, too.

"Fine."

He raised one brow as if to remark, "Funny way of saying thanks."

Gabe had always been able to convey enormous emotion using very few words. It was a quality she'd found intriguing from the time they were young. That, and his good looks. His Hispanic heritage, courtesy of his mother, blended beautifully with his Dempsey genes. Dark hair, silver-gray eyes, a strong jaw, tanned complexion and a wide mouth created for kissing.

Not that she had kissed him. Or even thought about it. Okay, not much.

She and Gabe had grown up neighbors, but also rivals, thanks to their fathers' lifelong feud. They'd steered as clear of each other as much as humanly possible in a small community the size of Mustang Valley.

Six months ago, she'd returned after a twelve-year absence. This afternoon was the first time she and Gabe had spoken since the night of their senior prom.

She should, she supposed, thank him for something else besides saving General. He'd kept his promise and said nothing about her pregnancy. If he had, she would have heard. Secrets like hers were too titillating to resist repeating.

Holding General's reins with her right hand, she clasped Gabe's outstretched one with her left. Then, putting her foot in the empty stirrup, she let him assist her onto the mare's back.

"Can she carry the two of us?" she asked, settling in behind Gabe. The mare was on the small side and worn out after her recent efforts.

"She'll manage."

The next moment, they were off. At the mare's first hop over a hole, Reese grabbed Gabe's middle rather than be dumped on the ground. She swore he chuckled beneath his breath. Or it might have been the wind.

"How's he doing?" Gabe asked after a few minutes.

Reese looked behind her at General, and her heart hurt. "He's limping on his right rear leg."

"Will he make it to the road?"

"I think so." Then she could call the house and have someone from the Small Change meet them with a truck and trailer.

If her phone had worked when General fell into the sinkhole, she wouldn't have had to rely on Gabe's help. She'd tried repeatedly to get a signal, but there had been none. She was lucky he'd ridden by. And that it was today rather than tomorrow, after the reading of August Dempsey's will.

"Thank you again," she said. "I owe you."

He simply grunted.

"For a lot more than saving General," she added, wondering if he understood her meaning.

"I'm a man of my word."

Okay, he did understand. "For which I'm very appreciative."

She waited for him to ask her what had happened to the baby. Where she'd gone when she left Mustang Valley. What she'd done. If she'd ever told Blake Nolan, the baby's father.

Gabe remained stoically silent, and she sensed an unmistakable tension coursing through him.

The next mile passed slowly. Every few minutes, Reese checked on General. His limp was getting worse, and she gritted her teeth. How far to the road? She craned her neck in order to look ahead over Gabe's broad shoulder.

In hindsight, she should have waited to take General out until later in the week when she was less busy. But she hated seeing the stout gelding cooped up day after day in his stall, barely ridden.

It wasn't her father's fault. He would exercise General every day if his health permitted. This morning, simply crawling out of bed to attend August Dempsey's funeral had been a challenge. Riding was out of the question.

"It was nice of you to come today," Gabe said, rousing her from her thoughts.

"My father may not have gotten along with yours, but he respected him greatly. We wouldn't have missed the funeral."

Gabe's response was another noncommittal grunt.

The mare stumbled on the steep incline, causing Reese to grip Gabe's waist tighter.

"Maybe I should get off and walk," she suggested, acutely aware of his broad, strong back through the thick fabric of his coat.

"We're almost to the road."

It was the longest fifteen minutes ever. Immediately upon dismounting, she examined General. The poor horse was on the verge of collapsing.

She got on her cell phone, and breathed a sigh of relief when her call connected.

"Hi, Dad." She summarized the situation, including how Gabe had rescued her and General.

"I'm glad you're all right and that Gabe was riding by." Relief filled his voice. "He's a good man."

Reese knew her father's praise was sincere. The rivalry between him and August Dempsey was strictly over business and had nothing to do with character. In another lifetime, under different circumstances, the two might have been friends.

"I'll tell him myself when I see him," her father continued.

"No, Dad. You've had a long day." She turned away from Gabe, who still sat astride the mare, and said in a low voice, "You need your rest. Send Enrico."

"He'll drive, but I'm damn well going with him."

It was the best she could hope for. Her father was a stubborn old fool when he set his mind to something. Like not telling anyone about his Parkinson's. How long could he realistically expect to keep hiding his disease? He was starting to show symptoms, and people were becoming suspicious. Like Enrico, who'd worked for the McGraws since before Reese had left.

"Fine." What choice did she have, short of telling Enrico? And her father would never forgive her for that. He was a proud man. "See you when you get here."

"Be careful, honey."

Reese glanced at Gabe, then chided herself. Of course, her father was referring to General. She had nothing to worry about from Gabe, who was scrutinizing her every move with those compelling eyes of his.

She said goodbye and disconnected the call. Returning to the weary horse, she gave his neck a loving stroke.

Eying Gabe, she said, "You'd better hurry if you want to get home before dark."

"I'll wait until your ride gets here."

"It could be a while."

Truthfully, she had no idea how long her father and Enrico would be. She was simply providing Gabe with an excuse to leave.

"I have time."

"Aren't you hungry?"

He shrugged one shoulder. "The house is filled with food."

She could well imagine. As expected, friends and family had stopped by, dropping off casseroles, covered dishes and baked goods as they paid their respects. Food and funerals seemed to go together.

"Are you?" Gabe asked. "Hungry?"

"A little." Between the service this morning, caring for her father and worrying about tomorrow's reading of the will, she'd missed lunch.

Riding General hadn't been solely to exercise the barn-bound horse. She'd needed a mental vacation in the worst way.

"Mostly I'm cold," she added.

Gabe dismounted, unbuckled the saddlebag and reached inside. A moment later, he produced a yellow rain poncho and a small, rectangular object she couldn't quite make out.

"Here." He approached her, his stride confident and, she had to admit, sexy.

A small thrill wound through her. She blamed the

stressful events of the day. It couldn't possibly be attraction. To Gabe Dempsey? No way.

"Here." He shook out the rain poncho, removed her hat and placed the poncho over her head.

"I don't need—"

"Shut up, Reese." He replaced her hat and fastened the top snap on the poncho, the one beneath her chin. "It'll help keep you warm."

The thrill turned into a flush as his fingers brushed her exposed skin. Who needed a poncho when Gabe's proximity was enough to warm her from the inside?

"O...kay." Please don't let him notice the effect he was having on her.

"Here." He lifted her hand and pressed the object he'd taken from the saddlebag into it. "Enjoy."

She stared at the energy bar. "I can't."

"Why not?"

"Because..."

"You're as stubborn as your father." A smile touched his lips.

She thought it might be his first one in days or even weeks. Nothing could be worse than losing a loved one.

"I'll eat this," she said, "but only if we share."

"You drive a hard bargain, Miss McGraw."

He hadn't seen anything yet. Just wait until they butted heads over his father's estate.

Ripping open the wrapper, she removed the energy bar and broke it in half.

He accepted the piece, his fingers brushing hers. Was it intentional? She wouldn't put it past him. Gabe had always been a ladies' man, starting in high school. She was surprised he'd reached the age of thirty without some woman snapping him up.

Then again, no one had snapped up Reese, either, though she'd come close once. Perhaps Gabe was like her, married to his work.

They didn't speak while they ate. Reese stared up the road. No sign of her father yet. When she was done with her half of the energy bar, she checked again on General, then returned to Gabe, pulling the poncho closer around her.

"Still cold?" Gabe asked.

"A little."

"We could huddle for warmth."

Her eyes widened. "You're kidding."

His smile returned. "I don't bite, Reese."

Sweet heaven, he was gorgeous. "I'm fine." She was not letting Gabe touch her, much less hold her.

Headlights appeared in the distance, about a mile up the road. Reese released a long sigh. As assistant manager of Southern Arizona Bank, it was her job, her duty, to conduct herself professionally and impersonally with the Dempsey family. Huddling with Gabe, even for warmth in extreme weather conditions, wasn't either of those things.

She waved as the truck and trailer neared. "Dad's here. You don't have to stay."

"All right," he said, his tone unreadable, and mounted the mare.

"What about your poncho?"

"Keep it." Gabe tugged on the brim of his cowboy hat. "See you around."

She watched him ride off into the darkness toward Dos Estrellas, barely noticing the truck rumble to a stop behind her.

He'd do more than see her around. Thanks to August Dempsey revising his will six months ago, Reese was about to become a fixture in the Dempsey brothers' lives, and there was nothing they could do to change it.

Chapter 2

"If you'll all please have a seat, we can get started." Hector Fuentes made a sweeping gesture that included everyone in the spacious living room. He lowered himself onto the cowhide upholstered recliner where Gabe's father had once dozed every afternoon while waiting for Raquel Salazar, Gabe's mother, to finish putting supper on the table.

Better it was the family attorney occupying his father's favorite chair than one of his half brothers, Gabe thought sourly.

Brothers. The word still sounded strange to him. Two full days in their company had made no difference. Neither had attending the funeral together yesterday or sharing coffee with them before spreading their father's ashes in the flower garden this morning. Gabe didn't know these men.

It was his mother's idea they take the guest suite in the house rather than stay at the Wild Horse Bed and Breakfast in town. "They're family," she'd told Gabe. "Your father would have wanted it. And we have plenty of room."

Gabe had seethed in silence instead of arguing. Did his mother have to be so nice to them? If they inherited the ranch, she'd be thrown out of her home.

After casting tentative glances at each other, the brothers in question sat in matching wingback chairs—which happened to be directly opposite Gabe, his mother and Cara Alvarez. Cara was the daughter of Raquel's childhood friend Leena and had lived with Gabe's family the past two years.

Consciously or subconsciously, Gabe, Raquel and Cara had made a united front on the couch.

No one else had been invited to the reading of the will, giving Gabe reason to believe those present were the only ones named as beneficiaries.

He swallowed, but the knot of pain residing above his heart didn't loosen. Those two men shouldn't be here. His father had promised Gabe the ranch. Many times over.

What had changed August Dempsey's mind at the eleventh hour? Was the cancer to blame? Had all the medications and treatments ravaged his body and mind? Or had he lied to Gabe and intended to give the ranch to his legitimate sons all along, leaving Gabe with nothing?

Using his briefcase as a lap desk, Hector Fuentes cleared his throat and tapped a thin stack of papers into a perfect rectangle. "If it's all right with everyone, I'll skip the standard legalese and get right to the bequests.

I've brought copies of the entire will for everyone and will distribute them later to those who want one."

Gabe wanted a copy. He'd bet his brothers would, too.

Hector smiled at Cara before beginning. "To Cara Alvarez, who has been like a daughter to Raquel and myself, I grant exclusive use of five hundred acres of Dos Estrellas pasture land, to include parcels six, seven and eight, for her mustang sanctuary."

Cara's hand flew to her mouth, and she inhaled sharply. The sanctuary and its horses meant a great deal to her. For his father to include her in his will showed how much he'd considered her to be part of the family.

His mother bit back a sob and placed an arm around Cara's shoulders.

"Cara is to have use of the parcels for as long as she wants," Hector continued, "or for as long as Dos Estrellas remains in the family."

Remains in the family. The words gave Gabe hope. His father wouldn't have allowed Cara exclusive use of nearly one-sixth of the ranch and not bequeath Gabe the entirety of it. Nothing else made sense.

Hector continued, outlining the specifics. "Do you have any questions?" he asked Cara when he was done.

She shook her head, tears filling her eyes.

"Raquel, the love of my life, and Cara both," Hector said, "will continue to reside at Dos Estrellas and occupy the ranch house for as long as they choose or for as long as the ranch remains in the family."

Again, Cara inhaled sharply and his mother softly sobbed. Gabe, on the other hand, began to worry. What was with the wording, *as long as the ranch remains in the family*? Twice his father had used it. There must be some significance.

"Any questions?" Hector repeated when he'd finished with the specifics.

"No," Gabe's mother and Cara replied simultaneously.

Hector then listed smaller bequests. Gabe's mother was to receive ownership of August's favorite dog. She, along with Gabe and a close cousin, were to get his jewelry, personal items and cherished mementos.

Gabe studied his brothers' faces during the reading. He wouldn't recognize either of them as being related to him or their father. Other than the fact they all three stood over six feet tall, there were no noticeable physical similarities. With their blond hair and blue eyes, Josh, the oldest brother, and Cole must resemble their mother.

Neither did they look like the boys he remembered from his childhood. Gabe had been in first grade, Josh second and Cole in kindergarten when an older child on the playground had pointed to the brothers and told Gabe in a taunting voice that they were his father's *real* sons. The boy had then called Gabe's mother a name he hadn't understood at the time, but instinctively knew was the worst of insults.

Angry and hurt and experiencing feelings he couldn't explain, much less process, Gabe had passed the rest of the day in a blur. Arriving home after school, he'd gone straight from the bus to his mother and told her about what the boy had said, omitting the bad name.

She'd hugged him, smoothed his hair and insisted he forget about it. Gabe might have, except the same thing happened two days later. Instead of retaliating against the boy, Gabe went after Josh, who was both older and bigger than him. The attack, poorly executed, nonetheless cost him three days' suspension from school for fighting.

His mother had been furious with him. She'd also been saddened. It was the first Gabe had learned that his father, who visited once or twice a week in the evenings, had a wife and children living on a ranch outside of Mustang Valley. It took Gabe several years to fully understand his family's unusual dynamics, long after he and his mother had moved to Dos Estrellas.

Did Josh remember the school tussle? Did he know it was Gabe who had hit him and what had made him so angry? Probably not. At least, his face gave no indication.

"Last, is my beloved Dos Estrellas Ranch, which has been in the Dempsey family for three generations."

Hector's voice jarred Gabe from his thoughts. Every muscle in his body tightened. He willed himself not to look at his brothers, but at Hector instead. They would not see how important this moment was to him, or his devastation if the rumors turned out to be true and Gabe lost the ranch.

Beside him, his mother shifted and murmured under her breath. Cara grabbed his hand and squeezed.

"I leave the ranch equally to my three sons, Josh, Cole and Gabe."

Pain sliced through Gabe, leaving him numb. He hadn't inherited the ranch. Worse, his father had named him third after his two legitimate sons, whom he hadn't seen in twenty-four years.

Betrayal. It was the emotion Gabe hadn't been able to define when he was six. It was also the emotion that gripped him now, fresh as the day on the playground with Josh.

"See, I told you, *mijo*," his mother said in a whisper, "your father did not forget you."

Not forget him? He might as well have. Gabe was supposed to share ownership of Dos Estrellas? With them?

"He promised to leave the ranch to Gabe," Cara hissed.

"Hush," his mother ordered.

"It's not fair." Cara's voice rose, loud enough to draw the stares of everyone in the room. "Gabe's worked the land. He knows the cattle business and how the ranch is run." She gestured to Josh and Cole. "They don't have the first clue. They're rodeo competitors, for crying out loud."

"We can hear you," Josh said.

Cole grunted and stared angrily out the large bay window.

Gabe fumed. What was the guy's problem? He had nothing to be angry about.

"If we could please continue," Hector scolded in an attempt to bring the reading back under control.

Cara didn't apologize. She didn't say anything, merely folded her arms across her middle.

With a warning nod in her direction, Hector carried on, reading August's words. "My good attorney has advised me to cover the many details on a separate page. I've done that, merely to satisfy him, mind you." A hint of amusement flashed in Hector's eyes. "But, in a nutshell, Dos Estrellas can't be sold in its entirety unless all three of my sons are in agreement. And while individual shares can be sold, it is my fervent wish my beloved ranch remains in the family for many future generations, and the grandchildren I didn't live long enough to see will grow up here, fine, strong and healthy like my own boys."

Gabe almost choked. Was his father serious? The

two men sitting across from him hadn't grown up at the ranch. As children they'd moved six hundred miles away to Northern California and never once come back, ignoring the requests to visit their dying father and say goodbye.

He half listened to the rest of the reading. Violet Hathaway, the ranch's livestock manager, along with the Dempsey housekeeper of twenty-plus years, were to retain their jobs. Lastly, there was a mention of selling shares to one another and how the profits were to be distributed.

Profits, right. What a joke. There weren't any, and hadn't been since August had become ill.

"Questions?" Hector asked, sounding a lot like a parrot.

Gabe shook his head. He would read his copy of the will later, when he was less agitated and better able to focus, though it wouldn't make much difference.

The empty hole inside him ached. He'd admired, respected and loved his father with boundless devotion. Now he feared he might have been wrong. Whether his father had realized it or not, he'd forced Gabe into partnership with his brothers and, by the looks on their faces, they were as unhappy about the outcome as Gabe.

"Are we done?" Cole asked, his tone sharp.

"Not quite." Hector set his briefcase on the floor by his feet. "There's the matter of the trustee."

"Trustee?" Gabe's mother leaned forward. "What is a trustee?"

"The Dos Estrellas and August's other property are actually held in the trust he established. As with all trusts, a person or entity is designated to oversee the trust and carry out the terms of the will according to the decedent's wishes. Typically, the trustee makes the distributions, and, in this case, will oversee the management of the estate per August's instructions."

"Dad hired a manager?" Gabe couldn't believe his ears.

"Not exactly. You and your brothers will run the ranch. But's the trustee's job to make sure you're running it according to the terms of your father's will. For instance, your mother and Cara continue to live here as long as they choose and Cara's mustang sanctuary is protected."

That sounded reasonable, Gabe supposed.

"You should know your father gave the trustee full financial powers until the ranch operates in the black for at least one full year, and all his medical bills are paid off. The trustee's duties will end only then or if the ranch is sold."

"I don't understand," Josh said.

"Essentially, while you and your brothers run the ranch, the trustee will be pulling the purse strings."

If Gabe wasn't already in a state of shock, this latest bombshell would have knocked him to his knees. His father had preferred for someone outside the family handle the ranch's finances over his son? His sons?

"Who's the trustee?" Gabe asked.

Hector waited a beat before responding. "The Southern Arizona Bank."

Mustang Valley's sole financial institution. Gabe was familiar with them, like everyone else in the community.

"Why?"

"A trustee is supposed to abide by the terms of the will." Hector shrugged. "Unfortunately, they don't always. It can happen when family members are put in charge. Emotions run high. As a result, some individuals choose an entity, such as a bank, or an attorney, to act as trustee. They tend to adhere more strictly to the terms of the will and keep emotions out of it."

Perhaps Gabe's father had the foresight to realize forcing his three sons into an unwanted partnership would guarantee high-running emotions.

The front doorbell rang, startling several of the room's occupants. Not Hector. He made his way to the large, ornately carved wooden door.

"Who could that be?" Gabe's mother moved as if to rise. "I specifically requested no visitors this afternoon."

"It's all right," Hector said. "I arranged for the representative from the bank to be here today in order to meet you all and put your fears to rest."

He opened the heavy door. It swung wide, revealing a feminine silhouette cast in dark shadows from the sun's slanting rays.

"Am I early?" the woman asked.

"Not at all, come in," he said. "We're ready for you."

Gabe blinked as the representative stepped across the threshold, convinced he was seeing things. It couldn't be. This had to be a mistake. Or someone's idea of a sick joke. He wasn't sure if he should shout in protest or laugh out loud.

Hector took the young, professionally dressed woman by the arm and led her to the center of the room as if she were on display.

"For those of you who haven't met her before, this is Reese McGraw, assistant manager at Southern Arizona Bank and the trustee of August Dempsey's estate."

"Thank you." Reese accepted the cup of coffee Raquel Salazar offered and smiled in appreciation. Other than the attorney Hector Fuentes, Gabe's mother was the only one to show Reese any friendliness so far.

It was to be expected. Even under normal circumstances, no one in the Dempsey or Salazar families would be pleased to welcome her, the daughter of Theo McGraw. To learn she was the employee at Southern Arizona Bank in charge of overseeing August Dempsey's estate, well, it must be a shock.

Gabe's features hardened each time he glanced at her, which was often. If he was trying to scare her off, it wouldn't work. Reese was here to stay.

It was, she mused, a far cry from the way he'd looked at her yesterday while waiting for her father and Enrico to arrive with the truck and trailer. When he'd buttoned her into the rain poncho, she swore the heat of attraction had flared in his eyes. Not to mention his touch lingered far longer than necessary.

The poncho had kept her warm, all right. That, and the effects of his proximity.

Reese silently scolded herself, alarmed by the direction of her thoughts. She'd known Gabe most of her life, but not once entertained any romantic notions about him. What had changed since their last conversation twelve years ago? Was it her or him?

"You are welcome," Raquel said in her lilting Hispanic accent. "How is your father doing? He looked a little pale yesterday at the service."

Reese gave a small start. Raquel had noticed her father's appearance? Surely, she'd had much, much more on her mind at the funeral than Theo McGraw. Reese swallowed. Soon, her father's symptoms would become increasingly apparent. Hiding his Parkinson's would be impossible.

Good. His constant care, and the tremendous burden that came with it, were taking a toll on her, physically and emotionally. He needed help managing his symptoms beyond her limited abilities. Yet he refused to hire an experienced health care professional, convinced people in Mustang Valley would view him differently. Think less of him.

She wished he could see how wrong he was. The same people he feared would pity him had rallied to comfort the family and offer support during August Dempsey's long illness. They would do the same for her father.

She blamed the damnable McGraw pride, which her father possessed in abundance. She, too, perhaps. Hadn't she left town shortly after realizing she was pregnant with Blake Nolan's baby, convinced people would talk behind her and her father's backs?

"He was tired," she explained to Raquel. "His arthritis has been keeping him awake at night."

Her hostess sighed expansively. "I understand. I have my own complaints. Give him my regards, will you?"

"Of course."

She patted Reese's arm before gliding away.

Reese admired Gabe's mother. While the sadness in Raquel's eyes showed evidence of her grief and sorrow, she remained strong and stalwart. Perhaps, in a way, she was relieved at his passing. August had been in considerable pain at the end, and no one wanted to see their loved one needlessly suffer.

Funny they'd never married. August and his wife divorced twenty-plus years ago. Reese was curious. Reading the entirety of his will hadn't provided any insight.

Sipping her coffee, she made her way to Cara Alvarez, who, by her estimation, was the one person with the least reason to dislike her. They had once been school friends, after all. Before the feud between August and Reese's father severed their budding friendship.

"Hey, how you doing?"

Cara glanced up from the spot on the floor she'd been staring at. "All right."

"I'm sorry for your loss."

"Thank you."

With her luxurious black hair and striking beauty, Cara might have been related to Raquel and not just the daughter she never had. One prominent difference was their eyes. While Raquel's sparked with a wide array of emotions, Cara's alternated between listlessness and despair. They had been that way since the tragic death of her toddler son two years ago.

"I hear you're doing great things with the mustang sanctuary," Reese said.

"I don't know about great." Cara shifted and resumed staring, this time out the window.

Was she remembering her son's funeral?

Reese decided her former schoolmate wasn't in the mood for conversation. "If there's anything you need, feel free to call me or come by the bank."

"Okay."

She touched Cara's arm before crossing the room. Feeling a prickling on the back of her neck, she turned and found Gabe staring at her from a far corner of the room. He stood by himself. No surprise, anger radiated off him in waves.

Reese squared her shoulders, refusing to wilt beneath the visual assault. She was at the ranch in an official capacity. Gabe and his family may not like the fact she was the trustee, but there was nothing they could do about it. August Dempsey's last wishes would be honored.

Lifting her coffee cup in acknowledgment, she nodded at Gabe. He responded with raised brows and a look of surprise. How about that? She'd bested him. Surely it was a first.

Pleased with herself, she continued her casual stroll of the room. Hector was currently immersed in conversation with Raquel. From what Reese could discern, he was answering the questions she'd have gladly done if asked.

She'd certainly chosen a rough road to travel, though she wouldn't have refused the assignment. Losing her credibility at the bank, and possibly her position, weren't options. She needed a job with decent income and one that enabled her to be close to her father. Assistant manager of Southern Arizona Bank fit the bill perfectly.

Besides, she liked her job. And, if she said so herself, she was good at it.

Finishing her coffee, she started for the kitchen, planning to dispose of her cup in the sink. At the large archway separating the dining room from the kitchen, she paused. The strains of what was clearly a private conversation reached her ears from the other side of the archway and around the corner. It was between Josh Dempsey and his brother Cole.

"What am I going to do with one-third of the ranch?" Cole demanded irritably. "I don't want it. I don't want anything that belonged to him."

"Let's get our copy of the will and read through it," Josh suggested. "The terms may not be ironclad."

"You heard what the attorney said."

Cole had understood correctly. The will was ironclad. August had been thorough, perhaps anticipating a conflict.

"Maybe we can contest it."

"And where are we going to find the money for that?" Cole scoffed. "Getting custody of your kids drained your bank account."

Reese recalled reading the background information Hector had provided on the Dempsey brothers. According to the report, Josh was locked in a bitter legal battle with his ex-wife over custody of their two young children.

"Take it easy, Cole. My financial problems aren't what's making you mad."

"You're right. I don't want to be here, and I'm sorry we came."

"Give it another day or two. We'll figure out a way to get your money."

"*Our* money, you mean. Don't forget, brother, you want your share as badly as I want mine. Attorneys aren't cheap."

Reese retreated, concerned by what she'd heard. Growing up in Mustang Valley, she knew about August's first family and that there was no love lost between him and his sons. But he must have wanted to make amends. Why else would he have modified his will six months ago? Obviously, his two sons didn't appreciate the gesture.

Should she tell Gabe? Was it her place? No, probably not. But nothing stopped her from dropping a hint or two about his brothers' intentions.

He hadn't left the corner. Seeing his hard expression, Reese had second thoughts. Perhaps she should speak to Hector instead. Though what could he do? The same as her, alert Gabe, who'd likely be more receptive to the family attorney than her.

She wavered, still debating and well aware she was drawing attention to herself. A moment later, she headed straight for Gabe.

He didn't so much as blink at her approach. The guy had nerves of steel.

"I wanted to thank you again for helping me yesterday," she said.

"How's the horse?"

"Fine. A bit sore, but otherwise unharmed. The vet prescribed pain relievers, an anti-inflammatory and a week's rest." She mentioned the vet's visit strictly to let Gabe know she wasn't lax when it came to the well-being of the McGraw horses.

"You were lucky."

"I was." She hoped he noted the sincerity she was trying to convey. "I can't imagine what I would have done if you hadn't come riding by."

"Gone for help," he said matter-of-factly.

"And might not have made it back in time to save General."

"I disagree. You're a resourceful woman, Reese."

"How would you know? We're not exactly friends."

Except he'd witnessed one of the worst moments in her life and had treated her secret like it was his own, telling no one. Did that give them some sort of bond?

"It shows." He angled his head in a way managing to be both confident and boyishly charming.

"I'm not that capable."

"No? You're the trustee of my father's estate. If you ask me, that's pretty resourceful."

Ah. There they were. The knives. And here she'd assumed they might have a normal conversation. "Believe it or not, I had nothing to do with your father's decision."

"Other than you returned to Mustang Valley and took a job at the bank a few weeks before he revised his will."

She stiffened. "A coincidence."

"Right."

"I can count on one hand the number of times I spoke to your father. The last was when he came into the bank and met with Walt, the manager. For the record, I wasn't in the meeting."

"Yet you were named as trustee."

"The bank was. I'm performing the duties because I'm assistant manager." Not entirely true, but Reese wasn't ready to reveal any private agreements between August and the bank.

"Does your father know?"

Reese stood straighter. "He doesn't."

"But he will soon enough."

"Gabe, I didn't strike up a conversation with you to bicker."

"Then why?"

There it was again, that flash of heat in his eyes. Darn him and darn her susceptibility.

"How well do you know your brothers?"

Her question elicited a sharp laugh.

"Have you had a chance to talk with them these last few days?"

"I've had the chance. Not the inclination." He studied her intently.

Reese resisted his close scrutiny. "I sense an animosity from them."

"No kidding." Gabe's tone rang with sarcasm.

"I'm serious. Josh and Cole appear to be…unhappy with the terms of the will."

"They aren't alone."

"I think Cole is only after money."

"What are you after?"

This wasn't going how Reese had hoped. She considered a different approach when Gabe's glance suddenly cut to the left.

"Quiet," he murmured and visibly tensed.

Reese peered over her shoulder. Josh and Cole weren't three feet away. Both wore suspicious expressions. How much, if anything, had they heard?

Gathering her wits, she said, "There you are. I was telling Gabe, the four of us need to schedule a meeting to review the financial records and discuss your father's plan for the ranch."

"We were about to suggest the same thing." Josh looked to his brother. "We have some questions."

"What kind of questions?" Gabe demanded, his jaw tightening.

Placing herself between the three men, Reese plastered a smile on her face. "How's tomorrow afternoon at the ranch? Say, two o'clock?"

Chapter 3

Gabe watched Reese bid goodbye to his mother and Hector, fetch her coat and purse from the back of a dining room chair and leave by the front door.

A moment later, when no one was looking, he followed her, catching up as she reached her parked car in the driveway.

"Reese."

She stopped and turned, her car key clutched in her fingers. "Oh, did I forget something?"

"You by chance have a second?"

"Sure."

She looked anything but sure. A second later, she popped the locks on her Honda sedan. Opening the car door, she deposited her purse on the passenger seat, then waited.

"Why didn't you tell me yesterday you were the trustee?" he asked.

She crossed her arms over her middle. "My instructions were not to tell anyone before the reading of the will."

"I helped you rescue your horse."

"Doesn't work that way, Gabe."

He shifted, the chilly November air penetrating his dress shirt. Why hadn't he grabbed his suit jacket before coming outside?

"Isn't there a conflict of interest?"

"Rest assured, I'm completely unbiased when it comes to my job, and completely professional."

"Your father has been after Dos Estrellas for years. Twice he tried to buy it when Dad fell behind on the property taxes. And he made an offer earlier this year. Dad was going through chemo. Nothing like kicking a man when he's down."

"What are you implying?"

"Can you be relied on not to use your position to advance your father's ambitions?"

She pivoted on her high heels. It was a miracle she didn't lose her balance and face-plant in the driveway. "I'm going to pretend you didn't say that."

Gabe took hold of her elbow. They both stilled. "It's a fair question."

"I have never used my job to advance my father's ambitions or my own. Nor would I. You asking such a thing is insulting."

"Look at me, Reese." He waited until did. "I'm protecting my family."

She sagged, some of the fight going out of her. "You're angry—about the terms of the will and your brothers inheriting two-thirds of the ranch. You were also taken aback learning I'm the trustee. For those reasons, I'll pretend you didn't just question my ethics."

"Our fathers didn't get along."

"I disagree. They actually liked and admired each other greatly. My father has always spoken very highly of yours."

"They were business rivals. And your father was considerably more successful than mine."

"Your father had two families to support. I'm an only child, and my mother left when I was eight. It makes a difference."

Her parents' divorce was another similarity they shared. While Gabe's father had taken a mistress, Reese's mother had abandoned her family, running away with her lover, who was, at the time, the Small Change's tax accountant.

"And your father came from money," Gabe said.

"Which gave him all the more reason to admire yours. August Dempsey made something of himself from humble beginnings."

Gabe didn't voice what was on his mind, that, in the end, his father had lost much of what he'd built. The family would be paying off his medical bills for years. Which meant Reese would be the trustee of his father's estate for a long, long time.

"Can we not argue about this?" She glanced down at her arm, which Gabe still held.

He let his hand drop and instantly missed the intimate contact. He'd felt warmth beneath the fabric of her jacket. And soft, supple flesh. It had stirred his senses.

"Does your boss know about the feud between our families?"

"Of course he does."

"And he doesn't care?"

"First of all, I'm the one who told Walt. I thought it would be best he hear it from me. Secondly, as I said earlier, I'm required by my position with the bank to be honest and fair. Also, every detail of my work will be scrutinized by the board." She squared her shoulders. "Should even one small detail come under question, my job could be at stake. I won't risk it."

"You don't need to work. Your father's well-off."

Reese inhaled sharply. "You're hardly an expert on my personal life."

Gabe could have kicked himself. "I'm sorry. I was out of line."

"Fine. Apology accepted." She reached for the open car door. "Now, if you don't mind."

"Would I also be out of line if I requested someone else at the bank be appointed as trustee? Surely, you aren't the only person qualified."

He expected her to be mad. She fooled him again by dismissing his question with an indifferent shrug. "You can ask. The answer will be no."

"Why?"

"I'm not at liberty to say."

"Sounds like a convenient excuse."

"It isn't."

Again, she'd barely reacted. Gabe found that interesting. Reese was either incredibly confident or she knew something she wasn't telling.

Her cell phone chimed from her jacket pocket. Extracting the phone, she glanced at the display and promptly answered with an anxious, "Yes, Enrico." After a pause, she said, "I'll be right there," and disconnected. "I have to go," she told Gabe.

"Is everything okay?"

"Yes. No." She fumbled with the phone before returning it to her pocket. "My father fell from the porch steps."

"Is he hurt?"

"Banged his knee. He may need to see the doctor."

For a banged knee? Gabe thought Reese might be overreacting. Theo McGraw was tough as nails and wouldn't be bothered by a little tumble off the porch steps. "Call me if you need anything."

She narrowed her gaze. "Really? After raking me over the coals, you're offering to be the good neighbor?"

"I, um…"

He'd started to say he was concerned for her, then changed his mind at the last second. He didn't give a damn about Reese McGraw.

Except, that wasn't true. He did feel something for her. Compassion and sympathy, at least. Why else would he have kept her secret all these years?

If not for their fathers' rivalry, their relationship might have taken a different path. They had been classmates and neighbors. Dating in high school wouldn't have been far-fetched.

Anything transpiring between them now, however, was out of the question, and Gabe was wise to maintain a safe distance.

The problem was he wanted to take her in his arms, give her a hug and tell her not to worry. Her father was going to be fine.

"I don't hate you, Reese. And I don't wish your father ill. If he needs help, or you, call me."

"Thank you." She slid onto the driver's seat, her hands

gripping the steering wheel. "I'll see you tomorrow at two."

Aware he was crossing an invisible line, Gabe covered one of her white-knuckled hands with his. She was obviously worried about her father. "Drive careful. It's getting dark."

For a moment, they remained where they were. If Gabe didn't know better, he'd think a part of her wanted to stay. But that was ridiculous.

Whatever spell they'd fallen under ended, and she started the engine. Gabe watched her depart, thinking he should return to the house. Why, then, didn't he? At the end of the long road leading from the ranch house to the main road, Reese's brake lights illuminated. She turned left, in the direction of the Small Change.

He might have spent more time contemplating why her father's seemingly minor fall prompted her to leave in such a hurry except he was interrupted by the last person he wanted to see. His brother Josh.

Dammit. What did the man want now? The shirt off Gabe's back?

"Hope I didn't interrupt anything."

Gabe ground his teeth together. His brother's timing was impeccable. Or, perhaps, intentional. He could have spotted Gabe and Reese from the living room window.

"You didn't." Gabe pushed past him. Whatever Josh wanted, he wasn't interested.

"Got a minute?"

Gabe halted and cursed under his breath. "For what?"

They'd hardly spoken these past few days despite living in close quarters. Gabe had no intention of changing the status quo.

"You and her," Josh hitched his chin in the direction Reese had driven in her car, "are you friends?"

Gabe's hackles rose. His relationship with Reese was no one's business. Especially Josh's.

"We're neighbors."

"I know. I lived here once."

He couldn't help thinking the reference to Josh residing at the ranch before Gabe came to live there was intentional.

"What I'm asking is, are you close?"

He stared his brother down.

Josh held his own. "It's a reasonable question. She's going to control the ranch's finances. If you and Reese are involved, there could be a conflict of interest."

Five minutes ago, Gabe had been asking Reese the same question. Now he defended her.

"She's a professional. She won't do anything to jeopardize her position at the bank."

"But you're friends."

"I'm not discussing her with you." Gabe once again started for the house and once again, Josh halted him with his words.

"I don't like this any better than you."

"We have nothing in common."

"Other than our father and this ranch and the fact we have to work together. Or agree to sell."

That rankled Gabe. "I'm not selling."

"Think about it before you decide. Dad left us with a lot of bills to pay and little means at our disposal. Selling would get us out of debt and free us to move on."

"There's no *we* as far as I'm concerned. Our father promised me the ranch. Not you and your brother."

Josh inhaled deeply as if to control his temper. "Cole and I have every right to inherit a share of Dos Estrellas."

"Because why? We happen to share the same blood?" Gabe snorted in disgust. "You haven't set foot on this place for twenty-four years."

"He cheated on my mother."

Josh had targeted Gabe's one weak spot, and the blow inflicted the desired damage.

He knew with all his heart his father had loved his mother deeply. That didn't make it right for him to disregard his marriage vows. Gabe's mother had raised him to be honorable. It was hard for him to accept the fact his father hadn't divorced his wife before becoming involved with Gabe's mother.

He'd asked once when he was twelve. His mother's face had immediately hardened, and she told him to never, ever bring up the subject again or she'd tan his hide. It was a private matter between her and his father.

In his early twenties, Gabe approached his father and got no further with him. The reason his father gave for not marrying his mother—that Gabe's maternal grandfather was very traditional and didn't approve—smacked of an excuse. When Gabe pressed, his father had stormed from the room. Only the love and devotion he felt for both his parents kept him from resenting them.

"We're done talking." Gabe strode ahead without looking back.

Good manners dictated he should return to the house and tell Hector goodbye. The attorney had been his father's closest confidant. But, like yesterday, Gabe needed an outlet to vent his frustration.

It was too late and too dark for a ride in the nearby mountains. Not too late to clean out the tack room, he decided. Nothing beat tossing a few crates and harnesses around to burn off steam. Dress shirt be damned.

"I remember," Josh called after him. "It was you who punched me in the nose at school. You had a pretty good right hook for a kid."

Gabe didn't miss a step, though it was the first thing his brother had said that made him smile.

Reese opened the jewelry box on her bedroom dresser, lifted out the top tray and removed a tiny framed picture hidden beneath. It was a ritual. Every year on this day, Celia's birthday, Reese studied the picture of her newborn daughter, let the memories of her birth warm her heart and then placed a phone call.

Today, Reese came home from the bank during her lunch hour in order to call Celia, but also to check on her father. His tumble off the porch yesterday could have been worse. Luckily, he hadn't fallen far, but he had *landed* hard and badly bruised his knee. Loss of balance was a common side effect of Parkinson's. As was stooped posture. Her father looked ten years older than he had mere months ago. She'd also noticed a slight tremor in his right hand and a quiver in his voice. Each new symptom increased her despair.

Feeling the weight of the little silver frame in her hand, Reese stared at Celia's infant face and was reminded of why she'd excused herself after lunching with her father and retreated to her bedroom. How could she not be thinking of her daughter on this special day? The problem with Parkinson's was it consumed the thoughts of the person afflicted with it, along with their family members.

While Celia's parents made no secret of her adoption,

they and Celia were the only ones who knew Reese was her birth mother. Shortly after her high school graduation, Reese had moved to Oregon to live with her older cousin Megan on the pretense of taking a year off before college. There, she'd given birth to Celia, who was then adopted by Megan and her husband.

They adored Celia. They also encouraged her to have a relationship with Reese, for which Reese felt grateful and blessed.

Ever since Celia could talk, Reese called her on a prearranged day once a month. Three times over the years, she'd flown to Oregon for a visit. In her closet, Reese kept a small trunk filled with letters from Celia, drawings, cards, photographs and, lately, school papers. Her computer contained numerous picture files organized by age.

Someday, when they were both ready, Celia would come to Mustang Valley for a visit and to meet her grandfather. Reese hoped it was soon, before the Parkinson's advanced to the point her father couldn't function or communicate.

"Hi, sweet pea," Reese said when Celia answered the phone. "Happy eleventh birthday."

"Reese! You called."

"Of course." Reese bit back a sob. Her emotions were getting the best of her today. "It sounds like you have a cold."

"We were supposed to go out for pizza tonight." Celia snuffled. "Now we have to wait for the weekend."

"That's too bad."

"I got your present. Thank you. The boots are exactly the ones I wanted."

They talked for twenty minutes until Reese had to

say goodbye. The meeting at Dos Estrellas was scheduled for two, and she wanted to check on her father one last time before leaving.

"I hope you feel better soon," she said.

"Me, too. But I get to miss school, so that part's good."

Reese enjoyed their easy banter. "Send me pictures of the pizza party."

"I will. Goodbye, Reese."

"Goodbye, sweet pea." Reese disconnected before softly saying, "I love you." She and Celia weren't quite close enough for her to speak the words. Not yet, anyway. Maybe one day. She refused to push.

In the kitchen, she found her father sitting at the table, having his customary afternoon coffee.

"I thought the doctor said caffeine was bad for you," she scolded.

"Would you rather I have a whiskey?"

"Dad!"

"I've given up everything worthwhile. You're not taking away my coffee."

"Fine." She patted his shoulder and kissed the top of his head. "I won't tattle on you."

"Your Aunt Louise sent me an email earlier. She wants to come for a visit at Christmas."

"Great!" Reese's mood brightened. She adored her father's younger sister, who'd been like a second mother to her after her parents divorced. "How long's she going to stay?"

"I told her no. That we were busy."

"What!" Reese dropped into the chair across from her father and gaped at him.

"It's not a good time."

"You can't hide your Parkinson's forever."

"I'm not ready to tell her."

"It won't be Christmas without family visiting."

"Your Aunt Louise is a busybody. Always thinks she knows what's best for people."

"She loves you."

"She'll interfere."

Reese bit her tongue. Her father was the one sick, not her. It was his choice whom he told and when, regardless if she disagreed.

"Off to your meeting at Dos Estrellas?" He was attempting to distract her, and she let him.

"Depending on how long the meeting lasts, I may come straight home and skip going back to the bank."

"I'm still trying to wrap my brain around you being the trustee of August Dempsey's estate."

She'd finally informed her father last night, when she was able to do so. "Strange, I know."

"August must be having himself one heck of a good laugh up in heaven."

"He did choose the bank to act as trustee."

"Probably didn't realize you'd be the one running the show."

There was no way for Reese to respond without violating her client's privacy, so she said nothing.

"Poor man," her father said. "He must have hated seeing the ranch fall to ruin like it did."

"Dos Estrellas is hardly in ruins."

"It's buried in debt."

Buried was an exaggeration. Waist-deep, maybe. "I can't discuss the ranch finances with you."

"He should have sold it to me when he had the chance."

Reese shook her head. "And what would you do with Dos Estrellas? Let's be honest, you're having enough trouble running the Small Change."

He grunted in displeasure. "Don't count me out yet."

"Never." She smiled and kissed his head again before retrieving her briefcase and a travel mug of coffee from the counter. "I'll see you later."

"Good luck," he called after her.

Reese passed Enrico on the way to her car, and they exchanged hellos. The ranch foreman was heading inside to give her father a report. The loyal employee had been doing that more and more of late, three or four times a day. And because her father was being regularly checked on, Reese was able to leave the house, confident he'd be all right.

In the indeterminable future, whether her father agreed or not, they would need to hire a caretaker. Reese could anticipate how their conversation would go and was dreading it.

During the ten-minute drive to Dos Estrellas, she mentally prepared for the meeting. This, she realized, was the third day in a row she'd see Gabe. She should get used to it. With her new responsibilities, they would be in frequent contact. The notion gave her a not-so-small shiver of anticipation—which she promptly squashed. Her attraction to Gabe was inappropriate, and even if they were to date, the timing couldn't be worse. He had a ranch in serious financial trouble to run alongside two brothers he didn't get along with.

Reese slowed to take the turn into the Dos Estrellas driveway. She parked in the same spot as yesterday, instantly reminded of her and Gabe's awkward, yet strangely intimate, parting. She'd have sworn he was about to say something revealing and romantic to her. When he didn't, she blamed her overactive imagination playing tricks on her.

But there was that moment between them on the hill-top when he'd fastened her into the poncho...

Enough, she told herself. *This has to stop.*

Raquel Salazar answered Reese's knock on the door, smiling affectionately. "Come in, *chiquita*."

Little girl? Reese could hardly call herself that. Raquel, however, was the motherly type who called everyone by an endearment.

"I have the office all set for you." Raquel indicated a door off the living room. "This way."

August's home office was a masculine mixture of functional and comfortable. Situated behind a heavy antique desk was an oversized executive chair. It nearly swallowed Reese when she sat down. Certificates lined one wall. August, it appeared, had been a member of several professional organizations, including the Arizona Cattlemen's Association.

On the other wall hung family portraits spanning several decades, back to the first Dempsey who'd originally purchased the land and built the ranch. A well-worn leather couch sat beneath the portraits and looked cozy enough to sink into for long hours of reading or listening to the old-fashioned stereo system.

Notably absent was evidence of modern technology. No computer. No TV, flat-screen or otherwise. No smartphone docking station or Bluetooth speaker. In fact, the one phone was an antiquated desktop model with a push-button dial pad, and the clock required a weekly winding to run.

Reese glanced around the room. "Where did August keep the ranch records?"

"In here." Raquel walked to a black lateral filing cabinet adjacent to the couch and opened the top drawer.

Reese could see rows and rows of hanging file folders with various headings: Payroll, Vehicles, Insurance, Veterinary Care, to name a few. "What about the financial information?"

"Ah." Raquel pulled out an elongated brown binder, which she placed on the desk in front of Reese. "Do you mean this?"

"Wow." Reese opened the binder and stared in amazement at the three-to-a-page checks and the thick stack of stubs. "I didn't know anybody used manual checks anymore."

"August didn't trust computers."

"So I see." Reese sighed, flipping through the stubs and noting the entries. "What about income? How did he track that?"

Raquel opened a side drawer of the desk. Inside were a half dozen green accounting ledger books stacked one on top of the other.

"Great." Reese definitely had her work cut out for her. "Prior year tax returns handy?"

Those were in the next drawer down. Reese was relieved to see they'd been prepared by a local CPA.

Thankfully, Hector Fuentes had given her a flash drive with August's plan for the ranch, including a month-by-month and year-by-year schedule. Reese wasn't sure what she'd have done with handwritten notes.

"I'll tell the boys you're here," Raquel said and left, her footsteps soundless on the thick, colorful area rug.

Reese removed her laptop from her briefcase and

powered it up. She also pulled out a copy of the entire living trust. When, a few minutes later, no one had yet arrived, she began examining the first accounting journal. It was meticulously updated until four months ago. After that, the entries were sketchy, then they stopped altogether.

August had probably gotten too sick to continue, which didn't bode well for the ranch finances.

Cole entered the office, removing his cowboy hat and running a hand through his windblown blond hair. Not the person Reese expected to see first.

"Hi." She greeted him in her best assistant bank manager smile. "Have a seat."

Raquel had brought in three chairs from the dining room and placed them across from the desk. Cole chose the one on the right and, sitting, balanced his hat on his knee.

"Will this take long?" he asked.

"I'm not sure. Depends on a number of things."

"Like?" He couldn't have a bigger chip on his shoulder if he tried.

"The number of questions you all have. How quickly we get through reviewing the records. What shape they're in." Terrible, these past four months. "How co-operative you are."

He answered by slouching in the chair, crossing his boots at the ankles and his arms over his stomach.

Reese wasn't impressed or intimidated.

Gabe entered the office next with Josh right behind him. If she didn't know better, she'd think they arrived together. But that was impossible, right?

"Hey, Reese." Josh grinned affably before taking the middle chair. "It is okay if I call you Reese?"

"Of course," she replied, trying not to stare at Gabe like a love-struck teenager.

He'd clearly come from the pastures or barn or wherever it was he'd been working. He smelled of the outdoors and looked ruggedly handsome with his tanned complexion and two-day growth of beard. With a nonchalance both unconscious and incredibly sexy, he sat, rolled down his shirtsleeves and rebuttoned them at the cuffs, but not before Reese caught sight of strong, prominently muscled arms with a light dusting of hair.

She remembered those arms from when they'd held her the night of their senior prom. She'd thought then they were the kind of arms a woman could rely on to take care of her and keep her safe.

"Are we ready to start?" Thankfully, her voice didn't betray the riot of emotions warring inside her.

Chapter 4

Gabe listened as Reese read from a document on her laptop computer. His father's plan for Dos Estrellas. Given the amount of detail, he'd trusted his legitimate sons no more than he'd trusted Gabe acting alone to make the right decisions for the ranch.

If it were possible for Gabe to move farther away from Josh without being obvious, he would. Why his mother had felt the need to place the chairs within inches of each other, he didn't know. To promote comradery was his guess. As if sitting close would dissolve years of animosity and resentment.

Admittedly, Gabe's opinion of Josh had risen the smallest fraction yesterday following his remark about Gabe's right hook. Cole, well, he continued to annoy Gabe. The guy took attitude to a new level with a temper to match. To be fair, he probably thought the same thing about Gabe. And, no, that didn't make them brothers or even pals. Simply two people with good reason to be angry at each other.

Struggling to stay focused, he concentrated on Reese. It didn't help. She was far too distracting.

Today, she wore dress slacks and a tan sweater that, despite being bulky, hinted at the lovely, lush figure beneath. She wore minimal makeup—something Gabe preferred. Her one exception, pink lipstick accentuating a very kissable mouth.

Come to think of it, the other day on the mountain she hadn't been wearing any lipstick, and Gabe had still thought her mouth was kissable. Was every red-blooded male who came into the bank like him, appreciating her looks?

He supposed his brothers were entertaining similar thoughts. Josh had intimated as much yesterday, and Cole was practically licking his chops, which didn't sit well with Gabe. Was she noticing Cole in return?

Gabe's sudden sense of possessiveness regarding Reese made him pause. He had no claims *on* her and no interest *in* her, other than as the trustee of the Dempsey Living Trust. Best he remember that.

"Your father's first recommendation," Reese said, "is to sell off any excess cattle."

"Which we've already done." Gabe's remark had everyone turning in his direction. "This past fall we sold off about a quarter of the herd. Had to in order to pay for Dad's treatment."

At his mother's insistence, they'd admitted his father to a cancer center in Tucson. There, he'd been poked and prodded and subjected to an array of experimental drugs.

The treatment may have extended his father's life by a few weeks. It certainly hadn't improved the quality of it.

"Can we sell more cattle?" Cole asked.

"We're down to sixteen hundred head. If we deplete the herd any more, we won't have enough breeding stock for next year."

"Can we buy more cows when the time comes?"

The question came from Josh, and Gabe resisted a biting reply. His brother clearly hadn't been listening to any of their conversations this week.

"Not unless you have a way of printing money."

Reese rested her elbows on the desk. "Your father did establish a line of credit with the bank before he died, secured by the ranch. One hundred thousand dollars."

Gabe hid his surprise. He had no idea.

"But I would advise drawing on the line very conservatively until the ranch is generating enough income to cover the interest payments."

"Beef is high now anyway," Gabe said. The elevated prices had been good when it came to selling their stock, but would be bad for buying. "We'd be smarter to wait on buying more cows until the spring or next summer when prices drop."

"In that case," Reese continued, "we'll move to the next item on your father's list. Maintain the current herd through winter."

Gabe reined in his impatience. "Which is going to be a problem."

"How so?" Josh asked.

At his brothers' blank stares, Gabe said, "We've had no rain since last fall, and grass doesn't grow without water. At this rate, we'll have to buy hay and grain to supplement the grass or the herd will suffer."

Reese nodded thoughtfully. "I see."

Gabe wondered if she did see. She was the daughter of a cattle rancher and must have some idea about weather and its effect on grazing lands. The Small Change was in the same position as Dos Estrellas; they would need to buy supplemental feed, as well. There was one big difference. The Small Change wouldn't be buying supplemental feed with the last cent to their name.

"How much money is in the ranch checking account?" Cole asked.

The question irked Gabe, though he'd wondered the same thing. From what he'd seen of Cole, all his brother cared about was money and getting his hands on some. Reese had tried to warn him yesterday after the reading of the will, specifically, about Cole's wanting money rather than part ownership of the ranch.

Reese returned to her computer screen. After a minute, she said, "Less than ten thousand dollars, I'm afraid."

"What about his life insurance? Was there a policy?"

Gabe bristled. Cole didn't even have the decency to refer to their father as Dad.

"Yes." Reese returned Cole's probing stare. Kudos to her, thought Gabe. She had no fear. Then again, he'd seen her trying to pull a thousand-pound horse out of a sinkhole by herself. That was the definition of no fear. "The proceeds went to Raquel."

"Aren't they part of the estate?"

She shook her head. "Gabe's mother is the owner of the policy and the beneficiary."

"Is that legal?"

"Perfectly."

Cole's mouth turned down. He wasn't happy about the policy or Reese's clipped tone, but he said nothing.

Good thing. Gabe's mother had stood faithfully by his father for years, including the last two, which had been the hardest. She deserved something, and Gabe's father had wanted her to have a small nest egg. If Cole had objected, Gabe would have been compelled to give him more than a piece of his mind.

Last night, over coffee, his mother had hinted at giving the money to Gabe. He'd refused and not because of his father's wishes. With all their futures uncertain, he, too, wanted his mother to have some money to fall back on.

"The next item on your father's plan is to slowly increase the herd."

"How do we accomplish that if we've sold off a quarter of the cattle and can't buy more?" Unlike his younger brother, there was no rancor in Josh's voice.

"Aggressive breeding," Gabe answered for Reese. "And choosing the right time of year."

"What determines that?"

"Availability of feed and beef prices."

"Which are high." Josh said.

He appeared interested, but Gabe remained skeptical. It would take a lot more than a token show of interest to change his mind about either of his brothers.

"Prices are high today," he said. "But they can change in a matter of weeks. And, like I mentioned before, weather's affected the growth of grass. Poor feed results in poor-quality cattle. Whatever extra money we have will pay for grain and hay. There's also the matter of land. Each acre can feasibly sustain only so many cattle. Right now, with a shortage of grass, it's about two head."

"That's all?"

Josh's question showed just how little he and Cole knew about the cattle industry. What was their father thinking when he left them two-thirds of the ranch? Gabe had his work cut out for him. He could either try to teach them the cattle business or watch them fail and drag him down, too.

There was a third choice. They could sell Dos Estrellas. And a potential buyer, Theo McGraw, was the father of the estate's trustee.

No. The latter two choices weren't options. Gabe refused to lose the ranch. Not to his brothers' glaring inadequacies and especially not to his father's archrival.

"What about the mustang sanctuary?" Josh asked. "With more land, we may not need to purchase supplemental feed."

Gabe scrubbed his face and groaned. Was the man not listening yesterday during the reading of the will?

"That land belongs to Cara."

"Technically," Josh said slowly, "it belongs to us."

"It's hers to use indefinitely." As long as they didn't sell the ranch.

Josh addressed Reese. "You're the trustee. You have control over the ranch's assets. If the land was returned to the ranch, we could buy more cattle and expand the herd."

"The bank's position is, barring extenuating circumstances, to follow the terms of the will to the letter." Reese closed her laptop. "I think demanding Cara give up the sanctuary is premature. You have the line of credit and several months to make a go of this."

Cole sat up straighter. "Maybe we should sell the ranch."

"No!" Gabe all but shouted his refusal.

"Fine. Then buy us out. We're allowed to sell our shares."

Gabe had read the will. He knew the terms. And what he'd give for the kind of money required to buy out his brothers. "Believe me, I would if I could."

"I'll cut you a deal."

Gabe knew what he wanted more than anything. "Give me six months, and I'll have the money."

"I'd rather sell now."

Before he could answer, Josh cut in. "I'm not ready to sell yet, either."

Wow. Really? That was hardly the response Gabe expected.

"Since when?" Cole demanded. "You need the money more than me."

Josh worked his jaw as if contemplating his brother's remark, then said to Reese, "I have two children. A boy, two and a half, and a girl, nine months. I'm in the process of gaining full custody. To satisfy the court, I need a permanent place to call home. Dos Estrellas fits the bill."

She smiled pleasantly. Almost wistfully. "There's nowhere better than Mustang Valley to raise a family."

Was she encouraging him to stay? Gabe suffered a stab of betrayal, though he had no reason. He and Reese weren't intimate or even friends. They were barely acquaintances.

"I need to go home for a few days," Josh said. "Maybe a week. Get more of my things. I'll be back before Thanksgiving."

"What about Brawley?" Cole asked.

Gabe wasn't a rodeo enthusiast, but he knew from overhearing Josh and Cole this morning at breakfast that Brawley, California, was home of the Cattle Call Rodeo.

"Looks like I'm making a career change. Ranching for rodeoing."

"Good luck," Cole grumbled.

"You, too, little brother. You're coming back here with me."

Josh's declaration wasn't well received, judging by Cole's scowl. By Gabe, either. Given his choice, both brothers would return to California and stay. Indefinitely.

Since they weren't likely to leave, the next best thing would be for him to acquire full ownership. For that, he'd have to come up with a game plan, and fast. Thanksgiving, and his brothers' return, was right around the corner.

"Get along little dogies, get along."

Hearing Violet's singing, Gabe laughed to himself. Dos Estrellas's livestock manager couldn't carry a tune to save her life. Then there was her song choice.

Pushing the four stragglers through the gate and into the next section of grazing land wasn't exactly the same as driving a herd of cattle across open range. But he appreciated her enthusiasm.

"We're done here," he called to Violet once the last young heifer meandered through the gate, lowing softly to her mates ahead.

"Okay, boss." Violet dismounted. Whistling the same tune she'd been singing, and just as off-key, she closed the wide gate and shoved the latch into place.

Boss. Gabe liked the sound of that. Ranch employees had called his father boss. What would they call his brothers, if anything? More interesting, what did they think of the brothers' part ownership and their staying on to run the place with Gabe?

It had been three days since Josh and Cole had left for California. Josh had called yesterday to say they'd be returning Thanksgiving Eve. Gabe was admittedly enjoying the peace and quiet. For now, and for the next few days, at least, he was the sole boss of Dos Estrellas.

Violet mounted and rode up beside him. Gabe nudged Bonita into a brisk walk. After some debate, he and Violet had decided to move the herd to a different section of grazing land, allowing the depleted vegetation in this section to regrow. With the help of their three best hands, the operation had gone smoothly, taking them all of yesterday and half of this morning.

The exception was a couple dozen strays who'd decided they'd rather hide in a stand of trees near the stock pond. These last four cattle were the most stubborn of the lot. And the craftiest. In the end, Gabe and Violet had prevailed.

"I have some news for you," she said, her jaw working as she chewed on a piece of dried grass.

"What's that?"

"It's about Mickey."

Violet had worked at Dos Estrellas for the past ten years, since she was eighteen. Gabe's father had originally hired her on as a wrangler. She'd worked her way up, from head wrangler to assistant livestock manager to senior livestock manager right before Gabe's father had become sick.

And while every bit a cowboy on the outside, she was one hundred percent girl on the inside. Back when she'd first started at the ranch, Gabe had asked her out. They'd gone on a few dates before mutually deciding they made better friends than romantic partners.

Gabe's father had also liked Violet, which was one reason he'd continually promoted her. The other was that she outperformed every other wrangler on the place, rightfully earning each of her new positions.

"What's with Mickey now?" Gabe didn't have a lot of patience when it came to the young wrangler, who worked hard one day and loafed off the next.

"He's leaving at the end of the week." Violet tossed away the stalk of dried grass. "Told me this morning."

"Not much notice."

"Said he got a better offer."

Gabe had his doubts. "From who?"

"Miracle Mile. They're near Tonopah."

He'd heard of the ranch. A little bigger than Dos Estrellas, but with a less-than-stellar reputation.

"Good luck to him."

Violet raised her brow, her head bobbing in rhythm to the horse's easy gait. "You're not mad?"

"Naw. Mickey's better off at Miracle Mile, and we're better off without him."

"Leroy's talking about leaving, too."

That did concern Gabe. "Why?"

"If you don't mind me saying, boss, the guys are a little worried. Talk is, money's in short supply, and what's left is going to the California Dempseys."

California Dempseys? That was what the employees called Gabe's brothers? Better than the California owners.

"I won't lie," Gabe said. "We aren't rolling in dough. But there's enough to carry the ranch for the next several months. I'm working on a longer-term solution."

"Good. I'll let the guys know."

"If they have a problem or want answers, they can come to me. I'll tell it to them straight."

"Wouldn't expect anything less from you."

Violet's respectful demeanor gave Gabe a warm feeling inside. It also motivated him to take action. His goal to buy his brothers' share wouldn't come together on its own.

Watching the last four strays reunite with the herd grazing contentedly on the green, rolling hills, Gabe envisioned what lay ahead and the course he must take. Cattle were what sustained the ranch, and increasing the herd was the best way to boost revenue.

"Can you finish up here?" he asked Violet. "I've got an appointment in town."

"Sure thing."

He trotted Bonita down the rocky rise and most of the way back to the barn. He hadn't been fibbing to Violet. He did have an appointment in town. Reese simply didn't know about it yet.

Smelling of cows was no way to make an impression. After unsaddling Bonita and returning her to the horse stable, he headed to the house. He showered and changed into clean jeans and a dress shirt.

Luckily, Cara was busy with some new arrivals at the mustang sanctuary and his mother had gone shopping in nearby Rio Verde for Thanksgiving dinner. Gabe could leave without having to answer their well-intended but nosy questions, about where he was going and why.

At the bank, he was informed by the teller that Reese was with a customer and he'd have to wait.

"How long will she be?"

"I'm not sure." The teller, a young man Gabe had seen on occasion, checked the wall clock. "Probably not long."

Gabe sat in one of the waiting chairs near an overly decorated seven-foot Christmas tree. Already? It wasn't even Thanksgiving yet. He'd noticed decorations in several storefronts on his way in, plus an empty lot next to the market cordoned off in preparation of tree sales. Signs for the community-wide annual Holly Daze Festival starting in a couple of weeks were posted all over town.

He typically didn't bother with the festival, but his mother had been talking about going for weeks. She'd missed last year's because of his father's illness. Gabe supposed he'd be the one recruited to take her and Cara.

His seat in the bank waiting area did offer one advantage: an unobstructed view of Reese's office. Through the floor-to-ceiling glass panel, he saw her sitting behind her desk, engaged in conversation with the customer who wasn't visible behind the solid wood door.

Hmm. She didn't look happy. If Gabe were to venture a guess, this particular customer was pushing all her hot buttons.

Well, finances could be a touchy subject. If she were turning down a loan request or collecting on a delinquent account, the person might be giving her grief. Gabe sat back in the deep cushioned chair and continued watching, intrigued by her expressive face.

She was lovely. Quite beautiful, actually, and obviously smart. Poised and confident. How had she flown so far under his radar until now? It wasn't like he hadn't seen her periodically, from a distance anyway, since her return. Probably because they worked diligently at avoiding each other.

Gabe noticed Reese twirling a pen between her thumb and forefinger as if venting her anger. Was she bored by her customer? No, Gabe clearly saw her face from where he sat, and her eyes were snapping. Whoever this customer was, he or she was getting to Reese while she struggled to maintain her cool.

Yet another quality to like about her. They were starting to stack up. Oh, yeah. Except for that one little obstacle: her tight grip on the Dos Estrellas purse strings.

The next instant, the door to her office flew open, startling Gabe. He glanced up and stared openly. The person with Reese was no customer. Blake Nolan strode angrily out of the office, his features dark and menacing.

He and Gabe were casually acquainted. Blake's mother was one of the town supervisors, and Gabe's father, like many of the local ranchers, had dealt frequently with the board of supervisors. Today, however, Gabe and Blake might have been complete strangers, for the other man walked past him without saying a word.

Gabe rose, considered hailing Blake, then thought better of it. He was more interested in Reese, how she was doing and—okay, fine—what had transpired between her and Blake.

He started for her office.

"Sir," the teller called out. "If you'll give me a second to buzz Ms. McGraw—"

"We're friends." At the door, he paused to take in Reese. "You all right?"

A flicker of surprise was her only reaction, which she quickly contained. "Gabe. What are you doing here? You're not on my calendar."

"I took a chance you were free."

"What can I do for you?"

He walked into her office and shut the door behind him.

She regarded him with suspicion. "Is this about the ranch?"

"You didn't answer my question. Are you all right?"

"Why wouldn't I be?" She tugged on the cuffs of her sweater, straightening the sleeves.

"Blake didn't appear very happy when he left."

"I'm not discussing him with you."

"Was it business or personal?" Gabe lowered himself into the visitor chair Blake had recently vacated.

"I repeat," she said in a clipped tone, "what are you doing here?"

He leaned forward. "I was concerned about you, is all."

"Because we're friends?" Though her tone remained clipped, her demeanor softened a bit around the edges. "I heard you say that to the teller."

"We're not?"

"We're business associates first."

"Funny isn't it?" He chuckled mirthlessly. "How did that happen, by the way?"

"Gabe, what do you want? I have another appointment in twenty minutes."

He sat back, striving to appear relaxed. In truth, he was a bundle of nerves. He'd sat in on several meetings with his father, always watching and learning, but he'd never conducted one. They'd both assumed his father had many more years ahead of him to run Dos Estrellas.

"I did some checking around this morning," Gabe said. "Made a few phone calls. Talked to a cattle broker. We can easily sustain five hundred more head. A thousand, even."

He waited for her to take what he saw as the logical leap. She didn't, simply stared at him and waited.

"I'd like to draw on the line of credit," he finally said.

"To purchase cattle?"

Was she intentionally baiting him? "Yes."

"Do your brothers know?"

"They're not back from California yet. Does it matter?"

"Yes. Any loans, including advances, must be approved of by all three owners." She didn't talk to him as if he were stupid or accuse him of not reading the will, which he appreciated.

That didn't lessen Gabe's frustration. "Can't you authorize it as the trustee?"

"Possibly. But I won't."

"This is a good time to buy. Beef prices are predicted to go up even higher."

Reese rested her clasped hands on the desk. "The ranch can't *easily* sustain more head, and you need the line of credit for supplemental feed."

"It could rain tomorrow. They're forecasting a ten percent chance."

She inhaled slowly. "I think we should wait. Stay the course for a few months. You said yourself at our recent meeting that summer is a better time to buy, when beef prices typically go down."

Gabe could also be stubborn. "Dad's plan was to grow the herd. You said so yourself."

"Slowly grow the herd," she reiterated.

"A few hundred head isn't exactly leaps and bounds."

"I'm sorry, Gabe."

"That's it?" He squeezed the chair's upholstered arm-rests hard enough to feel the metal bar inside. "You're in charge, so you can veto any request."

"I'll be glad to talk about it with all three of you when your brothers return."

And here he'd been thinking how attractive she was and smart. Right. He'd left out the part about her being obstinate and inflexible.

He abruptly stood. "Who's the manager here?"

"Walt Marshall." She also stood. "Why?"

"I want to talk to him about a change in trustee."

"It's not up to you. Your father named the bank."

"Then someone else here can take over. This Walt guy, for one."

Reese shook her head. "No, he can't."

"Why the hell not?" Gabe was getting pretty sick and tired of her countering everything he said.

"There are conditions."

"Like?"

"Gabe." She exhaled slowly. "I didn't want to tell you this." Her tone warned him not to ask.

He did anyway. "Tell me what?"

She hesitated. "Your father didn't just name Southern Arizona Bank as the trustee. He specifically requested me to oversee the trust."

"You're joking!"

"I'm afraid I'm not."

"How long have you known?"

"Since he arranged for the bank to be trustee."

He stared in amazement. "And you didn't say any-thing?"

"I couldn't. And even if bank policy didn't prohibit me, it wasn't my place."

"I don't believe you."

"Feel free to speak to Walt." She leaned back in her chair. "He'll tell you the same thing."

It was difficult for Gabe to see the sympathy in Reese's eyes through the red haze surrounding him. How could this be happening? Bad enough he had to share ownership of Dos Estrellas with two brothers who disliked him as much as he did them. He couldn't make a single decision about the ranch without the approval of Reese, the daughter of his father's rival.

None of this made sense. What could his father have been thinking? To specifically request Reese...

Gabe didn't say goodbye. Not that he remembered, anyway.

He knocked into the chair on his way out, muttering a curse under his breath. The next thing he knew, he was behind the wheel of his truck and driving across town to the attorney Hector Fuentes's office.

Maybe Gabe could contest the will. Or, there was a loophole giving him leverage over Reese. He had to find out, and Hector was the only one able to give him the answer.

Chapter 5

"Smells great, Mom."

"Gabriel, *mijo*. Did you put the extra leaf in the dining room table?"

"All done."

"And move the flowers to the living room?"

"Yep." Over a week had passed since the funeral and there were a dozen-plus floral and plant arrangements still alive and thriving. Gabe knew his mother didn't have the heart to throw them out.

"Good," she pronounced. "Now Cara can finish with the place settings."

Opening the oven door, Raquel checked the turkey and sides roasting inside. A blast of warmth filled the kitchen, along with an array of incredibly delicious aromas.

"You need any help?" he asked.

"I'm okay for now. Maybe in a little while." She shut the oven door, wiped her forehead with the back of her oven-mitted hand and sighed.

Along with the turkey, stuffing, sweet potatoes, cranberry relish and pumpkin pie, his mother had prepared a pot of beans, another pot of rice, two dozen beef enchiladas and a bowl of the hottest homemade salsa this side of Mustang Valley. In lieu of rolls or bread, warm flour tortillas would be served.

The Dempseys and Salazars had been a culturally blended family for as long as Gabe could remember. Being originally from Hermosillo, Mexico, the Salazars didn't celebrate Thanksgiving. It was different for August Dempsey. The holiday had a special meaning because it fell near the date his grandfather had purchased the land for Dos Estrellas. To please him, Gabe's mother prepared a big dinner, substituting favorite Mexican dishes for other, more common, American ones.

Gabe wondered what his brothers would think of the unusual menu. They'd returned from California late yesterday afternoon, driving two trucks and hauling two trailers. One was a rented moving van containing their personal belongings. The other, a horse trailer. They'd brought six of their personal mounts, four of which were Cole's championship calf-roping horses.

Without trying to be obvious, Gabe had looked the horses over last night as his brothers unloaded them. All appeared fit and stout with an alertness shining in their eyes. They weren't, however, ranch horses, and there was a big difference between roping calves in the rodeo ring and herding them across open range.

They might be trainable. Time would tell. He decided

to see how badly his brothers floundered before stepping in and giving them pointers.

Not his choice. Unfortunately, Gabe's visit to Hector's office last week had been a complete waste of time. The attorney, not bothering to hide his impatience with Gabe, assured him there was nothing to be done about either Gabe's brothers or Reese's position as trustee.

The sting had diminished, these past few days. Actually, who was he kidding? Gabe had chosen to ignore his frustration and anger rather than obsess about it. Perhaps after the holidays, when he had a better handle on the situation, he could try again.

Try what, exactly? Bang his head against the proverbial wall?

"*Mijo*, can you stir the beans for me?"

Grabbing the large wooden spoon, he did as his mother requested. There was hardly any space on the stove top. As usual, she'd prepared enough food to feed a small village.

Cara breezed into the kitchen. "The table's set. What else do you need, Tia Raquel?"

Gabe was glad to see her smiling. The holidays were difficult for her since she'd lost her young son two years ago. Gabe supposed it would be the same for him and his mother from now on.

"Where are Josh and Cole?" he asked.

"The backyard, last I checked." Cara stood on tiptoes and glanced out the window over the sink. "Yeah, they're sitting in the lawn chairs."

It annoyed Gabe that his brothers weren't inside with the rest of the family, helping with dinner or, at the least, socializing. Then again, he and Cara hadn't done much to make them feel welcomed. Just his mother.

"Cara, why don't you tell them we'll be ready to eat in about a half hour?"

"I think they're fine for the time being." Cara caught Gabe's eye and sent him the same conspiratorial look they'd often shared through the years. She was on his side and letting him know it.

The front doorbell rang.

"Who could that be?" Cara started across the kitchen.

With so many people showing up in recent weeks, and Gabe's brothers still settling in, his mother had suggested they limit dinner to immediate family. Gabe had heartily agreed.

"Let Gabe answer the door." His mother caught Cara by the shirtsleeve, and presented her with a strainer. "You drain the beans. My arthritis is bothering my hands."

Gabe had exactly one second to contemplate the oddness of his mother's remark—she'd been using her hands all day cooking without complaint—when the doorbell rang again.

"I'll get rid of them," Gabe said, already on his way.

"Nonsense." His mother's voice trailed after him. "Invite her in."

He didn't register his mother's use of the word *her* until he threw open the door. Seeing their guest, he silently cursed himself for not paying better attention.

Reese held a pink dessert box and a bottle of wine. Gabe stared like an idiot, struck dumb by her unexpected appearance and the killer tight jeans she wore, made sexier by her knee-high boots and a super-short jacket hugging her narrow waist. Her hair was pinned to the back of her head in a tidy knot that made Gabe think about removing the pins and sifting his fingers through the thick, silky strands.

If she had dressed like this the other day at the bank, he might not have been so angry at her for turning down his request.

After a moment, she tilted her head at an appealing angle. "Can I come in?"

"What are you doing here?"

She held up the dessert box and wine bottle. "These are for your mother. She invited me. Also my dad, but he can't make it."

"You're kidding." Gabe didn't know whether to be angry at his mom or impressed by her audacity. And at Reese's audacity for accepting the invitation. "Why would she do that?"

"I didn't ask her, but, if I was to venture a guess, I'd say she's trying to smooth out any difficulties in my working relationship with your family."

"Okay, but why did you agree to come?"

"The same reason."

He studied her one moment longer before standing back and allowing her to enter. He was glad he did for she gave off a hint of the most intriguing fragrance as she breezed past him.

One look at her walking away from him in those jeans and he wanted to investigate further.

She paused in the middle of the living room, waiting for him to catch up. He forced himself to not run.

"I'm sorry about the other day," she said. "I know you don't believe me, but I really didn't want to turn down your request."

"Too late now, the broker sold the cattle to another buyer."

"There'll be more cattle on the market. Maybe at a better price."

"And I'll still have to come begging to you with my hat in my hand."

"You didn't beg."

"And I never will." He hitched his chin toward the kitchen. "We're eating in the dining room, but everyone's in the kitchen."

Gabe was shocked his mother had invited Reese, and not because of the obvious reasons.

Their guests at holiday dinners were always close friends. Seldom family. The rift between Gabe's father and brothers wasn't the only one plaguing the Dempseys. His mother, while close to his grandmother, barely spoke to his grandfather. Gabe wasn't entirely sure of the reason for their estrangement, but he could guess. His *abuelo* Salazar hadn't approved of Gabe's father and the fact his mother began their relationship as an affair with a married man.

Gabe barely knew his maternal grandparents. They used to visit once a year in the summer when Gabe was little, staying at the bed-and-breakfast in town. That practice stopped years ago. They hadn't even attended August's funeral, though his grandmother had called, as she did frequently throughout the year.

"You first." Gabe gestured to Reese.

She walked confidently ahead of him into the kitchen. If she felt out of place or awkward, she didn't let it show. The same couldn't be said about his brothers. Since their return, their discomfort hung on them like ill-fitting shirts.

"You're here." Gabe's mother abandoned arranging the condiment tray and engulfed Reese in a friendly hug, which she returned as best she could with her hands full. "I'm so glad. How's your father?"

"He's sorry he couldn't come."

Gabe still couldn't believe his mother had invited Theo McGraw. Was she crazy? Maybe she was taking his father's death harder than he thought.

"These are for you." Reese held out the dessert box and wine to Raquel. "I hope you like pecan pie."

Gabe's mother beamed. "It was August's favorite."

How did Reese know that? Coincidence? Gabe wondered.

"Dad told me." She smiled warmly. "I guess August ordered it during the ranchers' monthly get-togethers at the Cowboy Up Café."

Gabe had attended those meetings numerous times with his father. August and Theo McGraw had always sat on opposite sides of the restaurant. Either Reese's father possessed superhuman vision and could see great distances or...

Was it possible the two men had been friendlier than they'd let on? His father had sometimes spoken well of Theo McGraw, when he wasn't cursing the other man's existence.

"Let me take that." His mother relieved Reese of the wine. "I'll put it in the refrigerator to chill. You can set the pie on the counter."

Gabe couldn't take his eyes off Reese. She busied herself with the pie, then flitted around the kitchen helping here and there as if she'd visited a hundred times before.

"Where's my china platter?" His mother had opened the cupboard and was staring at the top shelf.

"In the pine trunk, Tia Raquel." Cara, Gabe noticed,

was also watching his mother, with the same bewilderment on her face he felt.

"Ah, yes." His mother closed the cabinet and smiled with satisfaction. "I forgot."

She normally had the memory of an elephant. But she'd had a lot on her mind lately. Gabe could understand her forgetting where she left something.

"Will you get it for me, Gabe? The trunk is in the garage."

"Sure."

"Take Reese with you. For an extra set of eyes."

The request smacked of a setup. That would explain how his mother seemingly forgot the location of the platter.

"I can manage, Mom."

"Nonsense. What else is Reese to do with herself?"

"I'd be happy to go with you," she said, giving Gabe reason to wonder if she was in on things.

No. His mother worked alone, never able to make an ally of him or Cara when it came to her often-outrageous schemes. Reese was probably innocent. Like him. But he wasn't ignorant. Whatever reason his mother had for getting him and Reese alone, he didn't care. Her plan would fail.

"All right," he said. "Follow me."

They walked from the kitchen, through the laundry room and out the door leading to the garage. Gabe flipped on the light switch and indicated a step down.

"Watch it." He resisted taking her hand.

The pine chest sat against the wall, covered by an old quilt. In addition to the platter, his mother kept an assortment of other, seldom used, holiday relics.

Removing the quilt, Gabe lifted the lid on the chest,

trying hard to ignore Reese's proximity. She didn't need to stand right beside him.

"I'm glad your mother suggested I go with you."

He straightened, one hand resting on the chest lid. "You are?"

"I was rude to you the other day at the bank. This gives us a chance to talk."

"We cleared the air when you first arrived."

"I wanted to tell you why Blake was at the bank."

Not what Gabe was expecting to hear. "Like you said, it's none of my business."

"Yes...and no. You're one of the few people besides him who knows I was pregnant."

"You don't have to tell me."

"You're right. But I'd like to. You've kept my secret a lot of years, and I appreciate it."

"Okay." Gabe closed the lid on the chest without removing the platter. He sat, then patted the spot next to him. "I'm listening."

What had seemed like a good idea now felt like a colossal mistake. Had she lost her mind, suggesting she and Gabe talk? Yes, she regretted having to decline his request for a draw on the line of credit. That was no reason to reveal her past and what occurred after the night of their senior prom.

She paced the garage floor in front of Gabe, not accepting his invitation to sit beside him. The pine chest was small. Okay, not minuscule. But if she sat beside him, they'd be elbow to elbow. Thigh to thigh. Hardly conducive to pouring her heart out.

"I promise not to bite," he said, tracking her every step.

Bite? Her throat felt suddenly dry as she imagined

his teeth tugging playfully on her neck or on the inside of her arm. Swallowing didn't help.

"This is harder than I anticipated," she said.

Gabe grabbed her hand and tugged her onto the chest. Reese gasped softly. She'd been right. They were elbow to elbow. Thigh to thigh. His legs were strong and muscular, the result of hard physical labor every day of his life.

Her father had been strong once, with the build of a professional athlete. The Parkinson's had sucked every last ounce of strength out of him.

But that wasn't what she wanted to tell Gabe. Gathering her courage—they didn't have much time, dinner would be served soon—she began in a halting voice.

"The reason Blake stormed out of my office was because he didn't like my answer regarding his business with the bank."

"There's a lot of that going around."

She searched his face, unsure if he was teasing or serious. The corner of his mouth twitched ever so slightly. Teasing, she decided.

"It wasn't personal and wasn't about our daughter."

"Daughter?" Gabe studied her intently. "You had the baby, then?"

"Yes." She shifted, but there was no escaping. Short of her getting up, Gabe's body parts and hers would remain touching. With some effort, Reese refocused her attention. "And, to answer your next question, Blake knows about Celia."

Gabe shrugged. "I didn't ask."

"But you were wondering. His wife, Wynonna, knows, too."

"Did he tell her before or after they were married?"

"I never asked. It didn't matter."

"That must have been hard. Giving up your child. Or am I assuming wrong?"

She nodded. "You're right. About me giving her up and how hard it was. The hardest thing I've ever done." Even coping with her father's illness didn't compare. "But I was barely eighteen when she was born and incapable of providing for a child."

"Your father would have—"

"Not an option."

Reese would not discuss her family's complex dynamics with Gabe, and how disappointed and brokenhearted her straitlaced father would have been with her—for getting pregnant and having a relationship with an engaged man. She wouldn't have blamed him. But because of Celia, she didn't regret her actions. What she did regret was the difficult position she'd put Blake in, and she accepted full responsibility.

"Celia was adopted by my cousin Megan in Oregon," she continued. "We have a long-distance relationship. When the time's right, and Celia's ready, my cousin and I have agreed Celia can come to Mustang Valley for a visit. Hopefully, to meet my father."

"I thought he still didn't know about her."

"Things have…changed lately. I'm, well, ready to tell Dad, and I think he'll be more receptive." She exhaled. "Celia's asked to meet him. Maybe after the first of the year. Or her spring break from school."

"What about Blake?"

"He's less inclined to establish a relationship with her."

Gabe called Blake an unflattering name under his breath.

"Don't be so quick to judge." Amazingly, once she got started, she found talking to Gabe not hard at all. "Blake was involved with Wynonna long before I pursued him. I knew he was engaged from the start." She took a moment to collect herself. "I was young and stupid and thought I was in love. To my shame, I took advantage of a rough patch he and Wynonna were going through. My mistake was in thinking he'd break off the engagement and not get back together with her. His mistake, too, I suppose, for leading me on."

"Whatever the circumstances, he's still Celia's father."

"And the father of two other children with his wife, who may not want to or be ready to accept Celia in their lives. I respect their choice."

"That's no excuse," Gabe insisted. "He has a responsibility."

"Not financially, he doesn't. Any obligation was eliminated when he consented to the adoption. That was part of our agreement."

"He has a kid living in Oregon and doesn't care enough to see her?"

Reese could see how Gabe related to Celia and superimposed his own feelings onto her. He was also the illegitimate child of a parent with two legitimate sons. The difference was Celia, who had no conflicting emotions.

"Actually, it's up to Celia. She and I talk regularly, and I've visited her a few times. She loves her mother and father, and isn't compelled to seek out her biological father."

"That could change."

Reese didn't disagree. "When and if it does, we'll

figure things out. In the meantime, she's happy, which is the most a parent can hope for their child."

"Why are you telling me this, Reese?"

She sought the right words, needing Gabe to understand her reasons.

"I trust you."

"Huh. Didn't see that coming. I'm pretty sure I threatened you recently with having you removed as trustee."

"Oh, right."

He chuckled. "Am I to assume you aren't angry?"

"It was a knee-jerk reaction. Happens a lot at work." Returning his smile was difficult. Reese's nerves were getting to her. She and Gabe had never been like this before. Close physically and emotionally. "I trust you because you didn't tell anyone I was pregnant. That means something."

"What does it mean, Reese?"

The smooth timbre of his voice as he said her name caused a stirring in her middle. It was impossible to ignore and resist. Gabe was having an effect on her. And these intimate conversations they'd engaged in lately only heightened her awareness of, and attraction to, him.

He leaned in, and his breath caressed her cheek. She had to stop this. Right now. If not, they might be tempted to venture into dangerous territory.

"We should probably go inside." She made an effort to rise, but changed her mind when her shaky legs threatened to give out. "Your mom's expecting her platter."

"Not yet." He placed a hand on her arm.

"Gabe," she whispered right before his lips found hers and covered them completely. Her eyes drifted shut as he increased the pressure of their kiss.

This could not be happening. But, it was, and Reese

wasn't doing anything to stop Gabe or the incredible sensations his assault on her mouth elicited. Nor, would she stop him. Not yet, anyway. Another minute. Maybe two. The kiss was just too delicious. Too powerful. Too sensual. A soft moan filled her ears. Hers. It was followed by another moan as she angled her head to give Gabe greater access.

Her hand sought his jaw, and his short stubby whiskers tickled her fingertips. Truth be told, she'd imagined kissing Gabe and tracing her fingers along his jaw, more than once. That must account for her immediate and uninhibited surrender to him.

The next second, the assault intensified as Gabe slipped his tongue into her mouth. Reese didn't resist this either and melted farther into his embrace. His arms circled her, firm and strong, pulling her flush against him. She was trapped, exactly where she wanted to be.

The next low groan came from him, raw and desperate. Under different circumstances, Reese would have been thrilled with her ability to arouse this kind of excitement in him. Instead, the groan acted like a trigger and brought her to her senses. Their behavior was more than inappropriate. It was risky. Too much was at stake for her to make such a careless mistake.

Breaking off the kiss, she insisted, "We can't," in between short, shallow breaths. "Stop. Please."

He did. Sort of, in that he ceased kissing her. But he didn't move away and didn't give any indication he would. Lowering his head, he nuzzled the side of her face. The gesture was incredibly sensuous, sweetly tender and wildly romantic.

Who would have thought it? Gabe was an amazing kisser. With very little effort, he'd taken her to a place she'd never been before and might not ever go again. It was *that* good. And, she had to admit, her feelings for him were *that* strong.

"Gabe, we have to go inside." Sliding away from him, she all but leapt to her feet. This time, he let her go. Which was for the best because deep inside, she didn't want to leave the garage.

Rising casually—damn him for his composure; she was a basket case—he lifted the lid of the pine chest and retrieved the platter.

She hurried toward the door.

"Reese, hold up. We should go together. If not, my mom will think I did or said something to upset you." He paused, balancing the platter in the crook of his arm. The same arm he'd used to hold her tight moments ago. "Did I upset you?"

"No."

"Really? Because you look kind of flustered."

"I do?" She automatically smoothed her hair.

"Don't worry." He grinned. "You're gorgeous."

He'd been right the first time. She was flustered and more than a little mad at herself. She'd been wrong to encourage him.

"This is all my fault."

"I'm the one who kissed you."

"And I let you."

His grin widened. "Yeah, you did."

She rolled her eyes. He was such a guy. "Don't let it go to your head. I was simply curious."

"That wasn't the only reason you kissed me."

Of all the nerve! His confidence irritated her. "Whatever the reason, it isn't going any further and won't happen again."

"Because of your job."

"Yes."

And because this was exactly the sort of rash behavior that had landed her in trouble twelve years ago with Blake. He'd been unavailable. Engaged to another woman. But Reese had fancied herself in love.

She would not be that person again. She'd grown up since then. Learned her lesson.

At least no one had seen her and Gabe or knew of their momentary indiscretion. As long as he didn't say anything, and he'd proved himself dependable when it came to keeping his mouth shut, they could forget all about the kiss.

Who was she kidding? She'd remember this kiss for the rest of her life. But she would try and pretend it hadn't happened.

"Come on." Gabe nodded in the direction of the door.

Reese didn't need to be asked twice. She flew through the door, raced across the laundry room and burst into the kitchen before coming to a sudden halt.

"There you are." Raquel stood with her hands upon her hips, and taking them in, a wide smile spread across her face. "Cara was about to go searching for you. We're almost ready to eat."

Four pairs of eyes fixed on them—Josh and Cole had come in from outside while Reese and Gabe were in the garage. Seeing the suspicion in all of their eyes, Reese was convinced she and Gabe had been busted.

Gabe presented his mother with the platter, his manner unconcerned. "It wasn't where I thought. We had to look around." He sauntered over to the counter. "Need me to carve the turkey?"

Reese snuck a peek at her hostess, feeling heat climb her neck and travel to her cheeks. This was going to be a long, awkward dinner.

Chapter 6

Gabe could sense Reese's embarrassment from the opposite side of the dining table. She spoke little, fidgeted a lot and ate hardly anything.

He probably shouldn't have kissed her. Okay, fine. He'd been out of line and taken advantage of her in a weak moment. But, damn, he'd do it again given half a chance.

The kiss had been electric. Phenomenal. If he hadn't been sitting on the chest, he'd have fallen to the garage floor. Who would have guessed? Him and Theo McGraw's daughter, kissing in the garage. If his father were alive, he'd disown Gabe.

Or would he? He had named Reese as trustee. Gabe still failed to grasp his father's reasoning. It must have been the chemo or pain medication muddling his brain.

Gabe couldn't use that excuse. Kissing her had been

the furthest thing from his mind when they'd entered the garage. Then she'd told him about her daughter Celia. Thanked him for keeping her secret. Told him she trusted him and insisted he could trust her in return.

And what had he done? Abused that trust by kissing her. While she'd been a willing partner, he'd made the first move and elevated the kiss from a somewhat chaste, if not quite innocent, peck to a searing hot lip-lock.

It had been worth it. She'd shown him how good it could be between two people and how right it could feel.

"Gabe. Hey, Gabe. You listening?" Cara elbowed him in the side. "Josh asked you to pass the rice."

"Thanks," Josh said when Gabe roused himself from his stupor and handed over the large bowl.

"What's wrong?" Cara whispered.

"Nothing," Gabe insisted.

"I get it." She gave a tiny nod in the direction of his brothers, who were debating their favorite pie, pumpkin or apple. "I don't know what your mom was thinking, inviting them."

Gabe didn't correct Cara's assumption about his the reason for his distraction. "They *are* staying in the guest suite," he murmured.

"Yeah. Not to invite them would be rude. Too bad."

He ate mechanically, his gaze wandering the table. The next instant, Cara caught him staring at Reese.

"Well, well, well." A hint of amusement colored her voice.

"It's not what you think."

"You have no idea what I'm thinking."

"What are you two chatting about?" Gabe's mother asked, putting an immediate end to their private conversation.

"Nothing, Tia Raquel." Cara winked at Gabe.

He glanced away, not wanting to make Reese any more uncomfortable than she already was.

What was it about her that got to him? Before his father's illness, Gabe had dated. A couple of those former girlfriends had lasted long enough he'd considered making the relationship permanent. Considered, but hadn't acted on it. Something always held him back.

Until today, he hadn't realized what that was. Then he'd kissed Reese, and she had responded like no other. The incredible sparks were the missing component he'd been searching for.

"I was thinking," Josh said, "you could take me and Cole on a ride of the pasture lands tomorrow."

Gabe nearly choked on his bite of enchilada. "We're a little busy this week, vaccinating the calves and pregnancy checking the cows. I promised Violet I'd help her load the equipment and ready the vaccines."

"Cole and I will lend a hand."

At his mother's warning stare, Gabe ground his teeth together. "Be saddled up and ready to ride out at two."

Josh smiled, but Cole clenched his knife and fork as if attempting to bend them with his bare hands. "What about the morning?"

"Violet and I can handle it."

"If we're going to be partners on this ranch, Josh and I need to learn the ropes."

From anyone else, Gabe would have admired the man's persistence and determination. From Cole, it smacked of interference.

Again, his mother fired off a warning stare. Again, Gabe reluctantly conceded. Damn the holidays and having to behave during dinner.

"We start at seven o'clock sharp."

"Breakfast is at six," his mother added sweetly. "In the summer, when it gets light out earlier, we eat at five-thirty."

Did she have to tell them everything?

"Thank you again for inviting me," Reese said during a pause. It was her first contribution to the conversation in a while and probably made to ease the tension.

"My pleasure." Gabe's mother beamed.

"Isn't it a little late in the season to vaccinate?" Cole asked.

The question startled Gabe. What did Cole know about raising cattle?

"Normally, we vaccinate in October. Time got away from us, what with Dad dying and all."

Gabe purposely refused to look at his mother, knowing she was annoyed at his snide tone. But, hell, his brothers had been eight hundred miles away while their mutual father wasted away during the final stages of colon cancer. Vaccinating calves and pregnancy checking cows had been the last thing on Gabe's and anyone's minds.

"Tortillas, anyone?" His mother held up a ceramic warmer.

Gabe suspected she was attempting to diffuse the tension.

"Yes, thank you," Reese answered, too brightly to be genuine.

Cara, Gabe's mother and Josh carried the conversation for the next several minutes, long enough for them to almost make it through dinner. Then the shit hit the fan when Cole opened his mouth.

"Cara, why is it you got one-sixth of the ranch?"

She drew back, startled. "I beg your pardon?"

"Aren't you just a family friend? "

"Cara is practically a member of this family," Gabe's mother said, rushing to Cara's defense. "And I'm sure August wanted to remember her. The work she does with the sanctuary is important. Those poor horses need someone to look out for them. They're neglected, starving and sometimes abused."

"But wouldn't the ranch benefit if you turned the sanctuary land over to the cattle?" Josh asked.

Josh's question hadn't come across as an attack like Cole's. Gabe was irritated nonetheless.

"The land belongs to Cara," he said. "She fosters over two hundred horses. We'd have to find somewhere to place them. That's a big job."

"I'm simply trying to figure this out." Josh's gaze traveled from Gabe to Cara, "Don't you want the ranch to get out of debt? We'd have a better chance with five hundred more acres. We wouldn't have to supplement the grazing land with grain and hay."

"It isn't our habit to discuss business at the table," Gabe's mother said firmly.

"Excuse me for saying, ma'am," Cole stressed the last word, "but we were discussing business a few minutes ago, and you didn't have a problem with it."

Gabe pushed back from the table, his chair scraping loudly across the hardwood floor. "What my mother means is we don't argue at the table. My father wouldn't allow it. But, then, you'd know that if you were ever here."

"For the record." Josh tossed his linen napkin onto the table. "Dear old Dad refused to let us come out for a visit.

He told me so himself when I disobeyed my mother and called him fifteen years ago. He said I wasn't welcome."

Gabe's mother bit back a sob. "He always regretted that."

Josh's eyes flashed. "You're wrong, Raquel. He didn't have an ounce of regret. He couldn't have cared less about me or Cole."

"He loved you. It...it wasn't his fault." Her eyes filled with tears. "You don't understand."

"You're right." Cole ground out the words. "I don't understand a father who would turn his back on his children."

"The way I heard it, your mother left." Gabe could spar with the best of them and would be happy to oblige his brother.

Cole jumped to his feet. "Because of your mother."

Reese let out a small gasp.

"Stop it!" Cara cried out.

"I remind you," Gabe said stonily, "that you're staying in this house solely because of my mother's generosity."

Cole pointed at himself and Josh. "The house is two-thirds ours."

"She and Cara are entitled to remain here as long as they want."

"But the house doesn't belong to her, and she has no claim. She and our dad never married. Is that right?" He fired Reese a hostile look.

"I'm not an attorney," she said calmly. "My job is to carry out the terms of the will, not offer legal advice."

Gabe barely heard her. Cole's insinuations were another reminder Gabe wasn't legitimate. Was that the reason his father didn't leave him Dos Estrellas? Had he believed Josh and Cole would contest the will and try to take the ranch away from Gabe? As his legal offspring, they might have succeeded.

"My mother has been nothing but kind to you. Don't insult her."

Josh's face paled, and he and Cole walked away without excusing themselves.

"Good riddance," he said after them, then mumbled, "Greedy bastards."

Reese's eyes widened. Cara made a sound of disgust.

"What?" he demanded. "They are."

"Enough, *mijo*," his mother scolded in a tone Gabe hadn't heard since he was ten.

"They were ready to throw you from your home."

"Your brothers are our guests."

If he lived to be a hundred, he would never understand women.

"I owe you an apology," Gabe said.

"You've been doing that a lot lately." Reese hugged herself as if she might fly apart at the seams. "Apologizing."

"I had an outburst. Can you blame me?"

"You embarrassed your mother."

"They started it."

"Really, Gabe?"

Fresh anger surged, and he tried to tamp it down before he lost control again. "They were insulting and out of line."

"There's something to be said about taking the higher road."

"Right." He could hear his father making a similar remark when Gabe had punched Josh in the nose during their early school days. What would he have said back to his father if he'd known then what he knew now?

"It's Thanksgiving, Gabe. Holidays aren't a time for fighting with family."

"Can we save the lecture for another day?"

"You did ask me to stay."

"Sorry. Again."

She rolled her eyes.

Maybe he should quit while he was ahead and walk Reese to her car.

The two of them sat on the couch in the living room. She'd wanted to leave after the fiasco at dinner. Gabe had convinced her to remain and give him a chance to explain. Only he was doing a terrible job.

"It's been a difficult, weird day," she said.

"Not all of it." Gabe couldn't help smiling. "Parts of it were pretty darn good."

"Are you referring to…what happened in the garage?"

"We kissed, Reese. You can say it."

"Shh. Not so loud." She glanced worriedly around and whispered, "I thought we agreed to pretend that didn't happen."

"Speak for yourself. I, personally, am going to remember that kiss for a long time."

She closed her eyes and sighed.

"Okay, okay. I won't bring it up again." Today. He might want to talk about it again with her. Someday in the future, after he'd bought out his brothers' share of the ranch and was the sole owner. Then they'd be free to…what? Date? How would Reese feel about that?

"The argument between you and your brothers is the perfect example of why people choose a bank to be the trustee of their estate."

Gabe gave her a wry smile. "I'm beginning to see your point, much as I wish I didn't."

"Your father was a smart man."

"In some ways."

"No one's perfect."

"How's your father, by the way?"

She looked abruptly away. "Fine. Why?"

"His fall off the porch steps the other day. You left in a hurry."

"He's fine," she repeated. "Great."

"Glad to hear it."

She grabbed her purse on the floor beside her. "I should check on him."

"He'd call if he needed anything, right?"

"I suppose."

There was something off with her, more than the scene at dinner, and Gabe couldn't put his finger on it. She could feel guilty, he supposed, leaving her father alone on a holiday, even though she said he'd encouraged her to come.

"Speaking of fathers," Gabe said, "I remembered something the other day about mine that might interest you."

"Oh?"

"He liked you."

"You're kidding. We barely spoke." She seemed to relax.

"Well, I should say, he thought highly of you. He said it once. Admired you for going away."

"West Phoenix isn't exactly going away."

"You left the ranch and your father. That couldn't have been easy."

"I attended college. After Celia was born," she added in a quiet voice.

"But you didn't move back to Mustang Valley. Not for twelve years."

"There aren't many opportunities in a town this size for a person with a business degree. I was lucky to land the job at the bank. It was the first management position to open up there in four years."

"I think that's why Dad admired you. Because you chose a career you loved and didn't settle for being a rancher's daughter and marrying a local cowboy."

Her brows rose.

He might have been referring to himself, and she might have guessed.

"It's more than pursuing a career," she said. "I made a commitment to my cousin and her husband when they adopted Celia." Again, she lowered her voice. "I help with some of her expenses. Summer camp. Braces. Piano lessons. I also agreed to assist with her college education. I couldn't, won't, ask my father for that. Celia is my responsibility."

"That's very noble of you." He was sincere.

"I also like being my own person. I'm very independent."

Gabe nodded. "My dad was right to admire you."

She smiled, lighting up the room. "If he was still alive, I'd tell him thank you."

"Why *did* you come back to Mustang Valley?"

She stilled, taking her time to answer. "What's the old saying about coming home?"

"That's not an answer."

Reese ran her palms down the front of her jeans, then

moved her purse to her other arm. "I should leave. It's getting late."

He'd pushed her too far and not for the first time today.

"Maybe someday you'll tell me what's going on." Gabe searched her face.

"Nothing's going on," she insisted and rose.

At the front door, he leaned down, intending to kiss her on the cheek.

"Gabe." She stepped back.

"If our fathers weren't rivals, and you didn't work for the bank, you and I would be friends. More than friends."

She laughed wryly. "I'm not sure about that."

Gabe was. "See you soon."

He walked back to the kitchen, a spring in his step. That was the closest to a normal, casual conversation he'd ever had with Reese. Truth be told, he rather liked it and could almost—*almost*—forget she'd turned down his request for a draw on the line of credit.

"Hey, you two," he asked his mother and Cara. "Need some help with the dishes?"

They turned from the sink and gave him the evil eye.

"I'm assuming you're mad about dinner."

"You have to ask?" Cara resumed loading the dishwasher.

"Reese gave me an earful earlier."

"I like her," his mother said over the running water.

"I'm sorry, Mom." He was tired of issuing apologies. "I didn't mean to ruin dinner."

"Your father wouldn't have wanted you to fight with your brothers."

"What would he have wanted, Mom? Because I sure

as heck can't figure it out. Nothing makes any sense. He didn't care about his other sons until he got sick."

"You're wrong!" His mother shut off the water.

Cara grabbed a dishtowel and wiped her hands. "Why don't I leave you two alone so you can talk?" She didn't wait for an answer and left. He and his mother stood on opposite ends of the kitchen, each of them silently fuming. Gabe caved first. Sort of. What he did was ask the question he'd wanted answered all these years.

"Why didn't you and Dad ever marry?"

"He said once that he told you."

"Something about Abuelo not approving of him and you not going against your father's wishes."

"It's true."

"Seriously, Mom? You were an adult when you met Dad. If you'd wanted to marry him after he got his divorce, nothing Abuelo did or said could have stopped you."

"I don't want to talk about it."

"That's what you always say."

"You might think badly of your *abuelo*." She returned a pan to the cupboard.

"What did he do?" Gabe chuckled harshly. "Threaten you?"

She took a long time to answer. "Yes."

Gabe scowled. "With what? How?"

She sat at the table. Gabe did the same and gave his mother the moment she appeared to need in order to collect her thoughts.

"I promised your father I wouldn't ever tell you the details," she said with a sigh. "I suppose now it doesn't matter. Except…" She squeezed Gabe's hand, desperation shining in her eyes. "Please try and understand. Your *abuelo* did what he thought was best."

"Threatening someone is never best."

"Papi was raised in Mexico and didn't come to this country until he was a young man. His values and beliefs are those passed down to him from his father, and his father before him. Mexican men are revered as head of the household and their children, especially their daughters, obey them unconditionally. He is also very religious. Your father was separated when we met, staying temporarily with a friend, but still legally married."

Gabe hadn't heard that part of the story before. "He was separated?"

"He was intending to get a divorce. I was working in Scottsdale at a tree nursery. We met there."

Gabe had heard *that* part of the story.

"We started dating, fell in love and planned to marry. His wife, she changed her mind and convinced him to stay, using Josh as a reason. I was heartbroken, but didn't stop him. He had a son to think of." His mother paused. "He was gone a month before I realized I was pregnant with you. Hard as it was, I decided not to tell him."

"Dad didn't know about me." Gabe was stunned.

"Not until you were born. Someone at the nursery told him I was on maternity leave. Your father figured it out and insisted I move to Mustang Valley to be near him."

"And you did?"

"He told his wife he was getting a divorce. They weren't happy together. I wouldn't have moved here if I hadn't believed him."

"But was it true? They did have Cole after me."

"Yes. He had the papers drawn up when she told him she was pregnant."

"So, he stayed married, and you and he continued seeing each other." It was hard for Gabe to understand. His father had always preached honor and respect, yet he hadn't practiced those qualities. Not when it came to Gabe's mother.

"Eventually, your father did divorce. His wife left him and took their sons. My father still didn't approve. His religion doesn't favor divorce."

"You can't run your children's lives once they reach adulthood."

"My father ran mine," she admitted sadly. "He told me if I married your father, he would forbid me to have any contact with my mother and brothers."

"That's not only wrong, it's cruel." Gabe couldn't pick who he was madder at, his father or his grandfather. "What was he planning on doing? Ban you? Lock up Abuela and your brothers?"

"He would have forbidden them to see me, and Mama would not have disobeyed him."

"He's not in charge of—"

"You don't understand, *mijo*. You were raised by American parents. Mine have entirely different values. Your father understood and, for that reason, he refused to marry me. He didn't want to be responsible for cutting me off from my family. He'd already lost his sons."

"But Abuelo was all right with you two living together?"

"No, which is why they stayed at the inn in town and not at the house. But he believed a man has a responsibility to his children. He expected your father to raise and support you."

"He sounds like a hypocrite."

"Perhaps he is. But I respect him for his beliefs."

"Abuela would have found a way to see you and talk to you."

"Perhaps. And when Papi found out, he'd have made

her life miserable. Your father wouldn't put her in that position. He did what he thought was best."

"For him. Not for you. Or me." Gabe hated how childish he sounded, but he'd suffered his entire life from his parents' decision not to marry and, it seemed, his grandfather's bullying tactics.

"Your father had a lot of regrets. One was you not getting the chance to know your brothers."

"He cut them off."

"He didn't."

"Are you going to tell me that was Abuelo's doing, too?"

"To a degree. Josh and Cole's mother was also responsible. She turned them against your father. Filled their heads with half-truths. Made him out to be a terrible person."

"Can you blame her for being angry? He had an affair." Gabe had loved his father always, but he was angry at him. "I was born in between Josh and Cole, which means he was sleeping with both her and you at the same time." At his mother's beet-red face, Gabe felt ashamed. "I'm sorry, Mom. That was thoughtless of me."

"Try not to be so angry and bitter."

"It's hard to be anything but."

"Your father married because it was a good match, and he was of an age to settle down. Unfortunately, they were miserable together. When we met, it was like in the movies, fireworks exploding in the sky." She blushed anew. "We were wrong, I admit it. And our decisions caused a lot of hurt and pain for people we cared about. I would, however, do it again." She cupped Gabe's cheek. "Because I loved him more than life itself, and he gave me you."

"Why didn't he leave me the ranch like he promised?"

She returned her hand to her lap. "He was trying to make up to Josh and Cole for all the years he missed. And, I believe this with all my heart, he wanted to unite the three of you."

"Why didn't he try years ago?"

"He did. But, by then, the damage was done. Your brothers wanted nothing to do with him, and every overture he made was ignored or thrown back in his face."

Gabe was pretty sure if he looked up *dysfunctional family* in the dictionary, he'd read a description of the Dempseys and Salazars. If he wasn't so close to the situation, he'd laugh. Or get drunk. "Come on, Mom." He pushed back from the table. "I'll help you finish the dishes."

"You don't have to."

"The job will go faster with two people."

She smiled, relief in her expression, and chatted amiably about the upcoming Holly Daze Festival and the best time to haul out the Christmas decorations from storage.

Gabe understood that the causal banter helped take his mother's mind off her grief over his father's death and the unpleasant scene between him and his brothers. He wished he could say the same for himself.

Rather than feeling better, Gabe's anger and frustration continued to simmer. His mother had answered his question, but nothing had changed. He was still the illegitimate son who didn't inherit the ranch his father had promised him.

What an idiot he'd been earlier, thinking he could ask Reese out after this was all over. Without full ownership of the ranch and a respected place in the community, he had nothing to offer her. A woman like Reese deserved better.

when he gained full custody of them. Cole, well, he remained a mystery.

The man had a decent rodeo career that he'd put on hold in order to stay at Dos Estrellas. Josh, too. Their mother's parents owned a horse ranch in Northern California where the brothers had been raised and learned to cowboy. Gabe had heard the two of them talking the other day, and their grandparents' place also served as their home base when they weren't on the circuit. Point being, Cole didn't have a compelling reason to remain in Mustang Valley.

The only reason Gabe could think of was his loyalty to Josh, something he'd observed on more than one occasion. It was an admirable quality, and his estimation of Cole was raised a small notch, not that he'd ever tell his younger brother.

He'd also never tell Cole how good he was with horses. And Josh was a quick learner who showed a knack for cattle management. Had either of them been newly hired ranch hands, Gabe would credit them with potential. Because they stood between him and sole ownership of Dos Estrellas, he kept his mouth shut.

Gabe sat back in his father's office chair and stretched. Sitting at a desk and poring over papers wasn't his idea of a fun time. The past hour had dragged by like three. Neither Cole nor Josh had objected when Gabe stated he wanted to be the one in charge of record keeping. His motives had nothing to do with the fact that the task gave him an opportunity to talk to Reese almost daily.

She was patient with him and willing to answer his numerous questions. They'd covered balancing the monthly bank statements, updating income and expense spreadsheets, the liability insurance renewal and also a household budget. Gabe was learning a lot more about the business end of running a cattle operation than he'd thought possible.

One more thing the cancer had taken from him—Gabe's opportunity to learn this part of the family business from his father.

His anger from last week had dimmed, but the pain remained constant. How long until he stopped seeing his father's ghost everywhere in the house and barn?

His cell phone vibrated. Thinking it was the grain supplier, he was pleased to see Reese's name and number appear. This would be a nice break from the busy morning he'd had, crunching numbers and making calls.

"Hi, how you doing?" Funny, a month ago he couldn't have imagined himself happily answering a call from her. Neither could he have imagined kissing her. Yet, he'd done both and enjoyed it.

"We have a problem." She spoke in a rush.

"What's wrong?" His first thought was another unexpected bill. They'd received a whopper the other day, an overlooked co-pay balance from his father's specialist.

"Some of your cattle in section nine broke through the fence along the west line."

"Are they in with the Small Change livestock?"

"And some of ours are in with yours. Guess it's quite a mess up there, according to Enrico."

"I'll be right over." He shut off the ten-key calculator and desk lamp.

"Bring help," she said.

"That bad?"

"Apparently so."

The two neighbors had an unwritten agreement not to graze their cattle on adjacent land. Problem was, with the drought continuing, section nine had the best available grassland on Dos Estrellas. If Gabe and Violet hadn't moved a portion of their stock there, they'd be facing an even greater shortage of feed.

"Four-wheel, horseback or both?" Gabe asked.

"Both. We'll meet you there."

He assumed by *we* she meant her father, Enrico and any available Small Change hands.

"I'll call your father's cell when we're close." He had Theo McGraw's phone number, in case of an emergency, and Theo his.

"Call me," Reese told him.

"You're coming?"

"On my way now." She didn't wait for his response and disconnected.

Was she now? Gabe experienced a rush of anticipation. Passing his mother on his way out, he quickly filled her in on the problem and where he was going.

"Don't rush, I'll hold supper," she promised.

He kissed her cheek before racing from the house to the horse stable, all the while mentally composing a to-do list. He'd send Violet and one of the hands by road in two of their four-wheel-drive quads. He'd go by horseback along with...

He spotted Cole, who'd been repairing a leak in the automatic watering system. Evidently, he was done, for he emerged from one of the stalls, toolbox in hand.

Gabe made a decision. "Where's Josh?"

"He's saddling up to ride out and tend the heifer with the skin lesions."

"Good. We're going in the same direction. You saddle up, too."

Cole's eyes widened. "What's wrong?"

For a fraction of a second, Gabe saw his father in Cole's face, and his gut tightened. It was less his features and more his expression.

How could that be? Cole had left the valley when he was five, never seeing their father again. Were things like expressions inherited?

Gabe cleared his throat. "We have a break in the fence on the west side of section nine. Our cattle are getting mixed in with those from the Small Change. I'm sending Violet by road. The three of us will ride out."

"I'll get Josh." Cole set the toolbox by the tack room door.

"Meet you at the gate."

Cole hurried off.

Gabe grabbed a halter from the tack room wall and headed straight to Bonita's stall. He'd need a horse with good cow sense for this job. Leading her to the hitching rail outside the tack room, he saddled and bridled her.

While he worked, he thought about Cole. His brother hadn't asked a lot of questions. Instead, he'd immediately set off in search of Josh. It was the kind of response Gabe would have expected from anyone who worked for him. The kind of response he'd expect from someone who understood the necessity of responding quickly in a crisis.

Okay, he'd give Cole credit for that, too. The real challenge, though, would come in an hour when they were separating the cattle and herding theirs back through the hole in the fence. He would see how well his brothers applied their rodeo skills to a real-life roundup.

Ten minutes later, the three of them were riding the back trail to section nine, the same trail he'd ridden the day he had found Reese trying to free her father's horse trapped in the sinkhole. In the distance, Violet and Joey, a young hand who'd started working for Dos Estrellas this past summer, drove off in the Polaris quads. Twin plumes of dust rose from the rear wheels.

Before leaving, Violet had loaded the necessary tools and materials for repairing the fence into a crate strapped to the back of her quad. Maintaining the condition of the fences was her job, and Gabe had heard her disappointment with herself when they talked.

Once they arrived in section nine, separating the cattle wouldn't be hard. Each one was marked with an identifying ear tag. In case there was a question, Violet carried the log with her.

The actual rounding up of the cattle would be done with both vehicles and horses. The quads could cover more ground at a faster rate while the horses could turn on a dime and maneuver in between cattle, cutting one out from the group and moving it in the desired direction.

If all went well, they'd be done by dark, three hours from now, and Gabe would be twenty minutes late for dinner at most. His brothers, too, as his mother insisted they share meals together despite the continued awkwardness.

"How far is it?" Josh asked. He kept pace easily with Gabe.

"Two miles."

They pushed their horses along, alternating between a fast walk and a trot, depending on the terrain. They didn't lope, not wanting to tire out their mounts. The wind increased the farther away from the ranch they traveled, making Gabe appreciate his heavy coat. Cole lifted the collar around his neck and fastened the snap.

Talk was at a minimum. Over the next rise, they

reached the boundary of section six, part of the land designated to Cara's mustang sanctuary.

A herd of orphaned yearlings, grazing peacefully a half mile away, raised their heads and whinnied. The next instant, they galloped eagerly toward Gabe and his brothers. Over a dozen in all, they formed a small stampede, coming to a lumbering halt and walking the last hundred yards to the fence where they stood bunched together, staring.

Neither Josh's nor Cole's horses reacted much, which was a good sign. They might indeed do well with the cattle despite seldom being ridden outside the rodeo arena.

Gabe and his brothers arrived at section nine. Violet and Joey had beaten them to the site of the broken fence, along with Reese, Enrico and two other hands from the Small Change. Theo McGraw, Gabe noticed, was absent. Strange. The man diligently watched the goings-on at his ranch like a hungry hawk.

About twenty head of cattle were being kept clustered together on the Dos Estrellas side of the fence. Twice that many were on the Small Change side. Violet threaded her way through the nervous cattle on foot, verifying the ear tags. She spotted Gabe and motioned to him.

He waved in return, but didn't ride over. He had seen Reese. She sat astride her father's horse, wind tossing the hair peeking out from beneath her cowboy hat.

She made a striking picture, and Gabe wanted a closer look. To get there, he had to ride through the hole in the fence. Violet hailed him before he made it.

"Gabe, we have a couple injured heifers here. You should have a look."

Work came first, he thought with more than a little disappointment and reluctantly turned Bonita around.

* * *

Gabe and Cole pushed the last Dos Estrellas calf through the hole in the fence and onto ranch property. Bawling loudly, the calf ran to join its mother and the rest of the herd meandering down the hillside and the long stretch of flat land ahead. In just over two hours they'd finished dividing the cattle and treating the two heifers with nasty lacerations on their legs. His brothers had performed well, demonstrating skill and taking instruction without complaint.

They weren't the only ones. Reese, too, had done her share. She was a competent horsewoman, and years away from her father's ranch hadn't affected her abilities. She was Theo McGraw's daughter, all right. Born into the life.

Except, she hadn't chosen it and, instead, worked in a bank, which also suited her.

Watching her dismount and help Violet with the fence repair, he decided he liked her better in jeans and boots than slacks and dress shoes, though she certainly wore the business attire well. Maybe he liked her in anything.

"Gabe, can you lend us a hand?" Violet shouted. She and Reese were struggling with the posthole digger.

He was more than happy to oblige and pushed Bonita ahead, ignoring Josh's questioning look and Cole's dubious one. Dismounting, he dropped the reins to the ground, confident Bonita would stand obediently. She didn't disappoint him and, lowering her head, nuzzled at the sparse tufts of grass.

Therein was the problem. If not for grass being in short supply, the cattle wouldn't have gone searching for, as the saying went, greener pastures.

He would need to talk to his brothers about supplemental feed. And soon.

Reese handed the posthole digger to Gabe. Their gazes connected briefly, and a lovely smile touched her lips, mesmerizing him and reminding him of Thanksgiving when he'd tasted—

Reluctantly, he looked away. He didn't allow his eyes to linger, not with Violet standing right there. His livestock foreman wasn't blind or stupid.

Holding the posthole digger with both hands, he raised it level with his head, then drove it forcefully into the ground. The shovel blades hit with a solid *thunk*. Squeezing the two handles together, he lifted the posthole digger and deposited the dirt into a nearby pile started by Violet and Reese.

They'd been right to request his help; the ground was dry and hard.

"I heard from Banner Hay Sales today," Reese said. "One of their clients backed out, leaving them with ten semitrucks of hay for sale. They offered me a deal."

She named the price, and Gabe paused momentarily in his digging. Winter was a bad time of year to buy hay, prices were typically high. While still costly, the price Reese quoted was good. Better than good. And wasn't he thinking of talking to his brothers about supplemental feed?

"We can't afford ten trucks."

Thwank! The sound the shovel blades made when they hit the ground echoed inside Gabe's chest.

"I thought we could split the purchase," Reese said. "Five trucks each."

He sensed Violet's impatience. She knew how important it was they have enough feed to survive the winter.

Five truckloads wouldn't last them through more than a couple of weeks, but it might make all the difference.

Thwank! Another shovelful of dirt was added to the growing pile.

"We'd have to borrow from the line of credit."

"Yes." Reese adjusted her leather gloves.

"You'd approve the draw?"

"I wouldn't have mentioned the hay purchase otherwise."

Gabe slammed the posthole digger into the ground again, with such force, the shovel blades clanged loudly.

Reese was doing her job, seeing to the financial security of Dos Estrellas, of which the line of credit was a part. Yet, it galled Gabe. She wouldn't give him the money for buying more cattle, a practically guaranteed way of growing the herd. She would, however, authorize a draw to purchase hay, something that was her idea.

"How long do I have to decide?" he asked.

Confusion flashed in her eyes. She had assumed he'd readily agree. "Banner gave us until tomorrow. They have other buyers," she added.

Her comment struck Gabe as a threat rather than an incentive. If he were to decline, Dos Estrellas alone would suffer. The Small Change could easily afford five truckloads of hay. They could afford all ten trucks.

Violet's stare burned into Gabe.

"I'll let you know," he said.

"We can't wait," Reese protested.

Thwank! "You said I have until tomorrow."

She expelled a long breath. "Fine. Ten o'clock is our deadline. You should probably discuss this with your brothers."

That irked Gabe more than her blatant power struggle.

Without a word, he handed Violet the posthole digger, which she carried to the quad and secured to the crate with a pair of bungee cords.

"We don't have to do this," Reese told Gabe when they were alone.

"Do what?"

"Fight."

"I'm not fighting with you."

"Proving who's in charge, then."

"You said it. Not me."

She groaned. "Think about what your father would have done. We both know he'd buy the hay."

"And you can predict his behavior because the two of you were so close."

"I told you before, I barely spoke to him. But I did live next door to him for years and listened to my father talk about him all my life. Your father was smart, and he put the herd first. The entire ranch."

Gabe didn't need a talking-to. Not from Reese and not with their employees and his brothers in the nearby vicinity. He knew buying the hay was a good decision. And if he'd used the line of credit to purchase additional cattle, the hay would have depleted the line faster. What he resented was Reese calling the shots *and* reminding him he had to confer with his brothers. *He* should be the one making the decisions. No one else.

Picking up the fence post, he slammed it into the hole he'd dug. "Hold this," he ordered.

Reese grabbed the top of the post and kept it steady while he filled the opening with dirt and packed it down. By the time he finished, Violet had returned. Using a pair of pliers, she reattached the barbed wire to the post. When the fence was secure, Gabe started for his horse.

Reese appeared beside him. "Gabe."

"Is there something else?"

She hesitated, peering over his shoulder as if making sure they weren't being overheard. "I don't want it to be like this between us."

"You can't have it both ways." He didn't slow his pace to accommodate her shorter strides. "We're either friends—more than friends—or you're the trustee of my father's estate and the one running Dos Estrellas."

"Not running the ranch. I simply oversee the finances."

"There's a fine line. Especially since you're the one authorizing the purchases."

"We need to get along."

"Then quit kissing me," he snapped.

"You made the first move!"

"You're right. My fault."

"No, it isn't."

Several seconds passed, silent except for the sound of her soft panting and the crunch of their boots on the rocky ground.

She gave in first. "Don't let your personal feelings regarding me interfere with you making the best decision for the ranch."

"I'll call you tomorrow." Gabe reached Bonita's side. The mare hadn't moved but a few feet. Patting her neck, he lifted the reins over her head and mounted.

Gabe rode off with his brothers, following in the wake of Violet and Joey on the quads. His last sight was of Enrico joining Reese before he helped her crawl through the fence and onto Small Change land.

"You two have a fight?" Cole asked. He sat easy in

the saddle, not showing the least sign of fatigue despite putting in a full day. Josh, neither.

They were good workers. Gabe would give them that.

"Banner Hay Sales has ten semitruck loads of hay for sale at a fair price," he said, hating he was doing exactly as Reese had suggested. "Reese will authorize a draw from the line of credit if we want to buy it."

We. There it was again.

"Aren't we going to need hay?" Josh asked matter-of-factly. He clearly hadn't let Reese's position as trustee get under his skin.

They rode three abreast down the hillside. In the distance, the cattle they'd driven from the Small Change grazed on the sparse grass. By nightfall, they would join the main herd.

"Yeah, we'll need it," Gabe agreed with his brother.

"You tell her yes?"

"Said I'd—we'd—decide and call her in the morning."

"Why wait?"

Gabe pulled his horse up short. His brothers did the same.

"If we buy the hay, we're going to have to commit to maintaining the herd through the winter." Like their father's plan called for. "Find a means to purchase more supplemental hay. Not sell off stock."

"Didn't we already decide?" Josh asked.

"It's another debt. We'd have to make monthly interest payments."

"What's the weather forecast?" Cole asked.

"No rain for at least two weeks."

"Then we don't have a choice."

Cole's sudden change of heart made Gabe wary. "All you want is to sell the ranch."

"You and Josh won't agree to that, which leaves me stuck here."

"Not a good enough answer."

"What do you want from me?" Cole's voice carried an unmistakable edge.

"One year." Gabe couldn't quite believe what he was saying. All he'd wanted since his brothers first arrived at Mustang Valley was for them to leave. "We agree right here and now to give it our best effort. Grow the herd and pay off as many of Dad's medical bills as we can. Plus the interest on the line of credit. At the end of one year, we can discuss selling the ranch."

"You'd agree to sell?" Cole eyed him suspiciously.

"Yes."

"And if we aren't in a position to sell?"

"We will be, as long as we work our tails off."

Cole looked to Josh, and his brother nodded. "All right. One year."

Gabe held out his hand to Cole, who shook it. He then did the same with Josh.

"How 'bout that." Cole grinned.

No doubt he was happy. He saw himself getting a bundle for his share of the ranch at the end of a year. Josh, too, would have more than enough to take care of his children.

Gabe pushed Bonita ahead. He was okay with his brothers believing they were going to get out from under the burden of Dos Estrellas. In reality, he had every intention of being that buyer for the ranch and much sooner than a year. To accomplish his goal, he'd need to play by Reese's rules.

The thought left a bad taste in his mouth.

Chapter 8

Gabe dragged the last box of Christmas lights across the attic floor to the edge of the opening. He carefully lowered himself down the ladder one step at a time. When his shoulders were level with the opening, he grabbed the box of lights and carried them down to the garage floor.

Thank goodness this was a once-a-year job. Twice a year, if he counted a month from now when he'd be carting the half dozen boxes of lights back up to the attic.

His mother was getting a head start this year. Thanksgiving was just ten days ago. Usually, she waited until closer to Christmas to start decorating the house. Not decorating last year—his father had been too sick—made her want to go all-out this season.

He carried the box of lights to the front courtyard, and deposited it next to the others. "That's it, Mom."

She and Cara were bundled up from head to toe, as the weather had taken a turn. Colder, but not wetter. There was still no sign of rain. With their striped stocking caps, scarves and mittens, they resembled a pair of Christmas elves.

Gabe wished he were like them and more in the spirit of the season. He was anything but jolly. His mood hadn't gone unnoticed, and his mother was constantly trying to cheer him. Yesterday, she'd baked his favorite dessert. Double-layer chocolate cake. The day before, she'd made turkey soup with the Thanksgiving leftovers and mended his favorite shirt.

He suspected her motives weren't entirely selfless. She had her own troubles. She missed his father and worried about losing her home. Cooking and decorating kept her busy. This would be her first holiday in thirty years without August. Also, she missed her parents, who'd announced they wouldn't be visiting until the spring. Make that, his *abuelo* had announced it during their last phone conversation. Gabe doubted his *abuela* had much say in the matter.

"Can you help with this?" Cara asked. "I'm too short."

She was standing on a stepladder, attempting to hang a string of lights on the peaked eve above the front door.

Gabe didn't ask how she'd managed to hang the rest of the lights while he'd been going back and forth between the attic and the courtyard, carrying boxes.

"Let me," he pretended to grouse. "You're going to hurt yourself."

Cara relinquished the stepladder. Gabe's mother came over to supervise.

"It's drooping too much," she commented when Gabe attached the lights.

He grunted, but obligingly restrung the section of lights to hang evenly. For the next thirty minutes Gabe toiled, until his shoulders and back began to ache.

Cara handed him a red bulb. "There are too many blue ones on that string."

"I have better things to do on a Saturday afternoon than take this abuse." He thought of the hundred and one chores waiting for him. "The water troughs in the horse pastures need scrubbing."

"Everyone deserves a day of rest now and then," his mother said.

"Hanging Christmas lights isn't a day of rest."

"The troughs can wait until tomorrow. Josh and Cole went into town. Sightseeing, they said."

What was to see in Mustang Valley? he mused. The small community had only a diner, a halfway-decent market, one gas station and a couple of bars—

That was it. They were probably going to the Poco Dinero Saloon and Grill. Sightseeing his foot! As kind as Gabe's mother had been to them, they should be the ones helping her string these stupid lights.

"I promise, I'll make it worth your while." His mother smiled up at him. "Roast beef for dinner."

She might be cooking day and night in an effort to keep herself busy, but Gabe was reaping the benefits.

"Fine," he grumbled and plugged in the next string of lights.

They'd mostly finished when his mother called it quits. "That's enough for today."

Good. Gabe was starving.

She didn't make him wait long, and a half hour later, the three of them sat at the kitchen table, eating dinner. The roast beef was delicious.

"*Mijo*, do you have any plans tonight?"

He was contemplating crashing early. Quite the life of a bachelor. Pretty pathetic, actually. His brothers were still out, whooping it up, he assumed. Well, more chocolate cake for him.

"Nothing much." Gabe shoveled another bite into his mouth.

"Cara and I were thinking…"

Uh-oh. He recognized that tone and readied himself to say no. Whatever his mother had in mind, he wouldn't like it.

"I'm kind of tired, Mom."

"The Holly Daze Festival started last night." She sent Cara a conspiratorial look.

"Your mom would like to go," Cara said.

"Okay. Go." He'd get the TV to himself. Maybe watch the Phoenix Suns play and have a beer.

"She wants you to take her."

Gabe looked up from his plate. "Why me?"

"You should get out of the house," his mom said.

"I hate to disappoint you, Mom. But if I was inclined to get out of the house, it wouldn't be to attend the Holly Daze Festival."

"They added a new arts and crafts display. I hear there's a lot of great gifts for sale."

"I don't know." He did know—he'd rather stick sharp needles in his eyes than go to an arts and crafts display. "You can't drive yourself?"

"That truck is a pain."

Manual transmission. His mother had never mastered the technique. "What about Cara? Can't you ride with her?"

"I have to go early to help with the raffle booth."

He vaguely remembered her saying something about volunteering.

"Please, *mijo*," his mother implored.

"I'll drop you off. Call me when you're ready to be picked up."

"Won't you stay? The Powells will be there."

"They're running the booth with me," Cara said. "We're selling raffling tickets for carriage rides. The proceeds go to the mustang sanctuary. You know how much we need the money."

"We'll see."

"Thank you." His mother smiled as if he'd agreed.

Gabe did like the Powells, one of the more prominent families in Mustang Valley. Unlike Theo McGraw, they weren't in competition with Dos Estrellas. The Powells owned and operated a horse ranch and riding stable.

They were also responsible for Cara's mustang sanctuary. A few years ago, they'd captured Prince, the last wild mustang in the valley, and rehabilitated him. The stallion was now their prized stud horse and, between stud fees and selling his offspring, responsible for bringing Powell Ranch back from the edge of bankruptcy.

Gabe's family could use their own lucky discovery, like a pot of gold at the end of the rainbow. But rain was required for a rainbow, and there didn't seem to be any in sight.

The Powells had taken in refugee mustangs after Prince, most of them coming from other parts of the state. Cara, friends with the Powell brothers' wives, had helped. Cara was a talented horsewoman and had worked wonders with several incorrigible rebels in the past. Eventually, she brought a few mustangs to Dos Estrellas.

After her son died, she brought more and more mustangs to Dos Estrellas. No one complained, understanding she needed an outlet for her grief. Eventually, she took over the entire sanctuary, which was then moved from Powell Ranch to Dos Estrellas. Cara kept the mustangs she couldn't find good homes for. None were ever turned away.

When Gabe and his mother arrived at the Holly Daze Festival, he got out of the truck rather than go home.

The arts and crafts tables were on the north side of the square, which was illuminated from end to end with colorful lights. A fifteen-foot Christmas tree towered in the center, though it wasn't yet decorated. That community tradition took place next weekend with people encouraged to bring their own ornaments.

Gabe looked around. The Poco Dinero Saloon and Grill wasn't a far walk, across the street and up a block. His brothers might still be there. If not, there'd likely be a buddy or two with whom he could waste the next couple of hours.

There would also be members of the fairer sex. If Gabe was in the market, he could possibly coerce one of them into a dance.

It was an idea that should appeal to him and used to greatly. Instead, his mind was centered on one particular woman. Reese.

"Aren't you going to buy a raffle ticket?" his mother asked. "There's a drawing every hour."

"Who would I take on the carriage ride if I won?"

"You're missing the point." She steered him toward the booth where Cara and the Powells sat.

"Don't we already donate enough?"

"*Mijo.*"

"Fine. One ticket."

At the booth, Cara greeted them with a huge smile. He hadn't seen her that enthused in a long while and wound up buying two tickets.

"Thank you," Caitlin Powell said brightly when he handed over his ten-dollar bill. She was married to Ethan, the middle Powell brother. "Good luck."

Gabe had half a mind to tear up the tickets or give them to the nearest person. But, distracted by an acquaintance, he jammed the tickets into his coat pocket.

Five minutes later, he bid his acquaintance Merry Christmas and strolled in the direction of the saloon. A moment later, he came to an abrupt halt. There, not thirty feet in front of him, stood Reese.

The sight of her wasn't what glued his boots to the cement sidewalk. It was his brother Josh and the two of them conversing easily, as if they were old friends.

No, more than friends. Gabe wasn't born yesterday. He recognized the look of a man interested in a woman, and Josh had that look.

Why should he care? Gabe had no claim on Reese. She could talk to whomever she wanted. Except the burning sensation in his gut propelled him forward until he was literally upon them.

Startled, Reese turned wide eyes on him. "Gabe, what are you doing here?"

The loudspeaker attached to a nearby post crackled to life.

"Attention, attention. The winner of this hour's drawing for the carriage ride is ticket number 23853, Gabe Dempsey. Gabe, will you and your party please report to the carriage station at the south end of the square."

He took Reese's hand. "Come on."

"What!" She tried to pull away.

"You're my party. For the carriage ride."

"I happen to be talking to Josh, in case you didn't notice."

He glared at his brother. "You don't mind, do you?"

Josh chuckled. "Not at all. Have fun, you two."

"Thanks." Gabe dragged Reese down the sidewalk, ignoring her protests.

She should be mad. What right did Gabe have to tear her away from a perfectly cordial conversation with Josh to...what? A carriage ride? Of all the nerve! Could his me-Tarzan-you-Jane attitude be more annoying?

She *should* be mad. Secretly, Reese was pleased. Kind of giddy. And flattered.

"Can we go a little slower?" she pleaded.

Gabe reduced his speed by a fraction.

"What's with you?"

"We have to hurry."

"The carriage isn't going anywhere." Her words had no effect on him or how fast he walked. "Why, Gabe? Don't tell me you're jealous."

That made him slow down, then stop. "Of Josh?"

"He is the person I was talking to."

"No way."

"Then, care to explain this race we're on?"

"I can't."

"Because?"

"I'm not sure why." He started walking again, a frown darkening his features. She should pull away, but she rather liked the sensation of his strong, warm fingers wrapped firmly around hers. In some ways, it was more intimate than when they'd kissed, though not as enjoyable.

"Ask me." She struggled to keep pace, hampered by her knee-high, spike-heeled boots.

"Ask you what?"

"To go with you on the carriage ride. I'd like to be invited. Not forced."

He let go of her hand, making her regret her words. The loss of intimacy was that keen. "And what will you answer?"

"You won't know unless you—"

He caught her by the arms. People passed them on both sides. Reese barely noticed. She saw only Gabe. His eyes, seeming to take in every aspect of her face, and the five-o'clock shadow covering his jaw. It gave his appearance a dangerous and wildly sexy edge.

"Would you like to go on the carriage ride with me?"

For a guy who looked good enough to devour, the blandly delivered line was a letdown. Middle school kids selling candy for their fund-raisers had better pitches. She thought of telling him no. He deserved it after his ridiculous behavior.

"I would," she said. "Very much."

"Good," he grunted and resumed dragging her along. At least he was holding her hand again.

Ethan Powell waited by the horse-drawn carriage parked alongside the curb. With his cowboy hat, jeans, jacket and boots, he didn't look much like a carriage driver, but the carriage itself was right out of a fairytale. Illumination from the streetlight added to the magical illusion.

Reese caught her breath. "How pretty."

"I guess."

She rolled her eyes at Gabe's remark, then returned her attention to the carriage, committing the lovely sight to memory. A snow-white lacquer exterior set off the red velvet upholstered seats. Large-spoked rear wheels contrasted the much smaller front ones. Brass lanterns attached to the sides glowed a soft golden yellow. Even the horses, a matching pair of blacks with shiny silver accent trim on their bridles, were perfect.

"You're the lucky winner?" Ethan Powell pushed off from where he leaned against the carriage and sent them an amused smile.

"Gabe is. I'm his party." Reese ran her hand along the side of the carriage's gleaming exterior.

She'd been raised around horses. Her father had taught her to ride by the time she was three. But, like many little girls, she'd dreamed of being a princess. This carriage ride was probably as close as she'd ever get to realizing that dream.

"Thank you, Gabe." She sighed wistfully.

"Sure."

He didn't understand. He was a man, after all. Besides, it wasn't necessary. She'd enjoy every moment of the ride regardless.

Ethan opened the small door built into the side of the carriage and extended his hand. "Climb aboard."

She placed her foot on the narrow step. Ethan held her elbow, helping her up. The carriage rocked gently as she settled into the far side of the seat. Her hand brushed the velvet upholstery. The carriage rocked harder as Gabe climbed in and plunked down beside her.

He didn't appear concerned with the upholstery or anything else about the carriage, including her. Rather, he stared off toward the festival.

"You may need this." Ethan handed them a thick, fluffy blanket. "It's going to get cold."

He was right. Reese could well imagine the drop in temperature once they were moving. She took the blanket and spread it out across her and Gabe's laps.

"Cozy," he said.

His tone perplexed her. Was he being funny or serious? A glance at his profile offered no answers.

"All set?" Ethan asked.

Reese nodded, afraid if she spoke, she'd sound exactly like the excited little-girl-wannabe-princess coming to life inside her.

The driver's seat, situated in front, was considerably higher than where Reese and Gabe sat in the back. Ethan hauled himself up effortlessly—not an easy feat with a prosthetic leg. He'd lost his when he'd served in the Marines. He untied the reins from the brake handle, released the brake and clucked to the horses. The carriage lurched and they were off, the horses' iron shoes clip-clopping loudly on the blacktop.

Reese was instantly captivated. She'd seen the community of Mustang Valley thousands of times. She could probably travel the length of it blindfolded. But never had she seen it by carriage. The storefronts looked more charming, less stark and businesslike. The Christmas lights and tree in the center of town might have come straight from Santa's Village. The people, too, were different, smiling and waving gaily as they passed.

As the minutes flew by, Reese's heart soared higher and higher. Sitting with Gabe, snuggled beneath the blanket, increased her happiness. The ride couldn't be more romantic, and she thought of asking him how he truly felt about her.

"The hay was delivered the other day," he said.

Reese blinked. Really? A romantic carriage ride and he wanted to talk shop?

"It looks good," he added. "High quality. You were right to suggest purchasing it."

"I don't want to discuss the hay," she snapped, then bit her lip.

"Okay." Gabe resumed staring at the passing sights.

She suppressed a groan. He was either being intentionally obtuse or didn't get the hint. She decided to go out on a limb.

"If you and I weren't at odds—"

"We're not at odds."

"Weren't in a work relationship, then." She infused warmth into her voice. "This carriage ride might be going quite differently."

"How so?"

"For starters, you'd be looking at me and not the big sale sign in front of Valley Auto Parts."

He turned to face her. "I thought you wanted to keep our relationship strictly professional."

"I do." She should. "Just making small talk."

"So was I when I mentioned the hay."

Touché.

Several more minutes passed in silence.

At the next corner, Ethan pulled the horses to a stop and peered over his shoulder at Reese and Gabe. "You have a preference for which route we take?"

"No." Reese said.

"Hickory Street," Gabe countered.

She blinked in surprise. Hickory Street would take them to the outskirts of town. It would be dark there. No streetlights. And more isolated. Also...dare she think it?…romantic. But hadn't Gabe recently reminded her of their agreed-upon terms? Strictly professional.

"You got it," Ethan said and clucked to the horses.

With another lurch, they continued on, the horses resuming their slow, steady trot. Two blocks passed, then three.

"You guys are awfully quiet," Ethan said, this time without looking at them.

"Taking in the scenery," Reese answered, and she was. The distant mountains were blue-black against a star-filled sky. To the right of the rounded peaks, the lights of Scottsdale glittered, appearing much closer than the actual thirty miles away as the crow flies.

"Yeah, taking in the scenery," Gabe echoed.

Reese started at the feel of his breath on the back of her neck and the silky timbre of his voice. She turned in the seat and gasped softly when she found him mere inches away. Close enough to…

"Oh, my."

"You're prettier now than you were in school." His low whisper ignited a flurry of sparks in the place his breath had moments ago caressed. They quickly spread, making her both nervous and excited.

"Gabe. We have an agreement."

"I was never very good at following rules." He skimmed his fingers along the curve of her cheek. "And breaking them with you is very tempting."

She closed her eyes, savoring the moment. "This is a bad idea."

"It's the best one I've had since Thanksgiving."

"I thought you were mad at me about the hay."

"Didn't I admit you were right?"

She pressed her palm to his cheek. "Your father just

died. You're at odds with your brothers. The ranch is in debt. The timing couldn't be worse."

"I'm going to kiss you, Reese."

The sparks ignited a shiver. "You say that like I don't have a choice."

"You do. You can tell me no. But I happen to think you'd like me to kiss you, too."

He was obviously skilled at mind reading. "What about Ethan?" She shot their driver a concerned glance.

"Trust me, he's not paying us any attention."

Gabe's confidence was annoying. It was also very attractive. She was falling for him in a way she hadn't fallen for a man before. It was a little scary.

He lowered his head. Their mouths were almost, nearly, and then barely touching. "What do you want from me?" she whispered.

"Surrender."

That was all the encouragement Reese needed. The last barrier vanished, and she was in his arms, kissing him as if this moment were the one she'd been waiting for her entire life. Heedless, mindless and careless, she did as he wanted and gave in to him. It was glorious.

He drew her into the circle of his arms, flush with his hard, unyielding chest while his mouth played hers like a fine instrument. The motion of the carriage elevated the sensations. If Reese let her mind wander, she and Gabe could be floating adrift on a vast ocean, all alone, their problems nonexistent.

Nice, but not very realistic. Nonetheless, she reveled in their kiss. What would one more minute hurt?

There must have been a pothole in the road, for the carriage bumped hard, knocking them both sideways and breaking off the kiss.

Instead of coming to her senses, being embarrassed or chiding herself for her reckless behavior, Reese laughed.

"That's better." Gabe adjusted the blanket, which had slipped from their laps. "I like you when you're happy."

"When am I not happy?" The question was no sooner expressed then she remembered. The night of their prom. Her mood shifted, and she extracted herself from his arms. "We should probably…"

"Yeah."

She heard his reluctance as clearly as if he'd spoken it. "It won't always be like this. A lot could change in a year." Josh, not Gabe, had mentioned the brothers' agreement to work together.

"Nothing about our families will change. You'll always be Theo McGraw's daughter, and I'm the product of August Dempsey's affair with my mother."

"We don't have to let our past define us."

He smiled tenderly. "I didn't realize you were such an optimist."

"Be patient."

"What choice do I have?" His smile changed from tender to sad.

She suspected few people saw this side of him and was glad he felt comfortable enough with her to let down his guard.

"Next stop, the center of town." Ethan pulled on the reins, slowing the horses, who'd picked up the pace when they realized the ride was nearing an end. Ahead, the lights of the square blinked brightly.

Reese couldn't believe where the minutes had gone. She and Gabe had been completely absorbed—with their kiss and each other.

Unfortunately, none of her uncertainties had been

assuaged. She still had no clue where their relationship was heading.

She didn't like that. Reese always strove to maintain perfect order. Even when the rug was pulled out from under her, like getting pregnant, she found a solution and acted promptly. But when it came to her and Gabe, she had no solution. No expectations. No promises. It was scary—and thrilling.

Gabe's fingertips linking briefly with hers when she exited the carriage implied they shared a secret.

Another one.

Chapter 9

Finding a reason to go home at lunch was becoming a habit for Reese. For the fourth day in a row, she was making the fifteen-minute trek from the bank, this time with her father's prescription in her purse. He didn't need it until tonight and would most likely see through her excuse.

Big deal. If he objected, then they could hire a caretaker.

Seconds before Reese reached the Small Change, she saw a familiar-looking vehicle pull out. Her suspicions were confirmed when she and the truck passed on the road, and she got a good look at the driver.

Cole Dempsey! What was he doing here? Who had he seen? Did her father know?

Reese rushed inside the moment after she parked in the garage. "Dad, you here?"

There was no answer. Maybe her father was in the barn or at one of the livestock pens. He did venture outside at least once a day when he was feeling his best.

"Dad. Dad!"

"In here." His voice came from the TV den.

Reese breathed a long sigh of relief and dropped her purse onto the kitchen counter, along with the prescription. Her father was sitting in his favorite recliner, fiddling with the remote. "How you doing?" She was anxious to know about Cole Dempsey but unsure if she should ask. If Cole had been talking to Enrico or one of the hands, she'd prefer to grill them first, without her father's knowledge.

"I had a visitor." Her father wore a satisfied expression.

Aha.

"Who?" Reese asked, pretending ignorance.

"Cole Dempsey." He set down the remote. "Kid's the spitting image of his mother. You probably don't remember her."

"No." Reese decided to be blunt. "Why was he here?"

"Paying me a neighborly visit."

She knew better than that. "Come on, Dad."

"He's interested in selling his share of Dos Estrellas."

"You're kidding." Reese's knees weakened a little. She wobbled to the sofa and sat. "He offered it to you?"

"Yep." Her father leaned back in the recliner and pushed on the side handle, raising the foot rest.

Her father must be having a good day. With his tremors and loss of strength, he couldn't always manage his recliner.

"Did he happen to mention if his brothers knew?"

"What does it matter?"

"They're partners, Dad. It matters a lot."

"Is he prohibited from selling without their consent?"

"No. Consent is needed only for selling the entire ranch." Reese had found that part of the living trust unusual and interesting. Anyone could wind up owning a share of Dos Estrellas and partnering with the remaining brother or brothers, including, possibly, a rival. August Dempsey must have thought of that. He'd paid meticulous attention to every other detail.

Could it have been intentional? A test for his sons? She wouldn't put it past August. But, if true, he'd taken an incredible risk that could easily backfire.

Hearing her father's jovial chuckle, she was angry. "You can't seriously be considering accepting Cole's offer."

Deep furrows creased his brow. "I am. Why wouldn't I?"

"We've had this discussion before. Running the Small Change is hard enough. You're in no—" She'd started to say shape, but changed her mind. "No position to take on more responsibility."

"I could be the financial backer. Gabe and the other brother—Josh, right?—will run the ranch."

This was absurd. Her father talked like the purchase was a done deal.

Reese's heart pounded. "You cannot do this, Dad! Think of the problems it will cause."

Gabe would be furious. And he might think she was encouraging her father, though she'd assured him she had no personal agenda.

Her father leveled a finger at her. "You don't get to tell me what to do, young lady."

She stood, her legs now strong. "You're right. But I can tell Gabe about this, and I will. Right now."

Storm clouds gathered on her father's face, worrying her. She hadn't seen him this angry in a long time.

"Why would you go against me?" he demanded.

"Dad, I have a responsibility as trustee to oversee the finances of Dos Estrellas to the best of my ability."

"You also have an obligation to me."

"If owning a share of Dos Estrellas was in your best interest or good for your health, I'd support you a hundred percent. Neither one is the case. And I know for a fact Cole is after whatever money he can get his hands on. He has no loyalty to his brothers, Josh included."

She'd assumed, when he agreed to stay, he'd at least stick by Josh. Obviously not.

What a mess. She had to do something.

"He's making the decision that's best for him," her father said. "Nothing wrong with that."

"This isn't like you, Dad. It would be one thing for you to buy Dos Estrellas outright. Heaven knows you offered enough times. But to wrangle your way in the back door by taking advantage of a family dispute—"

"Now, wait a minute."

"I won't. In fact, I'm leaving now."

"Where are you going?"

To the only place that made any sense. "Our neighbors."

"Reese."

The pleading in her father's voice tore at her, and all at once she understood. He didn't want to own a one-third share of the Dos Estrellas, bought from a disgruntled brother. He would have owned the ranch outright, had the opportunity ever presented itself.

Her father was flexing what was left of his muscles in order to feel like his old self. She decided to cut him some slack.

"I have to tell Gabe. He has a right to know."

Her father stared at her, unwaveringly, for several seconds. Then he looked away. "Do what you must."

His obvious pain made her question her actions. She took his hand in hers, holding it to her chest, just above her heart.

"I love you, Dad."

He nodded.

"We're going to get through this."

He laughed without mirth. "Haven't you been listening to my doctors?"

"Parkinson's isn't fatal."

"Might as well be."

Tears pricked her eyes "New advances are being made every day."

"You talk like that support group leader."

Her father had attended exactly one meeting, declaring afterward that all those people moping and whining weren't for him. He'd go it alone.

But he wasn't alone. He had her.

"We have to keep hoping, Dad. *I* have to keep hoping. If not, I'll fall apart."

"You're a good daughter, Reese. I'm a blessed man."

He hadn't called himself blessed since being told his initial prognosis.

She kissed the back of his hand. "See you tonight when I get home. Call if you need anything."

"You fuss over me too much." His objection was delivered with affection.

Wasting no time, not even to eat, Reese returned to

her car and drove to Dos Estrellas. On the drive, she called Gabe. He answered on the second ring.

"Hi, there."

Minor static in the background didn't distort the fondness in his voice—which would change the moment she told him her news.

"Are you free?" she asked.

"Now?"

"If that's okay."

"Sure. I'm in the toolshed. Let me clean up, and I'll meet you at the house. Mom and Cara aren't home. They're making the rounds in town. Thanking some of our friends for their help these last few weeks by delivering homemade tamales. They won't be home until late tonight."

Was he dropping a hint that they'd have some privacy? Reese worried he might be recalling their kiss, and she didn't want to mislead him. "We can do this another time."

"No. Come on by."

She could tell him on the phone and avoid an awkward situation. No, she needed to tell him her news face-to-face.

"See you in a few minutes."

Standing at Gabe's front door, she smoothed her slacks before ringing the bell. Someone, she guessed Raquel, had gone overboard decorating the house exterior and courtyard with lights, ornaments and a giant inflatable snow globe with Santa and Rudolph inside. An evergreen wreath hung from the door with a puffy red ribbon at its center. The half dozen organ-pipe cacti to the right of the door wore fake beards and Santa hats, the white tassels falling at jaunty angles.

Reese smiled. The next instant, guilt overwhelmed her. She'd been too busy with work and caring for her father to worry about decorating the house. Perhaps she should. It might cheer him. She'd loved the holidays as a kid, in part because her father always made a big production of them.

When no one answered the door, Reese knocked again. Gabe must be delayed. She rummaged in her purse for her cell phone, found it and groaned. She should have paid attention to the low battery warning. Now the phone was dead.

She began walking in the direction of the horse stable. If memory served, the toolshed was a dilapidated structure behind it. Hopefully, Gabe was still there.

She took a shortcut through the stables, the pointy heels of her boots sinking into the soft ground and hampering her progress. Were it a different day, she'd stop to pet the horses, especially Gabe's pretty mustang mare Bonita, who watched Reese with wide, chocolate eyes.

Reaching the end of the aisle, she turned the corner and came to an abrupt halt. It wasn't the toolshed with its repaired sideboards, new roof and fresh coat of paint that had given her pause. Rather, it was Gabe. He'd stripped off his jacket and rolled up his shirt sleeves. Bending over the open hood of the tractor, with his right arm buried in the engine up to his shoulder, he grimaced as if in pain.

Was he hurt? Caught his hand in some metal mechanism?

Reese quickened her steps. "Gabe, are you all right?"

"Hey." He opened his eyes, but didn't extract his arm. "Sorry. Thought I'd be finished by now."

"What happened? Can I help?"

"Tractor died in the middle of feeding this morning. It's the carburetor. I have this one last bolt to screw on."

"Oh. Okay." Feeling silly at panicking for no reason, she brushed self-consciously at her hair.

"Almost there." Groaning, he wiggled his arm. The bolt was obviously difficult to reach.

She waited, then swallowed. Gabe looked good. Heck, he always did. But today, his strong, athletic build was visible beneath his snug-fitting plaid shirt. The collar was open at his throat, revealing the muscles of his neck, which stood out as he strained to reattach the bolt.

Business, she reminded herself. She was here on business. Unpleasant business at that.

"No hurry," she said and turned her attention to the pasture. It was empty, except for two remaining towers of hay; the other three had been distributed to the cattle—and the cattle moved to yet another section. Sound management, in her opinion. Reserve the hay if possible.

"Could you hand me that towel?"

"Sure." She grabbed a crumpled hand towel lying on the tractor fender.

Gabe had withdrawn his arm from the engine while her back was to him. She was greeted by his broad chest and bare throat, three inches from her face.

Reese gasped and involuntarily stepped back. Her heel caught on a rock, and her ankle threatened to turn. She flailed, arms wind-milling.

He grabbed her by the shoulders and steadied her. "Whoa there."

His words were teasing. His tone, seductive. Reese responded by turning soft inside. When he dipped his head as if to kiss her, she came to her senses and held up a hand. "Wait. I have something to tell you. Something you won't like."

"What is it?" He didn't move, didn't release her and looked at her with such concern, such caring, she momentarily lost her train of thought.

"Your brother Cole," she finally managed to sputter. "He met with my father. Not an hour ago. And offered to sell him his share of Dos Estrellas."

"That son of a bitch."

Reese wasn't sure who Gabe was referring to, his brother or her father.

He released her, his arms falling away, his stare now cold as steel. "Was this your idea?"

"Gabe, how can you say that?" They'd kissed during the carriage ride. Talked intimately. "I wouldn't betray you. Neither would I jeopardize my job."

He stormed off.

She chased after him. "Where are you going?"

"To pay a call on your father."

"Gabe."

His pickup was parked near the barn, and he was on a collision course with it. "Butt out, Reese. If this really wasn't your idea, then it doesn't concern you."

"There are things you don't know. About my father."

"I don't care." He yanked open the truck's driver's side door.

Reese couldn't let him get away. Couldn't let him storm her house and confront her father. Cutting in front of the truck, she hurried to the passenger side door.

"What are you doing?" Gabe growled when she climbed inside.

She prayed she was preventing a disaster. "If you're going to talk to my father, it'll be with me there."

* * *

Everything at the Small Change was twice as big as Dos Estrellas. The length of the driveway and the square arch adorning the entrance. The size of the main barn and livestock pens. The amount of grassland and grazing cattle. The height of the spouting water in the courtyard fountain. The damn wrought iron knocker on the front door.

Reese hadn't suggested that Gabe park around back, so he'd pulled his truck up parallel to the brick walkway leading to the front door. She'd come along, right beside him. So much for his plan of bursting in on her father unannounced.

They'd spoken once during the drive when she asked to use his phone, claiming hers was dead. He'd refused. Mean, yes, but he'd wanted whatever small advantage he could get.

Theo McGraw must have heard Gabe's truck screech to a gravel-spitting stop for he threw the door open just as Gabe crossed the threshold.

Taking in the two of them, he grinned affably. "Why am I not surprised?"

"Dad, Gabe wants to—"

Gabe cut her off. "I hope to hell you told Cole no."

He'd been in such an all-fire hurry to confront Theo, he'd forgotten to ask Reese how her father had responded to Cole's offer.

"Come in." Theo stepped back.

Gabe hesitated, afraid that accepting his enemy's invitation might show weakness. Ultimately, good manners prevailed, and he let Reese enter first. She'd hardly stepped across the threshold when he pushed inside.

Confronted by the beautifully appointed living room,

with its cowhide-upholstered sofa, hand-carved book-cases and framed original oil paintings depicting cattle drives and local wildlife, Gabe stopped. He'd been to the Small Change before. A few times. Never inside the main house, though.

Were he calling on anyone else, he'd have commented on what a nice place they had.

"Can I offer you a drink?" Theo said. "Reese made some iced tea this morning."

"No, thank you."

"Sweetheart." He turned to Reese. "Can you give us a minute alone?"

"I don't think that's a good idea."

"I'm pretty sure our guest will conduct himself civ-illy." He raised a bushy brow at Gabe. "And I promise not to hit him unless he throws the first punch."

Reese sighed. "I'll be in the kitchen."

"No need to check on us unless I call for you."

She left the room reluctantly. Gabe wouldn't put it past her to hover nearby and eavesdrop.

"Now that she's gone." Theo McGraw rubbed his palms together. "Maybe I can interest you in a drink. Your father liked whiskey."

"Did he come here much?" Gabe was suddenly curi-ous. "He never said."

"On occasion."

"What did Cole have to drink when he was here?"

Theo laughed and slapped his thigh.

Not that Gabe was well acquainted with the man, but there was something different about him. He looked older. Frailer. And there was a slight shakiness in his voice. When he walked over to the dry bar, his gait was slow and deliberate, as if he was carefully placing each foot in front of the other.

Going behind the bar, Theo removed two crystal tumblers from the shelf and a fifth of whiskey from the cabinet. "Straight up?"

Gabe was about to refuse. Again, he reconsidered, not wanting to appear weak. "Only if you'll join me."

"With pleasure." Theo's grin grew wider. "My daughter is going to have a fit. I'm not supposed to drink."

"Then I'll pass." Gabe ambled to the bar.

"Not on your life. It's not every day the son of August Dempsey pays me a visit. That's reason to celebrate."

Cole had visited Theo earlier, yet he'd referred to Gabe as August Dempsey's son. Against his will, Gabe warmed to his host.

Theo poured, a bit sloppily. Whiskey splashed onto the bar counter. He passed Gabe the first glass. When he was done pouring his own, he raised his glass in toast. "To August."

A moment ago, Gabe had been ready to throttle Theo. Now, they clinked glasses and tossed back their shots of whiskey. Gabe's burned going down. Not in a bad way.

"You didn't answer my question," he said when he could speak again.

Theo coughed, wheezed and pounded his chest. "No, I didn't offer Cole a drink."

Gabe almost smiled. Theo was no dummy, and he could play with the best of them. "Did you turn him down?"

"I said I'd think about it."

"Don't buy his share of Dos Estrellas."

Theo met his gaze head on. "Why shouldn't I?"

Gabe wasn't about to admit his plans to buy out his

brothers, to Theo. "Because you're a better man than to kick someone when they're down. And, much as I hate to admit it, we're down. Deep down in a financial hole."

"I've had my eye on your ranch for a lot of years. Here's my opportunity."

"You'd be buying into a lot of debt."

"True." He sipped at the remainder of his whiskey rather than gulping it, a look of contentment on his face. "This hits the spot. Reese complains if I drink, says it's bad for my...health."

"She doesn't want you to buy Cole's share."

Theo raised an eyebrow. "She tell you that?"

Gabe shook his head. "She came over to warn me about Cole. It's almost the same thing."

"Always had a moral compass, that one. She could have blamed me for her mother leaving. I wasn't the best husband." His expression turned tender. "She didn't. Stayed by me."

"Mr. McGraw."

"Call me Theo."

Gabe exhaled slowly. He wasn't in the mood to indulge the other man's stroll down memory lane. "Okay, Theo. I can't stop Cole from selling you his share, and I can't stop you from buying it. But I'm asking you to give me six months."

"What happens then?"

"*I'm* going to buy Cole's share. Hopefully, Josh's, too."

"Why would I wait?"

Gabe didn't have the chance to answer.

"How's it going?" Reese asked as she entered the living room, clearly defying her father's wishes. She glanced first at her father, then Gabe.

Theo laughed and slapped his thigh again. "The girl can't take orders. You should remember that."

Gabe wondered if Theo knew about him and Reese. No, impossible.

"As you can see, dear daughter," Theo continued, "we're both still in one piece. No punches thrown."

Gabe swore under his breath. He hadn't had a chance to finish his conversation with Theo, and he wouldn't in front of Reese. "I'd better go."

"Nonsense," Theo said. "You're my guest. Stay."

"Are you drinking whiskey?" Reese marched over to him, then frowned at Gabe. "Was this your idea?"

"Don't blame him," said Theo. "I'm the one who broke out the bottle."

"Dad!" She squeezed her eyes shut.

Gabe didn't need to witness the McGraw family dynamics. He had plenty of his own. "If you'll excuse me."

He started for the door and got no more than three feet before Theo lost his balance, banged into the bar and then hit the floor with an agonizing cry.

"Dad!"

Gabe rushed to Theo and knelt beside him. "Are you hurt?"

"I'm fine," he grumbled. "Damned rug."

It wasn't the rug. The older man's legs had simply gone out from under him.

By now, Reese was also kneeling beside her father. "Did you hit your head?"

"My elbow." He tried pushing up, only to collapse in either exhaustion or pain.

"Let me." Gabe stood and, getting a firm grip on Theo's uninjured arm, lifted him to a sitting position.

Theo sat and held his head as if the room was spinning. "Give me a minute."

Gabe gave him three before assisting him to his feet. Next, he carefully walked Theo to the nearest chair and sat him down.

"I'll get you some water," Reese said.

"I'm not thirsty."

"You shouldn't have been drinking."

"Please quit your nagging." Rather than harsh, Theo's request was imploring.

Gabe could see Reese struggled to keep quiet. "Should we call 9-1-1?" he asked.

"Maybe." She chewed her bottom lip.

"Hell, no!"

"If you can protest like that," Gabe gripped Theo's shoulder, "then you must be feeling better."

Neither Reese nor her father acknowledged his joke. Their worried faces indicated more going on. What was it Reese had told Gabe back at Dos Estrellas before he'd made a mad dash for his truck?

There are things you don't know. About my father.

Whereas Gabe had been anxious to leave a short time ago, he was now hesitant.

"I'm going to call your doctor," Reese said.

"And have him charge me another co-pay." Theo shook his head. "Not on your life."

"Let me see your elbow." She reached for him.

He, in turn, yanked his injured arm out of her reach. "Leave me alone, dagnabbit."

Various versions of this same exchange continued for several more minutes. Gabe saw that Theo was growing stronger. When he felt relatively certain his host was in no immediate danger, he said, "I'm going to let you two hammer this out alone."

"Wait." Theo grabbed Gabe's wrist. His grip was surprisingly strong. "I'll give you that six months."

Gabe nodded. "I appreciate it."

"On one condition. You tell no one what happened."

He didn't need to elaborate. Gabe understood. For whatever reason, Theo wanted his fall to remain a secret.

"Agreed."

"Reese." Theo hitched his chin at the door. "Would you be so kind as to see our guest out?"

"My car," she exclaimed, suddenly remembering. "It's at Gabe's house."

"I'll drive it here later. Have someone follow me."

"She needs to get back to work," Theo said.

"No, I don't. I called in while you two were talking and told Walt I was taking the afternoon off."

"Good." Theo smiled for the first time since his fall. "Then you can go back with Gabe and fetch your car."

"I'm not leaving you alone." She crossed her arms.

"I told you, I'm perfectly fine."

"You're not." Tears filled her voice.

"Call Enrico." Theo's shoulders slumped in defeat. "It's about time for his afternoon report."

Reese looked at Gabe. "Give me a minute."

Gabe sat on one of the two bar stools. "Take your time."

"She's become quite the mother hen," Theo said when Reese left the room.

"She loves you."

"I'm a lucky man."

"You are."

"The man who wins her heart will be lucky, too."

Gabe nodded, not sure how to reply.

Reese wasn't gone long. They waited another few minutes for Enrico to arrive. Gabe doubted his appearance was solely to report the day's activity to Theo, though the two of them discussed an upcoming cold front. Gabe noticed a look pass between Reese and the burly ranch foreman. If he interpreted it correctly, she was saying, "Call me later."

This arrangement, Theo falling and Enrico caring for him under the guise of ranch business, didn't appear to be anything new. Gabe remembered Reese getting a call when her father fell off the porch. And there had been that tremor when he'd poured the shots of whiskey. The man was ill.

Outside, Gabe opened his truck door for Reese, chagrined at his earlier behavior. When she asked if she could use his phone charger, he plugged it in for her.

At Dos Estrellas, he parked next to her car in the driveway. He knew he should let her leave, but he couldn't. Opening her car door, he took her hand and prevented her from climbing in behind the steering wheel.

"What's wrong with your father?"

Tears welled in her eyes.

"You came and told me about Cole. You didn't have to. I realize now I can trust you. You can trust me, too. I've proven myself."

His reminder of their prom night broke down her defenses, and she sobbed softly. "He has Parkinson's."

Gabe put an arm around her and pulled her to him. "Oh, honey, I'm sorry." He knew better than many what it was like to deal with a severely ill parent. "Come inside. We'll talk."

She shook her head.

"Call Enrico. Tell him to make up an excuse to stay with your dad. You need to vent before you have a breakdown."

Truthfully, he expected her to refuse. She didn't. Arm in arm, they walked inside the house.

Chapter 10

"Coffee?"

For a second, Reese almost answered Gabe's question with *I'd prefer a whiskey*, but instead bit her tongue. Much as she might like to follow her father's example and indulge in a dose of liquid courage, she was better off with caffeine. Whiskey might break down her last hold on her emotions, and she'd wind up a weeping mess. Once, in Gabe's company, was enough.

"Sure. Thanks."

A gourmet single-serving coffee maker sat on the kitchen counter. While Gabe prepared two cups with practiced ease, Reese threw her coat over the back of the nearest chair and sat at the table. The house was quiet, reminding her that his mother and Cara were gone until late this evening. His brothers, staying in the guest suite, used a separate entrance and, according to Gabe, came into the main house strictly for meals. She and Gabe were completely alone.

Good, when it came to taking him up on his offer for a heartfelt talk. Bad, when it came to their wildly exciting, but inappropriate, attraction. With the way she was feeling right now, getting cozy with Gabe was the last thing on her mind.

Well, maybe not the *last* thing. He did have a way of consuming her every thought by simply entering the room. And there was something deliciously thrilling about them being alone. Especially during Thanksgiving dinner when Raquel had sent them to the garage on the pretense of fetching the platter, they hadn't been truly isolated.

"Does anyone besides me know about your dad's Parkinson's?" Gabe set a steaming mug in front of her, then, removing his cowboy hat and setting it on the counter, occupied the adjacent chair. He cradled his own mug of coffee between his hands. "Besides you and Enrico."

"Enrico doesn't know. Not exactly. I'm convinced he suspects Dad's ill, but he's very loyal and won't say a word."

She stared at her mug. The coffee was black.

"Is something wrong?" Gabe asked.

"I hate to be a bother."

"You?" he teased.

A different day, a different moment when she wasn't hurting, she'd laugh. "Do you have any creamer?"

He produced three varieties from the refrigerator. "Cara's doing."

Reese selected the mocha-flavored creamer. "I got addicted to this stuff in high school."

"You used to go to the Java Stop after school. I'd see you there."

She and her group of friends had thought they were cool, frequenting the popular hangout and ordering specialty overpriced coffee drinks. How silly. "You noticed me?"

His tone became soft and low. "I noticed a lot of things about you."

Noticed *and* remembered. She was touched, flattered and more enamored than ever. "I wish we'd been friends back then."

"I wished we'd dated."

"As I recall, you didn't like me much."

"You never gave me a chance."

She didn't quite believe him. Their fathers had greatly influenced them when they were younger and not much had changed. Even now Reese could feel her father yanking the invisible strings attached to her.

"I appreciate you respecting Dad's request to not tell anyone about his Parkinson's."

"Like I said, you can trust me."

"You've kept my secret for twelve years. If I haven't said so before, I appreciate it."

He shrugged.

"You're an honorable man, Gabe. It's a quality not everyone has."

"Telling people about your father won't serve any purpose."

"He's afraid it would discredit him. If you wanted, you could use that to your advantage. Buyers might hesitate to deal with someone who's sick and throw business your way."

"Your father has some physical limitations. I can assure you, though, he's still sharp as a tack."

"Oh, yes. I can attest to that." The hot coffee felt good going down her throat. Holding back her tears this past hour had left it raw. "I just wish he'd let me hire a part-time caregiver. I can't provide everything he needs and half of what I can, he won't let me. Too proud."

She'd offered to help him bathe, shave, dress and a dozen other personal tasks. His response had been to snap at her. Yesterday, he'd sliced his finger with a pocketknife while trying to clean his fingernails, then refused to let her clean and bandage the small wound. He'd be lucky if he didn't get an infection.

"It's hard on me," she said, her voice cracking. "The extra work, the emotional stress, seeing him hurt himself. This wasn't his first fall."

"Have you told him how hard it is on you?"

"I don't want to get into an argument."

"He needs to know he's making your life difficult."

"Not difficult. I love my father."

"We went through the same thing with my dad. He ran Mom ragged. It got to a point where *her* health was in jeopardy."

Reese swiped at her eyes. She could see the same happening to her.

"I remember the name of the nursing service we used. They were good. We hired a male nurse. Dad was more comfortable with him than a woman."

Her father would be, too. "Maybe. Let me think about it."

"You'll be no good to your father if you're worn out."

"I'm more worried about my job. I'm finding it harder

and harder to concentrate. I don't want to start making mistakes."

Almost at once, she regretted her words. Would Gabe jump to the conclusion she wasn't doing her best as trustee?

"You're too smart for that," he said.

His assurances didn't ease her concerns. But when he folded her hand in his and squeezed her fingers, a calmness spread slowly through her, and she welcomed it.

"I like you, Gabe." Closing her eyes, she grimaced. "I shouldn't have said that."

"I'm glad you did. I like you, too."

"A lot." Oh, God, this was getting worse by the second.

His grip on her hand tightened. "I know."

"Oh? You do?"

"You kissed me, Reese. I may be an insensitive lug, but I can tell when a woman's into me."

"Into you?" She almost pulled her hand away, but didn't. "You sound pretty confident."

"What I am is glad. I'd hate to think I'm the only one losing my heart here."

Her pulse quickened. "Gabe, we can't let this go any further. It's okay to flirt a bit and maybe kiss, but no more and not again."

"Hmm." He grinned, and her pulse literally skipped a beat. "And here I was thinking of taking things further."

"You're terrible. That wasn't funny."

"I'm not joking."

He wasn't. She could tell by the look in his eyes, which roved her face as if trying to memorize every nuance. This intense scrutiny was incredibly more flattering and harder to resist.

"What are we going to do about it?" he asked.

She tensed. Was he serious? "Nothing."

"You're entitled to be happy."

"Not at the expense of my job."

"Is there a bank policy against dating customers?"

"Not exactly. Any romantic relationships must be disclosed." Reese imagined herself having that conversation with Walt and cringed. No way. "My boss would think I've lost my mind."

"You're right." Gabe let go of her hand. "It's a bad idea."

She hadn't expected him to acquiesce so quickly and thought of telling him she'd reconsidered. Maybe then he'd hold her hand again and stare into her eyes.

"I should probably get go—"

He cut her off. "You don't have to. Whatever it is you were going to say."

His voice was rich with promise and his smile contained a hint of mischief. The combination was too appealing for her own good.

"Yes, I do." Yes, she *should*.

"Keep looking at me the way you are and I won't be responsible for my actions."

She knew he wanted her. Like he'd said, they'd kissed. He wasn't the only one who could gauge a person's feelings. Neither was he the only one staring with an unmistakable hunger in their eyes.

"You could walk me to my car," she suggested.

"I'm going to do more than that." He pushed back from the table and stood. Taking her hand, he helped her to her feet and, before she could stop him, into his arms.

"Gabe. Didn't we agree—"

"To heed our better judgment and not make costly mistakes. Kissing you is no mistake."

"We're asking for trouble."

"I kind of like getting into trouble with you."

She might have said more but she couldn't. Her mouth was otherwise occupied. She let him take the lead, fusing her lips to his, then parting them. He wasted no time, tasting and teasing and satisfying her.

No, there was no satisfying. Regardless of what she'd said earlier, she craved more. While his hands roamed her back, she linked her arms around his neck and sifted her fingers through his hair. At his low moan of pleasure, she grew bolder and arched into him, her breasts making exhilarating contact with the hard planes of his chest.

He tensed and withdrew, gazing at her like she was everything in the world to him. "You're incredible."

"I think it takes two to achieve incredible."

"How did we not figure this out before?"

She shook her head, not sure what to say. Had she gone after the wrong man, Blake, because the right man, Gabe, was someone her father didn't approve of?

His hands settled on the curves of her hips and pulled her close. He moaned again. Reese didn't consider herself to be particularly sexy, but turning him on, obviously exciting him, gave her a heady sensation she could get used to.

Saying no to the many wonderful, exciting possibilities that could be hers if she'd simply give in would be harder than she'd imagined. "Gabe. Please—"

The floor shifted beneath her. She uttered a cry before realizing Gabe had picked her up. Turning in a half circle, he deposited her on the table. Not giving her a chance to catch her breath, he kneed her legs apart and positioned himself between them.

Speaking wasn't possible. At first, because he'd left her speechless. Then because he was kissing her again, with an intensity and passion that drove all but the last shred of good judgment from her mind.

He leaned into her. For an insane second, she thought he might be trying to lay her back on the table. The next instant, her relieved mind registered he was simply closing the distance between their bodies to nothing but a few molecules of thin air.

Heaven help her, she abandoned control and let him kiss her. His tongue swept into her mouth, evoking greater thrills with each stroke. His hands pressed into the small of her back and, when she moved her hips encouragingly, dipped into the waistband of her slacks. He must have realized she wore the briefest of panties for he let out a low, desperate sound that sent a shiver of pleasure coursing through her.

"I want you, Reese."

All at once, he really was laying her back onto the table. She immediately grasped that last shred of good judgment and ended their kiss.

"No. We can't."

He pulled back and, breathing deeply, lifted her off the table and onto her feet. "We could go to my room."

They could. His mother and Cara were gone for hours.

They *couldn't*! No matter how Reese felt about Gabe, and she was starting to care more than she'd have ever believed possible, she refused to endanger her job. They'd already crossed the line. Several times. To plunge headlong into dangerous territory was career suicide.

Placing her palm on the front of his shirt, she backed away. "I won't do something we'll both regret."

He hesitated a moment. Reese thought he might continue attempting to sway her. He didn't, surprising her once again.

"I understand." He tried a smile, which fell short. "I apologize for getting carried away."

"My fault, too."

"You have to admit." His smile widened. "It was a great kiss."

The best ever. He'd literally and figuratively swept her off her feet. "One for the record books."

He grabbed her jacket from the back of the chair and held it out for her. "I'll walk you to your car."

She slipped her right arm into the sleeve, then her left one and adjusted the jacket before buttoning it. Her exit did seem hasty, though under the circumstances, probably wise. Her defenses were at an all-time low.

At her car, he bent and gave her a sweet, yet lingering kiss that was completely intoxicating.

"Wait for me, Reese," he said and nuzzled her ear. "I've got a plan."

"For what?" He could be very distracting.

"Give me six months. I'm going to buy out my brothers."

She couldn't imagine how, as she'd turned down his one request to draw on the line of credit. Gabe was quite determined, though. Perhaps more now than before.

Rather than mention the many obstacles he faced, she hugged him to her.

"I'll help any way I can."

"I won't jeopardize your job."

Reese believed him. He hadn't let her down in the past.

She couldn't be with Gabe, not the way she longed to be, body and soul and heart. For now, she'd be content to wait. After today, and what had transpired between them, she believed they had what it took for a lasting relationship. That was certainly worth waiting a measly six months.

"Will your children be here for Christmas?" Gabe's mother asked Josh. "It would be so nice to have little ones in the house again."

Cara hadn't joined them for breakfast, otherwise his mother wouldn't have mentioned children and Christmas for fear of upsetting her.

"I'm afraid not," Josh said. "This will be their last time with their mother for a while. I agreed to let her have them for the holidays."

Gabe didn't know the whole story, but Josh had said something about his ex-wife going into rehab—her third go-round—for a drug addiction problem, which was one of the reasons he'd gained full custody of their kids.

"I won't be getting them until mid-January." Josh poured himself a glass of orange juice, then passed the pitcher to Cole.

Breakfast with his brothers had become something of a ritual for Gabe, thanks to his mother and her insistence. Conversation was mostly between her and Josh. Gabe and Cole preferred the roles of spectators.

He had yet to tell Cole he knew about his trip to see Theo McGraw. Gabe also hadn't told anyone about Theo's Parkinson's. Yesterday, Reese had called and asked him the name of the home nursing service they'd used when his father was ill. Perhaps she was making progress with Theo.

He hoped so. He was anxious for her to become a part of his life. But before that could happen, she needed to delegate some of her responsibilities for her father's care to a reliable nurse. Also, be done with her duties as trustee of Gabe's father's estate, which would occur when he bought out his brothers' shares.

"Oh, Josh." His mother clucked sympathetically as she crossed from the stove to the kitchen table, delivering a bowl heaped with scrambled eggs. "That is too bad for you, but good for the children's mother. It's important she have the support of her family during such a difficult time."

"Yeah. You're right." He didn't sound convinced.

Gabe's mother smiled delightedly. "I can't wait to meet them. A girl and a boy. The perfect family."

He didn't point out that if Josh was divorced and his ex-wife about to enter rehab for the third time, they were hardly the perfect family.

"I appreciate all you've done for us." Josh helped her find a place for the bowl, then sent his brother a sharp look.

"Yes. Thanks, Raquel," Cole said.

They'd been behaving better since the scene during Thanksgiving dinner. Perhaps due to Gabe and his suggestion they work together. He liked to think so, anyway.

"*De nada.*" His mother beamed as she took her seat.

What would she do if she learned that, a mere few days ago, Reese had been sitting on the table, right where his mother's arm rested, and Gabe had been kissing her like a crazy man, hoping to steal her off to his bedroom?

She'd box his ears, like she'd done that time when he

was seven and, on a dare, had stolen a pack of gum from the market. She'd also probably insist he make an honest woman out of Reese, though they hadn't let things go far enough to warrant a hasty wedding.

Funny, the idea of a future with Reese didn't scare Gabe like it had with his former girlfriends. Later, he'd give the notion some thoughtful consideration.

Or not. Frankly, it didn't matter. Gabe wasn't considering anything more serious than dating Reese. For now.

"Gabe, will you drive me to the lot by the market today for a Christmas tree?"

Gabe returned his attention to his mother. She'd been asking for this favor all week, and he couldn't put her off any longer.

"Yes, but not until after supper. We're meeting with the vet to decide on which cows to breed. If you can wait, I'm all yours."

Josh and Cole would also be at the meeting in order to learn, though Violet was technically in charge. Before the cancer had struck his father, Dos Estrellas owned several bulls, using them for breeding. The bulls, proven producers with outstanding lines, were the first livestock to be sold. As a result, this year they would artificially inseminate the cows.

The three brothers and Violet had much work ahead of them. To ensure the best results and produce a bumper number of calves at the least cost, the artificial insemination must be done as precisely as possible.

"I spoke to Tio Lorenzo yesterday," Gabe's mother said, referring to her favorite brother. "He's coming for Christmas."

"That's great, Mom."

His mother was very close to her brothers, Lorenzo in

particular. The upcoming visit had made her very happy. Just as his grandparents' refusal to visit made her sad.

"I'm looking forward to meeting him," Josh said.

He, at least, was being a good houseguest. Cole continued to eat in disgruntled silence.

What, Gabe wondered, had made his brother unhappy? Was being here, living in the home of the father he'd hated, the sole reason or was it something else? Why, Gabe wondered, did he care? He shouldn't waste his mental energy. Cole didn't spend one second thinking about him.

But Gabe did find himself thinking and caring. Reese was responsible for the change in him. Because of her, and their unexpected feelings, he had begun to look at his brothers differently.

"It's going to be a nice Christmas this year." His mother smiled at each of them.

Much better than the previous two. Though they would all miss his father terribly, and remember the loss of Cara's son, he, like his mother, had something positive to look forward to.

When they were done eating, Josh offered to help with the dishes, a chore Cara usually did. Not to be outdone, Gabe cleared the table. He was carting the last of the dirty plates to the counter when his cell phone rang.

He didn't recognize the number, but the voice that greeted him was familiar. Buck Sadoski, the cattle broker he'd spoken with several weeks earlier, was in high spirits.

"Hey, partner, how are you this glorious morning?" His booming voice resounded in Gabe's ear.

"Good. And yourself?" He hadn't expected to hear from Buck this soon; the cattle broker hadn't taken it well when Gabe turned down his previous generous offer.

"Fine and dandy."

"What can I do for you?" Gabe excused himself to his father's office with a wave to his mother. He didn't want his family to overhear his conversation.

"Partner, it's what I can do for you. I have four hundred of the best-looking steer calves you've seen in all your born days en route to Phoenix from Texas right this minute. They'll be hitting the borders of our fair city by tomorrow morning. I'm looking for a buyer, and the first person I thought of was you."

Normally, Gabe would be interested only in cows or heifers, seeing as breeding season was well upon them. And, after the last fiasco when Reese refused to advance him the purchase money, he was reluctant to jump in with both feet.

"Not sure I'm in the market for steer."

Buck laughed, low and grumbly. "Wait until I tell you the price."

He did, and Gabe's interest flared.

"You hold on to these little fellows until this spring, fatten 'em up, and you can sell them for a tidy profit."

That, he could.

"Beef prices are going to continue to soar," Buck added. "Count on it."

Gabe quickly ran the numbers in his head. If beef prices rose even half of what those in the business were predicting, they could stand to make 30 percent on their investment.

They, or him? What if he were to buy the calves on his own? Without his brothers?

Naw, he couldn't pull it off. Not without drawing on

the line of credit, and Reese had made it clear that was impossible without his brothers' knowledge and consent. There was also the matter of supplemental feed. With more head, they would have to purchase additional hay, and maybe not at the good price Banner Hay Sales had given them last time.

To make a purchase of this size, including the cattle and the hay, they'd quite possibly use what was left of the line of credit after paying for inseminating the cows.

Risky, yes, but not much of a risk. Young steers could be counted on to grow up.

"You don't take these pretty babies," Buck said, "and someone else will."

In a heartbeat. The man wasn't exaggerating. It was a good deal. If Gabe were to approach his brothers, he'd have to sell them on the idea. He had no idea how they'd react.

"Have the calves been vet checked?"

Buck chuckled. "I'm staring at the paperwork right here in front of me."

"Give me until the end of the day," Gabe said.

"Sorry." The cattle broker didn't sound sorry. "I've got to have these babies sold before the trucks arrive tomorrow. If you don't want them, I know ten other ranchers who do."

Buck wasn't exaggerating about that, either.

"Can you give me two hours?"

"Okay. But if I don't hear from you by nine o'clock, I'm gonna start making calls."

Gabe thanked him and hung up, then returned to the kitchen. Josh and his mother were finishing up with the dishes.

"Where's Cole?" he asked, then did a double take.

Josh wore a dish towel as an apron and was chatting amiably with his mother. They made a curious and unsettling picture. At Gabe's question, Josh glanced over his shoulder. "In the barn. He's driving out with Violet this morning."

That was right. They were distributing the last of the hay.

Gabe punched Cole's number into his phone.

"What's up?" Josh asked, his brows forming a deep V as he walked over to where Gabe stood.

"We have a lead on four hundred steer at a smokin' price."

"Can we afford them?"

"I don't think we can afford not to buy them. Hey, Cole," he said when his younger brother picked up. "Get yourself back to the house. We have an emergency meeting."

Gabe's father had conducted all his business in his office. Gabe broke with tradition. While his mother busied herself elsewhere in the house, he, Josh and Cole hammered out the details at the kitchen table.

It wasn't easy. They didn't always agree. Neither was it hard. Both Josh and Cole deferred to Gabe as the more experienced one among them.

At a quarter till nine, Gabe called Buck and told him that they would buy the steer. Their next call was to Reese. Gabe didn't ask for the money. Instead, he inquired when she'd be free to see them. He kept the conversation strictly business, never once slipping into the familiarity they'd shared often these past weeks.

"We have something to discuss with you."

"We?" Reese sounded busy.

"Me and my brothers."

"All right."

She agreed to see them after lunch. Gabe spent the time with Violet and his brothers, readying the pastures in the upper sections. He envisioned the young steers roaming Dos Estrellas pastures, growing fat and sleek, then using his share of the profits when the steer were sold to realize all his dreams.

It might not be a sure thing, but it wasn't impossible, either. Gabe could do it if he worked hard and stayed the course.

Chapter 11

Two wranglers lifted the ramp on the last trailer truck and closed it. The safety bar fell into place with a resounding clang.

The wrangler on the left, a wizened old-timer, secured the latch and called to his buddy, "We're done. Load up."

The pair jogged to the cab of the truck, one on each side of the long metal trailer, and clamored inside. They waved as they pulled out, joining the rest of the caravan waiting on the main road.

"Wow." Reese showered Gabe with a brilliant smile. "Been a while since I've seen this many young steer."

"I could say the same."

His gaze traveled the length of the herd, which stretched out nearly a quarter mile as the steer strolled leisurely across the pasture, enjoying their freedom as they familiarized themselves with their new home.

More hay would be delivered tomorrow. Gabe hoped this would be their last purchase for a while.

Finally, the skies were an ominous gray and heavy with cloud cover. Rain was predicted to fall by evening. It was the Christmas present Gabe had wanted most, and, while early by a couple of weeks, it appeared he was going to get his wish.

"I've *never* see this many steer," Josh added, a trace of awe in his voice. "Not all in one place."

The three of them sat astride their horses, Gabe on Bonita, Reese on her father's horse General, who was fully recovered from his fall in the sinkhole, and Josh on one of Cole's fancy roping horses he'd brought from California.

Gabe would rather he and Reese be alone. He'd like to express his excitement and appreciation in a way involving their mouths making intimate contact. Instead, he'd had to thank her the polite and proper way, by shaking her hand.

With the three brothers in agreement, Reese had reluctantly, but willingly, authorized the draw on the line of credit. There wasn't much remaining after paying the cattle broker and Banner Hay Sales. Barely enough to cover the cost of artificially inseminating the cows.

Reese worried that, should an emergency arise, Dos Estrellas would be at risk without the benefit of a reserve. However, purchasing the steer, inseminating the cows, growing the herd, it was all part of Gabe's father's plan. She'd been ultimately swayed by both the excellent price of the steer and the brothers' unanimous consent.

"How'd you convince them?" she'd asked at the bank after their meeting.

Gabe had leaned close and dipped his head. "I can be persuasive."

She'd gasped in shock and quickly shooed him out her office door. But when he'd asked her if she wanted to join them for the delivery of the steer, she'd heartily agreed, which had gladdened Gabe. He'd been missing her something terrible.

"I'm going to ride up the hill a bit," he said. "Inspect that fence we repaired. Make sure it holds."

They didn't need any of the steers to bust through the fence and onto Small Change land.

"I'll go with you." Reese turned General in Gabe's direction.

He expected Josh to tag along and was pleased when his brother begged off with, "I'm going to ride back to the ranch and give Violet a hand."

Finally, thought Gabe, some time alone with Reese.

Reese glanced back at his brother more than once as she and Gabe ascended the sloping hill, her lovely brow knitted in concentration. "Do you think he's interested in her?"

"Josh and Violet?" Gabe's first reaction was to laugh. His second was to frown. "I don't know. I don't think so."

"They've been working together a lot recently."

"I suppose." Gabe studied the sky. He could smell rain in the air, and it raised his spirits almost as much as seeing all those young steer roaming the pastures.

"They're both single," Reese continued, the wind stealing her words and swallowing them.

"He hasn't said anything to me."

"Would he?" She shot Gabe a sideways look that implied he was being a bit dense.

He shrugged, not the least offended. "Doubtful."

"I think they'd make a cute couple."

"He hasn't asked about her." If Gabe was interested in a woman, he'd find out what he could. "Besides, Cole spends more time with her than Josh."

"Well," Reese scoffed, "nothing's going to happen between *them*."

Gabe tended to agree. Cole told anyone who cared to listen that his ambition remained the same. Leave Mustang Valley at the first opportunity.

"How's your dad?" he asked, changing the subject.

"About the same."

Seeing the light leave her eyes, Gabe was sorry he'd brought up the subject.

"No more falls, thank goodness," she said. "And he finally told Enrico about his Parkinson's, though I think what actually happened is Enrico confronted him. Dad won't say."

By unspoken agreement, they stopped their horses and watched the steer nibble at the sparse grass on their slow trek to the stock pond over the next rise. Tomorrow morning, after breakfast, Violet would supervise the delivery of the first load of hay. Josh would probably help her.

Could Reese be right? Was an attraction developing between Josh and Violet? If true, Gabe wasn't sure how he felt about that. He wanted his livestock manager's undivided loyalty.

"I think it was hard for Dad, telling Enrico." Reese pulled her knit scarf up around her ears to ward off the cold, tucking the tails inside her jacket.

Gabe instantly recalled nuzzling those ears during

their heated kiss on the carriage ride. He'd nuzzled her neck during their kiss in the kitchen.

What would she say if he climbed down from his horse right now and—

"I hired a part-time nurse," Reese said, interrupting his thoughts. "It was a tough battle, getting Dad to agree."

"What changed his mind?"

"His doctor. They had a long heart-to-heart last week. Actually, I think what the doctor gave Dad was a severe talking-to, but that's not how Dad described it."

"You might want to consider getting medical power of attorney soon. We did with my dad. Saved us a lot of hassle in dealing with his doctors."

"I suppose I'll have to eventually." Reese sighed. "For now, I'm taking things slowly. Hiring the part-time nurse was a first step."

Because her mood had visibly changed at the mention of her father, Gabe dropped the subject. She could use a break from the stress at home, not have him add to it.

"Don't overwork yourself at Christmas," he said, remembering how his mother had run herself ragged. Her efforts to care for his father, play hostess to his visiting family and fill the house with as much cheer as possible had left her exhausted and miserable. "The holidays can be rough with a sick family member."

"My aunt Louise wanted to come for a visit. Dad told her no."

Reese sounded disappointed, and Gabe longed to comfort her. "You could visit her."

She shook her head. "I can't leave Dad."

"Why don't I invite you both for Christmas dinner at our house? Mom would love it."

Her lush mouth curved into a smile, reminding him of how much he wanted to kiss her. "We both know how that ended the first time."

"Strangely enough, I think it might go better than Thanksgiving."

"You three have made some amazing progress in getting along."

"Things are going to work out, Reese." He grinned.

"You sound confident."

"I am."

Her smile widened, some of its former brilliance returning.

He was captivated. "If you need any help with your dad, let me know."

"Thank you."

Impulsively, he reached across the small distance separating them and grabbed her hand, clutching it in his.

"We shouldn't," she warned, glancing around.

"No one's here to see us."

"I suppose not."

"I've missed you," Gabe said, feeling uncharacteristically vulnerable.

"Me, too." Her expression shone with sincerity. "Missed you."

Perhaps she wouldn't be opposed to that kiss after all. Gabe was wondering how to pull it off exactly when one of the young steer caught his eye.

It had wandered away from the herd, about one hundred feet away. Unusual behavior, as cattle were naturally wary of horses with riders, but not unheard of. It was the steer's stilted and awkward gait that set off silent alarms in Gabe's head. The steer walked stiffly as if its joints hurt.

"Look." He dropped Reese's hand in order to point.

"What am I looking at?"

"The steer separated from the rest. Something's not right with him."

Rather than ride over, Gabe dismounted. With any luck, he'd be able to get close to the steer on foot.

Fifty or so of the steer nearest them stared in comical, wide-eyed unison. They didn't bolt, which was a relief. Gabe was in a vulnerable position if they chose to run at him.

About twenty feet away from the steer, Gabe halted. He didn't like what he saw. Fluid dripped from the steer's nostrils and its nose gleamed a bright red color. Combine those symptoms with the steer's stilted movement and vacant stare, and Gabe had reason to worry.

He studied the other nearby steer for several minutes, which quickly lost interest in him and continued meandering down the hill. At first, all appeared to be in good health. Active, alert and munching grass. Then, Gabe saw it. Another steer with clear fluid dripping from its nostrils.

No point in panicking, he told himself as a jolt of fear shot through him. Returning to Bonita, he swung up into the saddle.

"I need to get back to the ranch. Fast."

"What is it?" Her voice rose with concern.

"A couple of the steer are sick. I'm going to call the vet. Have him get over here right away."

"Sick? The herd was vet checked. You got the papers."

He had. But, as anyone in the ranching business knew, cattle could appear perfectly healthy one day and drop dead the next. Some diseases progressed that quickly.

He urged Bonita into a lope. Reese rode beside him,

down the hill and toward Dos Estrellas. There wasn't a moment to waste.

Two or three sick cattle wasn't unusual. Viruses were common and not necessarily cause for concern. If the steer had contracted something more serious, then Gabe—and his entire family—could be in serious trouble.

As much as Gabe had wanted to be alone with Reese earlier, he'd have liked nothing better than for her to disappear when the vet arrived to examine the sickly steer. But she had remained. Not as his potential romantic interest and not as his friend. She'd stayed as trustee of his father's estate, watching and, he was sure of it, forming opinions.

She'd been present when the vet had delivered the agonizing news. The steer, over thirty in all, and with that number potentially growing by the hour, were stricken with infectious bovine rhinotracheitis. Red nose, the local ranchers called it. There was no definitive medical test, but the vet was adamant. He'd seen enough cases.

"I don't understand," Reese said. "Weren't the steer vaccinated?"

They stood outside the main barn, having returned minutes ago from meticulously inspecting and subsequently treating the infected steer. In addition to Gabe, Reese and the vet—a small, wiry man with impressive strength and stamina—Violet was also present.

At least Josh and Cole wouldn't see Gabe's humiliation. Cara had called asking for help at the mustang sanctuary, and he'd quickly dispatched his brothers.

"They were," Violet answered Reese's question. "I read the paperwork myself."

Four people in total had, including Reese, before the money changed hands. She knew that. Gabe wasn't sure why she'd asked. Unless it was to drive home the point that he alone was responsible as the person whose idea it was to buy the steer.

"Vaccinations are no guarantee a herd won't become infected," the vet said. They had gathered around his truck while he loaded supplies into the specially designed compartments built into the bed. "There are a lot of reasons why steer contract red nose."

"Such as?" Reese asked.

Gabe doubted her interest stemmed from a desire to learn. She was fishing, attempting to discover if Gabe had overlooked the obvious.

"Improperly administered vaccines." The vet slammed shut the door of the last compartment. "Poor nutrition, for another. Young calves without proper feed and mineral supplements won't respond to the vaccination. Failure to administer booster vaccinations, though that's not the case here. The stress of transportation could have played a role. It weakens a steer's immune system." He leaned against the side of his truck, directing his comment at Reese. "And, sometimes, the vaccines plain don't work."

She didn't flinch. Gabe had seen her go head-to-head with his brothers and her ex-boyfriend Blake Nolan. During those occasions, he'd admired her fortitude and grit. Now he was on the receiving end, and he didn't like it.

"Is there anything more we can do?" Violet asked. "Other than quarantine the infected cattle and continue with an antibiotic regimen?"

The vet turned to face her. "All manner of supportive

care. Rest, fluids, good food. Infectious bovine rhino-tracheitis never goes away. It resides in the brain indefinitely. You can treat the symptoms, but not eradicate the disease."

They would have to reserve the rest of the hay for the sick cattle, who'd need more than the sporadic tufts of grass growing on the hills.

Dammit, thought Gabe. Another unplanned expense. Reese wouldn't let him hear the end of this.

"Can the steer still be sold?" she asked the vet.

"Absolutely. Once they've recovered."

"Can they get sick again?"

"You'll have to watch them closely." The vet presented Gabe with a handwritten bill. "I assume I give this to you."

"What about antibiotics?" Gabe spoke for the first time in a while. He'd been too stunned after the vet's devastating announcement to say much. "Can you leave us a supply and add them to the total?"

"Would if I could." The vet barely came up to Gabe's chin, yet he had a way of looming over people like a much taller man. "Don't have any extra. Not that I can sell you. Need to save all I have for my practice."

Gabe was momentarily confused. "What? Why?"

"There's a shortage of cattle antibiotics," the vet explained. "I have an order in. More should be arriving next week."

Pushing back his cowboy hat, Gabe rubbed his forehead where an irritating pain resided. "The steer are sick. I can't wait until next week."

"You could always try the feed store."

Gabe felt the pressure from all sides. Reese's eyes bored holes into his skull like twin laser beams. Violet chewed a thumbnail. His brothers spoke to each other in low, conspiratorial voices.

Refusing to succumb, Gabe reached in his pocket and removed the check he'd brought from the office. He filled in the invoice amount, using the hood of the truck for a desk.

"Appreciate the business," the vet said, accepting the check. "Merry Christmas."

"Same to you," Reese replied.

He saluted the group before leaving.

Only when he drove away did Gabe notice the wreath attached to the truck's tailgate and its blinking colored lights. The wreath made a mockery of his earlier feelings when it seemed as if his greatest wish was being granted. What an idiot he'd been.

Gabe headed for his truck.

Reese hurried after him. "Where are you going?"

Wasn't it obvious? "The feed store."

"I could come with you."

He stopped in his tracks and glared at her. "Why?"

She hesitated. "To keep you company."

"Are you sure you don't want to chew me out for my bad decision?"

"You couldn't know some of the steer were infected with red nose."

"But I am the one who convinced my brothers to purchase the herd and you to grant the draw on the line of credit."

"Gabe, I just want to help. Let me come with you."

Had he been too harsh on her? Misjudged her? "I need to stop at the house first for another check. Unless you refuse to cover it from the line of credit."

"I'll cover it."

She waited in the passenger seat while he went inside. They didn't speak much on the short drive to the center of town. Luckily, Ray's Feed Depot was open till six on Saturdays, giving them plenty of time. Perhaps they'd caught the spread of red nose before any significant damage was done. Gabe prayed that was the case.

Chapter 12

At the same moment Gabe and Reese approached the entrance to Ray's Feed Depot, the door swung wide and Blake Nolan stepped out, lugging a large cardboard box. He stopped, took note of them and nodded curtly. Did he remember seeing Gabe at the bank a few weeks ago?

"Reese. Gabe. How goes it?"

"Good." Reese didn't hesitate speaking first and, evidently, on behalf of Gabe.

"All right," Gabe added despite being far from all right. But Blake didn't need to know that. "How are your folks doing?"

"Keeping busy with the holidays. Thanks for asking." Blake hesitated. "Sorry again about your dad. He was a fine man."

"Appreciate the kind words."

Blake and his wife, Wynonna, had come to the funeral. Gabe vaguely remembered seeing them among the throng of mourners.

"Well, take care." Blake nodded again, then left, the contents of the box rattling.

"Happy holidays," Reese said. By then Blake was long gone. She shrugged. "Clearly, he's still mad at me."

Gabe was more interested in what Blake was carrying. He swore the box contained bovine antibiotics. Was it a simple coincidence? Perhaps the vet had spread the news about Gabe's steer and the red nose outbreak. Yanking open the door, Gabe entered the feed store one step behind Reese. The life-size plastic horse just inside the entrance wore a wreath around its neck and a Santa hat on its head. Ray, the store's owner, dragged out the same tired decorations every year. Gabe paid them no mind. He was a man on a mission.

At the counter, he waited for Ray's niece and assistant manager, Alanna, to finish up with a customer.

"Hey, Gabe. Reese," she said when she was free. "What can I do for you?"

Several years older than Gabe, Alanna was short, plump and one of the hardest workers he'd ever seen. Without her, Ray would have been forced to sell the store when his son moved to Gila Bend last year.

Gabe leaned his elbows on the counter. Behind him, Reese waited, her booted foot tapping a staccato on the hardwood floor.

"We need all the bovine antibiotics you have in stock," he said, naming the brand the vet had recommended.

"Sure thing." Smiling pleasantly, Alanna disappeared through a door behind the counter. Gabe and everyone else who ever visited the store knew the supply room contained a large cooler where the medicines needing refrigeration were kept.

She returned a few minutes later, hugging five bottles to her chest, which she then set on the counter. Swiping her hands together, she asked, "Will that be all?"

He stared at the five bottles. "Where's the rest?"

"This is my entire supply."

"You're joking." He must have misheard, or she'd misunderstood him.

"Sorry. Blake Nolan bought up all our inventory but this. He heard there's been an outbreak of red nose in New Mexico and Texas and was stocking up before it traveled further west."

Gabe didn't clarify that the virus had already made its way to Mustang Valley. "What about a different brand?" The vet had mentioned other, less effective antibiotics that would do in a pinch.

Alanna shook her head. "Sorry. We're clean out of every kind."

"When will you get more in?"

"Next week." She then echoed what the vet had said. "Antibiotics are in short supply. Red nose is one of several respiratory outbreaks. This winter has been bad for cattle back East and in the Midwest, what with all the storms."

It was like a terrible dream from which there was no waking up. Buck Sadoski should have, but hadn't, mentioned the outbreak when he'd sold Gabe the steer. Buck had likely suspected, hence the low price.

Dammit! Gabe should have done his homework before agreeing to the sale. He'd heard about the storms. Who hadn't? It just hadn't registered. His oversight.

"Do you know where I can buy some?"

She scrunched her mouth to one side, thinking. "Let me call Rio Verde. They might have a supply." Alanna trotted over to the register and picked up a portable telephone handset. A minute later, she returned, her face saying it all. "Rio Verde is down to eleven bottles. If you want, they'll stay open an extra half hour."

Eleven bottles, plus these five, for thirty head of steer. That wouldn't last long. Nowhere near long enough to complete the number of days the vet had recommended Gabe treat the steer.

"You could always order online," Alanna suggested. "Might take a few days, assuming you find a supplier with enough product in stock."

What other choice did he have?

"Do you mind calling Rio Verde and letting them know I'm on my way?" He removed the check from his pocket.

"Tell me you aren't driving all the way to Rio Verde," Reese said, censure in her tone. They'd reached Gabe's truck, and she was opening the passenger door.

"I'll drop you home first," he said.

"I can ride with you."

"What about your dad?"

"He's resting. And Enrico's there."

Gabe handed her the paper sack of vaccine bottles to hold. "I don't need a babysitter."

"That's not the reason, Gabe."

"I'm going to save the steer. We won't lose the ranch."

"I know you're trying your best."

He bristled. More than censure, she was chastising him. "This could have happened to anyone."

"You're right." She adjusted the bottles more securely on her lap. He no sooner sat behind the wheel when she added, "But they may not be operating on a shoestring like you."

Here it comes, he thought, *the lecture*. Gabe jammed the key in the ignition.

"There's enough money left on the line of credit for the antibiotics, right?" he asked.

"You still have the artificial insemination to pay for. That's scheduled in a few days."

"We may have to impregnate fewer cows."

"May?" she asked.

He hastily threw the truck into Reverse and backed out of the parking space. "Don't patronize me."

She blew out a breath. "I deserve a share of the blame. I authorized the steer purchase even though I had my doubts."

"Except your livelihood's not on the line." And if it was, she still had her father and the Small Change to fall back on.

"It could be," she said, this time with noticeable worry in her voice.

Was it true? Could her job really be at stake? If so, Gabe would have more guilt to bear.

"Are you going to tell your brothers?" She glanced at him from across the seat.

"Yes."

"Today?"

"I'm well aware of my responsibilities, Reese. You don't have to keep nagging me."

She looked chagrined. "I'm sorry. I'm worried is all. Red nose is highly contagious."

He should be the one apologizing to her. "I didn't mean to snap at you."

"And I didn't mean to tell you what to do." She placed

a hand on his leg. "We're in this together. Not just as business associates. I'm also your friend."

He had thought they were more than friends. He now realized they hadn't talked specifics, other than asking her to wait. His plans, his dreams, were simply that. *His*.

They reached a fork in the road. To the left was the Small Change. To the right, the road leading out of town and to Rio Verde. Unable to make a decision, Gabe stopped, letting the truck idle.

"Tell you what," Reese said, giving him an out. "Drop me at home. While you drive to Rio Verde, I'll find a supplier online and place the order."

After the way he'd treated her, that was far more than he deserved. "Thank you."

"I'll call when I have some information. Maybe I'll come by tomorrow and pick up Dad's horse."

Gabe would see to it General was fed and given a clean stall for the night.

He took the left fork. Moments later, he dropped off Reese at her doorstep.

"I can be there when you talk to your brothers," she offered almost shyly. "Give them the bank's perspective on the situation."

His first inclination was to utter a resounding no. On second thought, her presence might show his brothers that the bank supported Gabe and the purchase of the steer.

"I'll let you know when."

He wanted to kiss her. Heck, he always wanted to kiss her. But now, more than ever, they needed to maintain the professional boundaries they'd set. If things went badly and more steer contracted red nose, he didn't want either of them or their actions to come under question.

Apparently, Reese had fewer concerns than him, for she leaned across the seat and kissed his cheek tenderly before hopping out of the truck.

Gabe drove to Rio Verde as fast as the law allowed. Daylight was disappearing, and he needed to get there before the store closed.

As the desert scenery blurred by, he realized he was fighting for more than full ownership of Dos Estrellas. His future with Reese was also on the line and that was quickly becoming the most important reason to fight.

A thirty-seven-mile round-trip, practically wasted. Gabe sat at the kitchen table, drinking his midmorning coffee and fuming about his drive to Rio Verde the day before. By the time he arrived at the feed store, only five bottles were left. Ray's niece must have forgotten to call and say he was coming.

"I've never seen a shortage like this in all my fifteen years," the clerk had commented while ringing up the sale. "The weather back East is a killer."

Last night's news had shown the results of another record-breaking storm—film footage of homes, cars and landmarks unrecognizable under piles of snow. Shipping services, hindered by the volume of holiday mailing, had stopped. Like Ray's Feed Depot, the store in Rio Verde wasn't getting a new supply of antibiotics for a week to ten days, if then.

Neither was Arizona immune from the harsh weather. Snow hammered the northern parts while heavy rain drenched central and southern areas. This morning, rain pelted the roof, causing a loud racket to fill the house. Sheets of water poured off the roof and flooded the courtyard, forming huge puddles outside the doors. The livestock pens and pastures had become muddy messes.

Gabe had been hoping and praying for just such a deluge. Now, he needed it to stop. The sick steer suffered worse in the cold and wet, and the healthy ones were more susceptible to infection.

Could his luck be any worse?

He, Violet and the two hands remaining at Dos Estrellas had risen at sunrise, donned their rain gear, and treated the infected steer. After that, they'd inspected the remaining herd for symptoms. They'd found three steer infected and moved them to section four.

As of late last night, Reese had yet to locate an online supplier. It was the same story everywhere. No antibiotics available until after Christmas. Perhaps not until the New Year. Since it was Sunday, most of the businesses were closed. The hunt had officially been put on hold.

Gabe briefly entertained the idea of delaying telling his brothers. They had some inkling of what was going on despite Gabe's efforts to keep them out of the loop. They weren't stupid.

Cole had gone to the Poco Dinero Saloon and Grill again last night, something he'd casually mentioned at breakfast. He'd heard the locals talking about the red nose outbreak in Texas and its swift move west to Arizona. If he'd said one word about the vet's visit yesterday, then half of Mustang Valley already suspected Dos Estrellas was in possession of infected steer.

To say the ranchers wouldn't be happy with Gabe was an understatement. If they suffered any losses because of red nose, he'd be vilified.

"Morning, *mijo*." Gabe's mother came up behind him and kissed the top of his head.

He absently patted her hand. "Hi, Mom."

"I thought, if you don't mind, I'd run into town and do some Christmas errands." With her brother Lorenzo definitely visiting for the holidays, she wanted to make sure they were well-stocked with his favorite foods.

"Of course I don't mind." Gabe drained the remainder of his coffee. "Where's Cara?"

"Visiting her mom. I hope Cara doesn't get stuck on the way home. You know how terrible traffic gets when it rains like this. Maybe I should call Leena's and tell Cara to stay the night."

Cara's mother had been a daily visitor at Dos Estrellas until she'd remarried and moved to Mesa a few years ago. Leena was more a sister than a friend to Raquel, and the reason Cara and her young son had moved to the ranch when she separated from her husband and stayed after the boy's death.

Gabe had contemplated asking Cara to be in on the talk with his brothers. Guess that wouldn't be happening now.

"Are you all right, *mijo*?" His mother sat down beside him, her smile a combination of affection and concern. "You seem distracted."

"I'm worried."

"It has been a difficult time for us."

"We're going to run out of antibiotics by tomorrow." Which was hardly his biggest problem. Feed remained in short supply, and they had almost no money for more.

"Something will come up. Reese is very smart." His mother's features softened. "I'm glad you two found each other."

Gabe tried to hide his reaction. "What are you talking about?"

"I'm your mother. I can see how you feel about her. And because I'm a woman, I can see how she feels about you. I approve. And your father would, too. He was right to pick her as his trustee."

"Wait a minute. Are you saying Dad picked Reese because he wanted us to hook up?"

"Of course not. He picked her because she was Theo's daughter."

"That makes no sense."

"Ah, but it does." She tapped the side of her head and winked. "Think about it. Your father wanted his will carried out to the letter and knew Reese would work extra hard to ensure there wasn't the slightest deviation."

"Because she's Theo McGraw's daughter."

"And because she's very good at her job. She wouldn't want to be accused of any... What is the word? Yes, improprieties."

Gabe could see the logic, though it was slightly skewed, in his opinion, and hurtful. "Dad trusted a person he hardly knew, a person who could well ruin the ranch, more than me."

"No, no, *mijo*."

"Funny thing is, I'm not sure Dad was wrong." Gabe thought of himself purchasing the sick steer, rushing headlong into a decision and thinking only of himself. "He was a lot wiser than any of us gave him credit for."

"He was worried his sons would fight."

"He had good reason to worry."

She sighed, more wistful than sad. "Your father and I made mistakes. We were young and in love. Even so, it wasn't fair to his wife. I don't blame her for being angry and for passing her anger on to her sons."

She rarely spoke of his father's ex-wife. Now that

Gabe thought about it, the two women must have crossed paths. Both had lived in Mustang Valley for a number of years. Surely, they'd run into each other at the market or the Holly Daze Festival. How would his father's ex-wife have felt, confronting her husband's mistress?

For the first time in his life, Gabe felt sorry for Josh and Cole's mother. She must have been deeply wounded by his dad. Which didn't justify her turning her sons against their father, but it did explain a lot.

Was that why Blake didn't acknowledge Celia? To protect his wife, their marriage and their sons?

"Your father's last wish was for you and your brothers to reconcile." His mother's voice penetrated his thoughts. "It wasn't possible while he was alive because Josh and Cole's mother refused to allow it. Now there's a chance. If you are willing."

Gabe wished he was a bigger person, one with more forgiveness in his heart. "I'm not sure I am. They knew Dad was dying, and they didn't come out. Not until Hector called them and told them they were named as beneficiaries in Dad's will."

"You assume it's greed that brought them here."

"Isn't it?"

"Their mother's parents have money, and they'll probably inherit a portion."

"Maybe they didn't want to wait or they aren't on good terms. Josh didn't ask his grandparents to help with his attorney costs when he was fighting for custody of his kids."

"I don't care what brought them here." Raquel's voice grew higher. "I'm glad they're staying. For your father and for you."

"Why for me?"

"You've felt all your life you weren't as good as them."

"Not true."

"It is." His mother gazed at him earnestly. "It's also true you're every bit as good as them and were loved by your father as much, if not more. Them being here will show you."

Gabe doubted that, but his mother could have a point. He was the son raised by his father his entire life. The one taught by him. Given his love. Not his brothers. Their anger and resentment might be because they didn't think they were as good as Gabe. It was something to ponder.

"I have to talk to them about the sick steer and our chances. It looks bleak, Mom."

"How bleak?"

"We're in trouble."

She stood and kissed the top of his head again. "You'll figure this out. You and Reese."

Her optimism was sweet. And naive. They were in for the battle of their lives.

His cell phone rang, and Gabe answered it, noting Reese's number. "Hello."

"I don't have good news," she blurted.

He propped an elbow on the table and rested his forehead in his hand. "You didn't find any online suppliers with antibiotics."

"None of them will promise a shipment until after Christmas. And that isn't all."

He didn't like the tone in her voice. "What?"

"Because of the shortage, prices are skyrocketing. Whatever supply we get our hands on will cost us top dollar."

Their situation was worse than yesterday.

"Okay." What else was there to say? Realistically, he'd expected this. Deep inside, he had hoped for more.

"What time did you want me over there?" Reese asked.

The meeting with his brothers, the one she was planning on attending. He'd momentarily forgotten.

"After lunch. One o'clock."

"It's going to work out," Reese said.

"I'm not sure how." With his mother nearby, he didn't dare say anything personal, even though she had correctly surmised he and Reese were involved. "See you soon," he said and disconnected.

"Not good news?" His mother came over when he'd disconnected from Reese.

He explained the situation, unable to hide his disappointment. "If I could put off talking to Josh and Cole, I would."

"Don't." His mother shook her head. "Your father would expect you to do what's right and take charge."

"Please stop defending him, Mom," Gabe bit out. "I loved Dad and hate that he died, but let's be honest. He really screwed things up. For all of us. You said so yourself."

"I'm not defending him." She sounded hurt. "I'm supporting you. I don't doubt for one second you will find the answers necessary to save Dos Estrellas."

She said *the answers* as if a red nose outbreak was no more serious than a skin rash.

"We have to face facts."

"*You* must have *faith*," she said before walking away.

Faith? They needed a miracle. For the skies to clear,

the grass to grow, the steer to recover and at least eight hundred healthy calves born next year.

Rather than his spirits lifting, Gabe experienced the weight of his mistake pushing him further and further down. He might well be buried under one of those piles of snow he'd seen on the news last night.

Chapter 13

Normally, the land between the horse barn and the ranch house was dry as dust. When the rain fell in torrents, like today, the shallow wash filled with water within a matter of hours. It now resembled a raging river ten feet wide.

Two years ago, Gabe's father had crossed in the quad and inadvertently flooded the engine, resulting in hundreds of dollars' worth of damage. Several times, when Gabe had been young and foolhardy, he'd daringly waded into the running wash, only to be swept away in the muddy water and carried a hundred feet before gaining his footing.

This afternoon, he wasn't so careless and crossed at the lowest point. It was a slow, arduous process, made more uncomfortable by his silently fuming brothers in the truck's rear seat. Violet sat beside him and, every few seconds, cast him a concerned look.

Moments ago, the four of them had come in from checking the herd yet again. More sick steer were discovered, bringing the total to over forty.

Gabe alternately looked out the side window at the rushing water and ahead, through the windshield, at the bank on the other side. Rain slammed the glass and, combined with the swiftly thumping wipers, hampered his vision. Finally, the truck bumped and rocked as the front wheels climbed out of the water and onto solid ground. He heard a collective sigh of relief from his passengers.

A five-foot-high slatted fence surrounded the house and yard, separating it from the horse stables, cattle barn, livestock pens, hay sheds and other outbuildings. Gabe rolled slowly through the gate and spotted Reese's car in the driveway. He pulled up beside her vehicle and shut off the truck. All four doors simultaneously opened, and everyone piled out. The flaps of Gabe's unfastened rain slicker blew open. He ignored the rain that pelted him, stinging his skin through his shirt and jeans, and soaking him to the bone.

At the back door, they stomped the water and muck from their boots and removed their slickers before entering the mudroom. They wiped their boots with rags before entering the house. Gabe's mother wouldn't be happy if they tracked dirt and water on her clean floors.

She'd opted out of the meeting, though Gabe had wanted her to attend. She'd claimed her presence might make his brothers uncomfortable and unwilling to express their opinions. She had fresh coffee waiting for them on the counter. Chai tea for Violet. They each grabbed a mug and a handful of Christmas sugar cookies.

Reese sat in the dining room at the end of the table,

holding a steaming mug. She glanced up as they entered the room. A musical, motion-activated Christmas tree on the buffet began playing "Jingle Bells."

Everyone stood stonily for the next ten seconds. After the music stopped, they sat.

"Quite the rain we're having," Reese addressed to no one in particular.

"It's supposed to continue until tomorrow," Violet remarked.

Complete silence. No one was in the mood for small talk.

Gabe's gaze wandered the table. He was reminded of Thanksgiving dinner, the last time they had all been in this room together. That gathering had ended badly, with Josh and Cole storming out. Would this one end the same? Studying his brothers' stern faces, he decided the odds were in favor of it. They hadn't appreciated Gabe putting off their questions about the sick steer.

"Shall we begin?" Reese deferred to Gabe.

He'd thought of little else all morning except this meeting, even mentally rehearsing what he'd say. Now that the moment had arrived, his preparation deserted him.

"You may have figured out we're dealing with a bovine virus outbreak," he began. "It's called red nose and over forty of our steer are affected."

"Is it fatal?" Josh asked.

"No."

"How did they contract it?" Cole demanded.

"Some of the steer were sick when we bought them."

"Didn't you check?"

"Gabe took every precaution," Reese insisted. "This could have happened to anyone."

Cole's eyes narrowed. "But it happened to us."

Gabe didn't rise to the bait Cole dangled, though he wanted to. Badly. "Between the snow storms back East and bovine virus outbreaks across the country, we're having trouble buying the necessary antibiotics." He paused. "We, all of us, need to decide a course of action."

"What do you suggest?" Josh asked.

Gabe evaluated his older brother, searching for clues to his frame of mind. "Continue our attempts to purchase antibiotics at the best available price. Inspect the herd twice a day and quarantine the sick steer. Feed them what's left of the supplemental hay and grain. Watch our other cattle for signs and isolate them if necessary."

"Quarantining is especially important," Reese added. "It's imperative we stop the red nose from spreading."

He'd been about to say the same thing. Coming from Reese, it smacked of criticism. He shifted uncomfortably.

"It would be best to get the cattle out of the rain," he said. "But we have no facility capable of accommodating that many sick steer."

Dos Estrellas had a cattle barn—a two-thousand-square-foot pen covered by a metal awning—but it was small, rundown and sorely inadequate for housing forty-plus head of sick steer.

Of the two original cattle barns, one had fallen to dry rot five years ago. Gabe's father hadn't gotten around to replacing it, mostly due to lack of money. The other cattle barn was on the land dedicated to Cara's mustang sanctuary and used for her horses.

"I was at the Poco Dinero Saloon and Grill the other night," Cole said. "Everyone was talking about the red nose outbreak."

"Your point?" Gabe asked.

"The ranchers are having some big powwow Tuesday night at the community center."

Gabe frowned. "I haven't heard anything."

"Just repeating the talk."

He was tempted to check his phone to see if he'd missed a call or text during their hectic day. Wait. What if the local ranchers didn't want to include him in the meeting because they believed he was responsible for bringing red nose to Mustang Valley? Or, maybe they didn't see him as the owner of Dos Estrellas.

A swig of coffee didn't alleviate the bad taste in his mouth.

"What's the worst that can happen?" Josh asked with far less attitude than his brother. "We need to be prepared."

"The infection spreads," Gabe said blandly. "We lose steer."

"How many?"

"Between the lack of antibiotics and the foul weather, it could be five, ten percent. More if any other cattle become infected."

"Can we recover from that?"

"Possibly. Probably," he amended. "As long as we can inseminate the cows as planned and they don't get sick."

"What if they do?"

Gabe, Reese and Violet all exchanged glances. Red nose was hardest on pregnant cows.

"They'll likely miscarry," Violet said.

"Great." Cole spat out a bitter laugh.

"There's still the mustang sanctuary." Josh said. "If we had the five hundred acres, we could use the cattle barn and extra grazing land for isolating the sick steer."

"Nothing's changed." Gabe should have anticipated this question and was mad that he hadn't. "We'd have to find a place for the horses."

"Why not sell them? We could use the money to buy antibiotics."

"Two hundred horses?"

"Only enough for the cash we need to carry us through."

Gabe shook his head. "Sale proceeds have always gone back into the sanctuary."

"Didn't Cara get money from the fund drive during the Holly Daze Festival?"

"She has a lot of horses to feed."

"Have you asked her?" Josh's demeanor changed with each question, going from civil to insistent to impatient to irritated.

Gabe's own irritation was rising. "I doubt we could sell the horses in time to make a difference. She has a detailed adoption process, matching the horse to the potential owner."

"You didn't answer my question."

"I have not asked her. Nor will I."

"Then, by all means, allow me."

"Stay away from Cara." Gabe was glad she was visiting her mother. He wouldn't have wanted her to witness how little his brothers cared.

"If you lose the ranch," Reese said, "she and your mom lose their home."

Gabe faced her. "You think I don't know that?"

"Josh's suggestion has merit."

"I thought you liked Cara."

Reese jerked as if affronted. "I do. Very much. But, as the trustee of your father's estate, I have to put the ranch first. Losing it will greatly affect your mother and Cara, who might be willing to help by selling some horses."

"No one buys a horse over Christmas."

"You didn't get a pony for a gift when you were a kid?" Cole asked.

"She could advertise them as Christmas presents," Violet added.

"That's not a bad idea," Reese remarked thoughtfully.

Gabe hated the satisfied expressions on his brothers' faces. This shouldn't be a contest, yet it felt like one, and Reese was choosing sides.

He tried telling himself she was being impartial; her job at the bank dictated nothing less. But her agreeing with Josh hit him like an invisible sucker punch to the sternum. He and Reese had kissed. Expressed their growing feelings for each other. Shared secrets and private wishes. Discussed a potential future relationship when the time was right.

And while he understood, the invisible blow still stunned him.

"Isn't it your responsibility to ensure my father's plan is carried out?" he asked her.

"Of course."

"Well, his plan included Cara keeping the mustang sanctuary."

"For as long as she wants it. She may choose differently, in light of the red nose epidemic."

"You can't really think that. Her son died. The sanctuary is all she has. I won't ask her to give it up."

"Like I said," Josh interceded. "I'll do it."

Gabe didn't realize he was standing until the musical Christmas tree started playing "Santa Claus is Coming to Town."

"Gabe, please sit down," Reese said.

He ignored her.

Reese ignored him and addressed his brothers. "There are other solutions than closing the mustang sanctuary or selling horses. We should explore those, too."

Take the higher road, Gabe's father and Reese had both advised. If he stormed out of the room, he would gain nothing and likely lose considerable ground.

"I'm listening."

He sat at the same time the musical Christmas tree stopped playing. Good thing, because he was ready to throw it across the room.

Reese had worked in the banking business for over six years. In that time, she'd seldom panicked. Today was one of those rare occasions. Gabe and his brothers didn't agree on anything and insisted on battling. It was her job to mediate, offer ideas and guide them in the right direction.

Frankly, she didn't know if she was capable of it. And if she failed...

No, not an option.

"The insurance settlement your mother received," Josh said to Gabe. "She could float us a loan."

"Forget it. My father took out that policy so she'd have a nest egg."

"You're right." Josh placed his palms on the table top and breathed deeply. "Because she's going to need the money when we lose the ranch."

Gabe clenched his teeth, then forced himself to breathe evenly. "Funny how every solution you come up with involves my family giving up what Dad left them. What are you willing to give up?"

"Now wait a minute," Cole snapped.

"Don't tell me you're broke. Your grandparents are loaded."

Josh's head snapped up. "We're not asking my grandparents for money."

"But I'm supposed to ask my family."

Reese had reached her limit—for the third time. "Your mother may want to lend you the money."

Gabe gawked at her.

"You should at least ask her."

"Me," he stated flatly.

"You did buy the infected steer," Cole reminded him.

Before Gabe could retaliate, Reese interrupted.

"This is every bit my fault as Gabe's. I authorized the draw on the line of credit."

"But you don't have to bear the consequences," Josh stated.

"My position at the bank could come under examination."

Cole stared at her hard. "When you authorized the draw, is it possible your judgment was affected by your relationship with Gabe?"

She'd wondered when this question would be asked and by whom.

"Gabe and I are friends." Not a lie. "Nothing more." An exaggeration. "We agreed to maintain a strictly professional relationship." The honest truth.

She shot Gabe the briefest of glances and was surprised to see his features harden. Wasn't that what they'd agreed on?

"I've heard a different version around town," Cole said.

Probably at the Poco Dinero Saloon and Grill. Reese swore men were worse gossips than women.

"You have nothing to worry about in that regard," she assured him.

He grunted indifferently.

"I authorized the draw because you three were in agreement and the price for the steer was very good. You could have said no. You could also have done more research before agreeing, possibly learning about the spread of red nose."

Cole nodded and he sat back. "I did agree. And it's a decision I hope I don't regret."

"What about our immediate plans?" Josh asked, his demeanor also less antagonistic.

Reese squared her shoulders. "I suggest we wait a week, until after Christmas. If the steer don't improve, then we sell off the healthy ones, using the money to pay the most pressing bills, buy antibiotics when they become available and supplemental feed for the remaining cattle."

"Should we talk to Raquel and Cara?"

"Let's revisit that next week. It won't make much difference before then, and why ruin the holidays? The steer could improve, after all."

She wished she sounded more convincing.

"There's one more solution we haven't discussed," Cole said tersely. "Selling the ranch."

Gabe slammed the table causing Violet to jump. "That's always your answer. Sell the ranch and get your share of the money so you can leave."

Reese hoped Gabe kept his raging emotions under control. To help, she delivered her next words calmly and rationally. "Selling may be a little premature."

"At the rate we're going," Cole said, "we could lose everything."

"We have weeks, if not months, to spare. And other solutions to try first."

Gabe pushed back from the table, setting off the musical Christmas tree again. He shot it a dirty look before turning that look on Cole. "You agreed to stay in Mustang Valley and work the ranch for a year."

"I did. Before you set out to ruin us by buying sick steer."

"Set out?"

"Why not? For all I know, you could have misled Josh and me on purpose."

"What would that have gotten me?"

"You want us gone."

"No fooling."

The Christmas tree finally stopped playing. Reese stood, picked up the tree and activated the off switch.

She faced the table and planted her hands on her hips. "The purpose of this meeting was to discuss viable options for the immediate future. Not pick fights with each other."

The three men quieted. She allowed herself a small sigh.

"Unless someone has a better idea, then I vote we wait a week and reassess the situation after Christmas. In the meanwhile, we focus all efforts on the sick steer."

"I assume we're done here." Cole pushed to his feet.

"Unless you have any objections."

Avoiding eye contact with each other, the three brothers exited the room. Violet followed, giving Reese a one-shoulder shrug.

She sagged into her chair. The last thirty minutes had been stressful. Rousing herself, she headed for the kitchen, the direction Gabe had taken. She assumed he'd be waiting for her and was surprised to find the kitchen empty.

Reese returned to the dining room, gathered up her briefcase, coat, umbrella and purse, turned on the musical Christmas tree then left out the front door.

Gabe waited for her by her car, his face unreadable. He'd donned his jacket and cowboy hat, which he'd pushed low on his head to ward off the rain and not, she assumed, to look tough.

Something told her he wasn't in the mood for a friendly chat. Nevertheless, she smiled in greeting. "Hi."

He nodded in return.

She stopped at her car, holding the umbrella over them both. Water pooled at their feet. "I know the meeting didn't go exactly as you wanted."

"Exactly?"

His sharp retort put her on the defense. "I was doing my job, Gabe. And from what I could tell, it went reasonably well. The decision to wait a week is a good one."

"I'm not arguing your decision."

She lifted her chin. "Is that what we're doing? Arguing?"

"You know how important the sanctuary is to Cara and how much my mother needs the insurance money."

"And you heard Cole in there. I can't, *we can't*, allow our romantic involvement for each other to affect our judgment or give anyone a reason to think it is."

He visibly bristled. "I couldn't have said it better myself."

She wasn't stupid. Something more was going on with Gabe than residual anger after the meeting. "Why were you waiting for me?"

"I still have no idea what there was between us other than a few kisses."

His remark stung. "It was more than that. Was I wrong?"

"You're the trustee of my father's will."

"For now. But later, when—"

"Not later," he said. "Not ever. I think today proved it."

The wind tugged at her umbrella, and she gripped the handle harder, feeling a little unsteady. "I don't understand."

Gabe shook his head and, for the first time, she noted the hurt in his dark eyes. "I'm not the man for you, Reese. I never was. And I was stupid to think we had a chance."

"Stupid?" Was that what he thought? Her chest hurt, more when she tried to draw a deep breath. "My mistake. I thought you cared about me."

"It's not going to work. You're Theo McGraw's daughter."

"That's not why I sided with your brothers."

"So, you admit it."

"No. I was..." She faltered, struggled. "Let's wait until after Christmas to continue this conversation. You're worried about the sick steer. Once they improve, you'll feel different about us."

"I won't."

"I see." She had her pride and refused to beg.

"I alone am to blame for buying the sick steer," he said.

"Not true. Me, your brothers—"

"It's completely true. And Cole was right about what

he said in the meeting, only he had it backwards. I let my feelings for you affect my judgment."

"I don't agree."

"I was gung ho to buy the steer because I thought I could turn a quick profit."

"There's nothing wrong with that, Gabe. It was a business decision."

"So I could buy out my brothers."

"Which would make them happy. And you, too."

"I also did it because the sooner I got sole owner-ship of the ranch, the sooner you and I could start see-ing each other."

"None of those are bad reasons."

"I could lose everything important to me." His voice changed. Deepened. "Because I wanted you."

"Quit being so hard on yourself." She was losing him. She could feel it, and her heart started breaking.

"Will you be saying the same thing when we're sell-ing what little is left of the ranch?" He shut his eyes. "It was a mistake. All of it."

"Not all of it. There were some incredible moments." She reached for him, but her hand fell short.

"I think you should leave."

Her lower lip trembled. Dammit, she wasn't like prone to tears. She was strong, and had been that way since her mother left. The night of her senior prom, when Gabe had held her, was one of the few times she'd al-lowed herself to cry.

She fumbled for the car door handle.

Gabe didn't stop her. Why would he?

She snapped closed her umbrella, practically drop-ping it as she slid into the car. Before she could close the door, Gabe bent low, one hand resting on the roof.

"I'm sorry," he said.

"Me, too." Despite her best efforts, her voice shook.

He stepped back. She shut the door and drove away.

God, how could she have made such a mess of things? She'd fallen for him. Gabe Dempsey. The most inappropriate man in all of Mustang Valley.

She didn't cry on the ride home. Silent tears streaming down her cheeks didn't count. Neither did quiet sobs. Crying wasn't real unless a person made noise.

That was what she told herself, anyway.

The moment she walked in the house, her father confronted her.

He took one look at her and pulled her into his embrace. "What happened, sweetie?"

Her reply was to make noise. Lots and lots of it as she cried hard enough to soak the front of his shirt.

Chapter 14

"That's the last of it, boss." Violet swiped her palms down her coat, brushing away the bits and pieces of hay clinging to her.

Gabe wondered how long she'd be calling him boss, then supposed it didn't matter. The name had lost its shine, the result of his short and disastrous run in charge of Dos Estrellas.

"What do you think?" he asked.

"We have enough hay for a few more days."

He'd been inquiring about the health of the steer, not the feed supply, but he could see how Violet made the leap. She and Gabe had just finished unloading a truck bed full of hay into the metal feeders, one on each end of the barn. The sick cattle, moving lethargically, vied for available space around the feeders. The fact they had an appetite at all was heartening.

"On the plus side," Violet continued, "the grass is making a comeback."

Good news indeed. The recent rains had worked their magic. Three days since the torrent, three days since his meeting with Reese and his brothers, and new shoots of grass could be seen poking up from the ground, encouraged by the shining sun and sudden warm spell.

Unfortunately, growing grass was the *only* good news. They had run out of antibiotics two days ago, after moving twenty-five of the sickest steer to the undersized cattle barn. Their inspection of the herd this morning had added six more infected steer, bringing the grand total to fifty-three.

Quarantining helped but not enough. Like humans, cattle were contagious for one or two days before displaying any symptoms. By then, the virus had continued its destructive rampage through the herd.

A larger cattle barn might make a difference. Like the one in the mustang sanctuary. Gabe refused to ask Cara. He might still refuse at the end of the week. Yesterday, Josh had remarked about them missing the opportunity to sell mustangs as Christmas gifts. Gabe had walked away in disgust, mostly at himself. He'd been thinking the same thing.

He'd also been thinking Reese was right to support Josh's suggestions. His mother and Cara deserved a say in the decisions and an opportunity to assist if they chose. Excluding them was unfair.

On the other hand, putting undue pressure on them was also unfair.

Reese was on his mind a lot. All day, all night. He regretted blindsiding her after the family meeting. It wasn't nice. Telling himself that a quick and clean breakup was best didn't alleviate his guilt. He felt precisely like the heel he was. He'd made the right decision, spared her from losing her heart to, and subsequently being hurt by, a guy completely wrong for her. It was his execution that stank.

"As least these fellows aren't getting any sicker." Violet patted a steer's brown rump through the railing.

"Yeah." Try as he might, Gabe couldn't muster any enthusiasm.

There were still the cattle in the pastures to consider. More could be coming down with red nose. The last of the line of credit was slated for the antibiotics due to arrive on the twenty-eighth—if the shipment wasn't delayed. Snowstorms back East were finally easing and shipping services resuming.

Hopefully, they could hold out until then. Less than a single tower of hay remained from the additional supply they'd purchased. Then again, if steer started dying, supplementing the feed would no longer be a problem.

Gabe was glad none of the other ranches were affected with red nose, and that he hadn't been run out of town. At the community center last night, the other ranchers had sympathized. It was a small consolation.

"I have something to tell you," Violet said, her manner reserved. "If you don't mind."

"Fire away."

"Whatever happens, I want you to know what a good job you've done."

He almost laughed. "You're in the minority."

"No, really. It can't be easy, and you've stepped up, Gabe. A lot more than your bro—" She winced. "Sorry, but that's my opinion."

He smiled. "Thanks for the support. It means a lot."

"We're going to get through this, boss."

"I hope you're right."

"Rest assured, you're stuck with me till the bitter end."

Smiling for the first time all day, Gabe pushed off the fence. "Come on. Let's get out of here."

A late model pickup traveling the narrow dirt road behind the horse pastures had them pausing. It turned onto the property and headed straight for them. Gabe didn't recognize the vehicle. Then he spotted the occupants. What in the world?

Enrico, the Small Change's livestock manager, pulled up alongside Gabe's truck and cut the engine. He and Theo McGraw emerged, Theo with some difficulty. Planting his feet on the ground, he used a cane to steady himself.

Gabe stepped forward, ready to assist if necessary.

Theo dismissed him. "I'm fine."

"Of course."

"Young lady." He spoke pleasantly to Violet. "Would you be kind enough to give us a minute?"

"Yes, sir." She glanced at Gabe, then backed away. After a brief, uncertain pause, she made for the Small Change truck.

She and Enrico met up at the tailgate where they began conversing.

Gabe studied Theo for a moment. How much did he know about Gabe and Reese, and was this unexpected visit related?

"What can I do for you?"

"I'm thinking, it's what I can do for you. I understand you're fighting a red nose breakout."

Theo hadn't been at the community center last evening, but had obviously heard the news from Reese.

"I am." Gabe was curious. This was no casual visit.

"I can help. I have a supply of antibiotics." Theo hobbled toward the fence, leaning heavily on his cane, his gait unsteady. "You're welcome to them."

Gabe chuckled. "I need a lot."

"I have over two hundred bottles."

Wow. That was more than enough to carry Dos Estrellas through until their shipment arrived.

"We've placed an order," Gabe said. "Should be here on the twenty-eighth. But, if you're offering, I'd like to buy fifty bottles from you."

"Take it all."

"I won't leave you in a lurch." The outbreak could hit the Small Change.

"Fine. But it's there if you need it."

"Thank you." Gabe was grateful. And overwhelmed by Theo's generosity. Removing his cowboy hat, he knocked it against his thigh, needing a moment to compose himself.

"Come by whenever you're ready," Theo said. "No cost. You can replace what you've used when your supply arrives."

Gabe couldn't accept the offer without first knowing the reason for it. "Why are you doing this?"

"Isn't it enough we're neighbors and should look out for each other?"

"You and my father were rivals."

"He would have done no less for me."

Gabe could easily see his father helping Theo in a crisis.

"But that's not the reason I'm offering you my supply of antibiotics." The older man smiled. "It's Reese."

Gabe said nothing, unsure how to explain what had transpired between him and Reese or how much to reveal. Theo should be reading Gabe the riot act, given he'd hurt his daughter, not offering him his precious supply of antibiotics. "About that…"

"You didn't have to keep Reese's secret all these years, but you did."

"Secret?"

"Don't play dumb. I know she had a baby."

Gabe's jaw dropped. He hadn't been this thrown for a loop since kissing Reese in the garage. "She told you?"

"No, though I wish she had." Theo seemed to lose himself in memories. "I gave her a difficult time when she set her sights on Blake Nolan, though I blamed him more than I did her. He was engaged. And older. In college. He took advantage of her naivety."

"When did you find out?" Gabe asked.

Theo leaned against the fence, his left leg trembling slightly. He absently rubbed it with his free hand. "Right before her high school graduation. I'd suspected something was going on for a few weeks."

That would have been about the time of Gabe and Reese's senior prom. Theo was clearly astute. Or, he loved his daughter and paid attention to her.

"She spent a lot of time in her room on the phone," Theo continued. "I became concerned. One afternoon, she thought I wasn't home. I heard her talking to her cousin Megan. They were making plans." He paused. "When she told me she wanted to take a year off before college and stay with Megan, I pretended I didn't know her real reasons. I agreed with her decision to give up the baby and figured she'd tell me when she was ready. She hasn't yet." His voice grew husky.

"She loves you, sir," Gabe said. "She didn't want to disappoint you."

Theo turned misty eyes on Gabe. "She couldn't if she tried."

"Maybe you should tell her and not me."

"Maybe I should." The older man studied Gabe. "You're pretty smart. Like your dad."

"I consider that a compliment."

"I owe you for protecting Reese."

"You don't owe me a thing, Theo." Gabe had never called his neighbor by anything other than Mr. McGraw. Using his first name felt right under the circumstances. "Certainly not your supply of antibiotics. It was my honor to help Reese. I…I care about her."

"The feeling's mutual, I assure you."

"Did she say anything?"

"No. But I know my daughter. She's quite smitten with you."

"She is?" The news pleased Gabe, though it shouldn't. He'd made it clear they had no future.

"Treat her well, or you'll have me to deal with."

"Actually, Theo, we're not involved."

"A situation you can easily remedy."

"Things aren't that simple."

"No?" His mouth curved in an amused smile.

Admitting one's shortcomings was never easy. "I don't have anything to offer her," Gabe said. "My family's on the brink of losing the ranch. Buried in debt. Fighting a red nose epidemic."

"You love her, don't you?"

Did he? Was there ever a question? "Yes."

"Then it is simple."

"I can't go to her until I have more to offer."

Theo scratched his bristled jaw. "You'll pull through this, son, and when you do, I expect you to make my daughter happy."

It was a pipe dream. "I imagine that's going to take some time."

"Then I suppose you should get after it." He started for his truck. "I'll see you shortly. When you pick up the antibiotics."

"Thank you again."

The older man kept walking. "Reese usually gets home from work about five-thirty."

Enrico appeared from behind the truck to open the passenger door. Theo waved him off.

Violet hurried to join Gabe. "Well?"

"I'll fill you in later."

She accepted his answer without comment.

He'd go to the Small Change today. Whether he arrived before Reese got home or afterward would depend on how the conversation with his family went.

Because of Theo's generosity, they had a chance. A slim one, but a chance. The rest was up to them.

Gabe and Violet arrived at the horse stables and he noticed two things—an unfamiliar truck and livestock trailer departing the ranch and Cole in the round pen, working a horse on a lunge line. Not just any horse, one of Cara's mustangs.

Gabe looked at Violet. That made no sense. His younger brother hadn't shown the slightest interest in the mustangs or the sanctuary, other than reclaiming the land for the cattle operation.

They strode over to the round pen. Josh was also watching his brother and turned at their approach.

"Afternoon." He tugged on the brim of his hat.

"What's going on?" Gabe asked.

Violet squeezed past the two men and rested her forearms on the railing.

Josh hitched a thumb at his brother. "Cole's working with one of Cara's more promising horses."

Gabe had always conceded his younger brother had a way with horses, and he was showing it now. Or showing off. The horse, a young, green broke gelding with a stubborn streak and flashy markings, had been testing Cara's patience for months. Yet, he responded to Cole's cues to walk, trot and lope on command like a docile lesson mount.

"Since when is he interested in training mustangs?" Gabe said.

Josh didn't take his eyes off Cole. "He's going to need a new saddle horse."

"What? He has four horses."

"Not any more. He sold them."

The unfamiliar truck and trailer Gabe had seen leaving. "Why?"

"He has his reasons."

None that made any sense to Gabe. "What's going on here?"

Cole tugged on the lunge line and commanded the horse to walk, then stand. The horse obediently halted, snorting and shaking his handsome head from side to side. Cole unhooked the lunge line from the halter. He gave the horse a friendly scratching between the ears before shooing him away.

"Get along, boy."

The horse trotted a few feet, stopped at the railing and hung his head over the side, no longer interested in the humans.

Gabe met Cole at the round pen gate. "Why did you sell your roping horses?"

He expected attitude from Cole. He didn't get it.

"I don't need them."

"You're going to quit rodeoing?"

"For now." Cole shut the gate, leaving the young mustang on his own.

Gabe was flabbergasted. "You're not making any sense." He stepped in front of Cole, blocking his path.

"I was going to tell you later." Cole shrugged.

"Tell me now."

Cole removed a small folded piece of paper from his coat pocket. He gave it to Gabe.

"What's this?"

"A check. I figured we could use the money for another couple truckloads of hay and inseminating the cows. Don't want to miss breeding season altogether."

Gabe opened the check. Seeing the amount, he swallowed. "You had them make it out to the ranch."

"Easier to deposit."

He pushed the check back at Cole. "We don't need this."

"We do, brother."

Brother? He'd never called Gabe that before.

"I don't understand."

Cole leaned his back against the round pen railing. Josh and Violet remained nearby, waiting expectantly.

"I'm a man of my word," Cole said. "When I make a commitment, I commit. Fully. I told you I'd give the ranch a year."

"Right." Gabe didn't believe him.

"If we lose Dos Estrellas because of the sick steer or a shortage of feed, I won't have given you a full year."

"If we lose the ranch, you get your share of the money and an excuse to leave. Without having to sell your horses." Gabe hadn't known until he saw the check just how much championship roping horses were worth.

"Who says I want to leave?" Cole's attention on Gabe didn't waver.

"It's all you've talked about."

"Josh needs a place to bring his kids next month."

All right. Gabe could buy that reason a little more. The two brothers were thick as thieves. Still....

"Why not give Josh the money?"

"He wouldn't take it," Cole answered offhandedly.

That was likely true. Josh was a proud man. A quality he probably inherited from their father. Like Gabe. When all was said and done, hadn't his battle with his brothers for the ranch really been a matter of pride?

"The only way I can make sure my niece and nephew have a home," Cole continued, "is to help pull this ranch out of the hole we've dug."

"You didn't dig the hole."

"I did." For the first time, Cole spoke without a giant chip on his shoulder. "I agreed to buy the steer. I did it for one reason. I wanted gone from this place as fast as I could get away. I made a bad decision that affected everyone in this family."

Gabe had recently said almost the same thing to Reese about himself. He, too, had let personal feelings affect his judgment.

"Still not your fault." He hoped no one noticed the slight crack in his voice. It had been an emotional day.

"You're splitting hairs." Cole put a hand on Gabe's shoulder. His grip was almost affectionate. "Buy the hay and get the cows bred. Let's make it through the holidays and the next month or two."

Gabe fingered the check. He could refuse. Tear it up and let the breeze carry the pieces away. Or he could take the check and put it to good use.

Cole had sold his most precious possessions to help the ranch *and* the family, which included Gabe's mother and Cara. His actions showed he was willing to put his resentment aside for the good of all. Gabe could do no less.

He stuffed the check into his jacket pocket—and felt a weight lift from him.

Theo and Cole, the two people Gabe least expected, had offered the greatest help. Dos Estrellas wasn't out of the woods yet, but a path lay ahead. Cole smiled. Josh was smiling, too, as was Violet. But she had tears in her eyes.

"You going to stand there like a lump on log?" Cole asked, "Or go inside and make a call to the hay company?"

"I have someone to see first." Gabe hadn't realized he'd made a decision until the words were out.

"Let me guess." Cole grinned. "Reese."

He considered telling his brothers about the antibiotics, then decided it could wait. He had something more pressing to do first.

"I'll see you at dinner." His glance took in Cole and Josh. His brothers. His family. There was a nice ring to it.

On impulse, he shook Cole's hand and then Josh's. They responded enthusiastically.

"Take your time," Josh said as Gabe hurried to his truck. "Don't rush home on our account."

He thought that was pretty good advice.

When he reached the Small Change ten minutes later, he found Theo just leaving. As before, Enrico drove the ranch truck. They stopped at the entrance to the driveway, each of them rolling down their window.

Theo winked at Gabe from his place in the passenger seat. "The antibiotics are in the main cattle barn supply room. Reese can show you. She's there now. I told her you were coming."

"I thought she didn't get home from work until five thirty."

"Appears she's anxious to see you."

Gabe's heart nearly exploded. She was waiting for him. Wanted to see him. Perhaps she regretted the other day and would give him another chance.

Please, he thought, one more small miracle.

"What are you waiting for?" Theo demanded, pretending impatience. "Get a move on."

The last thing Gabe heard as he rolled up his window was the older man's belly laugh.

Gabe drove straight to the main cattle barn, a giant structure about a half mile from the two-story ranch house. The supply room was at the south end. He took the corner too fast, causing the truck's brakes to squeal and the tires to cut wide grooves in the still-damp ground.

Reese burst from the supply room door and came to a sudden stop.

She wore a long, slim-fitting trench coat over something short. A skirt, maybe, or a dress. Gabe didn't care. All that mattered was he got a nice view of her legs.

Shapely, smooth and bare. Was she nuts? It was cold outside. She must have been in a hurry to see him. No less of a hurry than he was in to see her.

He wrenched open his door and jumped out of the truck. She didn't move. Had Theo exaggerated in order to orchestrate a reconciliation? Rather than run to her, as was his first inclination, he proceeded slowly.

"I saw your dad as he was leaving. He said you'd show me where the antibiotics are stored."

Reese gestured at the supply room. "Sure."

He closed the distance between them and would have taken her hand if she didn't abruptly turn and lead him through the door.

The supply room was large, but crowded. Half of the available space was taken up by shelving units, the other half by cabinets, crates and trunks of varying sizes. Gabe spotted an old refrigerator in the corner that probably contained the antibiotics. This time, he led the way, down the narrow aisle and between the racks. Reese followed closely.

Rather than grab bottles, Gabe spun, coming face-to-face with her. His plan all along.

"Cole sold his roping horses."

"He did?"

"Now we can buy more hay and inseminate the cows."

"Wow. I'm surprised."

"That makes two of us." Gabe reminded himself to breathe. She was so close. Within touching distance. "We're going to survive the red nose outbreak and get the ranch out of debt."

"I believe you."

She wasn't making this easy for him. If he wanted

her, he should make the effort. Maybe she knew that and was waiting.

Gabe had no intention of disappointing her. "I'm sorry, Reese. I was wrong."

"About what?"

She truly wasn't going to make this easy.

"Where to start?"

"Start with what's most important." Her warm, tender gaze melted the last of his doubts.

"I've been an idiot."

"It's not too late to change."

"You're what's most important. I shouldn't have let you go. What we have, what we could have, is incredibly special. The hell with you being the trustee or me not inheriting the entire ranch. None of that matters more than us."

She tilted her head appealingly. "Go on."

He drew her close. "I'd like to give us a try."

"There's still my job."

"I don't suppose you could quit." He squeezed her shoulders, wanting to kiss her, but waiting.

"No. But I could speak to Walt. I don't think this situation has come up at the bank before, but there has to be a workable compromise. If you and your brothers are in agreement, Walt could take over for me."

"If we're in agreement, you could stay on."

"Would Josh and Cole?" Hope blazed in her eyes.

"They like you."

"What about you?"

He hauled her against him, reveling in the feel of her soft, lush curves beneath her coat. Lowering his head, he brought his mouth to hers. "You know how I feel."

"Say it, Gabe."

"I fell in love with you that day in the mountains when I saw you trying to rescue your father's horse. I figured any woman crazy enough to think she could lift a thousand-pound horse by herself was crazy enough to love me back."

"You were right," she said and raised her lips to his.

Gabe lost himself in the wonder of Reese's kiss.

She was the one he'd been waiting for, the one worth fighting for, the one he could, and would, spend the rest of his life with. After today, and all the things he'd seen, nothing was impossible.

Epilogue

Christmas Day

Gabe couldn't remember seeing this many people gathered around the dining room table for Christmas dinner. The tradition of limiting the holiday meal to immediate family and friends was over. There were so many people they had had to set up an extra table.

In addition to Gabe's brothers, his mother and his *tio* Lorenzo, Cara was there with her mother and stepfather. Violet had also been invited, as well as the McGraws. *All* of the McGraws. Reese, naturally, her father and Aunt Louise, along with Reese's cousin Megan, her husband and—this was really incredible—Celia.

During one of their many moments alone over the past few days, Reese had told Gabe that, rather than wait until spring break, Celia had asked to come for Christmas. Reese had mustered up her courage and told her father about Celia, only to learn he'd known all along and couldn't wait to meet his granddaughter.

After that, the pieces had fallen into place. Celia's parents were able to wrangle three airline tickets, and they'd arrived yesterday for a week-long visit. Gabe had been honored and touched to be included in the family reunion. It was a moment he'd remember all his life.

As was this special holiday. He and his brothers still had a long way to go in repairing their relationship. Years of animosity didn't disappear overnight. And the ranch remained at financial risk, though no more steer had come down with red nose. There were bumps in the road ahead for Gabe and Reese, as well, one being her father's illness. Yet with all that, the future looked brighter than it had for a long, long time. Since before his father had become ill.

"Mommy," Celia asked Megan in a bright voice, "can I go riding tomorrow? Reese invited me."

"You're welcome to come with us," Reese added.

By us, she meant her and Gabe. He'd thought the idea was a good one when she'd mentioned it earlier.

"None of us have ridden much," Megan said, a bit dubiously.

"We have plenty of horses for beginners," Gabe said. "We promise to take it slow."

"All right." Megan smiled.

"Yippee." Celia nearly spilled her milk in her excitement. "Can Grandpa come, too?" She turned to Theo.

"I'll watch." He stroked her hair, his face that of a man ten years younger. Meeting his granddaughter was responsible.

Beneath the table, Gabe felt Reese's hand clasp his.

He didn't have to look at her to know she was deeply moved.

He squeezed her fingers in return.

"Here's to our many blessings." His mother raised her glass in a toast, which everyone readily joined in. "And to a happy, prosperous New Year."

When Gabe clinked glasses with Reese's, their eyes met. He couldn't say it at the table, but he tried to convey what was in his heart.

She must have understood, for she mouthed, "I love you."

The two of them had a chance at a future together, one of their own making. For Gabe, it included him and Reese and their brand-new combined family. The possibilities were endless.

Had his father known all along this would happen? Gabe liked to think so, and that he approved.

As if in answer, the musical Christmas tree began to play.

* * * * *

Marin Thomas grew up in the Midwest, then attended college at the U of A in Tucson, Arizona, where she earned a BA in radio-TV and played basketball for the Lady Wildcats. Following graduation, she married her college sweetheart in the historic Little Chapel of the West in Las Vegas, Nevada. Recent empty nesters, Marin and her husband now live in Texas, where cattle is king, cowboys are plentiful and pickups rule the road. Visit her on the web at marinthomas.com.

Books by Marin Thomas

Harlequin Western Romance

The Cowboys of Stampede, Texas

The Cowboy's Accidental Baby
Twins for the Texas Rancher

Cowboys of the Rio Grande

A Cowboy's Redemption
The Surgeon's Christmas Baby
A Cowboy's Claim

The Cash Brothers

The Cowboy Next Door
Twins Under the Christmas Tree
Her Secret Cowboy
The Cowboy's Destiny
True Blue Cowboy
A Cowboy of Her Own

Visit the Author Profile page at Harlequin.com for more titles.

To my editor Johanna Raisanen—
I don't know what I would do without you! I
can't thank you enough for the time and care you
put into each of my books. I'm probably one of
the few authors who look forward to her editor's
revision letter, but I'm always eager to see what
ideas and suggestions you have for my stories.
Your input and expertise are invaluable,
and I'm looking forward to writing many
more happy-ever-after tales with you!

Chapter 1

Conway Twitty Cash had only one rule when it came to women—never date one with kids. Period. No exceptions. Not even if the woman sent text photos of her hooters.

Friday afternoon at the Midway Arizona Cowboy Rodeo Days, Conway had been the recipient of a sexy text from a buckle bunny he'd met earlier in the day. Once his eyes had quit bugging out at Bridget's voluptuous tatas, he'd noticed a child's Batman cape draped over a chair in the background of the photo. Alarmed, he'd asked his rodeo competitors about Bridget and had learned she was a single mom. When they'd first met, he'd asked if she'd had kids, and she'd said no.

Too upset to focus on his ride, the bronc had tossed him on his head as soon as he cleared the chute. Afterward, Conway had made a beeline for the parking lot—he hadn't been about to wait for Bridget to catch up.

Miffed, ticked off and a whole lotta mad, he pulled into the Border Town Bar & Grill in Yuma—the employer of his good friend and pseudo-therapist Isadora Lopez. Two years ago when he'd first met Isi, he'd been drawn to her dark brown eyes and girl-next-door prettiness. He'd turned on the charm and she'd rewarded his flirting with fleeting touches, accidental bumps and sultry looks. Then he'd asked her to dance during her break and when their bodies had come in contact, a zap of electricity had shot through him. He'd been sure the night would end in Isi's bed, until she'd mentioned that she was a single mother of twin boys.

He'd told Isi that he had nothing against kids, but had no intention of ever being a father. From that day on, they'd settled into a comfortable friendship where Isi listened to his dating adventures and offered advice about how to find the perfect woman—one who didn't want children.

The bar was packed on this late-September afternoon. The crowd sitting in front of the big-screen TV watched a college football game between state rivals the University of Arizona and Arizona State University. Conway slid onto a stool and waved to the barkeep. Red was a mountain of a man—six feet seven inches—and bald with a crimson beard that ended in the middle of his chest.

After handing a pitcher of margaritas to a waitress named Sasha, Red brought Conway a bottle of his favorite beer. "You rodeo today?"

"Got bucked off."

"Too bad."

"Where's Isi?" Conway asked.

"In class." Red checked his watch. "She should be

here any minute." Isi was working toward a two-year business degree from the local community college.

Red went to fill a drink order, and Conway picked at the paper label on his beer bottle and silently cursed Bridget. Why was it so difficult to find a woman who didn't want children? After he'd discovered he came from a long line of deadbeat dads, he'd decided he didn't want to follow in their footsteps, but unlike his father, grandfather and great-grandfather Conway wasn't opposed to marriage. He really did want a committed relationship.

He wasn't a braggart, but the face he saw in the mirror each morning had garnered his fair share of female attention. At twenty-eight he'd thought for sure he'd have found "the one" by now, but every time he began thinking happy ever after, "the one" decided she'd like to have children after all.

Maybe he should take a break from his search. He'd been handed the responsibility of managing the family pecan farm, so he had plenty of work to keep his mind off his miserable love life. He lifted the beer bottle to his mouth and knocked his front tooth against the rim when a hand slapped his back. Startled, he spun and came face-to-face with Bridget's tatas.

How the hell had she known where to find him?

She planted her fists on her hips and glared. "Why'd you leave the rodeo after your ride? I thought we were going out on a date."

A date? He'd ended their conversation with "goodbye," not "see you later."

"Howdy, Conway." Sasha winked as she passed him with an empty drink tray.

"Is she special to you?" Bridget dipped her head toward Sasha.

"No."

"Hey, Conway." Isi strolled into the bar, backpack slung over her shoulder.

"What about her?" Bridget asked.

Isi stopped next to the bar and glanced between Conway and Bridget. "What about me what?"

Bridget glared. "Are you and Conway dating?"

"Heck, no."

Conway wasn't sure if he was offended or amused by Isi's fervent denial. It was true they were just friends, but she didn't have to act as if he was the last man on earth she'd consider going out with.

"You're not his type." Bridget gave Isi the once-over.

"Don't insult her," Conway said. Isi might not have been blessed with Bridget's bust size, but her long silky hair and exotic eyes were sexy as heck.

Squinting, Bridget asked, "Are you sure there's nothing going on between you two?"

"Positive." Isi and Conway spoke simultaneously.

"And Conway isn't dating Sasha, because Sasha's a lesbian." Isi's eyes sparkled with mischief.

"Then why'd you stand me up at the rodeo?" Bridget asked.

"I didn't stand you up," Conway said.

Bridget planted her hands on her hips. "You gave me your phone number."

"He gives all the ladies his number," Isi said.

Conway sent his "friend" an I-don't-need-your-help glare.

"You acted like you wanted to see me again." Bridget stuck out her lower lip in a pout.

"I don't date women with children," he said. "Never. Ever. No exceptions."

"Who told you I had a kid?"

"I saw the Batman costume in the picture you texted me."

"That belongs to my nephew."

Isi snickered.

"Get lost," Bridget said.

Isi inched behind Conway. He didn't blame her for being cautious. Bridget was getting really worked up. "I asked a couple of cowboys about you and they said you had a son."

"I swear he won't get in our way," Bridget said. "I'll make sure he's not there when you visit."

"Sorry, I don't date women with children or women who want children."

"Then why did you lead me on?"

"Hey, I never asked you out on a date. I never promised to call you and I never—"

Bridget cocked her arm and swung. Having grown up defending his name from bullies, Conway's reflexes were sharp. He ducked in the nick of time and Bridget's fist connected with Isi's nose. The blow sent her reeling. Conway dove off the stool and caught her before she crumpled to the floor.

"What the hell is going on!" Red's booming voice bellowed across the bar.

Bridget took one look at the giant man and sprinted for the door.

"I need a towel and ice," Conway said.

"Here." Sasha shoved paper napkins into his hand and he pressed them against Isi's bleeding nose then led her to a chair. "God, Isi, I'm sorry." He swallowed a curse as the skin beneath both her eyes began to bruise.

Red offered a towel packed with ice, and Conway placed it against her nose.

"I can't feel my face," she moaned.

"Hang on, honey." He wiped away the blood then spoke to Red. "I'm taking her to the emergency room." Damn Bridget. Already Isi's petite nose had swollen to the size of a kosher pickle.

He helped Isi to her feet and Sasha handed him Isi's backpack. Isi swayed after taking a step toward the door, so he tucked her against his side and practically carried her out of the bar.

They drove in silence to the hospital. He figured she was hurting pretty bad if she couldn't give him hell about Bridget. He parked in the visitor lot in front of the emergency entrance.

"I don't need to see a doctor. I'll be fine," she said.

"Let the doctor make that call." When he reached for the door handle, she snagged his shirtsleeve.

"I don't have health insurance."

He wasn't surprised. Isi worked part-time at the bar and by law Red didn't have to offer her benefits. "You got punched in the face because of me. I'll take care of the bill." It was the least he could do.

Once inside, Isi filled out the paperwork then waited almost an hour before a nurse took her to get an X-ray. Conway spoke to a billing representative and made arrangements to pay for Isi's E.R. visit. By the time Isi returned to the waiting room, the bruising beneath her eyes had worsened.

"A clean fracture," the nurse announced. She handed

Conway a bottle of pain pills. "No driving while she's taking this prescription."

Conway shoved the container into his jean pocket, thanked the nurse and escorted Isi to his truck. "Do you have a concussion?"

"No."

"Want to take a pain pill right now? I'll go back inside and buy you a bottle of water from the vending machine."

"No, thanks. I'll take a pill after I drive myself home."

"You're not driving anywhere tonight."

"I can't leave my car at Red's."

Conway didn't want to pick a fight with Isi when she was hurting. He drove her to the bar and parked next to her 1996 white Toyota Camry. "I'll follow you to your place."

"That's not necessary."

"Maybe, but I'll feel better knowing you got home safe."

She grabbed her backpack then hopped out and slammed the truck door. Conway drove behind her as she pulled out of the lot. He knew she lived in a trailer park nearby but had forgotten which one.

Isi headed southwest a mile then entered the Desert Valley Mobile Home Park. The neighborhood was well kept—mostly single wides. She pulled beneath a carport in front of a white trailer with faded turquoise trim. Instead of the traditional rock and cactus landscape, the yard consisted of dead grass and dirt. He parked behind Isi and followed her to the door.

"Thank you for taking care of the hospital bill," she said.

"I'll pay for any follow-up doctor visits."

"As long as your girlfriends stay away from the bar, I won't need to see any more doctors."

"I'm really sorry. I didn't think Bridget would follow me after I left the rodeo."

"You might have to compromise if you want to find the perfect woman, Conway."

He didn't want to discuss his love life. "Do you have a friend who will stay with you tonight?"

"I'll be fine."

When Isi opened the door, he heard a female talking. "Who's that?"

"The sitter. She's always on her cell phone."

Conway followed Isi inside.

"Oh, my God, what happened?" The teen's eyes widened in horror.

"I'm fine, Nicole." Isi sent Conway a silent message. "I ran into the kitchen door at the bar."

So she didn't want the sitter to know the truth—fine by him, because the truth made him look like an idiot.

"Conway, this is Nicole. She watches the boys when I'm at the bar. Nicole, this is Conway. He's a friend."

"Nice to meet you," Nicole said.

While Isi asked the sitter how the boys had behaved, Conway studied the furnishings. *Sparse* was the first word that came to mind. The furniture appeared secondhand—TV, love seat, chair and coffee table. Kids' artwork decorated the walls and colorful plastic bins filled with toys had been stacked in the living room corner.

"What time did the boys go to bed?" Isi asked.

"Fifteen minutes ago."

"I'm sorry to have to cut the night short." Isi faced Conway. "Where are those pain pills?"

He handed her the bottle and she went into the kitchen

and got a drink of water. "I won't be working at the bar this weekend, so I'll see you on Monday, Nicole." Isi disappeared down the hallway then a moment later he heard a door open and close.

"Do you need a ride home, Nicole?" Conway asked.

"No, I live here in the trailer park with my aunt." She walked to the door. "I left a note on the kitchen table for Isi. Will you make sure she reads it in the morning?"

"Sure."

After Nicole left, Conway stood in living room uncertain what to do. Was it okay to leave Isi and her kids alone after she'd taken a pain pill? What if a burglar tried to break into the trailer or the water heater caught on fire? Isi was in no shape to handle a crisis.

The least he could do after she'd taken a blow meant for him was stay the night and make sure she and her sons remained safe. As soon as she woke in the morning, he'd hightail it back to the farm.

A sixth sense told Conway he was being watched. He opened his eyes beneath the cowboy hat covering his face. Two pairs of miniature athletic shoes stood side by side next to the sofa. He played possum—not an easy task when his legs were numb from dangling over the end of the love seat all night.

"Is he dead?"

The question went unanswered.

"I bet he's dead." The same voice spoke again.

"Poke him and see." A second voice, slightly higher in pitch than the first, whispered.

Conway grinned, glad the hat hid his face.

"Get Mom."

"She's sleeping."

The sound of a food wrapper crinkling reached Conway's ears.

"Shh."

"I'm hungry." Crunching followed the statement.

Conway shifted on the couch and groaned.

"He's alive."

"Maybe he's sick."

"Look under his hat."

"You look."

"Chicken."

"Am not."

Conway's chest shook with laughter as he waited for his assailants' next move. Small fingers lifted the brim of his hat and Cheerio breath puffed against in his face.

On the count of three. *One...two...three.* Conway opened his eyes and his gaze clashed with the boys'. The kids shrieked and jumped back, bumping into each other. The Cheerio box sailed through the air, the contents spilling onto Conway's chest. He studied the mess then turned his attention to the daring duo.

"Sorry, mister." The brothers scooped oat rings off of Conway's shirt and stuffed them back into the box. Conway swung his legs to the floor and sat up. The twins were identical. They wore their hair cut in a traditional little-boy style with a side part and both had their mother's almond-shaped brown eyes.

He pointed to the kid holding the cereal box. "What's your name?"

"Javier."

Conway moved his finger to the other boy.

"I'm Miguel. Who are you?"

So Miguel was the outgoing one and Javier the shy one. "Conway Twitty Cash."

"That's a long name," Miguel said.

"You can call me Conway." It wasn't enough that his mother had slept with every Tom, Dick and Harry across southern Arizona, but she'd also possessed a strange sense of humor in naming all six of her sons after country-music legends. "How old are you guys?"

"Four." They answered in unison.

"Are you a real cowboy?" Miguel asked.

"That depends. You asking if I work on a ranch?"

Miguel nodded.

"I'm not that kind of cowboy."

Javier made eye contact with his brother and Conway swore the boys conversed telepathically. "What kind of cowboy are you?" Miguel asked.

"Part-time rodeo cowboy. When I'm not bustin' broncs, I work on a farm."

The boys stared with blank expressions.

"You know what pecans are, don't you?"

They shook their heads.

"Nuts that grow on trees. People eat the nuts or use them in pies."

Javier whispered in his brother's ear then Miguel asked, "How come you're in our house?"

Not sure what answer Isi would want him to give her sons, he asked a question of his own. "Have you ever seen a man in your house after you woke up in the morning?"

They shook their heads again.

For some stupid reason that pleased Conway.

Javier whispered in his brother's ear.

"You can ask me questions yourself, Javier," Conway said.

"I mostly talk." Miguel's chest puffed up. "Why are you sleeping on our couch?"

"Your mom wasn't feeling well, so I stayed the night in case something bad happened."

"Is Mom dying?" Miguel paused, then said, "Like what?"

"No, your mom isn't dying. For Pete's sake!" Conway had trouble following the conversation—he'd never talked with four-year-olds before. "Like what, what?"

"What kind of bad things?" Miguel asked.

"Well, there could have been a fire in the middle of the night."

Javier ran from the room then returned with a small fire extinguisher.

"We know how to put out a fire," Miguel said.

He doubted the boys had the strength to pull the pin on the extinguisher, but he was impressed that they knew what the canister was used for. "Or a bad guy could've broken into the trailer."

Javier set down the extinguisher then opened the closet door in the hallway and removed a baseball bat, which he dragged across the carpet. Conway got the impression the kid was trying to tell him that they didn't need his help protecting their mother.

"Can you lift that?" he asked.

Javier raised the bat and Conway intercepted the barrel before it hit Miguel in the back of the head. "Whoa, slugger." He confiscated the weapon and laid it on the couch.

"Javi...Mig... Where are you guys?" Isi's sluggish voice rang out a moment before she appeared in the hallway. Conway sucked in a quiet breath. The bruising beneath her eyes had deepened to dark purple.

"Mom!" Miguel dashed across the room, Javier following him. "What happened?" Both boys hugged Isi's legs.

"I had an accident at work last night. I ran into a door and broke my nose."

"Does it hurt?" Miguel asked.

"Yes. Did you have breakfast?" Isi dropped to one knee and hugged her sons. She whispered in Miguel's ear then he went into the kitchen, climbed onto the counter and retrieved two cereal bowls from the cupboard. Javier remained by Isi's side—he was definitely the insecure twin.

"Mom." Miguel set the bowls on the table.

"What?"

"Conway Twitty Cash slept on our couch."

"You can call me Conway."

"*Mr.* Conway," Isi said.

"I told them I stayed last night, because you weren't feeling well and I needed to be here in case of an emergency."

"We don't need his help, do we, Javi?" Miguel said.

Javier wouldn't look at Conway.

"It was nice of Mr. Conway to stay, but I'm fine now." Isi sent him a time-to-leave look.

Conway stood up and the Cheerios that had gotten caught in the wrinkles of his shirt spilled to the floor. He stepped over the Os to avoid smashing them into the carpet. "Your sitter left this for you last night." He handed her the piece of paper Miguel had pushed aside on the table. "She wanted you to read it first thing in the morning."

While Isi read the note, Conway said, "I'd really like

to make it up to you for what happened last night. Is there anything I can—"

Isi glanced up from the note a stunned expression on her face.

"What's wrong?" he asked.

"Nicole quit."

"What?"

"She's moving to Tucson to live with her father."

"When?" Conway asked.

"Today." Isi sighed. "If I don't find a sitter by Monday, I'll have to skip class and I have an exam that day."

"Maybe your mother could help out with the boys."

She frowned. "My mother's dead."

That's right. She'd told him her mother had passed away right before she'd immigrated to the U.S. He inched closer to the door. "Maybe a relative—"

"Conway—"

Hand on the doorknob he froze. "What?"

"I told you a long time ago that I don't have any family. It's just me and the boys."

Really? He couldn't recall Isi talking about her family. He was always wrapped up in his dating dilemmas and the information had probably gone in one ear and out the other. He swallowed hard. That Isi was all alone in the world didn't seem right. He might have had a mother who cared more about chasing after men, and a father who hadn't wanted the responsibility of raising him, but he'd had siblings and grandparents who cared about him.

"You offered to help," she said. "Would you watch the boys until I find a replacement sitter?"

Babysit? *Him?* "I don't think that's a good idea."

"It would be for two or three days at the most."

"I don't know anything about kids."

She ignored his protests. "I'd need you to drop them off at preschool and bring them back here afterward."

"I'm sure—" he winked at the boys "—they'd rather have anyone but me watch them."

"Never mind." Her shoulders sagged.

Did she have to act so dejected?

"I'll take the boys to school with me and hope the professors allow them into the classroom."

"I don't want to go to your school, Mom," Miguel said.

It's because of me that Isi's nose is broken.

Oh, hell. How hard could it be to watch a couple of four-year-olds? For two years Isi had listened to him bellyache about women. He couldn't turn his back on her when she needed him most.

"Okay, I'll watch the boys," he said.

She flashed him a bright smile. "You'll need to be here by noon on Monday."

"See you then." Right now, Conway couldn't escape fast enough.

Chapter 2

"I don't want a babysitter."

Isi ignored Javier, who sat under the kitchen table playing with his toy cars, and focused on memorizing the Visual Basic code for her exam later in the day.

"How come Conway Twitty Cash has to watch us?" Miguel asked.

Ever since her son had learned Conway's full name, he insisted on using it. For the tenth time, she explained, "Nicole moved to Tucson to live with her father and Mr. Conway is helping us out until I find a new sitter."

Her child-care search had stalled over the weekend. The manager at the preschool had offered Isi the names of three women but none of them had been available to watch the boys at night while she worked at the bar. She worried she'd have to resort to the want ads in the newspaper.

"Mr. Conway's not a girl," Javier said.

"He certainly is not." Conway was all male. Not only did he have a movie-star face, but the way he filled out a pair of jeans turned female heads when he strolled into the bar. Add a boyish grin to his cowboy appeal and every woman on this side of the border was in love with the man.

Too bad he wasn't interested in being a father, because she still experienced an occasional romantic dream about Conway. The day he'd come into the bar and hit on her had been the stuff of fairy tales. Then when he'd learned she was a single mother, he'd cooled toward her. She'd wanted to stay mad at him forever, but he'd continued to visit the bar and joke around with her and in a matter of weeks they'd settled into a cozy friendship. He'd been and always would be her favorite cowboy.

Javier drove a Lego car over the top of her shoe. "Only girls babysit."

"Boys can be sitters, too," she said.

"Conway Twitty Cash, Conway Twitty Cash, Conway Twitty Cash, Con—"

"Enough, Miguel!" Isi shut the textbook. "Names are special and you shouldn't make fun of someone's name."

"Our names are special," Javier said.

She'd named her sons after their twin uncles Javier and Miguel whom they'd never met and never would. Surprisingly, the boys favored their namesakes. Isi's brother Javier had been shy and her brother Miguel had been outgoing—neither had lived long enough to meet their nephews. Isi wished there was a man in her life to help raise the twins, but she'd rather go it alone as a single mom than trust the well-being of her sons to a here-one-day-gone-the-next boyfriend or their biological father, who refused to claim them.

One of the reasons her friendship with Conway had grown was because she enjoyed listening to him talk about his family. When she heard stories about him and his brothers' antics she felt like one of his siblings.

"He's too big for our house," Javier said.

Isi poked her head beneath the table, wincing at the stab of pain in her nose. "Mr. Conway seems tall because we're all short."

"Do we have to do what Conway Twitty Cash says?" Miguel asked.

"Yes." Isi opened the refrigerator door. "You two wash up while I make lunch." Miguel raced to the bathroom but Javier remained beneath the table. Isi peered at him. "What's the matter?"

"I don't want you to go to school."

"I have an important test this afternoon," she said.

"Are you gonna go to school forever?"

"I hope not." This was her final semester and as long as she passed all her classes, she'd earn an associate degree in business before Christmas. She pulled on her son's shirt until he crawled into the open then she sat him on her lap. "Tell me what's really bothering you, *mi corazón?*" Javier laid his head against her chest. "Mr. Conway's a very nice man," she said. "Did you know he has five brothers and a sister?"

Javier shook his head.

"Maybe when he gets here, you can ask him what it's like to have to share toys with all those brothers." She checked the wall clock. Conway would arrive shortly to drive the boys to preschool—three hours during which she wouldn't have to worry about her sons. It was what went on after Conway picked them up from school that concerned her.

"Everything's going to be okay." She set Javier on his feet and gave him a gentle push in the direction of the bathroom. "Wash your hands."

A half hour later, the boys had eaten their peanut butter and jelly sandwiches and had fetched their backpacks from the bedroom when the doorbell rang.

"It's Conway Twitty Cash!" Miguel raced to the door.

"Use the peephole," Isi said.

Miguel climbed onto the chair next to the door and peered through the spy hole. "It's him." He hopped down and flung open the door. "Hi, Conway Twitty Cash."

Conway grinned. "Hi, Miguel Lopez."

"How come you know I'm Miguel?"

"Because you talk more than your brother." Conway stepped inside. "Hello, Javier."

Javi peeked at Conway from behind Isi's legs. "Thanks for arriving early," she said.

"No problem." His brown-eyed gaze roamed over her body and she resisted glancing at herself to see if she'd spilled food on the front of her blouse.

She motioned to the kitchen table where she'd left a notebook open. "Important numbers are in there. The boys need to be dropped off at school by twelve-thirty and picked up at three-thirty. Supper's between five and six. Bath time is seven. Bedtime eight. I should be home shortly after midnight."

"Where's the school?" Conway asked.

"Over there." Miguel pointed at the kitchen window.

"The Tiny Tot Learn and Play is a mile down the road next to the McDonald's." Isi peeled Javier's arms off her legs, kissed his cheek then gathered her backpack and laptop before kissing Miguel. "Be good for Mr. Conway. If I get a bad report, we won't be going to the carnival this weekend."

She took two steps toward the door before Conway blocked her path. His cologne shot straight up her nose and she sucked in a quick breath. He always smelled nice when he came into the bar. Her eyes narrowed. "What's different about you?"

"I got a haircut," he said.

His shaggy golden-brown hair usually hung over the collar of his shirt. The shorter style made him appear older, more mature. Less like a playboy. "I like it." His lips curved in his trademark sexy smile. If she didn't leave soon, she'd be tempted to run her fingers through his locks.

He followed her outside. "Don't you want my number in case you need to get in touch with me?"

Duh. She dug her phone from her purse. "What is it?" He recited the digits. "Thanks. My cell number is in the notebook." She turned away then stopped. "I notified the school that you'd be bringing the boys and picking them up for a few days. You'll need to show your license each time. And don't forget to put their booster seats in your truck." She waved at the seats on the porch. "Thanks again!"

Conway watched Isi get into her clunker and drive off then studied his charges. The boys stood side by side, their backpacks strapped on. They wore the same outfit. Jeans, striped T-shirts—Miguel's was red and blue and Javier's was green and blue.

"Aren't we gonna leave, Conway Twitty Cash?" Miguel asked.

"We can't."

The brothers looked at each other, then Miguel asked, "Why not?"

Conway stared at Javier's feet.

Miguel shoved his brother. "You got different shoes on, stupid."

"I know." Javier jutted his chin.

Conway suspected the kid hadn't meant to wear mismatched shoes and was trying to save face. "Cool. I used to wear a different cowboy boot on each foot when I first began rodeoing."

"Why?" Miguel asked.

"For good luck," Conway said. "Is that why you wear different shoes, Javier?"

The boy jiggled his head.

"I wore my good-luck boots all the time and you know what happened?"

"What?" both boys asked.

"They ran out of luck."

Javier raced from the room and returned with matching sneakers.

"Smart man, Javier. Gotta save the good luck for stuff that matters." Crisis averted, Conway ushered the boys out of the trailer and they raced to his truck.

"Hey, does your mom lock the door when she leaves?"

Miguel returned to the porch and plucked a key from the flowerpot of fake daisies on the first step. After Conway secured the trailer, he slipped the key into his pocket and picked up the booster seats. "You guys sit in the front while I figure out how to install these things." Five minutes later, he said, "Okay. Get in them."

The boys climbed in the truck, their shoes dragging across the front seat of the cab as they crawled into their boosters. "Watch the shoes, amigos." Conway's black

Dodge was only a year old—he didn't even allow his dates to put their makeup on in his truck. Once the boys were buckled in, he drove off.

There was nowhere to park his big truck in the preschool lot when he arrived, so he pulled into a handicapped spot. He'd no sooner turned off the engine than a woman knocked on the window.

"You can't park here," she said. "You don't have a permit."

"I'm dropping the boys off."

"I'm sorry, but you'll have to use the lot across the street."

"I'll only be a few minutes."

"Doesn't matter." She planted her hands on her hips and he had no doubt that she'd tackle him to the ground if he tried to get out of the truck.

"Hang on, guys." Conway backed out of the spot.

"That's Mrs. Schneider," Miguel said. "We call her Mrs. Spider 'cause she's creepy." The boys giggled.

"She is creepy." Conway parked across the street then helped the boys out of their booster seats. The school bell rang, echoing above the noise from the traffic.

"We get a flag by our name if we're late," Miguel said.

Conway tucked both boys against his sides like footballs and said, "Hold on." Bypassing the crosswalk he dashed across the street then set his cargo on their feet. "Lead the way."

As soon as they entered the building, Miguel marched up to the front desk and said, "This is Conway Twitty Cash."

The day-care employee rolled her eyes. "And I'm Loretta Lynn."

Conway fished his wallet from his pocket. "Isi Lopez

called the school and informed someone that I'd be dropping the boys off and picking them up." He set his license on the counter.

The woman read his license. "You're kidding, right?"

"No, ma'am. I'm Conway Twitty Cash."

Miguel grinned at the lady.

"Shouldn't you guys hang up your backpacks?" Conway asked.

The lady handed him a clipboard and pen. "Fill out this form."

He wrote down his full name, cell phone, social security and license numbers plus the color, make and model of his truck. Hell, he was surprised they didn't ask for a credit card. When he finished, he turned away from the desk and plowed into Javier, who'd been standing behind him the whole time.

"Javier doesn't like to come here," the lady whispered then walked off to speak with a parent.

Conway guided the boy to a chair in the waiting area and sat down. "You don't like to come here?"

The kid scuffed his shoe against the floor.

"Are the teachers mean?"

Javier shook his head.

"Are the kids mean?"

He shrugged.

Javier's shyness probably made him an easy target for bullies. Conway peeked into the main room and saw that Miguel sat on the floor with a group of boys. He didn't know what to do. If he left Javier at the school, he'd worry about him being picked on.

"Are you ill?" He touched the boy's forehead. "You feel kind of warm. You think you might be coming down with a cold?"

Javier's eyebrows scrunched together.

"Because if you're getting sick, you shouldn't stay here and infect the other kids."

The boy blinked then he faked a sneeze.

"You are coming down with a cold." Conway spoke with the head of the preschool then waited while she asked Miguel if he wanted to go home with his brother. Miguel elected to remain at school.

Now what? Conway sat in his truck staring at Javier in the rearview mirror. He'd planned to use the time the boys were in school to browse orchard sprayers at a local farm-equipment store. He needed to apply insecticide to the pecan trees before the weevils got out of hand. "You ever been to a tractor store, Javier?" The boy shook his head. "Then it's about time you met John Deere."

Isi turned in her exam early and left the classroom. The test had been a breeze—then again she'd studied all weekend. She didn't have the luxury of failing a class or retaking it. She'd qualified for a scholarship to attend the community college and she had to maintain a 3.0 grade point average to keep her financial aid.

She stopped at the school cafeteria for a bite to eat before her next class and while she waited in the sandwich line, she skimmed through phone messages. When she saw the missed call from the preschool, alarm bells went off inside her head. She gave up her place in line and stepped into the hallway to call the school. After learning Conway had signed out Javier because her son hadn't felt well, she dialed Conway's cell. No answer. She left a voicemail, asking him for an update then returned to the cafeteria.

By the time her final class of the day ended, she still

hadn't heard from Conway. She contacted the preschool again and they confirmed that Conway and Javier had returned to pick up Miguel. As soon as Isi arrived at the bar, she texted Conway. When he didn't answer, she left another message, pleading with him to get in touch with her. Two hours later, she was about to ask her boss if she could leave work early when Conway strolled into the bar with the twins.

Relieved the three males appeared no worse for wear she delivered a drink order to a table while they claimed seats at the bar. When she approached the group, she felt Javier's forehead. "No fever."

Conway came to her son's defense. "He was warm when we got to the school and I didn't think it was a good idea to leave him there." He ruffled Javier's hair and Isi's heart melted at the affectionate gesture.

"Are you feeling better, Javi?" she asked.

"Yes."

Isi switched her attention to Conway. "Why didn't you return my calls?" This gig wasn't going to work, if they didn't communicate with each other. "I was frantic wondering what was wrong with Javier."

"I'll try to remember to check my phone more often."

She waved a hand in front of her. "What are you doing here?"

"Conway Twitty Cash doesn't cook, Mom." Miguel's gaze swiveled back and forth between Isi and Conway.

Isi got a discount on her meals, but she didn't have the extra money to pay for the boys' food.

As if sensing her dilemma, Conway said, "It's my treat."

Isi guessed it wouldn't hurt for the boys to eat at the bar this one time. She put in an order for three cheeseburger baskets with fries. While she waited tables, she kept an eye on the trio and couldn't help feel a tiny smidgeon of envy that she wasn't sitting with them. Whatever Conway said appeared to amuse her sons, because they giggled an awful lot. Miguel was a talker, so it didn't surprise her that he chatted with Conway. What amazed her was that shy Javier appeared more animated. Maybe Conway's relaxed personality put her son at ease.

That nonchalant attitude would drive Isi nuts after a while. She was a go-getter, get-things-done-do-it-now-not-later kind of woman and Conway came across as a man who went with the flow. Instead of going after the future, he was happy to let the future find him.

A half hour later, the boys had finished eating and were fooling around with the jukebox in the corner.

"That's too much," Isi said when Conway left forty dollars next to the empty food baskets.

"You can never tip enough for great service." He ran his finger along the bridge of her nose. "The swelling's gone down."

"It's not as sore, either." She didn't want to tell him that last night when she'd rolled over in bed and had pressed her face into the pillow, it had felt as if someone had stabbed her up the nose.

"I don't think you'll have a bump."

"I'm not worried about that."

"You should be, because you have a very pretty, petite nose."

She scoffed.

"What?" He leaned closer and whispered. "Just because we're friends, doesn't mean I don't still find you attractive."

Sheesh. The guy was an incurable flirt. The last thing

she needed was to allow Conway to slip past her defenses when they both knew they were all wrong for each other. "Javier wasn't really sick, was he?"

"No. And he wouldn't tell me why he didn't want to stay at school."

"There are a couple of boys who tease him, because he's shy. Give him a little encouragement when you drop him off tomorrow."

"You want me to give him a pep talk?"

Conway made her handling of the situation seem stupid.

"Sounds to me like someone needs to tell the bullies to keep their distance from Javier."

"Stay out of this, Conway." The last thing she wanted was her babysitter threatening her sons' classmates. "Red said I could leave early if it's not busy tonight."

He slid off the stool. "How'd your test go?"

Startled by the question, she didn't immediately answer.

"You did have an exam today, didn't you?"

"It went fine. Thanks for asking." She wasn't used to anyone inquiring about her schoolwork.

"See you later." Conway called to the boys and they left the bar.

Isi ignored another sharp twinge of envy when neither of her sons waved goodbye or acted as if they'd missed her. As a matter of fact, they seemed downright gleeful that they were stuck with Conway.

She returned to work, hoping the night would pass quickly. By the time her shift ended and she arrived back at the trailer, she was exhausted and she still had schoolwork to do before going to bed. When she got out of the car and surveyed the mess in the yard, she groaned.

Bikes, pogo sticks, footballs, basketballs, baseballs, mitts, bats, scooters and skateboards were strewn about.

Why hadn't Conway demanded the boys put their toys away before turning in for the night? She thought about doing it herself, but she was too tired. When she entered the trailer, the place was dark, save for the light above the kitchen stove. She stood by the door until her eyes adjusted to the dimness.

Conway slept on the love seat, legs hanging over the end, boots off. His sexy sprawl triggered a vision of her coming home to him every night—until he found the perfect woman and left Isi out in the cold.

She padded closer to the couch and studied him. Why had he cut his hair? Had he wanted to impress her? *Dream on.* The shorter hairstyle drew attention to his square jaw and full lips—a mouth made for kissing as she'd discovered a long time ago.

They'd only shared a couple of kisses before Conway had learned she was a single mother, but those kisses had been amazing. The instant their lips had touched, sparks ignited. He'd nibbled her lower lip, making her yearn for more then he'd thrust his tongue inside her mouth and… Isi swallowed a groan and shoved the memory aside.

She glanced at the living room—toys scattered everywhere. When had her sons accumulated so much junk? She'd bought the toys at second-hand stores and rummage sales, but maybe she'd gone overboard. She was the first to admit that she spoiled the twins because she felt guilty for not spending more time with them. Guilty that they didn't have a father. Guilty that they didn't have any family except her.

She retreated to the kitchen, where a sink full of dirty dishes greeted her. The boys must have used a clean cup each time they'd gotten a drink. Next, she went into the bathroom and felt their toothbrushes. Dry as a bone— they'd gone to bed without brushing their teeth. She didn't have dental insurance, so she was strict about making the boys brush and use a daily fluoride rinse. She walked down the hall to their bedroom and poked her head inside. They were sound asleep in their twin beds—fully clothed.

Isi brushed her teeth, changed into her sleeping shorts and T-shirt then slipped into bed, forgetting all about waking Conway and sending him home.

Chapter 3

The rumble of a truck engine woke Isi at the crack of dawn.

Conway! Had he slept on her couch all night long?

She sprang from the bed and raced through the trailer. When she stepped outside, only the taillights of his truck were visible as he turned out of the neighborhood. Her gaze skimmed the yard. Bless Conway's big cowboy heart—he'd put all the toys in the box next to the storage shed and had left the boys' booster seats on the steps. When she went inside to make coffee, she noticed he'd also picked up the living room. Every Lego and building block, toy car, board game and action figure had been stowed in the colored bins against the wall. And in the kitchen, there wasn't a dirty dish in sight.

A lump formed in her throat. She'd thought she'd known Conway pretty well after their talks at the bar.

So how had it escaped her notice, that hiding beneath all that sexy charisma and charm was a considerate man?

Conway's thoughtfulness reminded her of how much she missed her best friend, Erica. Isi had met Erica three years ago at the community college when they'd worked together on a class project. Erica had always been there for Isi, helping her out with the boys when the sitter had become ill. This past spring, Erica had transferred to the University of Southern California to pursue a nursing degree and live closer to her boyfriend.

Feeling weepy, she made coffee and decided to read a chapter for class before the boys woke up. After the twins ate breakfast, she'd resume her search for a sitter.

"You were MIA last night."

Conway stepped away from the tractor where he was in the process of attaching the mist sprayer he'd rented in Yuma the day before. Will hovered in the barn doorway.

The second-eldest Cash brother had once been a tie-down roper, but the past few years he'd spent more time working construction jobs than he did riding the circuit.

"Since when did you start keeping tabs on me?"

"It was Mack's birthday yesterday, you dumb shit."

Well, hell. He'd forgotten. "I was helping a friend out."

Will walked farther into the barn. "I suppose your *friend* needed help with her bed."

His brother's words prompted a vision of Conway slipping between the sheets with Isi. Disturbed at how easily his mind put him and Isi together as a couple he said, "You need to go off and rodeo for a while."

"Why's that?"

"Lately you've been as sociable as a rotting tooth."

"We all can't be as popular with the ladies as you are," Will said.

Normally Conway would relish a game of verbal sparring with his brother, but he didn't have time. "I'll call Mack and wish him a happy birthday." He tested the lock that held the fan sprayer in place then hopped on the tractor seat.

"Where'd you get the sprayer?" Will asked.

"Jim Baine leased it to me."

"Since when did the feed store start renting farm equipment?"

"I don't know, but when I went to Tractor Supply in Yuma to browse sprayers, the salesclerk told me to stop by Jim's, so I did."

"How much did he charge you for it?"

"A hundred dollars for the week." Several months ago their oldest brother Johnny had informed the family that the farm was in financial trouble. Conway and his brothers had pitched in their savings to make up the missed mortgage payments so any new equipment purchases would have to wait.

"I hope you know what you're doing, because I sure as hell would like to get paid back the money I contributed to produce this crop," Will said.

Ever since Johnny had handed over control of the pecan groves to Conway, the rest of his brothers believed it was their duty to comment on how he did things. Will wasn't a farmer, but Conway felt a special connection with the land and he intended to do everything in his power to produce a healthy nut crop and that meant doing things by the book—like spraying for insects during the month of October.

"Don't worry, bro, I've got things under control."

Conway grinned. "But if you're willing to help out, you can—"

"No way." Will raised his hands in the air. "I build things. I don't grow them."

"Is the construction business improving?"

"Ben's got several small jobs lined up to keep us busy."

Not busy enough to prevent Will from harassing Conway. "I'd love to chat, but I need to spray a few rows before I leave."

"Where are you going?"

"I'm watching a friend's kids while she goes to school and works at night."

"Your friend wouldn't happen to be a waitress at the Border Town Bar & Grill, would she?" Will asked.

"Why?"

Will chuckled. "You're the guy two women were fighting over when one of them got her nose broken."

"They weren't fighting over me. Isi—"

"Who's Isi?"

"The waitress at the bar. She took a punch that was meant for me."

"Ouch." Will shook his head. "I don't get why women fawn all over you."

"Because I'm the handsome Cash brother." Conway grinned.

"Yeah, right. Wait until word gets around that you're a pecan farmer and not the swaggering rodeo hero you want everyone to believe you are."

Conway didn't give a crap how his new career might affect his image. For a while now he'd been wanting to settle down and it was only a matter of time before he found the right woman.

"This Isi must be special if you're sprucing up for her." Will motioned to Conway's short hair.

Isi was special, but not in the way Will meant. Conway ignored his brother and started the tractor. The engine sputtered and coughed before settling into a loud roar, then he shifted gears and drove out of the barn.

He lined up the sprayer then moved through the first row of trees, contemplating Will's words. There was no reason he couldn't work on the farm and rodeo weekends until he found the woman of his dreams. As a matter of fact, he'd head up to Payson on Saturday and enter the Frontier Days Rodeo. Who knows, maybe he'd run into his soul mate.

"And he let us sit on the tractor," Javier said.

Isi listened to the boys chatter about their day with Conway while she made grilled cheese sandwiches for lunch.

Miguel set two plastic cups on the table. "Next time I get to go."

"And he let me push the brake and—"

"Okay, enough," Isi interrupted Javier, hoping to ward off a fight. Miguel was jealous that his brother had gone to the tractor store with Conway while he'd stayed in preschool.

"I wanna tractor when I grow up," Javier said.

Isi cut the sandwiches in half, placed them on paper plates then added apples slices to the meal. "What would you do with a tractor, Javi?"

"I'd help Mr. Conway on his farm."

"Does Conway Twitty Cash have cows and pigs on his farm?" Miguel asked Isi.

"I don't know, honey." She joined the boys at the table

and smoothed the hair off Javier's forehead. "You don't feel warm." He wouldn't make eye contact with her and she reminded herself to tell Conway not to give in to her son if he complained about going to school.

Once the boys ate and brushed their teeth, she sent them outside to play in the yard and began making phone calls. Fifteen minutes later, she'd gotten nowhere—each of the women she'd found in the Sunday want ads had already taken babysitting jobs. Later today she planned to put up a flyer on the campus bulletin board and hoped a student wanting to earn extra cash before Christmas would contact her.

A knock rattled the door. "It's me." Conway stepped into the trailer and his smile faltered. "You're upset. What's wrong?"

For a man who spent yesterday chasing after two demanding four-year-olds and sleeping on a dollhouse-size couch, he looked well-rested.

Well-rested? That was a unique way to describe *sexy*.

Isi ignored the voice in her head. "I'm not upset. I'm discouraged." She closed her notebook. "I haven't had any luck finding a sitter."

"Did you try the online classifieds?" He stopped next to the table and his half smile tugged a sigh from Isi.

"I don't trust those online sites," she said.

"Why not?"

"They're full of child predators." Poor Conway. He was really clueless about raising children.

"Can you put them in day care after school?" he asked.

"There isn't a facility open until midnight." She waved a hand in the air. "Besides, I don't have the money for extended child care."

"I suppose I could keep watching the boys until you find a new sitter."

"You can't be serious."

"Why not?"

She laughed. "The twins are a lot of work."

"They aren't so bad."

Wait until he spent more time with her sons, then the novelty would wear off. She went to the window to make sure the boys were in the yard. "I told Javier that he has to stay at school. Please don't let him talk you into signing him out."

"I wanted to speak to you about that."

She stuffed her books into her backpack.

"Javier told me that he's getting picked on at recess."

"You mean teased?" she said.

"Why haven't you spoken to his teacher about it?"

Isi jerked as if he'd slapped her. "You think I've ignored the problem?"

He shrugged. "Then why are the brats still tormenting Javier?"

Angry that Conway believed she was an uncaring mother, she lashed out. "I don't know what he told you, but his teacher assured me the situation is being dealt with." An image of her son cornered by miniature thugs on the playground popped into Isi's mind. She felt bad that the boys had been placed in day cares and preschools the past three years, but she'd had no choice—not if she intended to make a better life for them. Isi blinked hard.

"You're not going to cry, are you?"

"No." She fussed with her backpack.

Conway wiped the pad of his thumb across her cheekbone, catching the tear that escaped her eye. "I didn't mean to upset you."

She sniffed. "It's... I don't have... Never mind."

"Never mind what? Talk to me."

"I'm doing the best I can, Conway. I complained to the head of the preschool that Javier said kids were picking on him, but she insisted that the boys would work things out on their own."

"How long ago did you speak to this lady?"

"I guess it's been a month."

Conway's jaw hardened. "I can help. Will you trust me to handle this?"

"You don't have any experience with kids."

"I grew up fighting bullies who picked on me because of my name."

His comment triggered more tears. "The teacher said I should encourage the boys' father to become more involved in their lives, but that'll never happen."

"Why?"

"Their father refuses to acknowledge that the boys are his."

Conway scowled. "Make him take a paternity test."

"He's already married with kids."

"You slept with a married man?" Conway gaped at her.

"He didn't tell me he was married."

"And you didn't ask him?"

"He wasn't wearing a wedding band, so I assumed he was single."

"The boys' father should be paying child support. If he helped out financially, you could afford day care." Conway swept his hand in front of him. "You're barely getting by raising them on your own."

"We're fine." She wasn't proud of accepting government assistance to help meet her monthly expenses and put food on the table, but as soon as she earned her degree, she'd find a full-time job with benefits and be able to support herself and the boys all on her own.

"Being a single parent isn't easy." She swallowed hard. "I have no one to—"

Conway cut her off midsentence by pressing his finger against her lips. The tip of his finger slipped past her lip and touched her tongue. A spark of heat warmed her brown eyes as they locked gazes.

"What are you doing?" she mumbled against his finger.

"Trying to stop you from talking."

Did he have any idea how long it had been since a man had touched her so intimately? Feeling short of breath, she said, "Don't do that again."

Good grief. No sense playing with fire when they were both destined for different futures—Conway wanted marriage without kids and if she ever committed to a man, he would have to love her boys as much as she loved them.

"Is my touch that awful?" His eyes sparkled with humor.

"Stop trying to distract me."

"Isi. You're a great mom and the boys are lucky to have you in their corner. Let me help Javier."

Just because you accept his help doesn't mean you're a failure. "Fine." She slung her backpack over her shoulder. "See you after midnight."

Isi stepped outside and blew kisses to the boys. "Be good." Then she drove off, thinking she'd better keep her guard up around Conway in case he turned out to be an authentic Mr. Nice Guy—a Mr. Nice Guy who rocked her world. Again.

When Conway entered the preschool, he strode up to the desk and announced, "I'm staying with the boys."

Both Miguel and Javier smiled.

"You can't stay," the lady said.

Conway peered at her name tag. "Why not, Rose? I'd like to observe what the boys do during their time here."

"I can tell you what they do. First, they sit in a circle for story time then—"

"I don't want to hear about it, I want to experience it." Conway tapped his finger against the sign-in sheet on the clipboard. "Is there a guest form I need to fill out?"

Flustered, Rose said, "Wait here, Mr. Cash. I'll get the director."

Miguel tugged on Conway's pant leg. "Now you're in trouble. Ms. Kibble's mean."

"You guys go hang up your backpacks. I'll be there in a minute."

After the boys walked away, an older woman with a salt-and-pepper bob stepped from her office. "Mr. Cash, I understand you'd like to observe today."

"Yes, ma'am." He held out his hand.

"Is there a problem with Miguel or Javier?" she asked.

"Well, ma'am, there is. It seems Javier is being picked on and nothing's been done to address the problem."

The director's eyes rounded and Rose made a hasty exit.

"This is the first I've heard of any bullying going on in my school," Ms. Kibble said.

"No, ma'am, it's not. According to the boys' mother,

she's spoken to you about this before, and because the teasing hasn't stopped, Javier doesn't want to come to school anymore."

"Which boys are bothering him?"

"He won't say, but I intend to find out."

"I appreciate your concern, Mr. Cash. I'll make sure the teacher is aware of the situation."

"Good. I'm eager to see how she deals with the bullies."

Ms. Kibble's mouth tightened, but she backed down. "Enjoy your afternoon."

When Conway joined the boys for story time on the floor, Miguel whispered to the kid next to him, "That's Conway Twitty Cash. He's my new friend."

Javier inched closer to Conway but remained silent. Story time turned out to be boring as hell and it was all Conway could do to keep his eyes open. When the teacher—Ms. Haney—closed the book and asked if anyone had questions, Conway raised his hand.

"Yes, Mr. Cash?"

"When's recess?" The room erupted in giggles, which earned Conway a dark scowl from the teacher.

"Go to your tables and start your work sheets," the teacher said.

When the kids bolted in all directions, a boy walked past Javier and elbowed him in the back. Conway noticed the teacher's attention was elsewhere. The boy with the sharp elbow sat at the same table as Javier, and Javier refused to make eye contact with the kid.

One bully identified. Now he needed to find the others. The only way to do that was to sit away from Javier. He joined Miguel at his table and Conway's gut twisted at Javier's hurt expression. It was all he could do not to rush to the boy's side and reassure him.

While the group worked on their alphabet sheets, Conway watched Javier. Nothing out of the ordinary happened until the teacher asked the students to pass the papers to the head of the table. A freckled-faced boy swept Javier's paper onto the floor then stepped on it before putting it back in the pile and handing it to the teacher.

Bully number two identified.

The class spent the next hour moving from activity to activity until snack time. Fruit punch, crackers and small boxes of raisins were doled out to each kid. Miguel stuffed his face, eating everything in front of him and asking for seconds of the punch. Javier didn't touch his food—or rather he didn't have a chance to, because the red-haired bully had stolen his box of raisins and Javier hadn't protested.

By the time recess arrived, Conway was spitting mad that the teacher hadn't noticed what was happening right under her nose. He followed the kids outside and Javier raced to the swings while Miguel veered off toward the monkey bars and a group of gossiping girls.

When the bullies closed in on Javier, Conway made his move. "Mind if I join you guys on the swings?"

The freckle-faced boy crossed his arms over his chest. "We were playing here first."

Insolent bugger.

"Yeah." The chubby kid kicked dirt at Javier. "He's on our swing."

"This is your swing? You brought this from home?" Conway asked.

Javier giggled then sobered quickly when the bullies glared at him.

"I think you guys have got it wrong. This swing belongs to the school."

"Get off, stupid," the redhead told Javier.

Javier made a move to vacate his seat, but Conway set his hand on his shoulder. "You'll have to wait your turn, carrottop."

"Says who?" the kid glared.

"Says me, Rico." Javier stood and faced his adversary.

Rico laughed. "You can't stop me."

"Yes, I can." Javier shoved Rico in the chest and the kid tripped over his feet and stumbled. Once he gained his balance, Rico swung his fist, but Javier ducked and tackled the boy to the ground. Conway sent the overweight bully a stay-where-you-are glare while Javier and Rico wrestled.

Tiny fists punched mostly air, then a student alerted the playground monitor and the woman hurried over and separated the boys. Holding each by the back of the shirt collar she spoke to Conway. "You stood there and did nothing."

"The boys had to settle this between themselves," Conway said.

"Well, I've never heard of—"

"Lady, if you'd have been doing your job rather than texting on your phone, you'd know that Rico and his buddy like to torment kids."

The woman marched the boys into the building and Conway followed at a distance. Twice Javier peeked over his shoulder and grinned at him. Now that Rico and the other kid knew Javier could stand up for himself, they'd leave him alone.

Conway stood outside Ms. Kibble's office while the playground monitor explained the situation. All three boys were suspended for fighting and told not to return to school until Friday. Grinning from ear to ear, Javier followed Conway out of the school.

"Is my mom gonna be mad at me?" Javier asked.

"Nah." *She's going to be mad as hell at me.*

Conway heard Isi's car pull beneath the carport and he braced himself. When the trailer door opened, he said, "I can explain, Isi."

"Explain what?" She flashed a nervous smile.

"Didn't the school call you?"

The blood drained from her face. "What happened? Are the boys okay?"

"They're fine." He hadn't meant to scare her.

She set her backpack by the door. "What's going on?"

He didn't think this would be hard but the speech he'd rehearsed after the boys had gone to bed suddenly didn't sound so clever. "Javier's been expelled from school until Friday."

Isi's eyes widened. "What happened?"

"It wasn't his fault. You can blame me."

"What did he do, Conway?"

"He got into a fight on the playground."

She gasped.

"None of the boys were hurt. I watched the whole thing and—"

"You watched the fight and didn't break it up?"

"Let me explain." He shoved a hand through his hair. "I stayed at school and monitored their class. As I suspected, Javier is being bullied by two boys, one named Rico and the other one was a chubby kid."

"Mathew."

"During recess Javier got to the swings first but the bullies tried to make him get off. I told the boys Javier didn't have to give up his swing and all of a sudden Javi shoved Rico. The boys rolled on the ground until the recess monitor intervened and took them to the principal's office."

"Was Javier upset?"

"Nope."

"What did Ms. Kibble say?"

"Not a whole lot."

"Were all the boys suspended?"

"Yep. You'd have been proud of Javier, Isi."

"I'm supposed to be happy that you taught my son to solve his problems by fighting?"

"I didn't teach him to fight. I taught him to stand up for himself."

"Do me a favor and don't offer my sons any advice, okay? I'm their mother. I'll handle their problems." Isi walked down the hall to check on the twins and Conway made a hasty escape before he got suspended from his babysitting job.

Chapter 4

When Conway stepped inside Isi's trailer Friday at noon, he came face-to-face with two pouting grumps.

"What's wrong?"

"I found a sitter," Isi said.

A weird feeling gripped Conway's stomach, but he blamed it on the three breakfast burritos he'd eaten earlier in the morning. "Is it—" he motioned to the boys "—because of the school suspension?"

"Not at all," she said. He noticed she didn't make eye contact with him. "A customer at the bar recommended her aunt."

The swelling in Isi's nose had gone down and the bruising beneath her eyes had faded to a yellow hue. If she wore makeup, no one would be able to tell she'd broken her nose. His gaze drifted to her shirt—she looked hot in the black tank top that hugged her small breasts and the threadbare jeans that made her short legs appear a lot longer than they were. He imagined sliding the strap of the shirt off her shoulder and caressing the exposed skin with his tongue, then licking a trail up her neck toward her ear....

Whoa. Hold on, cowboy. What the heck was wrong with him? When had his brain decided to travel south and vacation in his crotch?

Since you started watching the twins.

Isi was an attractive woman and it wouldn't take much effort on her part to jumpstart his libido, especially because he wasn't dating other women. As of right now, Isi was the only female taking up space in his thoughts.

"The new sitter's name is Maria," Isi said. "She'll take the boys to school and pick them up and stay until bedtime. Then my neighbor Mrs. Sneed will come over and watch TV until I get home from work." Isi handed him a sheet of paper.

Conway caught her scent. The combination of flowery perfume and warm female sent a blast of testosterone through his bloodstream. He focused on the note. Isi had written down Maria's full name, address, birth date and a bunch of numbers—driver's license, social security and cell phone.

"What's this for?" he asked.

"I need you to take Maria to the school and show her the ropes." Isi took a deep breath. "She doesn't speak English very well and Rose is the only employee at the school who's bilingual. If she's not working, please give Maria's information to whoever's at the front desk."

"How am I supposed to show Maria anything, if I can't communicate with her?"

"Javier and Miguel will interpret for you."

"I didn't know they spoke Spanish," Conway said.

"They're not fluent, but they should be able to understand most of what Maria says." Isi slung the backpack over her shoulder. "I have to meet with my academic advisor before class, otherwise I'd stay and introduce you to Maria."

"Are you sure this is a good idea?" What if he and Maria got their messages mixed up?

"Stop worrying. Everything will be fine." Isi opened the door. "Thanks for helping with the boys this week."

"No problem."

She paused on the porch. "I'll probably see you at the bar."

"Yeah, I'll drop by." As he watched Isi's sashaying fanny walk to her car, he worried that their relationship would never be the same as it was before he'd offered to watch her sons. Once she drove off, he said, "Are you guys going to be grouchy all day?"

"We don't want Maria," Miguel said.

"I bet she can cook." His comment drew no response.

After the short amount of time he'd spent with the twins, it was nice to know they'd miss him. "You gotta give Maria a chance. I can't watch you guys forever."

"Why not?" Javier asked.

"The pecan harvest starts next month in November. There's a lot I need to do on the farm to get ready for it."

"We could help." Miguel tugged his brother by the shirtsleeve and dragged him across the room until they stood in front of Conway. "We can pick nuts."

"I appreciate the offer, but you guys have to stay in school."

"How come?" Javier asked.

"Because that's what kids do. They go to school to

get smart and then they go to college like you're mom is doing."

"Did you go to college?" Miguel asked.

"Nope."

"How come?"

"Do you always ask a lot of questions?"

Both boys bobbed their heads.

"I didn't go to college because I didn't have anyone telling me I should. Then I got older and figured out that what I wanted to do with my life didn't require a college degree."

"What did you want to do?" Miguel asked.

"I wanted to be a pecan farmer."

Javier's nose wrinkled. "I thought you were a cowboy."

"I'm a cowboy when I rodeo on the weekends."

"Can we rodeo?" Miguel asked.

Conway wasn't about to let the munchkins change the subject. "I bet Maria's a nice lady."

"What if she's mean?" Javier's brown eyes pleaded with Conway.

"Then we'll tell your mom." And let Isi deal with the situation. From now on he'd keep his advice to himself.

The sound of a vehicle pulling up to the trailer drifted through the screen door. "That's Maria. You guys be on your best behavior." Conway stepped onto the porch.

Holy moly. The woman was as old and gnarled as the root of an ancient oak tree. She had more wrinkles than a ten-year-old road map. Polyester slacks, a silk-printed long-sleeve blouse with a navy blazer and low-heeled shoes was hardly proper attire for chasing after boys. Then again, this woman was so old, if she chased anything, she'd drop dead of a heart attack.

"*Hola,* Maria." *Hola* and *sí* were about the only words Conway knew in Spanish.

She smiled, the gesture generating more facial wrinkles. He motioned for her to follow him inside. "Miguel, ask Maria what she'd like you to call her?"

Miguel translated Conway's words then Maria spoke.

"What did she say?" Conway asked.

"She said we can call her La Anciana."

Javier giggled.

"Okay." Conway pointed at Maria and smiled. "La Anciana." Then he indicated himself and said, "Conway" before moving his finger to the kitchen wall clock. "Miguel, tell La Anciana that it's time to leave for school and she should follow us in her car."

After Miguel spoke, Conway waited for the boys to get their backpacks then he held the door open for everyone. When Maria walked by him, her mouth curled in a snarl and he couldn't figure out what the heck he'd done to tick her off.

When they arrived at the school, Rose wasn't working. Conway turned over Maria's information to the lady at the counter and explained that the boys' new sitter didn't speak English and that she'd be dropping the boys off and picking them up after school.

While the employee filled out Maria's paperwork, Conway spoke to the boys. "Miguel, play with your brother at recess." This was Javier's first day back after his suspension. "And no fighting, Javi." Conway hoped Miguel would stick by his brother's side and ward off any threats by the bullies.

"Are you gonna pick us up?" Miguel asked.

"Yes. Tell Maria that she's to meet me back here at

three-thirty." He wanted to make sure she didn't forget to return for the boys.

Miguel translated and Maria responded.

"What did she say?" Conway asked.

"She wants to know if she's supposed to wash our clothes."

Conway was certain Isi would appreciate help with the housework. "Sure. Tell her she can wash clothes if she wants."

Miguel translated then said, "She wants to know what you're going to do."

"I'll be at the farm."

After Miguel conveyed the information, Conway said, "Have fun." He tipped his hat to Maria then left the building.

Anxiety gnawed at his gut as he drove away from the school. Isi was desperate to find a sitter for the boys, but Maria wasn't the right fit. The twins needed a young energetic person who would play outside with them. By the time he reached the edge of town, he'd broken out in a cold sweat. Instead of heading to the farm, he made a U-turn. He'd feel better if he stayed close by in case Javier got into trouble again at school.

A sixth sense told Isi she needed to go home after her classes and see how Maria and the boys were getting along, so she'd called in sick to work. She hoped the day had gone well and her sons had been on their best behavior, but she couldn't ignore a nagging suspicion that not all was right. When she'd interviewed Maria over the phone, the woman hadn't sounded very peppy but after raising five children of her own, she was certainly experienced enough to handle the twins. Even so,

Isi worried the boys would be too taxing on the seventy-year-old woman.

She turned into the mobile home park and saw Conway's truck next to the trailer. *Uh-oh.* She parked beneath the carport and got out of the car. Conway was throwing the football with Miguel and Javier played with a Slinky on the porch steps.

"Watch this, Mom." Miguel tossed the ball to Conway.

"Where's Maria?" she asked.

"She left," Conway said.

"She was supposed to stay with the boys until Mrs. Sneed came over at eight o'clock."

"I don't know what happened," Conway said. "Everything was going fine until she took her purse and stormed out of the trailer."

"I thought you'd planned to work on the farm after you dropped the boys off at school," Isi said.

"I had errands to do in town."

Something smelled fishy. Isi noticed that Javier wouldn't make eye contact with her. "Miguel, what happened?"

He shrugged.

"Come to think of it," Conway said, "Maria seemed agitated when we called her La Anciana, but—"

Isi gasped.

"What?" Conway's gaze bounced between her and Miguel.

"You called her La Anciana?"

"That's what Miguel said she wanted us to call her."

"You insulted her. *La Anciana* means old lady. It's a derogatory term." Isi glared at her sons. "We'll discuss this later."

"I thought you were working at the bar tonight," Conway said.

"I called in sick, because I had a funny feeling about today. Good thing I listened to my instincts."

"I'm sorry. I didn't mean to insult Maria," Conway said. "I'd be happy to apologize to her."

Isi appreciated his offer, but waved it off. "What else happened?"

"Maria asked if she should wash clothes while the boys were in school and I said sure, thinking you'd appreciate the help. When we got home from school she had all the laundry done."

Dear Lord, there had been at least six loads of clothes piled on the laundry room floor.

"And I told her to clean our bedrooms and do the dishes," Miguel said.

"Cleaning the bedroom is your responsibility, Miguel." Isi rubbed her aching forehead. "What else did you tell Maria to do?"

"Nothing."

Javier tattled on his brother. "He dumped all the toys out of the bins after Maria picked them up."

Isi thought she'd hired a woman experienced enough to stand up to her sons and not let them run roughshod over her. "Is Maria coming back on Monday?"

Miguel played with the laces on his sneakers.

"She's coming back, right?" Conway nudged Miguel's shoulder.

Her son shook his head.

"Why isn't she coming back?" Isi asked.

"'Cause I told her not to." Miguel stamped his foot. "We want Conway to take care of us."

"You two go inside and wash up for supper while I speak with Conway," she said.

Miguel glared at her and she was tempted to paddle his bottom for being disrespectful.

Once the trailer door closed and the boys were out of earshot, Conway spoke. "I had no idea what Miguel was saying to Maria. Had I known he was being rude and misleading her, I would have stopped him."

"I shouldn't have put you in this position." She felt bad for Maria and bad for Conway, both having been duped by a pair of four-year-olds. "I'll call Maria later and apologize. Hopefully, she'll agree to return on Monday."

"What if she doesn't?"

"Then I'll ask Mrs. Sneed to fill in until I find a sitter."

"Will she watch the boys for free?"

"Probably not. I'll have to scratch a few items off the boys' Christmas lists to come up with the money to pay her." Isi abruptly shut her mouth. Since when did she unload her problems on Conway? She was the advice-giver not the advice-seeker.

"I'll tell you what," he said. "I'll watch the boys until you graduate at the end of the semester." Then he added. "For free. It'll be my graduation gift to you."

For a man dead set against fatherhood, it was a generous offer. "You're busy with the farm, and what about your rodeos?"

"I'll manage. Well, there might be a problem unless…"

"Unless what?"

"You allow the boys to miss a few days of school the middle of November when I harvest the pecans."

"The boys will get in your way."

"I'll put them to work. Once I drive the shaker machine through a row of trees, they can collect the twigs and sticks that fall to the ground. And we've got extra beds in the bunkhouse they can sleep in."

"I don't know, Conway. They could be more of a hindrance than a help. I have to nag them to do their chores."

"Farming isn't sissy work like making beds or washing dishes."

"Sissy work?" Isi struggled not to laugh. "There's nothing wrong with a man who picks up after himself and keeps a clean house."

"You were the one who said their teacher suggested you ask the boys' father to become involved in their lives. I'm not their father, but I'm offering the boys a chance to do guy stuff."

She shook her head.

"What?"

"I can't believe what I'm hearing." When he frowned, she said, "I've spent the past two years listening to you insist you don't want kids and now you're offering to watch mine 24/7."

Conway flashed a grin and her breath caught in the back of her throat. All the man had to do was smile to get his way. "What happens if the boys decide they don't want to stay at the farm all day and night?"

"Then you threaten to bring Maria back."

"That might work." It would be a weight off of her shoulders not having to worry about child care while she studied for finals and worked on her research paper. "Okay, but I'll pay you."

He chuckled. "I've used you for my personal therapist the past two years."

"You consider me your therapist?"

His gaze roamed over her body, and a delicious heat spread through her belly. "Yes, ma'am, I do." He winked. "And I'm sure I'll need more therapy, if I'm to survive the next two months with Mig and Javi."

"I'll think about it, Conway, but until I make up my mind, please don't say anything to the boys."

"Tomorrow's Saturday," he said. "Do you have to work at the bar?"

"No, I'm taking the boys to the carnival."

"What carnival?"

"Every year a small carnival sets up in the Walmart parking lot. It's only a few rides, games and lots of junk-food vendors." It was cheap entertainment.

"Can Conway go with us?" Miguel asked, smashing his face against the screen.

"Conway has better things to do than ride the Ferris wheel and eat cotton candy. And stop eavesdropping, Miguel."

"Do you like cotton candy, Conway?" Javier asked.

"Sure do."

It hadn't escaped Isi's notice that Javi had opened up to Conway this week. If anyone had told her that this man, who never wanted to be a father, would be great with kids, she would have thought they had a screw loose.

"What time are you leaving for the carnival?" he asked.

"I'd like to get there when it opens at ten." As the day wore on the boys would become cranky.

Conway dug his keys from his pocket and walked to his truck. "I'll pick you up at nine forty-five."

Isi hurried after him. "You don't have to do this," she said. "They'll understand if I tell them you're busy."

He opened the truck door. "Isi?"

"What?"

"I'm not doing this for the boys."

"You aren't?"

He shook his head. "I'm doing it for me."

"You've been dying to go to a carnival?"

"No." He slid on his sunglasses then flashed a devil-may-care smile. "But it beats the heck out of getting bucked off a bull."

As soon as Conway drove off, Javier's "I'm hungry" snapped Isi out of her trance.

"Hey, Dixie." Conway climbed the farmhouse steps early Saturday morning and quietly walked to the end of the porch where his sister, the baby of the Cash clan, sat on the swing with her three-month-old son, Nathan. He leaned against the rail and whispered, "How's the little guy doing?"

"He finally fell asleep."

Nate had been colicky since birth, but Dixie's husband, Gavin, had the patience of a saint and walked the floors with the baby. Keeping his voice low, he asked, "Has he been up all night?"

"Yes. I took over walking him an hour ago so Gavin could sleep."

Conway peered at the fuzzy dark head. "I can't believe he's got all that hair."

His sister released a deep sigh.

"What's wrong?"

"I never thought I'd say this, Conway, but I'm ready to buy a house in Yuma. Commuting to the gift shop every day with the baby is too exhausting."

"But you love this place." Their grandmother had

willed the farmhouse to Dixie, trusting her granddaughter to keep it in the family.

"After Nate was born I realized it's the memories of growing up here that I love most. The house is only walls and doorways and light switches. It's what went on in each of the rooms that will stay with me the rest of my life."

"Is Gavin pushing you to move to Yuma?" Conway's brother-in-law worked for the city on water reclamation projects and spent most of his day in his truck driving to various sites.

"Not at all. But it seems like the only time Gavin sees Nate is in the middle of the night when he's crying. And maybe if Nate didn't have to spend so much time in the car, he might sleep better."

"What do you want to do with the house? Rent or sell?"

"Neither."

Conway gaped at his sister. "You made us all move out because you and Gavin wanted privacy. Now it's going to sit empty?"

"I thought maybe Johnny and Shannon might want the house."

"Johnny works at the Triple D. It wouldn't make sense for them to drive back to the ranch every day when Johnny's out of bed at the crack of dawn feeding cattle."

"Okay, then whichever of my brothers marries next can lay claim to the house."

"The place will sit empty forever."

"Considering how picky *you* are when it comes to women, you'll never get the chance to live in this house."

"What do you mean picky?"

"Women swoon when you walk by them." Dixie smiled. "But you find fault with every female you date."

It wasn't that he found anything wrong with his dates, it was that the ladies weren't always truthful with him when they claimed to be on board with his no-kids itinerary. The women who'd said they didn't want kids tried to change Conway's mind after they'd gone out on several dates.

"I'm picky," he said. "So what?"

"Does your father have anything to do with you not wanting kids?"

Dixie was too perceptive for her own good.

"Have you ever been in contact with your dad?" she asked.

"Nah." He dropped his gaze so she wouldn't catch him in a lie.

No one in the family knew that when Conway turned eighteen, he'd tracked down Zachary Johnson—the man who'd gotten his mother pregnant but had refused to marry her. Since Conway and his brothers had been fathered by different men, their mother had put her surname on all their birth certificates, but she'd listed Zachary Johnson as Conway's father. Conway found the man working as a ranch hand on a spread in northern Arizona. To his surprise the man hadn't been upset that Conway had found him. When asked why he'd walked out on Conway and his mother, his father said he hadn't known how to stay. Zachary Johnson's father and grandfather before him had all walked out on the women they'd gotten pregnant.

From that day forward he'd decided he wouldn't be like his father or grandfather and abandon his children.

The only way he could guarantee breaking that cycle was marrying a woman who didn't want kids.

"Now that I have Nathan, I think it would be nice if he had a grandfather."

"Nate's got plenty of uncles." An image of Miguel and Javier flashed before Conway's eyes and he felt bad for the boys that their father wasn't involved in their lives. The twins were still young, but it wouldn't be long before they asked Isi why their father wanted nothing to do with them. Conway had been seven the first time he'd asked his mom that same question.

Nate began fussing and Conway held out his arms. "Give to him to me."

The baby was the size of a football. "He's getting fat—you're feeding him too much."

"Since when are you an expert on babies?"

"Hey, I can be objective, because I don't intend to have kids."

"You'd make a great father."

He shook his head. "When I marry, I plan to spend all my free time with my wife." That's what he told everyone whenever the subject of marriage and kids came up. Better to have others believe he was selfish rather than admit he was afraid if he had kids he'd leave them high and dry for no good reason other than an inherited genetic instinct to flee.

"You'd feel differently if you had your own child," Dixie said.

"I'm sure Nate will have plenty of cousins to play with in time."

"You'd better get going if you want to catch up with Porter. He left for the rodeo a half hour ago."

"I'm not going to the rodeo."

"Why not?"

"I'm not telling." He kissed the top of Nate's fuzzy head. "He smells good on top, but his bottom stinks." He handed his nephew back to Dixie.

She sniffed his diaper and made a face.

"I won't have to worry." He skipped down the steps.

"Worry about what?" Dixie called after him.

"My house smelling like baby vomit and dirty diapers."

As he drove away from the farm, he reminded himself to stop at the bank once he got to Yuma. He sure hoped the pecan harvest was abundant this year—making amends for Isi's broken nose was costing him a fortune.

Chapter 5

Conway stood in the middle of the Walmart parking lot holding the twins' hands as they gazed up at the Ferris wheel while Isi waited in line to buy tickets for the ride.

"Have you ever been on a Ferris wheel?" he asked the boys.

Javier nodded, then Miguel said, "Our mom loves the Ferris wheel."

As Conway watched the huge wheel rotate, its occupants waving to friends and family on the ground, he struggled to understand how he'd reached the age of twenty-eight and had yet to visit a Six Flags amusement park, SeaWorld, Disneyland or a circus.

He didn't often allow his thoughts to drift back to his early childhood, because of memories he'd just as soon forget—a mother who'd been in and out of his life and a father who'd gone AWOL six months after his birth. His grandparents did their best to love seven grandchildren, but caring for their daughter's brood had worn them out and stretched their finances to the limit—there had never been extra money to take the family to a carnival.

Javier squeezed Conway's hand. "Are you afraid?"

"I don't know. I've never been on a Ferris wheel."

"We got a deal on the tickets," Isi said when she joined them.

"What kind of deal?" he asked.

"Early-bird special—two-for-one." She smiled. "That means there's an extra ride in the budget."

"Conway's never been on a Ferris wheel, Mom," Miguel said.

"Really?" Isi leaned in and whispered in Conway's ear. "Are you afraid of heights?"

"I don't know. Guess I'll find out," he said.

Isi smiled. "I'll hold your hand."

"Me, too," Javier said.

After the riders got off, the carnival worker ushered the four of them into one seat, the boys squeezing between Isi and Conway. When the seat lurched forward, Conway clutched the safety bar across their laps. As they made their way to the top of the wheel, he decided he definitely didn't like heights. Instead of staring at the ground he focused on Isi. He reached behind the boys' heads and ran his finger lightly down her dainty nose. "No bump."

"I was wondering when the swelling went down if I'd be left with a hockey player's snout," she said.

Isi was a pretty girl—any guy would be lucky to have her and the twins.

As long as it's not you.

Startled by the voice in his head, he pulled his arm

back and glanced down too quickly. His head spun and he closed his eyes.

The pressure of a tiny hand on his thigh forced his eyes open. Javier's brow scrunched with worry and Conway grasped his fingers. Javier smiled, the gesture tweaking Conway's heart. He pulled in a deep breath and stared straight ahead, spotting a hot air balloon in the distance. "Check that out, guys." He pointed to the west.

"Can we ride in one of those, Mom?" Miguel asked.

"No, honey," Isi said.

Miguel leaned in front of his brother. "Will you ride in a balloon with me, Conway?"

"Conway's busy with his farm, Miguel," Isi said before he could answer the boy.

After one more rotation, the ride ended. "What's next?" Conway asked.

Javier motioned to a game booth where a girl held a giant stuffed polar bear. "Win us one of those, Conway."

"Yeah—" Miguel chimed in "—win us a bear."

Nothing like pressure. "Let's go see." Conway had been the second-string pitcher on his high-school baseball team—he ought to be able to knock over a few milk bottles.

"Five balls for five dollars! Everyone wins a prize!" The carnival worker shouted at the passing crowd.

"I might need a few warm-up throws," Conway said. Ten dollars later, he still hadn't thrown a strike.

"That's okay, we don't need a bear." Javier was letting Conway off the hook and that made him feel worse.

"You can do it." Miguel didn't want Conway to give up.

"Boys, we've spent enough money. Let's find a new

game." Isi attempted to steer the twins away from the booth.

Miguel wouldn't be deterred. "Wait, Mom. Conway can do it."

The boys had too much faith in him and he didn't want to disappoint them. "I'll give it one more try." He handed the carnival worker a ten-dollar bill and ignored the soreness in his elbow as he wound up for the throw.

No luck. When the booth attendant handed Conway his last ball, he whispered, "Don't throw so hard and hit the pin left of the center."

Conway threw the ball and the milk bottles tumbled like dominos.

"You did it, Conway!" Miguel jumped up and down and Javier clapped his hands.

He high-fived the boys, relieved he hadn't made a fool of himself in front of Isi.

Since when have you ever cared what Isi thinks of you?

Since he didn't know when—he just did.

The game attendant handed the boys the huge polar bear, which had ended up costing Conway forty dollars. "I'll take the bear to the truck." He handed Isi a twenty. "Buy the boys some cotton candy and I'll catch up with you."

"Meet us at the Scrambler," she said.

Later when Conway arrived at the ride, Isi said, "Perfect timing." Their turn came, but she blocked Miguel from boarding first. "Let Conway sit on the end, then me, then you two."

"You don't want them to sit between us?" Conway asked.

"The person who boards first gets smashed the worst during this ride."

With Isi pressed tightly against his side, it was impossible not to breathe in the scent of her perfume. Conway broke out in a sweat that had nothing to do with the sun beating down on his head.

The ride began, building momentum, pushing Isi's body into his. He swore the friction between their limbs was going to set their clothes on fire. Her laughter rang out along with the boys, but Conway didn't find anything funny about the feel of Isi's breast rubbing his arm.

When the ride slowed down, her gaze connected with his. He'd lost himself in Isi's eyes before but had never felt short of breath like he did now.

When the ride came to a complete stop, the attendant released the safety latch on the seat and they piled out. As they walked away, Conway heard someone call his name and he stopped. An attractive blonde waved a balloon in the air. *Sara...* He couldn't recall her last name. Sara approached with a child in tow and Conway felt Isi stiffen next to him.

"Long time no see, Conway."

"Sara, this is Isi and her sons Javier and Miguel. Isi, this is Sara…"

"Reynolds." Sara stroked the girl's hair. "My niece, Tiffany."

"Nice to meet you," Isi said, noticing Sara's perplexed expression.

"I never expected to run into you at a kids' carnival," Sara said.

The lightbulb finally went off inside Isi's head. Sara had been the woman Conway had dated this past February. He'd told Isi that he believed she'd been *the one* but like all the other women he'd pursued, Sara hadn't been truthful in the beginning with him about wanting children. It wasn't until they'd been together almost a month that she'd admitted she'd like a baby one day.

There was no mistaking the predatory gleam in Sara's eye—obviously she believed Conway had changed his mind about children. Isi might as well set the woman straight. "Conway, take the boys to get a hot dog. I'll catch up in a minute."

Isi told herself she was looking out for Conway's best interests and warning Sara away from him had nothing to do with her own growing feelings for the cowboy.

After Conway took Miguel and Javier by the hand and walked off, Sara asked, "Are you two dating?"

"No, we're just friends."

Sara sighed dramatically. "Conway and I dated for a brief time."

"I know. You're Miss February." Isi enjoyed Sara's startled expression. If she recalled correctly, Miss February had a killer body but was also spoiled and demanding. "Conway and I talk a lot."

"He said he didn't want kids. That's why we broke up."

Isi had advised Conway to be up front about his feelings toward children before he got serious with any woman.

"I don't understand why he has such an aversion to kids. He seems comfortable with your boys," Sara said.

"That's because he's not responsible for them."

"Too bad. He'd make a great father."

Isi agreed. She thought back to all their talks but couldn't recall Conway ever revealing the reason behind his objection to fatherhood.

Sara dragged her gaze from Conway's retreating figure. "He's such a hottie."

That was Conway—making women's hearts throb all over southern Arizona. "I better go," Isi said. "Nice meeting you, Sara."

"You, too."

As Isi hurried to catch up with Conway and the boys, she wondered if spending time with the twins would show him that having children could actually strengthen a couple's relationship.

How would you know?

Fine. She didn't know if her theory was right or wrong, but couldn't a girl dream of finding a man who'd love her and be a loving father to her sons? The twins were Isi's whole world and she'd never take a chance on a man who didn't treat her sons as if they were his own.

Conway would never be that man, but it didn't hurt to pretend they were a family—for today anyway.

"You think they'll sleep through the night?" Conway asked when Isi tiptoed from the boys' bedroom Saturday night.

"I hope so," she said. "Are you in a hurry, or do you have time to sit outside and drink a glass of lemonade?"

"I'm not in a rush to leave." Heck, his plans for the day had been shot a long time ago. He'd woken this morning, intending to take Isi and the boys to the carnival for a couple of hours, then head back to the farm to work. Instead, he'd spent the whole day with the little family. And he didn't understand why that didn't bother him more.

"Here you go." She handed him a plastic cup filled with pink lemonade and they went outside on the porch.

They sat in silence, listening to crickets chirp. A breeze blew the faint scent of Isi's perfume past his nose, reminding him that he found her attractive, and nice and smart. And it depressed him. Why did all the perfect women either have kids or want them?

"Thank you for being kind to Miguel and Javier, Conway."

"They're good boys. You've done a great job raising them." He tapped his cup against hers. "To superhero moms."

"I was terrified when I brought the boys home from the hospital."

Conway gaped at Isi.

"What's the matter?" she asked.

"I just realized…"

"What?"

"I don't know much about you and your family."

"I didn't know you were interested in pecan farming. That took me by surprise." She winked and Conway felt an electric zap in his chest.

He cleared his throat. "I've always possessed a connection to the land but then I grew up and—" he flashed a grin "—became popular with the ladies and forgot all about pecans."

"What changed your mind about becoming more involved with the farm?"

"Johnny wasn't able to find an agricultural company to lease the orchards, so I stepped up and said I'd bring in this year's crop." He chugged the lemonade. "Time will tell if I'm able to turn a profit."

"Do you still plan to lease the groves?"

"Depends on how things go with the harvest." If the nuts brought in enough money to cover expenses, he was certain his siblings would approve of him taking over the farm on a permanent basis.

"Are your brothers helping you?"

"Nope. It's all on my shoulders."

"Isn't that going to cut into your rodeo schedule?" she asked.

Heck, it wasn't the orchards that interfered with rodeo—it was Isi and her sons. "I'll catch a rodeo here or there."

"Oh, dear." Her brow scrunched.

"What?"

"Missing all those rodeos is going to decrease your chances of finding *the one*."

"I suppose I'll have to hunt for my true love at farm auctions." He sobered. "You did it again."

"Did what?"

"Steered the subject back to me." He set his empty glass aside. "Tell me about your family."

"I don't like to talk about them."

"Why not?"

"Because when I block out the past, I'm less frightened of the future."

Her honesty caught Conway by surprise. He'd never pictured Isi as a woman intimidated by anything. "Tell me. Please."

After a long exhale, she said, "I was born in La Boca, a poor neighborhood in Buenos Aires, Argentina."

"Argentina? I assumed you were from Mexico."

She rolled her eyes. "One of the first things I learned coming to the Unites States was that most people assume anyone who speaks Spanish is from Mexico."

"Do you miss Argentina?" he asked.

"Yes, but I'd never go back."

"What happened to your family?"

"One morning my father went to work at the factory and he never came home. I was five years old. My twin brothers were eleven. My mother waited an entire week and when my father still hadn't returned, she took me with her to the police station to report him missing."

When Isi went silent, he asked, "Did they find your father?"

"No. It was as if he'd vanished into thin air. My mother was a housemaid for a well-to-do family but in order to cover our rent, she had to pick up a second job cleaning business offices at night. My brothers and I were left on our own."

"But you were only a year older than Miguel and Javier." Conway couldn't imagine leaving a young child home alone all day and night.

"Three or four months after my father disappeared, my mother received an eviction notice because she'd fallen behind on the rent. My brothers dropped out of school, joined a gang and sold drugs to help keep a roof over our heads."

"Your mother allowed your brothers to do that?"

"She wasn't the same after my father disappeared. She went through the motions for us kids but a part of her died when she lost my dad."

"How long were your brothers in the gang?"

"Almost four years. They'd bring me supper in the evenings and ask about my school day then take off again and spend the rest of the night on the streets."

"What happened to them?"

"I was nine when they didn't show up at the apartment with my supper. The next morning the police knocked on our door and told my mother that her sons had been gunned down in a drug raid."

Conway squeezed Isi's hand. "I'm sorry." Sorry didn't convey the hurt he felt for her.

"My mother cried for days, missing work at both her jobs. Then one morning she said, 'Isadora, you will stay in school and graduate.' Then we moved out of the apartment and rented a room in a boarding house, where I helped with chores in exchange for my meals."

"And you stayed in school?"

"I went to class every day and studied hard. I learned English and promised my mother that one day we would move to the U.S. and make a better life for ourselves. After I completed my education, I got a job tutoring students in English and I began saving money. Then my mother was hit by a bus on her way to work."

Conway couldn't find his voice to express his sympathy.

"There were a lot of pedestrian accidents in the city and my mother wasn't paying attention when she crossed against the light."

At eighteen Isi had been the only surviving member of her family. His chest physically ached as he envisioned her burying her mother next to her brothers and an empty grave for her father.

"I had an aunt and uncle who lived in Buenos Aires, but they didn't offer to take me in, so I packed my bags and came to the U.S. by myself."

"Your mother would be proud of you."

"I hope so."

"Are the twins named after their uncles?"

"Yes."

"The boys are lucky to have you for a mother. They're going to grow up to be fine men."

"I want them to have a good life and be happy."

"Mind if I ask who Miguel and Javier's father is?"

"Tyler Smith," she said.

"The bull rider?"

"That's him."

Smith was in his early thirties and was the construction foreman for Desert Builders—a company that competed against Will's boss for projects in the Yuma area.

"I'd gotten a work permit in the U.S. and began waitressing at the pancake house on Main Street when Tyler walked in after a rodeo and asked me out on a date." She sighed. "I knew he was trouble, but he was handsome and I was lonely."

Conway clenched his jaw, refusing to picture Isi with Tyler. "What did he say when you told him you were pregnant?"

"He insisted the baby wasn't his." Isi's soft brown eyes implored Conway to believe her. "I didn't cheat on Tyler."

"He's an ass." A surge of protectiveness filled Conway. Isi had no one to defend her and a part of him wanted to confront Smith and demand he do right by his sons.

"You know what?" she said. "All the times you've talked about your family, you've never mentioned your father."

"I told you that my brothers—"

"I know you were all fathered by different men, but how did growing up without a father affect you?"

"I never really gave it much thought." He hoped Isi wouldn't read the truth in his eyes. When he'd been a kid, Conway had thought about his father a lot. It wasn't until after he met the man that he quit thinking about him.

"Does it bother you that he wasn't involved in your life?" Isi asked.

"Not really." His standard response—the one he gave to avoid telling the truth.

"Right now the boys are young and they don't know any different because Tyler hasn't been involved in their life, but I worry that down the road they'll ask why he never visits."

The twins would ask. And when Isi's explanation wasn't good enough, her sons would go to bed at night feeling sick to their stomachs like Conway had.

"Javier is more sensitive than Miguel. I worry he'll believe there's something wrong with him and that's the reason Tyler doesn't visit." She nudged Conway's side. "Is that how you felt when your father stayed away?"

Conway didn't know how to address Isi's concern without making her more anxious. It had bothered the hell out of Conway that his father hadn't wanted a relationship with him, but after meeting the man, he didn't see any point in getting to know him better. "I had my brothers and grandfather to make up for an absentee father."

"It's amazing the changes I've seen in the boys since you began watching them. Javier isn't as shy and Miguel is more cooperative." She finished her drink and set the cup aside. "Once I graduate and find a full-time professional job, I'll get back into dating. You've proven to me that the boys need a male in their lives."

"Don't rush into anything. It'd be worse for Javi and Mig if you date a guy and break up with him soon after."

"True, but there will come a time when I'm going to have to take a leap of faith."

Conway stood. He didn't care to discuss Isi's plans for her love life. "I better head to the farm."

She followed him to his truck. "Thanks for spending the day with us. I enjoyed the carnival as much as the boys did."

"See you on Monday." He offered a quick wave then drove off. The trip to the farm lasted forever as Isi's words rang through his head....

I'm going to have to take a leap of faith.

With his paternal family history a leap of faith was the worst thing Conway could take. After spending a week with Javier and Miguel he admitted that he enjoyed being with the twins, but he wasn't so naive as to assume the fun and newness wouldn't eventually wear off and be replaced by the heavier burden of responsibility. And then what? Would the itch to move on hit him?

As much as he might be tempted to open himself up to dating single mothers or women who wanted children, the risks were too great.

Chapter 6

Thursday night Isi marked off the last day in October on the calendar. November sure had taken its sweet time arriving. She'd been buried under midterm exams on top of waitressing at the bar, but it was more than school and work that had caused the days to crawl by—she and Conway hadn't spent much time together.

And she hadn't expected to miss him.

After Erica had left for California, Conway had been the only person she'd had regular contact with outside school and her job. Listening to Conway's girl troubles had made her feel connected to the real world. The two weeks that had passed since the carnival made her admit how alone she and the boys really were. She wished she could go back to the days when Conway swaggered into the bar after a rodeo and flashed his sexy grin. Now, she woke each morning to the boys chattering about the fun they'd had the previous day with Conway.

You're jealous.

She was jealous of her sons and wished she could switch places with them. She wanted to ride the tractor with Conway and learn how to shell pecans. She wanted to watch TV in the bunkhouse where Conway and his brothers slept. And she wanted to see Conway hold Dixie's son, Nathan, and stop him from crying.

Blast it, she wanted to see and experience all the things her sons had with Conway, but not once had he asked her to visit the farm. She didn't understand why he was pulling away from her, especially after the day they'd spent at the carnival. The heated looks they'd exchanged and Conway's accidental touches proved their attraction to one another was as strong and hot as it had been two years ago when they'd first met.

She wasn't foolish enough to believe she might be Conway's *the one,* but at the pace he was going, he might not find that woman for years. In the meantime, why couldn't they flirt? And if flirting led to sex…was that so terrible? She was a grown woman—a mother of four-year-old twins, whose sex life was as dry as the desert landscape outside the trailer. Didn't she deserve a night of steamy sex once in a blue moon? She'd never been promiscuous. The boy's father had only been the second man she'd slept with—the first had been her high school crush, but they'd been forced to break up when his parents discovered she lived in La Boca.

The twins were getting the best of Conway—why couldn't she have the best of him, too, for a short while?

"When's Conway gonna get here?" Miguel stood by the window.

"Soon," Isi said. Conway had offered to take Miguel and Javier trick-or-treating because Red had scheduled her to work at the bar tonight. When Sasha learned that Isi wouldn't be able to go trick-or-treating with the boys, she'd insisted on covering Isi's shift. Isi had texted Conway that he was off the hook, but he still wanted to go out with them.

She studied her son's costumes. The superpower duo had been decided upon months ago, making it easy for Isi to save the money and buy them before the stores sold out. Miguel was Captain America and Javier was the Green Lantern. "Let me take your picture." She grabbed the disposable camera and moved closer. "Smile." One day when she had the money, she intended to make a scrapbook using the photos she'd taken through the years and then add the few pictures she had of her brothers, mother and father, so the twins wouldn't forget their family.

"What are you, Mom?" Javier asked.

"I'm a sheriff, silly." She'd worn tight-fitting jeans and strapped the boys play pistol belt around her hips then pinned a sheriff's star to her long-sleeved Western shirt. Her straw cowboy hat and leather cowboy boots completed the outfit.

A knock on the trailer door sent the boys running across the room.

"Is that you, Conway?" Miguel shouted, his hand on the knob.

"It's me."

Miguel opened the door and Javier's face lit up with excitement. "What superhero are you, Conway?"

"I'm not a superhero, Javi. I'm a caveman."

Isi nearly swallowed her tongue when Conway stepped into the trailer wearing a fur cape. Her gaze traveled over his muscular bare chest, across his leatherlike kilt and down his naked legs—which she'd never seen before now—to the flip-flops on his feet.

"What's a caveman?" Miguel asked.

"A man who lives in a cave." Conway smiled.

Isi couldn't take her eyes off him. He'd thought of all the details—a battery-operated torch and armbands that showed off his biceps muscles. He'd spiked his sandy hair with gel, leaving the ends sticking up in all directions. He was the sexiest caveman she'd ever seen.

Fighting a smile she said, "For a cowboy you sure have tan legs."

"There's a swimming hole at the farm," he said.

"How come we don't get to go swimming?" Miguel asked.

"Because I don't know if you guys can swim."

"They've never had lessons," Isi said.

"Maybe next spring when the water warms up, I'll teach you two how to swim."

Isi winced at Conway's promise. Spring was a long way off and what if he found *the one* before the pond warmed up?

"Mom's a sheriff," Javier said.

Conway studied her outfit then he flashed a sexy grin and raised his hands in the air. "I surrender."

The boys giggled, but Isi wasn't laughing at the heat in Conway's eyes. She swallowed hard when she imagined his strong, naked legs entwined with hers on the bed in the room at the back of the trailer.

"Conway switched his attention to the boys. "What superheroes are you guys?"

"I'm Captain America," Miguel said, then motioned to his brother. "Javi's the Green Lantern."

"See?" Javier held out his hand.

Conway examined the plastic ring on Javi's finger. "What does it do?"

Miguel answered for his brother. "Javi has to think real hard and then he can make stuff happen."

"And Captain America can throw his shield and it'll come back to him," Javi said.

"You guys will give Superman a run for his money." Conway turned to Isi. "Ready to leave?"

"Let me take a picture." She'd buy double prints of the photo—one for the scrapbook and one for her night-stand drawer. "Move next to Conway." Isi snapped the photo. "Go fetch your candy bags." The boys raced to their room.

"Where do you usually trick-or-treat?" Conway asked. "In the trailer park?"

"Not many of the neighbors hand out candy, so I take the boys to the mall. Most of the merchants give out treats."

"I have a better idea. One of Dixie's friends lives a few miles away in a subdivision. We'll go there."

"Are you sure we're allowed to do that?"

"Dixie used to trick-or-treat there when she was younger."

"The boys would love to walk from house to house with other kids," she said. Once the twins returned with their bags, they piled into Conway's truck.

As they drove through town, Isi couldn't stop her-self from admiring Conway's naked thighs and the way the muscles bunched when he pressed the brake or ac-celerator. She recalled the first time he walked into the bar and turned his smile on her—she'd almost fainted. And for a short while she'd lived in a fantasy world, be-lieving Conway might be her "the one." Once she understood how strongly he opposed becoming a father, she'd accepted that they'd only ever be friends. Would he rethink his stance on fatherhood after helping her with the boys, or was she reading too much into the time he spent with them?

"Hey, Conway," Javier said.

"What?"

"When I grow up I'm gonna be a farmer like you."

Isi smiled.

"I'm gonna ride broncs like you," Miguel chimed in.

"When I grow up," Conway said. "I want to go to Tiny Tot Learn and Play like you guys."

The boys erupted in laughter, but Isi wasn't smiling. She stared out the window at the passing cars and second-guessed her decision to allow Conway to take care of her sons. She'd believed the boys would benefit from having a man in their lives, but she hadn't considered how the twins would react when Conway stopped coming by.

You'll have to find a man to replace him.

No one could replace Conway, but the idea had merit. If she had a boyfriend by the time she graduated, then when Conway quit babysitting, the twins wouldn't feel his loss as deeply.

Conway turned into a neighborhood and parked at the end of a block. "This is a good place to start." After they got out of the truck, he said, "You guys stick together. Don't walk off by yourself."

As they followed the boys, Isi whispered, "You'd better be careful, you're sounding like a father."

"Sorry, that slipped out."

"No need to apologize. You've been watching the boys almost a month. It's only natural for you to take charge." And surprisingly it didn't bother Isi that he took the lead with her sons. After four years of having sole responsibility for the twins, she enjoyed the brief respite.

Isi and Conway waited on the sidewalk as Miguel and Javier walked up to the first door. "Don't forget to say thank you," she called after them.

Miguel rang the bell and they hollered, "Trick-or-treat!" After receiving their candy they shouted a thank-you then cut across the lawn to the next house.

"The weather's beautiful tonight," she said, feeling nervous as she walked beside Conway.

"You can't beat southern Arizona in the fall." Conway set his hand against her lower back and guided her through a crowd of kids. They continued walking, but he didn't remove his hand, and Isi's pulsed raced as the skin beneath his touch warmed.

"You look hot in your sheriff's getup," he whispered in her ear.

"I bet you say that to all the ladies." She forced a smile. "Speaking of ladies…we haven't talked about your latest 'the one.'"

"Who's that?"

She shrugged. "I assumed you'd found a new woman."

"Between watching the boys and working on the farm I haven't had time to date."

They strolled to the next house in silence, Isi lost in thought. She'd been so relieved when Conway had volunteered to take care of the boys while she finished out the semester that she hadn't given a thought to how it would affect his personal life. "I'll keep searching for a permanent sitter."

"Why?"

"Because you said you don't have any time to yourself."

"Neither do you."

"I'm not supposed to. I'm a single mother."

"Mom!" Javier raced toward her, holding out his bag. "The lady gave us a giant candy bar."

"She sure did." Isi waved at the woman. "Did you thank her?"

"Yep." Miguel pointed to the house at the end of street where a large crowd of kids gathered. "She said that man gives out lot of treats to kids who don't get scared and run away."

"It's a haunted house," Isi said.

Miguel tugged his brother's arm. "C'mon, Javi."

The boys ran off and Isi and Conway both called, "Stay together!"

"We'd better catch up." Conway took Isi's hand and they walked fast, keeping the boys in sight.

"This guy went all out," Conway said.

Ghosts hung from tree branches. Skulls and skeletal hands stuck out of the ground next to tombstones. The dark porch was filled with cobwebs and scary music blasted from an open window. The front door had been covered in white butcher paper with the words *Keep Out* painted in red.

The boys were at the back of the line, so Isi settled in for a long wait. "You've more than made up for Bridget punching me in the nose, Conway. There's no reason your love life should suffer any longer."

The heat in his eyes burned the side of her neck. "Is that all you think I care about—having sex?"

The group of women standing nearby stopped talking. Isi lowered her voice. "C'mon, Conway. It's me, Isi, you're talking to. Finding 'the one' has been your main preoccupation since we met two years ago."

"Hey, a guy's entitled to take a break from romance every now and then."

She snorted.

"I'm not a stud machine who can switch on and off, you know."

"I'm still going to try to find a sitter."

They stood for a few more minutes, watching the fray of kids then Conway stiffened next to her. "I see Miguel, but where's Javier?" He didn't wait for Isi to respond before charging up the sidewalk. "Javi?" he shouted.

Miguel raced toward Conway.

"Where's Javi, Mig?" Isi asked when she caught up.

"He was next to me when the man gave us candy."

"Did he go inside the house, Miguel?" Conway asked.

"No, the man didn't open the door."

Conway noticed a hand poked through the hole in the paper that covered the door and dropped candy into the waiting bags." He glanced down the block. "I'll follow that group. You two stay here in case Javier comes back."

Heart racing, Conway caught up to the mass of goblins and fairies. One by one he surveyed the kids' costumes but didn't see a Green Lantern in the group. Panic squeezed his gut. Javier had most likely gotten swallowed up by a wave of kids as they passed by him.

Where are you, Javi?

If Conway hadn't suggested trick-or-treating in a larger neighborhood, the boy wouldn't have gotten lost. He reached the end of the block then called Javier's name.

"Excuse me. Did you lose your child?" A woman pushing a stroller approached Conway.

"Yes, ma'am. He's wearing a green superhero costume. Have you seen him?"

"I'm sorry, I haven't." She motioned to a crowd up the block. "That's our church group. We'll keep an eye out for him."

"Thanks. His name's Javier." Conway jogged ahead of the group and caught the next crowd. "Has anyone seen a kid wearing a Green Lantern costume?"

The children shook their heads and Conway's chest felt as though it would explode from fear. There was no way Javier could have walked much farther. When he turned the next corner, he spotted a woman standing on a front lawn, holding Javier's hand.

Thank God. He hurried toward them. When Javier noticed him, he raced to Conway.

Weak with relief Conway dropped to one knee on the sidewalk and hugged the boy. "I'm glad you're okay, buddy."

"I told him that his mother or father would find him." The lady held the hand of a ballerina in a pink tutu.

"Thank you for watching out for him," Conway said.

"Stay by your father now." The lady smiled then walked off with her daughter.

Conway was so relieved he'd found Javier unharmed that he didn't care if the woman thought they were father and son. "Why did you leave your brother?"

Javier squeezed Conway's neck and sobbed.

"Whoa, buddy. You're safe now."

"I didn't run off." Javier's chest shuddered when he took a deep breath. "Mig left me."

"Mig didn't leave you, Javi. He's still back at the haunted house."

"I couldn't see him."

"It's all right. All that matters is you're safe. Let's find your mom." Instead of holding Javier's hand, Conway scooped him off the ground and carried him. As his heart rate slowed, his thoughts raced. The boy had been lucky tonight—he could have been abducted by a crazy pedophile. Losing track of Javier was more proof that Conway wasn't meant to be a father. He just couldn't handle the responsibility or worry that came with keeping kids safe.

As he drew closer to the haunted house, Isi hurried toward them. "Javi, where were you?"

Conway set the boy on the ground and Javi shoved Miguel. "You left me!"

"No, I didn't!" Miguel pushed Javier back and the boys tumbled to the ground.

Conway snagged the backs of their costumes, holding them apart while their tiny fists pummeled the air.

"Stop right now or we go home," Isi said.

"You left me," Miguel said.

"Did not!"

"Did, too!"

"We're done for the night." Isi took Javier's hand and motioned for Conway to hold Miguel's, but the kid crossed his arms over his chest and marched off behind his mother and brother.

Conway followed. After a block Miguel whispered, "I didn't leave, Javi."

"It's easy to lose track of each other in a crowd," Conway said.

"It's not fair."

"What's not fair?" Conway slowed his steps so their conversation wouldn't be overheard by Isi and Javier.

"Mom always makes me take care of Javi."

Conway felt bad for Miguel. He had to find a way to salvage the night. Halloween came once a year and he hated for the boys to go home mad at each other with only a handful of candy in their bags.

When they reached the truck, the twins hopped in back, refusing to speak to each other. Conway pulled away from the curb and said, "I've got an idea."

"What's that?" Isi asked.

"Have the boys ever been to a drive-in theater?"

"What's a drive-in theater?" Miguel asked.

"A place you can watch movies in your car." Conway shrugged. "We could see what's playing?"

"But a movie rewards them for being naughty," Isi said.

"Maybe you could put off their punishment until to-morrow?" Conway pointed to the boys. "They look so sad."

Isi almost laughed when her sons' mouths pouted and they batted their eyelashes at her. "If we go to the movie that means no TV tomorrow. Understood?"

The twins nodded.

By the time Conway backed into a parking spot at the rear of the drive-in the second movie was beginning— *Invasion of the Spiders*. He helped the boys out of their booster seats then lifted them into the truck bed.

"I can't hear anything," Miguel complained.

Conway turned on the outdoor speakers.

"Cool," Miguel said.

"Yeah, cool." Javier smiled at his brother and the boys were back to being best friends.

"Who wants popcorn?" Conway asked.

The twins raised their hands.

"What kind of sodas?" Conway asked Isi.

"No soda. They can share a bottle of water."

Conway left to buy the snacks, and when he returned the twins were lying down and Isi leaned against the cab at the back of the truck bed. He crawled over the boys and joined Isi. They shared a bag of popcorn in silence. It wasn't long before her sons dozed off, and Conway watched Isi instead of the movie. Without thinking, he tucked a strand of hair behind her ear.

"I've never been to a drive-in," she said.

"Really?"

"I'm guessing you've broken your fair share of hearts in the back row."

"You'd guess wrong. You're the first woman I've been with at a drive-in."

"No way."

"Yes way. I've been here twice with my brothers when we were younger and once with Dixie after she coerced me into taking her and a group of her junior high friends."

"I'm your first official drive-in date?" she asked.

"Yes, ma'am."

"You were always the one who did most of the talking in our relationship," Isi said. "Now I need your advice."

"Sure."

"After my experience with Tyler, I've avoided dating, believing I was better off raising the boys on my own."

"I sense a *but* coming," he said.

"But seeing how happy Javi and Mig are after they spend time with you…" She took a deep breath. "Do I need to get out there and start dating again?"

Conway felt a stitch in his side and winced. "It doesn't matter what I think. You have to do what's best for you and the boys."

"What if I date a guy I like, but the boys don't like him? That could be a disaster. Maybe I should focus on finding a man who wants to be friends but enjoys being with the boys."

"You know what?" Conway said. "You're nothing like the women I date."

She laughed. "You just figured that out?"

"Seriously. The women I end up with only think about themselves. You think about the boys."

"I'm their mother, Conway. The boys will always come first."

"I understand you wanting the best for Mig and Javi, but what if after a while the guy wants more than friendship from you?"

"That would be great," she said, surprising Conway. "I'm only telling you this because we're friends and you won't blab to anyone." She leaned closer. "I haven't had sex since I got pregnant with the boys."

Wow.

"I'm in a four-year drought and right now sex with a guy friend seems mighty appealing."

Conway couldn't shake the image of a faceless man stripping Isi of her clothes.

"It's time I find a man who'll be good for the boys and for me."

Conway didn't think that was a smart idea at all. "You're the boss," he said, reluctantly.

"What do you mean?"

He tapped the plastic star on her shirt. "You're in charge."

"You're right. A sheriff calls the shots." She smiled. "It's not like I haven't had offers." She'd been hit on at the bar a number of times. The heat radiating off

Conway's body interfered with her concentration. She scooted over until his bare thigh no longer brushed against her leg.

"Aren't you concerned about how the twins will react if you bring home a boyfriend?" Conway asked.

"Not anymore."

"What changed your mind?"

"You."

"Me? What did I do?"

"The boys love being with you. It's obvious they're starved for male attention."

"Whatever guy you date isn't going to be me."

She punched him playfully in the arm. "You're full of yourself."

"Hey, I'm being honest."

"I'm guessing the boys will measure any man I date against you and find him lacking, but you're not going to be here forever." She snapped her fingers. "Maybe I should date behind the boys' backs until I find the right man to introduce to them to."

"That's a good idea." Conway grinned despite his reservations. "I wouldn't want your new man to jeopardize my rock-star status with Javi and Mig."

Chapter 7

The first week of November was drawing to a close. Conway stood in the pecan orchard and peered into the canopy of a tree.

"What are we looking for?" Javier asked.

"I'm not sure." Conway had followed his grandfather through the groves many times and every few trees he'd stop and study the leafy branches—as if he sensed which ones would yield the most nuts. Conway checked over his shoulder, making sure Miguel remained in sight. That kid was definitely not a farmer. He couldn't stand or sit still for more than a few minutes, unlike Javier who had the patience of Job and did whatever Conway asked of him.

"What do you think, Javi? Is this tree going to drop a lot of nuts when I bring the shaker machine through?"

"I don't see any nuts."

Conway lifted the boy above his head. "Grab hold of that branch and climb up."

"Me, too!" Miguel raced toward Conway.

Once Javier had settled on a limb, Conway said, "Don't fall." The last thing he wanted to do was call Isi and tell her that one of the boys had broken an arm or leg.

Miguel impatiently hopped up and down, waiting his turn. Conway hoisted him into the tree. "Pick a branch and count the nuts on it."

The boys called out different numbers. After a few seconds, they counted in unison. Javier stumbled at fifty, but Miguel corrected him and they continued until they reached a hundred.

"There's got to be more than a hundred nuts on that branch," Conway said. The boys ignored him and started a pecan war.

"Hey!" Conway said when he felt a nut ping his head.

The boys giggled as they bombarded each other. Conway scooped a fistful of nuts off the ground and joined the battle. The twins combined forces against Conway and he shouted, "No throwing at the face!" As soon as he turned his back to gather more ammunition, the boys pelted his butt with nuts. "You'll pay for that."

"Who are you talking to?" Isi walked toward Conway, her gaze scanning the trees.

"Where'd you come from?" Conway couldn't stop staring at her tight-fitting jeans—the ones that hugged her fanny to perfection and sported tiny tears in the thighs.

"My class was canceled." She shrugged. "So I drove out here to see my favorite guys before I go to work." The warmth in her brown eyes convinced Conway that he was included in Isi's group of favorite guys.

"Where are the boys?" She stopped next to him.

"Up here." Miguel poked his head through the branches.

Isi moved closer but froze when a pecan flew past her face. "Miguel! You better not throw any nuts at me, young man."

The boys scrambled to a lower branch and Conway lifted them out of the tree and set them on the ground.

Isi threw a pecan at Miguel, hitting him in the chest then she tossed a nut at Javier. "Got you both."

Miguel collected ammunition from the ground and Conway handed the nuts he'd collected to Javier.

"No fair." Isi ran off, dodging pecans as the boys chased her through the trees.

"Don't let her get away!" Conway jogged after the group.

The boys' laughter and Isi's squeals filled the groves, reminding Conway of days gone by when he and his siblings had played tag in the orchard. It wasn't long before the twins ran out of gas and stopped, their chests heaving as they sucked in air. Isi bent at the waist, gasping for breath.

"I'm out of shape." She laughed.

"We helped Conway count pecans," Javier said.

"And I helped rake the branches." Miguel neglected to tell his mother that he'd raked for two minutes before handing the chore over to his brother.

"You guys go ask Porter for a drink of water," Conway said.

"C'mon, Javi, maybe we can share Porter's Skittles." The boys raced to the bunkhouse.

Isi watched her sons run off. "I thought bunkhouses were like big log cabins not giant metal sheds."

"The Cash brothers aren't your traditional cowboys." He grinned.

She scuffed the toe of her shoe in the dirt and he had a hunch she hadn't dropped by the farm for a visit.

"What's on your mind?" he asked.

"I need a favor."

"What kind of favor?"

"Would you be willing to stay later than usual tonight to watch the boys?"

"Got a hot date?"

"As a matter of fact, I do."

A sudden coldness gripped his chest. "Really?"

"Yes, really." Frowning, she said, "I told you I wanted to start dating again."

He thought she'd been venting in the back of his pickup Halloween night. "Who are you going out with?"

"Sean Mason."

"The name doesn't sound familiar. Does he rodeo?"

"I'm not sure. Sasha set me up with him. He's been to the bar a few times."

"What else do you know about this guy? You can't be too careful these days," he said.

"Thank you for being concerned, but I can handle myself."

"Sure, I'll watch the boys." He planned to grill *Sean* after he dropped Isi off.

"Thanks."

The bunkhouse door opened and Javier and Miguel stepped outside, their pockets bulging with candy. "You two be good for Conway." Isi kissed their cheeks. "And don't forget to brush your teeth tonight."

"They'll brush twice." Conway laughed when the twins groaned.

After Isi drove away, he got the weirdest feeling in his gut. He didn't like the idea of her dating a guy she barely knew.

Or maybe he didn't like the idea of Isi dating—period.

This date was a bust.

"You wanna dance?" Sean Mason asked.

I'd rather call it a night. Conway would have pulled out the chair for her, but Sean walked off, expecting her to follow him to the dance floor.

The Desert Lounge in Yuma was a popular dance club where local bands performed for free. The Rattlers provided tonight's entertainment and the middle-aged trio—two guitar players and a drummer—sang country music from days gone by. Sean stopped in the middle of the floor and pulled Isi into his arms, then twirled her in circles. *Show off.*

Once her head stopped spinning, she struggled not to squirm. Nothing felt right about Sean. He was too short. She didn't like the spicy scent of his cologne. His hands were soft. And he rarely smiled.

He's not Conway.

The song ended and the lead singer cleared his throat, the gravelly sound rumbling through the speakers on the stage. "We got any Conway Twitty fans out there tonight?"

Isi's gaze flew to the exit, hoping for the impossible— Conway waltzing through the door.

"Hold your ladies close, cowboys—" the musician grinned "—because…'It's Only Make Believe.'"

When Sean pulled Isi closer, she braced her palm against his shoulder and locked her elbow to keep their bodies from rubbing against each other. What had possessed her to let Sasha set her up on a date?

Conway.

She'd wanted to prove her feelings for Conway were those of a girl with a teenage crush and nothing more. The only thing tonight had established was that she'd rather be with Conway.

A couple bumped into Sean's back and Isi cringed when their lower bodies came in contact and she felt the bulge in his jeans. If the cowboy expected her to invite him into her bed, he was in for a big surprise.

After the song ended, the band took a break, but Sean made no move to leave the dance floor. A quarter found its way into the jukebox and they continued dancing. Isi made a second attempt at conversation. "Sasha said you're a wrangler at a local ranch.

"The Flying S." He didn't elaborate.

Sean hadn't strung more than two sentences together the entire night. Each time she asked him a personal question, he changed the subject. When she attempted to talk about her classes at school, he cut her off and argued that too much education made a person uppity. Who used the word *uppity* anymore? "Any vacation plans for Christmas?"

He shook his head.

She gave up trying to salvage the date. When the song ended, Sean headed back to their table. She'd finished her beer an hour ago, but he hadn't offered to buy her a second. The time on her cell phone showed midnight.

"I better get home," she said. The boys would be up early in the morning.

Without a word, Sean led the way outside to the parking lot. He hopped into his truck—again not bothering to open the passenger side door for her.

No wonder women fawned all over Conway—he was a true gentleman and knew how to treat a lady.

Sean drove Isi to the Border Town Bar & Grill where she'd left her car. As soon as he shifted the truck into park, she opened her door and flashed a quick smile. No sense lying and telling him she'd enjoyed their date. "'Night."

She caught a glimpse of his surprised face as she shut the door. Too bad if he expected a good-night kiss— Conway was the only man she wanted to smooch with. She got into her car and the headlights from Sean's truck moved across her back window when he left the lot.

As Isi drove home, she decided that finding a nice guy to fill the void in her and the boys' lives was going to be more difficult than she thought.

Conway peered between the blinds in the front window of Isi's trailer. He'd put the boys to bed five hours ago then watched a marathon of *Hawaii Five-0* shows on TV. If he heard "Book 'em, Danno" one more time, he'd throw his boot at the wall.

One in the morning. Pretty soon the bars would close down, then where would they go—back to Mason's apartment? Isi was a good mother. She worked hard at school and her job. She deserved to be happy, but not too happy—at least until the end of the semester when his nanny services would no longer be needed.

Isi sleeping with a man bothered him.

No. Yes. Conway's stomach growled. He went into the kitchen and surveyed the contents of the fridge. A few apples and oranges. A plastic container of leftovers.

Two gallons of milk and a variety of condiments. The freezer contained a box of waffles, a bag of French fries and a tub of cheap ice cream.

He moved to the cupboards, finally settling on SpaghettiOs and eating them cold from the can. Finished with his snack he stepped outside and sat on the porch. He dug his cell phone from his pocket for the umpteenth time and checked for messages—none. He was positive that if Isi went to a motel with Mason, she'd let him know she wouldn't be home until morning. Besides, she wasn't the kind of woman to sleep with a guy on the first date.

How do you know? She hasn't had sex in four years.

A pair of headlights turned into the mobile-home park. Conway bolted back inside and switched the TV on so she wouldn't know he'd paced the floor waiting for her. He peeked out the window and watched her park beneath the carport. Why hadn't Mason followed her to make sure she'd gotten home safe?

The trailer door opened and Isi stepped inside.

Conway noticed her neat hair and clothes. Her lips weren't even swollen. He hadn't realized he'd been holding his breath until it whooshed from his body.

"What are you smiling at?" She set her purse on the table.

Unwilling to examine why her neat appearance made him happy, he rubbed a hand down his face, erasing his grin. "How was your date?"

Her eyes shimmered with tears.

Uh-oh. "I take it the evening didn't go well."

"Hardly." She made a move to pass by him, but he snagged her arm.

She looked so dejected he couldn't help himself—he

hugged her. "I'm sorry, Isi." He wasn't really. "What happened?"

"Sean was a jerk."

"You want me to beat him up for you?" he said, hoping to coax a smile out of her.

"No." She wrapped her arms around his waist and snuggled closer. "I never got my good-night kiss."

Don't even think about it. But that's all he'd done tonight—imagined Isi kissing her date. Ignoring the voice in his head warning him not to overstep his bounds, Conway tilted her chin until she made eye contact with him.

"What are you doing?" she whispered.

"Giving you a good-night kiss." The scent of faded perfume and warm woman surrounded him, drawing his mouth closer to hers. He hesitated, waiting to see if she'd pull away. She didn't.

He held himself back, keeping the first press of his mouth against her lips light and gentle, reacquainting himself with their flavor. Their softness. When her mouth relaxed beneath his, he eased his tongue inside and tasted her.

She swayed closer, her fingers fluttered over his ribs. A groan rumbled through his chest when her small breasts flattened against him. Could she feel his heart pound?

He was playing with fire, but he relished the burn and deepened the kiss. She didn't shy away. Instead, she grew bolder, engaging in a game of dueling tongues that robbed him of oxygen. He had to end this insanity before he lifted her into his arms and carried her into the bedroom.

He broke off the kiss and stepped back. She stared wide-eyed, pressing her fingers against her moist lips.

Neither said a word for the longest time, then she asked, "Do you kiss all your first dates like that?"

"Sorry, I got carried away." He sensed Isi would have allowed him get a lot carried away if he'd wanted to.

Needing a moment to gather her wits, Isi walked into the kitchen and got a drink of water. Good Lord, Conway's kiss had sucked all the oxygen out of her, leaving her light-headed. She set the empty cup in the sink and faced him. "I'm not giving up." There had to be a man whose kiss could rock her world the way Conway's had. "Just because Sean turned out to be a dud doesn't mean the next guy will be one, too. I'll ask Sasha if she—"

"After tonight I wouldn't trust Sasha to find you a date," he said.

"I need a friend to set me up, because I'm not the kind of girl who asks guys out."

"I'll find you a date," Conway said.

"Seriously?"

He nodded.

"It would be nice to go on a date before Thanksgiving."

"Done."

She didn't know whether to be miffed or appreciative that Conway was eager to push her off on another guy. "No jerks."

"Don't worry. The man I find for you will be harmless."

He was in trouble. *Big trouble.*

Conway sped down the highway toward Stagecoach, putting as many miles between him and the Desert Valley Mobile Home Park as fast as possible.

He'd been a fool to kiss Isi, but her sad eyes had

begged him to erase the bad memory of her date with jerk Mason.

Don't blame Mason. You've been waiting for an excuse to kiss Isi for a long time.

He clenched the wheel tighter until his knuckles ached. He'd wanted to kiss Isi since he'd begun watching the twins. It wasn't a big deal. He'd kissed her before—

A long time ago.

Maybe, but he hadn't forgotten how great that kiss had been.

You got it out of your system, now forget it.

Easier said than done. Their kiss tonight had proven that the attraction he'd felt for Isi the first time he'd met her hadn't faded with time as he'd believed.

Why Isi? She'd be the perfect woman for him—if she didn't have the twins. He felt sorry for the boys growing up without a dad. Conway knew what it felt like and he wished differently for the boys. It was because he felt protective of Isi and her sons that he wanted to find her a decent man.

You mean possessive, not protective.

The damned voice in his head playing devil's advocate irritated the hell out of him.

Conway ran through a mental list of his rodeo buddies not sure who he could trust with Isi. They were good guys, but they were rodeo cowboys—anything could happen. There had to be a man who'd treat Isi like a lady and not push her into doing more than she was ready for.

Will.

Finally the voice in his head had said something worth listening to.

Why not his older brother? Will had quit chasing after buckle bunnies years ago. He was older than Isi, mature and harmless. He'd treat her right and show her a good time without coming on strong.

Problem solved. Now all he had to do was convince Will to go along with his plan.

Sunday morning Conway poked his head inside the bunkhouse door. Will sat at the table, leafing through the Home Depot ads while Buck and Porter played a game of chess. "Hey, Will, you got a second?"

"Sure." Will scooted his chair back then stepped outside. "What's up?"

"I have a favor to ask." Conway motioned for his brother to follow him to the barn where they could talk in private.

"Let me guess." Will chuckled. "You've got too many women chasing after you and you want me take one of them off your hands?"

Conway skidded to a stop. "How'd you know?"

Will sobered. "I was joking."

After they entered the barn, Conway took a seat at the workbench. "You're not dating anyone, are you?"

Will leaned against the tractor tire and crossed his arms over his chest. "No."

"I want you to take a friend of mine on a date."

"I'm almost thirty-four, Conway. I quit dating buckle bunnies a long time ago."

"That's why you're the perfect date for this woman."

Will narrowed his eyes. "What's wrong with her?"

"Nothing. She doesn't have time to meet guys, because she works, goes to school and she's a single—"

"Oh, no." Will shoved away from the tractor. "If you're referring to that gal from the Border Town Bar & Grill then—"

"Isi's a great catch." Conway stood and paced in front of his brother.

"If she's so perfect, you date her."

"I can't."

"Why not?"

Conway leveled a meaningful glare at his brother. His siblings knew how he felt about being a father.

"Oh, yeah. You won't date her because of the twins."

Bingo.

"How old is Isi?" Will asked.

"Twenty-four."

"She's way too young for me."

"Johnny married Shannon, and he's nine years her senior. Besides, Isi acts older than her age. She's responsible, independent and—"

"Forget it."

Conway went on as if Will hadn't spoken. "Isi had a date with a jerk the other night and now she's down in the dumps."

"Then you take her out and cheer her up," Will said. "You don't want kids but that doesn't mean you can't date a single mother."

His brother's suggestion made Conway squirm.

"You like her, don't you?" Will said.

"Of course I like her. She's a great person."

"But you're afraid to date her, because you might start liking her too much."

"Quit trying to psychoanalyze me. It's better for both Isi and me if we remain friends." Conway shoved his fingers through his hair. "I want you to make her feel special for one night."

Will quirked an eyebrow. "How special?"

"Not *that* special." Conway scowled. "C'mon, Will. You owe me."

"Owe you, how?"

"You never help on the farm, so you can pay me for all the work I—"

"Watch yourself, buddy." Will motioned to the bunkhouse visible through the open barn doors. "I built that without much help from you or Porter. I think we're even." Will walked away. "Ask Porter to take her out. He's easy-going and gets along with anyone."

Conway dogged his brother's heels. "Porter's too immature for Isi."

"When do you plan to harvest the pecans?"

"Around Thanksgiving. Quit changing the subject." Conway tugged his brother's shirtsleeve. "You're the only one I trust to not take advantage of Isi."

"Fine." Will jerked his arm free. "I'll take her out next Friday."

"She doesn't get off work until midnight," Conway said.

Will's mouth dropped open.

"I know it's late, but can't you pick her up at the bar after her shift and go for a bite to eat?"

"Whatever. We'll figure it out. Give Isi my cell number in case she gets off earlier."

"Thanks, Will. I knew you'd come through for me."

As soon as his brother went inside the bunkhouse, Conway phoned Isi and left her a message. Now that he knew she'd be in good hands, he could relax and stop worrying.

Chapter 8

"Hey, quiet down in there and go to sleep," Isi hollered from the kitchen Sunday night. She and the boys had spent most of the day outside, and she didn't understand how they weren't tired after all that fresh air.

She'd finished drying the last of the supper dishes when she heard a faint jingle. She cocked her head, trying to identify the noise. She'd heard the same muffled sound earlier in the day, but had been too busy chasing after the boys and doing chores to think much of it.

Cell phone.

Good grief, she'd left her cell in her backpack by the front door. She rummaged through the bag and discovered Conway had left her a voicemail message.

Her heart gave a little jolt. No matter how hard she'd tried to keep busy, she hadn't been able to forget the kiss she and Conway had shared last night. She dialed her inbox and listened to his deep voice.

"I've got a surprise for you," he said.

What kind of surprise?

"You're going on a date Friday night."

I am? She held her breath.

"I set you up with my brother, Will."

The excitement fizzled out of Isi. *Thanks, but I can find my own date.*

"Will's going to pick you up after your shift at work."

She had a whole week to think about dating Conway's brother. *Yee-haw.*

"Here's Will's cell number in case you get off early from work on Friday."

While Conway repeated the number, it occurred to Isi that he really didn't want to start anything between them. She'd been an idiot to hope that their kiss meant more to Conway than it did. It was probably best they stayed friends since she already knew how he felt about being a father.

"Will's a great guy, Isi. He'll enjoy hearing about the boys and the classes you're taking at the community college."

She racked her brain, trying to recall conversations she'd had with Conway about Will, but he'd talked mostly about Johnny—the eldest Cash brother who Conway idolized.

"Call me if you can't go out with Will Friday night. See you tomorrow."

End of messages.

Isi set the phone on the kitchen table. She'd go out with Will if only to stop Conway's meddling.

Late Friday night Isi sat in a booth across from Conway's brother at the All-American Diner in Yuma and ignored the butterflies fluttering in her stomach. She'd been a nervous wreck since Will had picked her up at the bar. And she had no one to blame but herself for her anxiety. Will was a polite, well-mannered, handsome man—exactly the kind of guy she wanted to date.

But he's not Conway.

"I hear my brother's a regular at the Border Town Bar & Grill," Will said.

"I've known Conway almost two years." She forced a smile, hoping Will would stop talking about his brother.

"I think we should get it out of the way," Will said.

"Get what out of the way?"

He leaned over the table, his mouth closing in on Isi's. Caught by surprise, she froze. A moment later, his lips pressed against hers. The kiss was warm and firm. Squeezing her eyes closed she analyzed the feel of Will's mouth against hers. There was no zing, zip or zap like she felt when Conway kissed her. The breath she'd been holding in her lungs escaped in a dramatic sigh and she opened her eyes to Will's devilish grin.

He cocked his head. "Nothing?"

Startled by his bluntness she answered honestly. "No."

"Didn't think so. My loss."

She laughed. "You're too much of a gentleman to admit that you didn't feel any sparks, either."

"Now that we got the kiss out of the way, we can relax and enjoy ourselves."

The queasiness Isi had felt since Will had picked her up at the bar magically disappeared. "I'm sorry you were coerced into taking me out tonight, but Conway's determined to find a man for me."

"Hmm."

"What?" She noticed a sparkle in his eye.

"I'm trying to figure out why Conway's so invested in your love life." Will frowned. "You're sure you two are only good friends?"

"Sure." She dropped her gaze.

"C'mon, Isi. Tell me the truth."

Face flushing, she said, "Conway and I hit it off when we first met, but—"

"Then he found out you had the twins."

"Yes."

"How well did you two hit it off?"

"Well enough." She resisted the urge to press her fingers against her burning cheeks.

"Did you kiss?"

"We shared a few kisses."

Will grinned.

"But nothing happened after that," she protested.

"Tell me if I've got this right," he said. "You two were attracted to each other. You kissed a few times, maybe several. And you were working your way toward the bedroom when he found out you were a single mother. Then he backed off and you settled for being friends."

"Wow. You're good."

"After all this time being friends, what rocked the status quo between you two?"

Will wasn't going to drop the subject, so Isi spilled the details of her date with Sean and how Conway had kissed her later that night, because he'd felt sorry for her.

"I think I know what's going on." Will's smile stretched into a full grin.

The waitress arrived with the food, halting their discussion. After she promised to return with drink refills, Will spoke. "Conway wants you for himself, but

he's afraid things might get serious between the two of
you and—"

"That wouldn't be good," she said. "Because Conway
doesn't want to be a father."

"You nailed it."

"I like Conway a lot." Her feelings went deeper than
"like" but she was afraid to voice them. "And I don't
want to lose his friendship."

"Hate to break it to you—" Will shoveled a forkful
of omelet into his mouth, chewed then swallowed. "As
soon as Conway finds the perfect woman, she'll put a
stop to his visits to the Border Town Bar & Grill when
she finds out you're the reason he goes there."

Isi hadn't considered how Conway's "the one" might
feel about her friendship with him. The thought of him
not visiting her wherever she worked in the future depressed her. She changed the subject. "Conway said
you're thirty-three."

"And still single."

"Confirmed bachelor or playing the field?" she asked.

"I don't play the field anymore, but I haven't found
the right woman yet." He sipped his water. "I proposed
to a woman a few years back but things didn't work out."

"Conway never mentioned anything about you or any
of his brothers being engaged."

"My brothers didn't know about it," he said.

"What happened?"

"The night I'd proposed, I had a dream about a girl
I'd gone on a date with my senior year in high school."
He shook his head. "Craziest thing. After that dream I
couldn't get her out of my head."

"Did you try to contact the girl?"

"No. We have nothing in common. The last I heard she was living in California."

"But the memory of this girl was enough to break things off with your fiancée?"

"I'm afraid so."

"I'm a believer in fate," Isi said. "Things happen for a reason."

"Maybe, but I also believe we control our own destinies," Will said. "I hear you've been working your way through college and you have a job. That's no easy feat with twins."

"I've had help along the way," she said. "My boss has been great about adjusting my work schedule so I can take the classes I need to graduate. And when my babysitter moved out of town, Conway offered to watch the boys." She smiled. "They love being with him."

The diner waitress returned with their drinks then asked if they needed anything before she disappeared again.

"It's because of Conway that I decided I should start dating. The boys need a male role model in their lives."

"Speaking from experience, I'd wished my father would have wanted to be involved in my life."

"Conway spoke highly of your grandfather," she said.

"Grandpa Ely was a good man, but it was Johnny we all turned to as we grew older. He kept us in line and taught us how to defend ourselves against the bullies."

"I'm envious of you and your brothers," she said.

"Why's that? You always wanted to fight six siblings to use the bathroom?"

"I've dreamed of being part of a large family." She shrugged. "It's just me and my sons."

"You've got a lot going for you, Isi. You'll find a man who'll love your sons as much as you do."

They finished their meals in silence and Isi ordered coffee instead of dessert. "Conway mentioned you work in construction. Do you do any handyman work on the side?"

"Need a few repairs?"

"There are always things that need to be fixed in the trailer. My elderly landlord charges me next to nothing for rent, so I don't pester her about sticky windows and leaky faucets."

"I'll stop by your place next week," he said.

"That would be great." She smiled. "Thanks."

When they ran out of things to talk about, Isi pulled out her cell phone and said, "Oh, dear."

"What?"

"Conway sent a text message an hour ago, asking when we'd be back." She texted him saying they were on their way. Will drove her to the bar to pick up her car then followed her to her trailer.

When Will got out of his truck, she said, "You were a good sport tonight. I enjoyed getting to know you."

"Me, too, Isi. You're easy to talk to." He followed her up the porch steps.

When she walked into the trailer, Conway said, "'Bout time you got home."

Will ignored his brother's comment and spoke to Isi. "Dixie and Shannon are putting on a big spread for Thanksgiving. You and the boys should come out to the farm and spend the day with us."

"That's nice of you to offer, but we couldn't interfere in a family—"

"You won't be interfering," Will said. "Besides, it will give me a chance to get to know the twins better."

Conway's mouth sagged. Isi smothered a laugh behind a fake cough then said, "If you're sure, the boys and I would love to come."

"Great."

"Thanks again for the nice evening," Isi said.

"See you next week." Will closed the door behind him.

"What did he mean he'll see you next week?" Conway asked.

"Will offered to fix a few things around the trailer," she said.

"Why didn't you ask me for help?"

"I didn't think you did home repairs." The glower on his face worried her. "Did the boys misbehave tonight?"

"No, they were fine." Conway's gaze zeroed in on her mouth.

Was he thinking about the kiss *they'd* shared or imagining the one Will gave her tonight?

"I guess you and Will hit it off," he said.

"Your brother's very nice."

"What did you talk about?"

She yawned. "It's late, Conway, and I'm beat."

He grabbed his keys off the kitchen table. "I'll see you Monday."

"Conway?"

He stopped at the door and faced her.

"Thank you for setting up the date with Will." She smiled. "He was a big improvement over yucky Sean." She waited for Conway to speak but he remained silent, his brown eyes glowing with an emotion she couldn't identify.

Then he was gone. She crossed the room and flipped the lock on the door then thought about the twists and turns her relationship with Conway had taken the past couple of months. If anything good had come out of her date with Will, it was that they'd become friends. Once Conway found "the one" and moved on from her life for good and she'd need all the friends she could get to fill the hole he left behind.

The third week of November had ushered in a dip in temperatures, nature's way of signaling the beginning of the pecan harvest. Conway stood at the edge of the grove, deciding how best to collect the nuts.

"Getting ready to start up the shaker machine?"

Startled, Conway spun and came face-to-face with Will. "I thought you were at a job site with Ben."

"We finished early." Will held out a key.

"What's that for?" Conway asked.

"Isi's trailer."

Isi had given Will an extra house key? "You're moving awfully fast with Isi, aren't you?" That his brother was spending time at the trailer when Conway wasn't there rubbed him every which way but right.

"I stopped by her place this afternoon to fix the window over her bed."

Will had gone into Isi's bedroom? Hell, Conway had yet to venture inside her private quarters. "Was Isi there?"

"Why all the questions?"

Conway wanted to wipe the smirk off his brother's face but refrained from throwing a punch. Isi would have a fit if he picked a fight in front of the twins. "I hope you know that Isi's not ready for anything serious."

"That's funny," Will said. "She told me she thought the boys needed a male role model in their lives."

Frustrated, Conway walked over to the shaker machine and adjusted the settings.

Will followed him. "You surprised Johnny."

Grateful for the change in subject, Conway asked, "How's that?"

"Johnny wasn't sure you meant it when you said you wanted to take over the farm."

If the eldest Cash brother had doubts, why hadn't he said anything to Conway? "I wouldn't have volunteered if I didn't intend to follow through."

"Grandpa would be proud of you."

Yeah, he would. "He loved his pecan trees."

"It was a good place to grow up, wasn't it?" Will said. "Plenty of room to run without disturbing any neighbors."

"That's for sure."

Will pointed to the farmhouse, where Javier and Miguel played. "What do the boys do while you work in the orchards?"

"I made them bring their crayons and coloring books and told them to stay on the porch." Conway didn't want the kids anywhere near the shaker machine when he drove it through the rows.

"I could take the boys into town for root beers at Vern's Drive-In," Will said.

No way was Will honing in on his charges. "They're fine right where they are."

"If you say so."

"I say so." Conway gritted his teeth, pissed off that his brother had riled him.

"Think I'll say hi to the boys." Will walked off and it was all Conway could do to not tackle him to the ground.

Will stopped at the porch steps and spoke to them. Miguel laughed at whatever Will had said and it irked Conway that his brother amused the twins—that was his job.

Conway marched toward the group determined to find out what was so dang funny. He climbed the steps then froze. The boys had colored a highway system of roads from one end of the porch to the other. What happened to coloring in their books?

Miguel made *vroom-vroom* sounds as he moved a toy car over a bridge.

"Pretty ingenious if you ask me," Will said.

Conway glared at his brother. "No one asked you."

"Can I have a ride on the tractor?" Javier set his car aside.

"Not now. I want both of you to stay on the porch. It's too dangerous to be in the groves with pecans flying everywhere."

"I don't care if I get hit by one," Javier said.

"I'll make a deal with you," Conway said. "I'll give you a ride on the tractor after I finish each row." He figured one row up and down would take thirty minutes. He hoped the boys had enough patience to wait an hour. "Deal?"

"Okay," Javier said.

"What if we get hungry?" Miguel asked.

"I could—"

"I'll take care of that right now," Conway said, cutting off Will. He marched inside the house and rummaged through the pantry and fridge then returned with a stash of food—boxes of cereal, bags of chips, cans of soda and water bottles. "Don't eat all of this at once."

"What if we have to use the bathroom?" Javier said.

Before Will had a chance to offer his services again, Conway said, "Don't you have somewhere to go?"

Will raised his hands and backed away. "See you later, guys."

Conway motioned for the boys to follow him. "I'll show you where the toilet is." They trailed Conway through the kitchen and up the stairs to the second floor. He opened the bathroom door and the boys poked their heads inside. "Make sure you flush the toilet and wash your hands, okay?"

"Okay," the twins echoed.

They returned outside and Conway issued one last warning. "Don't leave the porch."

"We know," Miguel said.

"I'll be back when it's your turn for a ride on the tractor." Conway skipped down the steps and walked to the orchard where Will waited. "What are you still doing here?"

"I forgot to tell you Johnny said he got a call a few days ago from an agricultural company."

"What company?"

"Bell Farms out of southern California. They want buy the orchard."

"Why didn't Johnny tell me?" Conway asked.

"I think he's waiting to see how you do with this year's harvest."

"Grandpa would spin in his grave if we sold the place," Conway said.

"Johnny wants to discuss selling at Thanksgiving and put it to a vote."

Conway deserved more say in the decision than a simple vote.

"Good luck this afternoon." Will got in his truck and drove off.

After Conway started the tractor he decided he was more determined than ever to show his siblings he could bring in the harvest by himself. He steered the tractor into the second row of trees, where the vibrating robotic arms shook trunk after trunk until it rained pecans.

After the fifteenth tree he noticed Miguel and Javier waving their arms at the end of the row. He turned off the tractor and shouted, "What's the matter?"

Miguel spoke but Conway was too far away to make out the words. He hopped off the machine and walked toward the boy. "What's wrong?"

"We don't want to color anymore," Miguel said.

Swallowing his irritation, Conway said, "You can watch TV in the bunkhouse." Isi had told him that she didn't allow the boys to watch TV very often, but he was running out of ideas to entertain them. Inside the bunkhouse he turned on the big-screen TV mounted against the wall across from the row of single beds. "What channel?" Will had installed a satellite dish behind the shed and they got over a hundred different television programs.

"Disney," Javier said.

While Conway flipped through the directory, he noticed Miguel studying the posters of rodeo cowboys above the beds. "Do you like rodeo?"

Miguel shrugged.

"Have you ever been to a rodeo?"

The boys shook their heads no. Shoot, Conway had competed in his first mutton bustin' contest when he'd turned five. He positioned the sofa toward the TV. "Sit down." After they crawled onto the cushions, he said, "Don't get into any trouble."

"Is it my turn for a ride?" Javier asked.

"Not yet." The way things were going Conway would be lucky to drive the shaker machine through five rows before dark. "I'll come get you in a while."

A half hour later, Conway had made it to the end of the row and was about to head down another when Miguel dashed across the yard. The kid couldn't sit still for a minute. He raced up the porch steps, gathered an armful of snacks and attempted to carry them to the bunkhouse. He made it halfway, before he lost his load.

Conway considered helping Miguel, but he didn't have time. An hour later he shut down the machine and went into the bunkhouse. "You guys ready for a ride?" He gaped at the table covered in candy wrappers. "Did you eat all Porter's candy?"

"He lets us eat his candy," Miguel said.

"You didn't ask him."

"Can we ask him when he gets back?" Javier said.

"Forget it. You want a ride on the tractor or not?" He hated losing his patience, but he'd yet to make decent progress and half the afternoon was gone. When they reached the tractor, Conway sat Miguel next to him on the seat and Javier in his lap. He wasn't wasting time giving separate rides.

When they pleaded for Conway to show them how the shaker machine worked, he gave in and allowed the twins to remain on the tractor as he drove down the row, shaking tree after tree. Javier appeared fascinated by the process, Miguel not so much—he grew antsy and wanted to get off the tractor. When Conway reached the end of

the row, he sent the boys back to the bunkhouse with
the promise to check on them in an hour.

Time flew by and Conway shut down the tractor and
shaker machine and made his way through the orchard.
He got to within fifteen yards of the bunkhouse and
heard shouting.

"You're in big trouble!" Miguel's voice carried
through an open window.

"No, I'm not, you are!" Javier said.

Conway opened the door and stepped inside.

Both boys looked at each other and said, "He did it."

Conway stared in disbelief at the large-screen TV
resting facedown on the cement floor. "Don't move." He
crossed the room, grasped both boys by the seat of their
pants and lifted them away from the broken glass, then
carried them outside. "What the heck were you doing
in there?" He didn't give the boys a chance to answer.
"That TV cost over a thousand dollars."

The boys' eyes widened.

He shoved a hand through his hair. "How am I supposed to harvest the pecans if you two won't stay out
of trouble?"

"We didn't mean to break the TV," Miguel said.

"Stay here." Conway retrieved a broom and dustpan
from the storage closet then spent the next twenty minutes sweeping up glass. When he returned outside, the
boys were lying on their backs in the dirt staring up at
the sky.

"How much is a thousand dollars?" Miguel asked,
crawling to his knees.

"A lot of money."

Miguel kicked Javier's leg. "It's your fault." Miguel

faced Conway. "Javi threw his pillow at me, but I ducked and it hit the TV."

"Are you gonna be mad at us forever?" Javier asked, getting to his feet.

"No, but I need time to cool off." He walked the boys back to the porch.

"Are you gonna tell our mom we broke your TV?"

"I haven't decided." Conway's anger was dying a fast death at the scared expressions on the boys' faces. He'd broken his share of things as a kid and Grandma Ada hadn't punished him harshly.

"We're gonna be grounded forever." Miguel sighed.

The boys walked to the end of the porch and sat on the swing.

"We won't leave the porch," Javier said.

Conway trusted them to keep their word. No doubt they were more than a little worried about what their mother would say when she found out what they'd done.

Chapter 9

Isi reread the first paragraph of her term paper, satisfied she'd nailed the opening. Three sentences later, her mind wandered. The boys should be awake by now. Rarely did they sleep in and she worried they were coming down with colds.

Last night when she'd arrived home from the bar, she'd been surprised to find Conway's truck parked in front of her trailer, because they'd agreed that the boys would sleep at the farm while he harvested the pecans. When she'd asked why he'd brought them home, he'd said he thought it was best that they sleep in their own beds.

She shut down the computer and left the kitchen. When she opened her sons' door, she discovered them dressed and sitting on their beds, wearing glum expressions. "Hey, you two, what's the big secret?" Their eyes widened—not a good sign.

"Aren't you hungry?" she asked.

They hopped off their beds and filed past her, shoes dragging across the carpet. *Oh, dear.* They sat at the kitchen table and she felt their foreheads—no fever. "What's going on?"

"Conway's mad at us," Miguel said.

"Why?" When neither of them explained, she pulled out a chair and sat. "What happened at the farm yesterday?"

Javier refused to make eye contact with her, so she swung her gaze to Miguel. "I'm waiting…"

"We broke Conway's TV."

Isi gasped. "How?"

Miguel stamped his foot. "It was Javi's fault!"

"Was not!"

"Was so!"

"Stop." She slapped her hand against the table, startling her sons. "Javi, how did the TV break?"

"We had a pillow fight 'cause we were bored."

"Where was the TV?" she asked.

"In the bunkhouse," Miguel said.

Why had the boys been in the bunkhouse by themselves? Conway had promised to keep them close by while he worked.

"How big was the TV?" Isi mentally calculated the meager amount she'd saved for the boys' Christmas presents.

"This big." Javier spread his arms wide.

"It cost a thousand dollars," Miguel said.

A thousand dollars?

Why hadn't Conway told her about the TV last night?

Because he knows you don't have the money to replace it.

Isi rubbed her brow. Conway had done so much to help her—more than he should have, and the boys breaking his TV made her feel horrible. "We're going to have to pay for a new TV."

As she cooked breakfast, she worried over how she'd come up with the money to replace the TV. Maybe Conway would allow her to make monthly payments. Poor Conway—he needed a break from her sons. She could skip class but not work—she couldn't afford to lose any hours when she lived paycheck to paycheck. There had been many times when she'd almost given in and confronted Tyler Smith, demanding he pay child support but pride had stopped her. If she'd had to choose between her pride and feeding the boys she would have pursued Tyler with relentless determination, but things had never gotten that bad.

A half hour later Conway's truck pulled in front of the trailer and Isi's heart pounded with dread. "Conway's here." She turned from the window and caught her sons fleeing to their bedroom. *Chickens.*

She met a sober-faced Conway at the door. "The boys told me about the TV. I'm sorry."

He shrugged off her apology. "It was my fault. I shouldn't have left them alone in the bunkhouse."

"The boys knew better than to have a pillow fight when they were a guest in someone else's home." She squeezed his hand. "I want to cover the cost of the TV, but I'll have to make monthly payments."

"You're not paying for the TV," he said.

When the boys' bedroom door banged open, Isi realized she still held Conway's hand. She released her grip as her sons walked into the living room with their ceramic piggy banks.

"You can have our money to pay for a new TV." Miguel held out his pig to Conway.

"Mine, too," Javier said.

Isi was so proud of her sons.

"And you can smash 'em 'cause we smashed your TV," Miguel said.

"I have an idea on how you can make up for breaking the TV," Conway said.

"How?" Miguel asked.

"You're both going to collect the branches and twigs that fall from the trees after the shaker machine knocks the nuts loose."

"How many sticks do we gotta collect?" Javier asked.

"All of them." Conway kept a straight face, and Isi bit her lip to keep from laughing at her sons' astonished expressions.

"Let's get going. We've got a lot of work to do." Conway held open the door and waited for the boys to put their banks away.

"Be good." Isi watched them walk off as if marching to the gallows. Once they were out of earshot, she said, "Please let me make payments on the TV."

"Forget about it, Isi. It was an accident. Porter and Buck are shopping for a new TV right now." He stepped onto the porch. "See you tonight."

"You're bringing the boys back here to sleep then?"

"I think it's best for all three of us to have a break from each other at night."

"Would you mind staying a bit longer then? Will and I are going to a late movie at the mall after I get off work."

"You're going out with Will again?"

"You sound surprised," she said.

"Will never said anything to me."

"Is it okay if we go to the movies?"

"I guess."

He didn't sound too enthusiastic. Maybe Conway was jealous of his brother.

She could only hope.

"How come we gotta get boots?" Miguel asked, following Conway through Boot Barn with Javier.

"'Cause that's what rodeo cowboys wear. Jeans, a long-sleeve shirt and boots." Conway had felt guilty the past week while he'd harvested the nuts. Since breaking the TV, the boys had been on their best behavior and hadn't stepped off the porch—not once—unless Conway said it was okay. He'd finished most of the harvesting and was ahead of schedule, that's why he decided to surprise the twins and take them to a rodeo, where they could enter a mutton bustin' competition.

"Can I help you, sir?" An older gentleman approached them.

"These wranglers need a pair of boots," Conway said.

"Have a seat." The salesman pulled up a bench. "Be right back." He brought two boot boxes from the storeroom and knelt before the twins. He slid a brown pair on Javier's feet and a black pair on Miguel's. "Walk in them and tell me if they fit."

The boys shuffled up and down the aisle.

"What do you think?" Conway asked.

"I want the black ones," Javier said.

"I want the brown ones," Miguel said.

The salesman shook his head. "Thought for sure I had the right colors picked out for them."

"Okay, switch boots," Conway said.

Once the boys traded pairs, they raced to the end of the aisle. "Can we wear 'em now?" Javier asked.

"You bet." The salesman placed the boys' sneakers into the boot boxes then escorted them to the register and Conway got out his credit card.

After they left the store, he drove to Somerton, a small town twelve miles south of Yuma, where the Tamale Festival was in full swing. The annual event was sponsored by an Arizona State University Alumni chapter and the proceeds benefited local students attending ASU. Mutton bustin' happened to be one of the moneymakers at the festival and Conway hoped the boys would have fun.

"Where are we going?" Miguel spoke from the backseat.

"The Tamale Festival."

"My mom makes tamales," Javier said.

"What are we gonna do at the festival?"

Conway glanced at Miguel in the rearview mirror. The kid never stopped talking. "Wait and see." Fifteen minutes later, he parked in a gravel lot next to a small outdoor arena then opened the back door and helped the boys out of the truck. As soon as their boots hit the ground, Conway said, "Wait here." He rummaged through the truck toolbox and removed a pair of straw cowboy hats then set them on the twins' heads. "Now you're ready to rodeo."

After paying for their admission, he bought hot dogs then they sat in the stands and ate, while watching rodeo helpers set up the arena for the mutton bustin' contest.

"Ladies and gents, welcome to the twenty-first annual Tamale Festival and Rodeo. Hold on to your hats, we're about to kick off the mutton bustin' races." After the announcer spoke, one of the chute doors opened across the arena and a sheep ran out with a young boy clinging to its back.

Both Javier and Miguel watched the sheep race through the arena. The kid finally fell off then he got to his feet and waved to his parents in the stands.

"Well, folks, Billy Baker will have to keep working on his technique. Better luck next time, buckaroo!"

"What do you guys think? Would you like to ride a sheep?" Conway asked.

"Can we?" Miguel's eyes shone with excitement. Javier inched closer to Conway.

"You don't have to ride, Javi. Only if you want to."

Javi poked Miguel in the shoulder. "You go first."

"Let's sign you up, Miguel." Conway guided the boys through the throng of rodeo fans to a table next to the chutes. While they waited in line, he studied a man and his daughter a few feet ahead of them. The cowboy looked familiar. He turned and Conway recognized him. Tyler Smith's gaze clashed with Conway's then he spotted the twins and stiffened. Even though Isi had told Conway that Smith had rejected his sons, the cowboy had probably seen her and the boys around town.

"Smith," Conway said.

"Cash." There were questions in Smith's eyes, but damned if Conway would answer them. "Is your daughter entering the contest?"

"Yes." Smith's gaze strayed back to the boys.

"We gotta move up." Miguel tugged on Conway's hand.

"Hold on, Miguel," Conway said.

"Are you gonna ride a sheep?" Javier asked the young girl standing with Smith.

She smiled shyly and nodded.

"Me, too," Javier said.

Hell, the boys had no clue the little girl was their half sister. Talk about ironic—Tyler Smith's kids all chatting together as if they were best friends. Smith's face paled as he took his daughter's hand and pulled her out of line. "Let's go."

"But, Daddy…"

Conway didn't catch the rest of the girl's words as her father walked off with her.

"How come they left?" Javi asked.

"I don't think her father was feeling well." Served Smith right to see what he'd tossed aside. They moved up in line and Conway paid Miguel's entry fee then pinned his contestant number to the back of his shirt.

Next they stood behind the sheep chute, waiting their turn. The boys took in all the action, watching the rodeo helpers put helmets on the kids before setting them on the sheep.

"Ready, cowboy?" a rodeo worker asked when Miguel arrived at the front of the line. Once he sat on the sheep, Conway said, "Wait a second. I want to take a picture." He removed the camera he'd purchased at the drugstore earlier in the week after he'd decided to take the boys to the rodeo. Isi was always snapping photos of the boys, and he figured she'd be upset if she didn't have pictures of them mutton bustin'.

"Done," he said.

The gate opened and the sheep trotted into the arena.

He climbed the rails to take a second picture. "Go get 'em, Miguel!"

Miguel had no trouble hanging on until the sheep switched gears and ran hard. Conway thought for sure the boy would fall, but he clung to the sheep's fur. The cheering crowd rose to their feet.

Hang on, Mig. Hang on, buddy.

Miguel made it all the way across the arena before the rodeo helpers caught up with the sheep and cornered it.

"Folks, I think you witnessed a future National Finals Rodeo bronc rider!"

As applause echoed through the stands, Conway felt Smith's eyes watching him from two chutes away. He'd thought the man had left the rodeo. Pissed off, Conway hopped down from the rails. "Stay here, Javi. I'll be right back."

He approached Smith. "You're an ass, you know that? And wipe that grin off your face. You haven't earned the right to smile at your son." Conway didn't know what had possessed him to speak that like to Smith, but he felt protective of the boys.

"This is none of your business, Cash."

"The hell you say?" Conway noticed a woman talking to the little girl Smith had been with at the sign-in table—probably his wife. "You're wrong. It is my business, you know why?" Smith didn't rise to the bait. "You abandoned your sons. I know all about fathers who walk out on their kids. Those kids never want anything to do with their fathers after they're grown-up. When you're old and wanting to make amends for your sins, don't expect forgiveness." He nodded to Javier and Miguel back at the sheep chute. "Kids don't forget and they don't forgive." He'd had his say, so Conway walked off.

"Are you mad, Conway?" Javi asked.

"No. You did great, Miguel. I'm proud of you." He gave the boy a high five.

"Javi you gotta try it," Miguel said.

Conway bent down and looked Javier in the eye. "You ready?"

Javier slipped his hand inside Conway's. "What if I get hurt?"

"You won't, 'cause you gotta wear a helmet," Miguel said. "C'mon, Javi, you can do it."

Javier straightened his shoulders. "I'm gonna ride."

Once Conway paid his entry fee, the rodeo helpers put a helmet on Javier and set him on the sheep's back. The gate opened and Conway snapped two pictures before Javi slipped sideways and dropped to the ground. He got up, brushed off his jeans and raced back to the chute.

Out of breath Javier said, "Can I do that again?"

"Sure." Whether Isi knew it or not, her sons were rodeo cowboys in the making and Conway couldn't be prouder of them.

Isi waved as she watched Will drive out of the trailer park. They'd skipped stopping for dessert after the movie. Will insisted Conway wouldn't mind, but Isi hadn't wanted to take advantage of her sitter by staying out too late. When she stepped inside the trailer, she spotted Conway asleep on the couch. She treaded closer to the sofa. He was such a handsome man. If only...

"I'm a light sleeper, if you're thinking about pulling a prank on me." He opened his eyes.

Isi lost herself in his warm gaze.

"Where's Will?" Conway sat up.

"He left." She shrugged out of her jacket. "How did the boys behave?"

"Fine. We played hooky." He stretched his arms above his head, drawing her gaze to his chest.

"You didn't work at the farm?" she asked.

"We drove over to Somerton for the Tamale Festival."

Isi had always wanted to attend the festival. "Did you rodeo?"

"Nope, but the boys entered the mutton bustin' competition."

"Really?" She'd heard about the event for kids. "Javier rode, too?"

"He was nervous, but after watching Miguel he wanted to give it a try." Conway grinned.

"What?"

"Miguel rode his sheep 'til the buzzer and won a blue ribbon."

Isi smiled. That sounded like her competitive son. "How did Javier do?"

"He fell off after a few seconds. Miguel said he'd share his ribbon with him."

"Did you by chance take any pictures?"

Conway went into the kitchen then returned with a photo envelope from a local drugstore.

Isi browsed through the pictures. "These are great," she said. "Where did they get the boots?"

"We stopped at Boot Barn on the way out of town."

"You shouldn't have spent money on them," she said. She'd be indebted to Conway for life if he continued to buy things for the boys. As it was, she doubted she'd be able to pay for the bunkhouse TV until she landed a new job after she graduated. "Thank you for taking the photos."

"So you and Will are really hitting it off," he said.

"Will's a nice guy." She noticed his frown and asked, "What's wrong?"

"Will's too old for you."

"He's not that much older than you."

"Maybe not, but if you two get serious, I—"

"Right now we're friends, Conway."

"That could change, but my brother's not the right man for the twins."

"You can't be serious."

"Hey, I've been with the boys long enough to know who would make a good dad for them."

"Oh, really?" *This ought to be interesting.* "What kind of man do you think the boys need in their life?"

Conway shoved a hand through his hair and paced across the room. "They need a man who won't get upset when they make a mess with their toys."

Like you. "Go on."

"A guy, who doesn't mind being interrupted and asked a million questions."

Like you.

"A guy who'll teach them to stand up for themselves."

Like you did.

"A man who'll appreciate their differences and not compare one to the other."

Oh, Conway, can't you see you're describing yourself? "If Will's not the right man for me and the boys then who is?"

Was it a trick of the light or had Conway's eyes sparked at her question?

"I don't know, but it's not my brother." He closed the distance between them and Isi felt the air squeeze out of the room. He stared into her eyes, the sexy tilt of his mouth making her heart race. Would it always be like this between them—his brown eyes making her knees go weak?

"Isi?" he whispered, drawing her gaze to his lips.

"What?" She couldn't think with Conway standing so close.

The next thing she knew, Conway's breath fanned her cheek and her skin broke out in goose bumps.

"Tell me what kind of guy rocks your world and I'll find him for you."

She held her breath. He stood so close all she had to do was lift her face and her mouth would brush his jaw. "You'll never find him."

"Why not?"

Because he's standing right here in front of me, and he doesn't want to be found.

She swayed forward, bringing their mouths closer. *Kiss me, Conway.*

He must have heard her silent plea. His lips brushed across hers and her body tingled as if he were running his hand over her naked flesh. He pulled back, his gaze piercing. "This isn't a good idea." He didn't allow her a chance to speak before he kissed her again, this time, his mouth lingering.

"Tell me to stop." His dark eyes gleamed. He wanted her, but he couldn't promise her anything more than this night in his arms.

Is one night enough?

Isi had dreamed of making love to Conway for weeks. She hadn't had sex since the boys were born and to end a four-year drought in Conway's arms was nothing short of a dream come true. But once she got a taste of his passion, would she be able to distance herself from the experience and return to being his friend and confidante?

She caressed his scruffy cheek, relishing the prickly feel of his five-o'clock shadow. The yearning to be intimate with him overpowered her common sense.

Standing on tiptoe, she whispered, "I don't want to stop you."

He grasped her face, sweeping his tongue inside her mouth, leaving no doubt in her mind what he wanted.

Her.

Chapter 10

Like a drunken cowboy, Conway stumbled after Isi through the hallway. As soon as he entered her bedroom, she shut the door and flipped the lock. The light from the street lamps behind the trailer park flooded the room, casting Isi in a mystic glow.

Not a hint of doubt showed in her beautiful brown eyes. When she ran her tongue across her lower lip, leaving a moist trail on the pouting flesh, Conway's testosterone level went through the roof.

There was no doubt Isi wanted him. Her fingers moved with confidence over the buttons of her blouse until the sides fell open revealing the creamy swells of her breasts above her black lace bra.

"You next," she said.

So that's how they were playing this game. He ripped open the snaps on his shirt, baring his chest. She flashed a wicked smile that jolted his heart. She unbuckled her belt then slid the zipper down on her jeans. A bit of black lace peeked at him and Conway scrambled to undo his belt and release the buttons on his fly.

"I guess we both prefer black undergarments," she said, staring at his briefs.

Conway shrugged out of his shirt then closed the distance between them. He brushed her blouse aside, exposing her shoulder then he kissed her skin. The scent of perfume and warm female made him crazy hungry for her.

"You're beautiful." He cupped her small breast and kissed the nipple through the lace. Her moan echoed in his ears, and when her hand found his arousal, he knew he wouldn't last long. He lifted her into his arms and carried her to the bed. He kissed her once, twice, three times before coming up for air. "How do you want this? Hard and fast or slow and easy?"

"Let's save the slow and easy for next time."

"I was hoping you'd say that." He reached for his jeans on the floor, but Isi intercepted his arm. "I've got it covered." She rummaged through her nightstand drawer and held out a new box of condoms. "After getting pregnant with the twins, I don't want to be caught unprepared again."

"Are you sure?"

"I've never been so sure of anything."

He slid her panties off then sheathed himself and thrust inside her, groaning in pleasure. Everything about Isi and this moment felt right. Perfect. His fingers coaxed her to keep pace with him and when he heard the quiet hitch in her breath followed by her muffled cry against his chest, he let himself go, and followed her to paradise.

* * *

Soft guttural snores and the hot press of naked flesh
dragged Isi from slumber. Conway spooned her body,
one arm stretching beneath her pillow and the other resting along her thigh.

Conway's chest pushed against her shoulders when
he inhaled, then a sliver of cool air rushed between their
bodies when he exhaled. The hair on his thighs tickled her bottom, but it was the rhythmic puff of air hitting the back her neck that made her skin break out in
goose pimples.

The muffled wail of a police siren echoed in the distance, reminding her of the stark contrast between their
childhoods—Conway having been raised on a pecan
farm in the country and Isi having grown up in the poor-
est barrio in Buenos Aires. How different her life would
be right now if her father had been a farmer and not a
factory worker.

Isi didn't often allow herself to think too far into the
future, beyond earning her degree and landing a stable
job—mostly because of fear. Fear that another roadblock
would prevent her from graduating. Fear that she'd never
find a job that made enough money to move her and the
boys out of the trailer and into a real home. Fear that her
sons would grow up without a father.

Fear that she'd spend the rest of her life alone.

In Conway's arms, she felt safe enough to dream. She
imagined waking in the mornings on the farm, hearing
the boys arguing down the hall in their bedroom. She
envisioned cooking a country breakfast before walking
her sons to the meet the bus. When the boys returned
from school, they'd jump on the tractor and help Conway in the pecan groves.

But happy ever after on a farm would never be a reality, because Conway didn't want to be a father.

No matter how much Isi wished otherwise, she'd known from the get-go that raising children was not in his future. She'd experienced plenty of disappointment in her young life—more than most women her age. No matter what happened between her and Conway, she'd survive, because she had her sons. Javier and Miguel were her greatest joy. Her purpose in life. Her reason for living.

Forcing her thoughts from the boys and the future, she basked in the glow of Conway's lovemaking. If Isi had learned one thing after their conversations about women, it was that Conway needed to be a priority in his lady's life. He wanted to be the center of her world, but when their clothes had come off, he'd focused on her pleasure, not his.

He'd been amazing in bed. Of course, she'd only had two lovers to compare him with—her high school boyfriend and the twins' father. Neither had come near to the passion she'd found in Conway's arms. She doubted she'd ever close her eyes without hearing his deep voice murmur how much he adored her body. He'd made her feel young, sexy and carefree and for a short time she'd forgotten she was a mother, student and waitress. She glanced at the nightstand clock.

If only time would stand still.

If only she, Conway and the boys were a real family.

If only Conway would wake up and ask her to marry him.

Wishful thinking.

Of course he wouldn't propose, but what if they could be friends with benefits until "the one" happened along?

What about Javi and Mig?

There were times she hated the voice inside her head, always challenging her decisions. Even if she hid her affair with Conway so the boys wouldn't get their hopes up that he'd become their dad, would she be able to stop herself from falling in love with him?

If there was one thing she'd learned about herself the past few years, it was that she was a survivor. When Conway found his perfect woman, she'd pick up the pieces of her broken heart and move on.

He stretched behind her, his hand moving over her breast, caressing her. Then she felt the press of his mouth on the top of her head.

She turned in his arms and he spread tiny kisses over her face, drawing sighs and moans from her before he sheathed himself and took her on another fantasy ride.

When their breathing returned to normal, he whispered, "You're amazing."

His smile melted her heart. "So are you."

"It's almost five." He squinted at the bedside clock. "I'm usually out in the barn by now."

The sun wouldn't be up for two hours. They had time… "Stay." She squeezed his bicep. "You work too hard."

"Not as hard as you." Conway kissed her forehead. "I don't know how you do it, taking care of the twins, going to college, working at the bar then studying when you get home." He slid down on the mattress and nuzzled her breasts.

"I want you to know…"

Conway stiffened. He'd woken up in enough beds with pink-flowered sheets to have learned that most morning-after conversations didn't bode well for him.

"That last night was special," she said.

He couldn't concentrate when she toyed with his nipple. "Isi...we can't do this again."

Her eyes widened and he felt like an ass. He'd shared an incredible few hours with Isi, which had been way better than any fantasy he'd had about her the past two years. The least he could do is wait until they had their clothes on to discuss whether or not there would be a repeat of tonight in the future.

He didn't want to be the bad guy, but there was no way he'd take advantage of Isi and keep carrying on with her when he had no intention of making their relationship permanent.

"I'm not going to change how I feel about being a father," he said. "You deserve to be with a man who'll make your sons a priority in his life. I'm not that man."

She raked her fingernails down his back and he shivered. "We could be friends with benefits."

Was she saying what he thought she was saying? A creaking sound in the hall startled Isi and she flew off the bed, dragging the sheet with her.

"Oh, my God!" She motioned to the window above the bed as she backed against the door. "Get out!" she whispered.

He shoved his legs into his jeans then stuffed his bare feet into his boots, wincing at the tight fit.

"Mom? My throat hurts."

When the door handle jiggled, Isi gestured frantically.

"Mom?"

"Be right there, Miguel."

Conway yanked the blinds up and opened the window, then punched out the screen with his fist. "Sorry," he mumbled as he stepped on her sheets and launched himself out the window. When his boots hit the ground, he poked his head through the window. "My keys."

Isi tossed his keys and wallet. He caught them then raced bare-chested to his truck.

It wasn't until he reached the city limits that he caught himself smiling in the rearview mirror. Good thing Will had fixed Isi's sticky window or he would have had to explain to Miguel what he'd been doing in his mother's bedroom.

"Look who came crawling home before dawn?"

Conway froze when he stepped from his truck and heard Porter's voice echo in the darkness.

"Over here." Porter sat up in the bed of his truck.

"What are you doing?" Conway asked.

"I couldn't sleep."

Couldn't sleep? "Twenty-seven is too young to be suffering from insomnia."

"Not being able to sleep has nothing to do with my melatonin levels and everything to do with Betsy."

Although he'd earned a reputation of being a ladies' man, Porter never lacked for female attention. And while Conway was on a mission to find the right woman to settle down with, his brother played the dating game for the sake of competing, not caring in the end if he lost or won.

Of all the brothers, Conway and Porter resembled each other the most in appearance, but they couldn't be more different. Porter was a goof-off, who took life one day at a time. Conway liked having fun as much as the next guy, but the past couple of years he'd been thinking there was more to life.

"Where's your shirt?" Porter's white teeth flashed in the predawn light.

If given a choice Porter was not the brother he'd have picked to have a serious conversation with, but Conway was rattled by what he and Isi had done and he needed to vent. "I crossed the line with a woman I shouldn't have."

"What happened?"

"I slept with Isi."

"The twins' mother?"

What other Isi was there?

"She's single," Porter said. "What's the problem?"

"I have no intention of marrying her, so we shouldn't have slept together."

"I have no intention of marrying Betsy, but I still slept with her."

"Who's Betsy?"

"Betsy Brumfield. We met at Vern's Drive-In a few days ago and hit it off."

"That was quick."

"Betsy invited me back to her apartment after the movie." Porter shrugged. "I wasn't going to say no."

"Do you ever think about settling down with one woman?"

Porter waved a hand in the air. "Quit talking about me. Why are you upset about sleeping with Isi? Does she already have a steady boyfriend?"

"No!" Conway shoved a hand through his hair. "But I let my emotions get the best of me. I was frustrated."

"By what?"

He didn't want Porter to know he was jealous of Will. "Isi went out on a date with a guy and the whole night I worried that she was having sex with him."

"If you don't like the idea of Isi dating, then you must have feelings for her."

"We've been friends for a long time."

"How come you've never invited her to spend a holiday with us?" Porter asked.

"Because we're not that kind of friends."

Porter stared at him with a perplexed frown. "What the hell kind of friends are you?"

When had his younger brother become so pushy? "I stop by the Border Town Bar & Grill a few times a week and we talk."

"Ah."

Conway quirked an eyebrow. "Ah, what?"

"Isi's your therapist."

Not only was Porter pushy, he was perceptive, too.

"Let me see if I have this figured out." Porter sat up straight. "You and Isi are friends and she listens to all your problems, offers advice and basically keeps you focused on your goals, whatever those are."

"Right."

"So the reason you're all worked up over having sex with her is that you're afraid she won't view you as a friend anymore and you won't be able to bend her ear like you used to."

"Not at all. I—"

"Wait," Porter interrupted. "You're afraid that if Isi becomes involved with a guy, then he'll put the brakes on your friendship with her."

"No." Conway's anxiety had nothing to do with being cut off from Isi's counsel—did it? He'd grown close to her and the boys these past weeks, and accepted that he couldn't have her and the twins for himself but that didn't mean he wanted some other guy to have them.

"If you value Isi's friendship that much, why did you sleep with her?" Porter asked.

"When she walked in the door, all I could think about was kissing her and—"

"Staking your claim on her."

Had he wanted to stake his claim on Isi? "She didn't try to stop me when I kissed her."

"I have that problem all the time," Porter said. "I usually hesitate right before I kiss a girl in case she changes her mind, then I—"

"Hey, back to my sex life, not yours."

"Sorry."

Agitated, Conway paced. "Making love with Isi was off-the-charts amazing." After they'd made love the first time, Isi had fallen asleep for a few minutes, giving Conway a chance to study her without her knowing. The sight of her pretty face relaxed and her breathing even and quiet had moved something deep inside him. His chest had swelled with tenderness and he'd felt connected to her in a way he'd never experienced with another woman. The intensity of that emotion had scared him but at the same time it had felt exhilarating.

"And good sex is a bad thing?"

"I can't have serious feelings for Isi because of her sons."

"What's wrong with Miguel and Javier? Aren't they good boys?"

"I don't want to be a father, Porter." He felt protective of the twins and he'd do everything possible to make sure they didn't get hurt, which meant he could never be their dad.

"Is it because the twins aren't yours?"

The fact that Conway hadn't fathered the twins had nothing to do with not wanting to be their father. He feared that if he continued sleeping with Isi, it would only be a matter of time before his feelings for her developed into love. The boys were a part of Isi—if he fell in love with her, how could he not love her sons?

"I like the twins fine, but I don't want the responsibility of raising them." That sounded better than telling his brother the truth—that he didn't trust himself not to cut out on Isi down the road—he was his father's son after all and abandoning women and children was in his DNA. What if he and Isi married and the boys accepted him as their father then six months later, the pressure of all that responsibility got to him and he split? Isi had already lost too many people she loved—he didn't want to be one more.

"A lot of guys can't envision themselves as fathers until their girlfriend or wife becomes pregnant. It happened to Gavin," Porter said. "He panicked when Dixie turned up pregnant. Now, he's a natural at taking care of Nathan."

Gavin was a better man than Conway. After the things his brother-in-law had witnessed in the army and the nightmares that had followed him home from the war in Afghanistan, it astonished Conway that Gavin always put Dixie and their son first in his life.

"Not wanting kids has nothing to do with a lack of confidence in my ability to be a father." Conway scuffed the toe of his boot on the ground. "I want to keep my life simple. Me and my wife. No kids." He was already taking a huge risk by committing to a woman he wasn't sure he could stay with a year much less a lifetime. "Lots of married couples choose not to have kids."

"True, but you grew up with five brothers and a sister," Porter said. "Won't the quiet drive you nuts?"

"Maybe."

"So what are you gonna do about Isi?"

"I'm for sure not going to have sex with her again." After she suggested friends with benefits, abstinence might prove challenging. He'd have to avoid being alone with her. "She'll understand. She knows I don't want kids."

"What if she doesn't care that you don't want kids and she's only in it for the sex?"

Conway gaped. Had his brother been spying on him and Isi from inside her bedroom closet?

"I guess the only problem with sleeping together—" Porter stretched his arms above his head and yawned "—is that sex would interfere with Isi trying to find a potential husband and you the perfect wife."

Exactly. Isi might want a brief affair until she finished her degree, but they'd been lucky they hadn't been discovered by the twins. Once she graduated, he'd have to end their friendship for good.

"Are Isi and the boys coming for Thanksgiving this Thursday?"

"Yeah, Dixie invited them," Conway said, unwilling to admit it had been Will's idea.

The sky glowed pink as the sun rose higher. "I better get to work," Conway said. "I have to watch the boys again on Monday and I need to get the orchard cleaned up this weekend."

"If you want, I can drive into Yuma and get the twins Monday morning."

"No rodeos?"

Porter shook his head. "I told Betsy I'd hang out with her this week."

"Where does she work?"

"The Pancake House in Yuma."

His brother was seeing a waitress, too. What was it about waitresses that attracted the Cash brothers? "If you're sincere about picking up the twins, I accept your offer."

"What time should I be at Isi's?" Porter asked.

"Eleven-thirty. I'll leave directions to the mobile-home park in the bunkhouse."

"Think I'll go to bed now and dream about Betsy." Porter hopped down from the truck.

Conway watched his brother walk off, thinking he didn't need sleep to dream about Isi—he could do it standing up with his eyes wide open.

"Conway's here!" Miguel raced to the front door after hearing the bell ring.

Isi drew in a deep breath and exhaled slowly. Two days had passed since Conway escaped her trailer through the bedroom window and she'd been a wreck, waiting for his call or text. She'd received neither, which had only added to her anxiety.

She zipped her makeup bag and stowed it in the bathroom drawer then studied her reflection in the mirror. She looked the same, but she felt different—when she thought of Conway, her body tingled in places it had never tingled before.

Unsure how Conway would react after they'd crossed the friendship line, she left the bathroom then stopped dead in her tracks.

"Hey, you're not Conway." Miguel flashed a smile.

"Hi, Porter." Javier joined his brother at the door. "Did you eat all your Halloween candy?"

Porter stepped inside the trailer. "I think you guys ate all my candy."

When he looked Isi's way she said, "Hello, Porter." Worried Conway had been hurt at the farm, she asked, "Is Conway okay?"

"He's out in the orchard on the tractor right now."

Had Conway sent his brother to get the boys because he hadn't wanted to face her after they'd had sex? She tried not to read too much into the situation but couldn't help wondering if he regretted sleeping with her. The thought hurt more than she cared to admit.

"I'm not rodeoing this week," Porter said. "So I volunteered to fetch the troublemakers."

"We're not troublemakers. Are we, Mom?" Miguel asked.

"That's up for debate."

"What's a debate?" Javier asked.

"A big dispute," Porter answered.

"What's a dispute?" Miguel asked.

"A fight." Porter raised his arms and curled his hands into fists then punched the air above their heads. "It's a winner-take-all, knockout brawl."

The boys giggled and joined in the fun, swinging their arms at Porter as he dodged out of the way. Clutching her car keys Isi said, "Would you tell Conway I won't need his help during the day the rest of the week? I don't have classes again until after the holiday."

"Sure." Porter slapped a hand against his thigh. "I almost forgot to tell you. Dixie says we're eating at one o'clock Thanksgiving Day and not to worry about bringing anything."

Suddenly Isi wasn't so sure she should attend the Cash Thanksgiving celebration. What if Conway didn't want her there but couldn't say so without hurting the boys' feelings? Darn it. Why did morning-afters—make that two-day-afters—have to be so difficult?

"Tell Dixie I'd planned to make my mother's chorizo stuffing. It's spicy, but I think everyone will like it."

"Sounds great. Okay, guys, let's go. I've got to get ready for my hot date with Betsy." Porter ushered the boys out of the trailer and Isi locked the door behind everyone then handed the booster seats to Porter.

"Who's Betsy?" Miguel asked.

"A girl."

"What's a hot date?" Javier trailed after Porter and Miguel.

"Um…" Porter grinned over his shoulder at Isi. "A hot date is when you do lots of fun stuff."

The devilish gleam in Porter's eye gave Isi pause. Had Conway told his brother they'd had sex? *No.* Conway wasn't a sleep-and-tell kind of guy.

"What fun stuff?" Miguel moved out of the way while Porter installed the child seats.

"You know," Porter said. "Play with new toys and go fun places."

Javier climbed into his chair. "What fun places?"

"You two always ask this many questions?" Porter shut the door on the twins in the middle of their answer. He waved to Isi. "Don't worry. They won't hear any sex talk from me. Promise."

Porter's comment had Isi wondering all over again if Conway had confided in his brother about his relationship with her. Blushing she slid behind the wheel of her car and drove off. She'd have to wait until tonight to find out if sleeping with Conway had been the biggest mistake of her life.

Chapter 11

Conway had put the boys to bed a few minutes ago, but they'd yet to settle down. He sat on the sofa then reached for the remote and turned on the TV. A few minutes later the twins marched into the living room.

"What's wrong?" Conway asked, noting the brothers had put on their rodeo boots, only they must have done it in the dark, because they each wore one black boot and one brown boot.

"Here." Javier shoved a piece of paper at Conway.

He scanned the note. "This is your Christmas wish list."

Miguel shook his head. "We don't want 'em anymore."

"Why not?" He hoped Isi hadn't already purchased the toys.

"'Cause," Miguel said.

"Okay. What do you two want then?" Conway asked.

"We want you to be our dad," Javi said.

If Conway hadn't already been sitting down, his legs would have folded beneath him. The boys stared wide-eyed, waiting for his response. When he opened his mouth to speak, the words stuck to the sides of his throat. He swallowed hard, ignoring the panic building inside him. "I'm flattered, guys, but—"

"What's flattered?" Miguel asked.

"It means I appreciate you wanting me to be your father, but I can't."

"Why not?" Javi inched closer and set his small hand on Conway's thigh. "Don't you like us?"

"Of course I like you." Conway squeezed his hands into fists to keep from hugging the boy. How the heck did he get himself out of this mess without hurting their feelings? "I've had a lot of fun hanging out with both of you."

"You could be our dad and have fun with us all the time," Mig said.

Feeling like a cornered rabbit, Conway sprang from the couch and walked to the opposite side of the room then faced the boys. How could two kids three feet tall be so intimidating? "You guys don't understand. I'm not going to be anybody's father. Ever."

"Why not?" Javi asked.

"Because—" He shut his mouth. He couldn't very well tell them that if he became their father, odds were one day he'd wake up and walk out on them. "Don't worry, guys. Your mom will meet a really great man one day and he'll be your father."

"But we want you," Miguel said.

Feeling lower than pond scum, he said, "Get back in bed."

The twins didn't move and Conway feared they were going to defy him, then Miguel huffed and walked off.

Javier stood his ground and pointed to his mismatched boots. "You lied."

"About what?" Then Conway remembered telling the boy not to wear mismatched shoes all the time because the good luck would wear off. "I'm sorry, Javi."

The kid walked back to his bedroom and slammed the door hard, shaking not only the trailer walls but Conway's heart. He'd handled the situation badly—more proof that being a father wasn't in the cards for him.

He waited an hour before opening the bedroom door and peeking in on the twins. They were asleep in their beds—thank goodness. He wouldn't have been able to stand it if he'd found them crying. As he closed the door his gaze landed on the garbage can across the room. They'd thrown both pairs of cowboy boots in the trash.

Feeling like the cruelest man on earth, Conway closed the door and returned to the living room. He had no idea what he was going to say to Isi when she got home tonight. They'd yet to talk about making love and now the boys had asked him to be their father.

Conway had been given a reprieve when Porter had volunteered to fetch the twins earlier in the day, but there was no escaping a face-off with Isi tonight. He still hadn't wrapped his head around the fact that he'd had sex with a woman who'd been his friend and confidante the past twenty-four months.

Every once in a while his thoughts of Isi would stray into X-rated territory when he remembered the past— like the night she'd worn a tight spandex top at the bar.

When she'd caught him staring at her breasts, her nipples had hardened and it had taken all his willpower to act as if he hadn't noticed. Then there had been the night when she'd tripped over a bar stool and he'd caught her by the waist—except her waist had actually been her breast. He'd suffered erotic dreams for a month after that incident.

His attraction to Isi had always been there, simmering below the surface. If she hadn't had the boys, Conway would have fallen hard for her within the first week of meeting her.

He wanted to wipe the slate clean between them and return to the way things used to be—before he'd offered to babysit for the boys. He yearned for the days when he stopped by the bar and shared his latest dating dilemma with her and she'd make sense of it all for him. Now Isi was his dating dilemma, and he sure in heck couldn't her ask for advice on how to deal with *her*.

At twelve-thirty he heard Isi's clunker park beneath the carport. When she entered the trailer, their gazes clashed and his first thought was how hot she looked in her bar T-shirt and tight jeans. A surge of testosterone flooded his bloodstream as his mind flashed back to their clothes flying off in her bedroom.

"How was your day?" he asked.

"Fine." She set her backpack on the floor. "How about yours?"

"Fine," he lied. He swore he saw wavy tension lines hovering in the air between them.

"Conway."

"Isi."

They spoke simultaneously. "Ladies first," he said.

"That's okay. You go."

"About the other night." Damn, why was it so hard to tell her that making love with her again was never going to happen? "I don't think we should…you know…have a repeat of…" *Oh, hell.* For a guy who had a reputation of being a ladies' man, he sounded like an idiot. "It's not that I didn't enjoy what we did," he said. "It's that I don't want kids and—"

"I have the boys."

And tonight he'd discovered how much power kids wielded over adults and how they could make a grown man feel like crap.

"It's okay." Her sad smile tugged his heartstrings. "I didn't invite you into my bed, hoping you'd change the way you feel about kids." She strolled past him into the kitchen and he caught a whiff of her perfume—the same stuff she'd worn the night they'd slept together. She drank a glass of water then set the cup in the sink. "I'm fine with keeping things between us casual until I graduate at the end of the semester and we go our separate ways."

Two very good reasons why he couldn't keep things casual with Isi were sleeping a few feet away behind a closed door. Heck, it was bad enough that he cared about the boys as if he were their…uncle or *something*. If he gave Isi half the chance, he'd begin caring for her like a steady boyfriend or… He couldn't make himself say the word *husband* out loud much less in his head.

"Porter said you don't have classes the rest of the week."

"That's right."

"I think it would be best if you found a new sitter to watch the boys when you go to work."

Isi's eyes widened then she dropped her gaze. Conway backed up a step to keep from taking her in his arms and begging for her forgiveness.

He edged toward the door, his stomach dropping when he caught her wiping a tear.

She sniffed. "Conway?"

"Yeah?"

"Would it be better if the boys and I don't show up at the farm for Thanksgiving?"

He'd forgotten Will had invited them. "You should still come."

"Are you sure?"

"Positive." *Leave. Don't stay no matter how badly she acts like she needs a hug.* Conway closed the door behind him and jogged to his truck. When he started the engine it occurred to him that his actions tonight proved he was no better than his own father—for all intents and purposes he'd turned his back on Isi and the boys. Better that he found out now rather than later after all their hearts became entangled.

As soon as Conway's truck pulled away from the trailer, Isi broke down in tears and swiped angrily at the moisture that leaked from her eyes. What an idiot she'd been to believe that if Conway made love to her once he'd want to share her bed again.

Suck it up, girl.

Conway had done so much for her and the boys that she refused to make him feel guilty for not wanting to carry on an affair with her. She hated to be the one to break the news to her sons, but first thing in the morning she'd continue her search for a new sitter. If she didn't have any luck, she'd beg her neighbor for help.

Mrs. Sneed might not be as exciting as Conway but at least she wasn't a pedophile or a crazy lady.

After turning out the lights, she stopped in the hallway and poked her head inside the boys' bedroom. Javier was wide awake. "What's the matter, honey? Did you have a nightmare?" She sat on the bed, pulled him into her arms and rocked him.

"Conway doesn't want to be our dad," he said.

Isi stiffened. What was Javi talking about?

"I asked him to be our dad for Christmas instead of getting presents from Santa, but he said no."

So it wasn't sleeping with her that had scared Conway off. "When did you ask him?"

"Tonight."

When Isi turned her head away so Javier wouldn't see her tears, she noticed the trash can. "Why did you throw your boots in the garbage?"

"They're bad luck."

She had no idea what Javi was talking about, but she didn't want to ask for an explanation. "Honey, Conway is a nice man and he really likes you and Mig, but he never planned to be with us forever." She didn't know how to explain Conway's fear of fatherhood when *she* didn't fully understand his reasons for not wanting children.

"We don't want Conway to watch us anymore."

You're getting your wish. "Tomorrow we'll find a new sitter."

Miguel lay wide awake staring at her. She waited for him to say what was on his mind, but he kept silent. "You okay, Mig?"

He rolled away and flung the covers over his head. His heart was broken, too. She gave Javi an extra hug then tucked in his blankets. "We have each other, guys. The three of us will always be a family."

She left the door cracked open before retreating to her bedroom where she changed into her pajamas and slipped into bed.

Then she cried, her sobs muffled by the pillow pressed against her face.

Isi dried the last of the Thanksgiving dishes and set the damp towel on the counter. She'd volunteered to help Dixie in the kitchen so she could escape the awkwardness between her and Conway. Even the boys had chosen to stick by Will's side this afternoon—not that she blamed them.

"This is a lovely home, Dixie."

"The house is over a hundred years old and Will is constantly repairing leaky faucets and creaky doors. The place needs a facelift, but no one has the time or money to update the rooms."

"I wouldn't change a thing." Isi strolled into the dining room off the kitchen. She studied the wallpaper pattern of elegantly intertwining white blooms against a faded burned-gold background. The space was cozy and inviting.

"Would you like a tour of the house?" Dixie asked.

Isi had been dying for such an invitation. "I'd love to see the other rooms."

"Let's start upstairs."

She followed Dixie out of the kitchen and asked, "Does Shannon want to come?"

"Shannon practically grew up in this house. She spent more time here than at her father's ranch." Dixie stopped by the front door and looked in the parlor. "I don't know where she disappeared to."

"Maybe she's outside." Those who weren't helping clean up after the meal were playing touch football in the yard.

"There are three bedrooms upstairs," Dixie said.

Isi stepped on a squeaky stair. "Are these the original wood floors?"

"Yep. They've taken a lot of abuse over the years and need to be refinished."

"I like the noise, it's charming."

"My grandparents never minded the loose boards, because they warned them when one of my brothers snuck into the house past curfew." Dixie stopped outside the door at the top of the stairs. "This is where Gavin and I sleep."

"Nice," Isi said.

"It's considered the master, but all three bedrooms are the same size. The only difference is that this room has three windows, not two." Dixie opened the next door.

"Cowboy and Indian wallpaper."

"Believe it or not this was my mother's room," Dixie said. "She picked out the paper. The other bedroom has fire trucks and police cars on the walls."

Isi strolled over to the window. She spotted Conway in the midst of his brothers and their girlfriends, but it was Will who her boys stood next to. Will played quarterback and Javier and Miguel blocked for him. When the ball was snapped, Buck and Merle—called Mack by family and friends—tackled the twins to the ground. Her heart ached at the thought that she and her sons would never be part of this family. "The boys haven't had this much fun in a long while."

Dixie peeked over Isi's shoulder. "They're sweet kids."

"They don't get a chance to roughhouse very often." Isi's attention shifted to Conway. Maybe she was biased, but he was by far the handsomest of the males playing football. Each Cash brother was charming in their own way, but Conway was special—he was...or had been for a short time...her Cash brother.

"You'd think my siblings would have changed the wallpaper or painted over it, but since my mother had picked it out..." Dixie shrugged.

"Conway told me that your mother passed away when you were all young."

"It was a difficult time, but Johnny was our rock, and we had our grandparents."

Sensing Dixie would rather not discuss her mother, Isi asked, "Where did you sleep, if your brothers used these two rooms?"

"Follow me." Dixie walked to a door at the end of the hall. "This used to be an old linen closet. When I came along, Grandpa Ely knocked out the back wall of the closet and sealed off a portion of the attic, turning it into a bedroom for me." Dixie ducked inside and Isi followed.

"This is adorable." Isi's gaze took in the slanted ceiling and stained-glass window near the roof line. A second window had been cut into the side of the house to hold an air conditioner. "You must have felt like a princess in a castle tower."

"You're the only one who's ever come in here and said that. My brothers view it as a cramped, unappealing attic," Dixie said.

"This is definitely a girl's room and it should never be changed."

"I agree. Let me show you the bathroom. It has all the original fixtures."

When they stepped into the hallway, the bathroom door opened and Shannon emerged, her skin pale.

Dixie rushed forward, but Shannon held up a hand. "Don't say a word."

"How far along are you?" Dixie asked.

"Two months, but—" Shannon wiped at a tear that escaped her eye.

"But," Isi said, her expression softening. "Because Dixie had a miscarriage you're afraid it might happen to you, too."

Dixie frowned. "Conway told you?"

Isi nodded.

"It's true, Dix. I've been so worried, thinking about what you went through. I don't want to tell Johnny until I'm sure everything will be okay. All he talks about is how cute Nate is and how it would be fun having our own baby." Shannon winced. "He's got my father pestering me for grandchildren."

"I thought you were going to wait to start a family?"

"We were, but…"

"Johnny really wants to be a father," Dixie said. "He misses riding herd over me and our brothers."

Isi wished Conway felt the same about fatherhood.

"Then by all means have kids now if it'll keep Johnny from sticking his nose in our business," Dixie said.

"I want to surprise him at Christmas with the news."

"Don't worry." Dixie hugged Shannon. "Isi and I will keep your secret. In the meantime, smile and enjoy the moment. You're pregnant!"

The women went outside and Dixie took over watching Nate so Gavin could play football. Shannon sat on the swing with Dixie while Isi retrieved her disposable camera from her purse and snapped pictures of the game. This was the first Thanksgiving she and the boys hadn't spent alone, and she wanted more Conway memories for their scrapbooks.

Will stepped back to pass, but when he released the ball, Porter got his fingers on it, changing the flight path and sending it straight at Isi. Instinctively she put her hands out to protect her face and ended up catching the ball.

"Run, Isi, run!" Will shouted.

She raced down the steps and darted past hands that tried to capture her. Miguel and Javier ran alongside her then Will came out of nowhere. He scooped her into his arms and dodged his brothers. Isi clung to his neck, the football smashed between their bodies. When they whizzed past Conway, she caught him gaping.

Mack dove at them and Will stumbled. Isi buried her face in his neck and squeezed her eyes closed, bracing for impact. Right before they hit the ground, Will spun and Isi landed on top of him. Hanging on to her, he rolled Isi over the goal line and everyone erupted into cheers. Will broke out in laughter and she joined in. After a minute, he crawled to his feet and helped her off the ground then twirled her in the air.

"You won the game for us, Isi!" Will flashed a cocky grin at Conway who strode toward them.

"What the heck are you doing?" Conway said.

Isi attempted to step aside, but Will's arm tightened like a steel band against her waist.

"What do you mean, what am I doing?" Will said. "I'm celebrating our victory." He smiled at Isi as he slid his hand over her hip. "We make a great team, don't we?"

"That's cheating." Conway grabbed Isi by the arm and tugged her free of Will's hold.

Isi gasped. The two brothers weren't aware that everyone had stopped playing to watch them.

Will pulled Isi back to his side. "I didn't cheat."

"Yes, you did." Conway claimed her again.

"Isi's catch was made fair and square." This time when Will reached for her, Johnny stepped between the brothers.

"I get the feeling that you two aren't talking football anymore." Johnny narrowed his eyes. "It's Thanksgiving. Behave."

Miguel and Javier wiggled their way between the adults and hugged Isi. "You won the game, Mom!" Miguel gave her a high five.

"Next year Isi's on our team." Will's gaze challenged Conway.

"Time for dessert!" Dixie hollered from the porch.

"Before everyone fills up on pumpkin pie, we need to take a vote on whether or not any of us are interested in selling out to Bell Farms."

"You know where I stand," Conway said then walked toward the barn.

Isi rushed after him. Before she left she wanted to tell him that she'd found a new sitter. "Conway!"

He stopped and waited for her to catch up. "I need to talk to you." When he didn't say anything, she asked, "Show me the pond?"

"Can we come, too?" Miguel skidded to a stop at Isi's side.

"Can we, Conway?" Javier asked.

"Lead the way." He motioned for the boys to walk

ahead. He wasn't in the best mood—not after watching Will plaster himself all over Isi as if she belonged to him.

Jealous?

Damn straight he was jealous. Some brother Will turned out to be—honing in on Isi. Conway should have never asked his brother to take her out on a date.

Then why did you?

Because I thought he was harmless! Will was supposed to have been a safe bet—a guy Conway could trust to show Isi a good time, not steal her out from under him.

You have no claim on her.

He'd made love to Isi—that meant she was off-limits to his brothers—no exceptions.

As they strolled along the path that skirted the barn, Conway couldn't ignore how much he'd missed Isi the past few days. Why did she have to be the one who touched him in a way no other woman ever had? If he could go back in time and intercept the punch Bridget had thrown at Isi's nose, he would. Then all would be right in his world.

"I wanted you to know that I found a sitter for the boys," she said.

"Who?"

"My neighbor Mrs. Sneed agreed to watch them."

"Will she drive the boys to school and pick them up?"

"Yes."

"And she's willing to stay late when you work at the bar?"

"Yes, but the boys will have to sleep at her house until I get home."

"Why can't they sleep in their own beds?"

"Mrs. Sneed won't give up her television programs, and I don't have satellite TV." Isi continued walking.

"The boys will fall asleep quickly once they're back in their own beds."

Conway didn't like the new arrangement for the twins.

You're not their father. You don't have a say. Before he pestered Isi with more questions about her neighbor, the boys raced toward the pond.

"Wait for us!" he shouted. Once they reached the water's edge, he said, "Stay here." Conway walked the perimeter of the pond then announced, "Coast is clear."

"What were you doing?" she asked.

"Searching for snakes."

Isi held fast to the boys' shirt collars. "Are you sure it's safe?"

"Positive. I haven't seen a snake in months. Not since Porter and Buck cleared out a den a mile from here last spring."

She released her hold on the twins. "You can stick your toes in the water, but don't get your clothes wet."

Mig and Javi removed their shoes and socks then waded a few feet into the water, squealing at the cold temperature.

"I can't thank you enough for all the help you've given me this semester," she said. "I don't know what I would have done if you hadn't stepped up after Nicole left me high and dry."

"I was glad to help."

"Now you can get back to farming and not worry about interruptions."

He'd finished the pecan harvest. All that remained to do was clean up the debris in the grove and next month prune the dead branches from the trees. He wouldn't be doing any of that if his siblings voted to sell out tonight.

As if Isi read his mind, she asked, "What was Johnny talking about when he said you were all supposed to cast a vote on selling the farm?"

"An agricultural company made an offer to buy the orchards."

"You don't think they'll sell, do you?"

"I don't know. I'm the only one who's willing to harvest the pecans."

"I can't picture your sister getting rid of the farmhouse. She loves your grandmother's home."

"I'll find out later tonight."

"If they decide to sell, what will you do?"

"Go back on the rodeo circuit full-time." The prospect didn't excite him.

He changed the subject. "When's your graduation ceremony?"

"They don't have one for students who finish school in December."

That wasn't right. Isi had worked her butt off to earn a degree. She deserved to celebrate her success. His gaze cut to the boys. Who would throw Isi a party—she had no family and her best friend was in California.

"Hey, Conway," Miguel said. "Can we ride on your tractor?"

Now that Isi no longer needed him to babysit this might be the last time Miguel and Javier visited the farm. No more tractor rides. No more naps in the hammock. No more visits to the pond. "Sure. We better head back before it gets dark."

The boys giggled and fell backward as they struggled to pull their socks on over wet feet.

Isi watched with a wry smile. "They're a riot, aren't they?"

Conway chuckled, but his chest felt as if it was cracking wide open. He was going to miss the little troublemakers more than he'd ever imagined.

Chapter 12

"I don't like Mrs. Sneed. She has bad breath," Miguel said.

Her son made their neighbor sound like a troll who lived under a bridge. "It's not nice to talk about people like that."

The Monday after Thanksgiving was proving to be a difficult one. The boys had been down in the dumps all weekend since they'd learned their neighbor would be babysitting them.

"How long does Mrs. Sneed gotta watch us?" Javier shoved a bite of hot dog into his mouth.

"I'll be finished with school in three weeks. Hopefully it won't be long before I find a new job and I'm able to stay home at night with you guys."

Miguel grunted as he carried his empty plate to the sink.

"Is Red gonna be mad if you get a new job?" Javier asked.

"No, honey. He wants me to use the skills I learned in school."

Javier took his plate to the sink. "What skills?"

"Stuff I learned how to do on the computer. Like keep track of product sales, orders and inventory."

"What's a product?" Javier asked.

"An item that a business sells. A product at Red's bar would be a cheeseburger basket."

Javier came back to the table and sat down. "Are toys products?"

"Yes."

"Are we gonna get products for Christmas?" Miguel asked.

"I'm sure Santa will bring you a toy."

Javier shook his head. "Katie said Santa isn't real."

The boys' classmate was supposedly the smartest kid at their school. By the time she'd turned two, she'd probably figured out Santa Claus was a myth.

"You'll have to wait until Christmas morning to see that Santa isn't a fake."

"Can we get a real tree this year?" Miguel asked.

She almost caved in just to erase the hangdog expressions from their faces. "No real tree but we'll string up Christmas lights on the trailer like we did last year." There was no money in the budget for a real tree or an artificial one—not if she hoped to purchase Christmas gifts.

"Get your backpacks and I'll walk you over to Mrs. Sneed's."

Isi prayed this day would go well and that the older woman would have patience with the twins, because if things didn't work out, she'd end up having to bring the boys to school with her and that was a no-win situation for everyone.

"How come you let the twins color with their crayons all over the porch floor?" Will asked when he stopped next to Conway in front of the farmhouse.

"I didn't let them. They got bored with their coloring books." He shrugged. "It wasn't a big deal. The porch needed painting anyway."

Will motioned to the paint can in Conway's hand. "You're going to need more than one coat to cover the marks."

"I think I can handle this." He scowled. "What are you doing at the farm in the middle of the day?"

"I stopped by to pick up a shovel then I'm heading back out." Will glanced behind him. "Where are the twins?"

"In school." Conway hadn't told anyone that he'd stopped watching the boys. He wasn't sure if it was because he didn't want to answer their nosey questions or because he thought he might change his mind and re-apply for the job.

"I get a kick out of the boys. Miguel never stops talking and—"

"What are your intentions toward Isi?" Conway set the paint can on the ground and faced his brother.

"What are you talking about?"

"You're always over at her trailer making repairs," Conway said.

"I've been helping her out. So what? I enjoy her company. She's easy to talk to."

Conway had been miffed at his brother since Thanksgiving when the twins had ignored him and followed Will around the farm all day like lost puppies. He'd didn't like being replaced.

Will eyed him suspiciously. "As a matter of fact, I'd planned to ask Isi out on a third date."

A burning sensation spread through Conway's chest. "Isi's not the kind of girl you date casually, Will. She's got kids. She needs a guy who'll be a good father to the twins not a guy who only wants to get into her bed."

"Who said I want to get into her bed?" Will grinned. "Not that I'd ever turn down an invitation from a pretty girl like—"

Before he realized what he was doing, Conway swung his fist, the punch hitting Will in the jaw. His brother stumbled backward and landed on his rump.

"What the hell did you do that for?" Will rubbed his jaw.

"Don't use Isi for sex." Conway was more worried that Isi might want to use Will to warm her bed than the other way around.

Will stared thoughtfully at Conway. "You're in love with her, aren't you?" he said.

No! Yes! "Maybe." He'd marry Isi in a heartbeat, but she had the twins…and Conway wasn't good enough to be their father. The boys deserved a man who would never turn his back on them.

Will got to his feet and brushed the seat of his pants off. "What's keeping you from asking her to marry you?"

"It wouldn't work out in the end." No way was he bringing up his long-ago visit with his birth father. It wasn't that he didn't think Will would understand or be sympathetic—after all, Will had grown up without a father, too. It had more to do with Conway's insecurities.

"If you're not willing to take a chance on Isi, then you're going to have to let her and the boys go, Conway. I'll tell you right now, there's probably more than one guy out there who'd give anything to make a life for himself with a woman like her. It's only a matter of time before that guy finds her." Will brushed past Conway and headed to the barn. "And by the way, next time you sucker punch me, I'm going to kick your ass." A minute later, he emerged with a shovel and dropped the tool into his truck bed.

Will opened the driver's-side door. "Any luck selling the pecans?"

Conway's siblings had voted to keep the farm in the family and had given him complete control over managing the orchards. Now it was up to him to find a buyer for this year's crop. "I've got two bids. I'm waiting on a third then I'll decide."

"Good luck."

Conway had a feeling his brother's well-wishes were meant for him and Isi and not the pecans. Before his brother's truck had cleared the yard, Conway's cell phone rang. He didn't recognize the number.

"Conway Cash."

"Mr. Cash this is Sandy London. I work at the Tiny Tot Learn and Play preschool."

Why was the school calling him?

"Javier and Miguel picked a fight on the playground, and they're being sent home for the day. We called their mother, but she isn't answering her phone."

"Isi's in class right now," he said.

"You're listed as an emergency contact. Would you be able to come get the boys?"

"I thought Isi's neighbor Mrs. Sneed was dropping them off and picking them up now?"

"She's not answering her phone, either."

"I'll be there as soon as I can," Conway said.

"Thank you, Mr. Cash."

He disconnected the call then jogged to his truck. Wait until Isi found out the boys had been in another fight. She was going to be spitting mad—at him. He'd been the one to tell the twins to stand up for themselves and not allow bullies to threaten them.

The drive into Yuma took longer than usual—probably because his mind wouldn't stop envisioning Isi and Will together. By the time he turned into the school parking lot he was in a bad mood. He sat in the truck and took several deep breaths, willing himself to calm down before he went into the school to get the boys.

When he entered the building, Mig and Javi were sitting in the waiting room slouched in their chairs gazing at the ceiling lights. He cleared his throat and the woman behind the desk set aside the magazine she'd been reading. He waited for the boys to smile at him, but they ignored him.

He was no longer a hero in their eyes.

"I'm Conway Cash," he said.

"Hello, Mr. Cash. Please sign here that you're taking Miguel and Javier home." She handed him a clipboard. "Thank you for coming to get them."

He scribbled his name on the paper then spoke to the boys. "Your mother isn't going to be happy about this."

Heads held high, the twins marched outside. As soon as the door shut behind them, Javier said, "What are we gonna do?"

"We're going back to the trailer to tell Mrs. Sneed she doesn't need to pick you up this afternoon."

"This sucks," Miguel said.

Conway was sure Isi didn't allow the boys to say the word *suck,* but he didn't reprimand Miguel, because… well, because.

They made the drive to the mobile-home park in silence. Conway struggled not to laugh at the boys' sullen expressions. He wanted to say he was proud they'd stood up for themselves, but he doubted Isi would approve.

Conway parked next to the trailer and helped the boys out of the backseat then motioned for them to sit on the porch steps. "Wait there." He cut across the yard to the neighbor's trailer.

Mrs. Sneed answered the door on the second knock. "Who are you?"

"My name is Conway Cash, ma'am. I'm a friend of Isi's."

The old woman nodded. "You're the young man who watched the boys for Isi."

"Yes, ma'am." Conway explained what had happened at the school.

"I don't answer my phone when my game shows are on," she said.

Did Isi know that? "I was listed as one of the emergency contacts."

"Are you taking care of the boys then?" she asked. "My game shows won't be over for a while."

"I'll watch them until Isi gets home tonight."

The relief on Mrs. Sneed's face suggested that she regretted offering to watch the boys. "Thank you," she said then closed the door.

When Conway returned to Isi's yard, the twins looked

bored. He sat on the bottom step and stretched out his legs. "Okay, let's hear it."

"Hear what?" Miguel asked.

"The reason you started a fight at recess."

Javier surprised Conway by speaking up first. "Katie said that Santa Claus is a fake."

"You fought with a girl?" Conway asked.

"No." Javier nudged Miguel and his brother explained.

"Katie told everyone that Santa was a fake and Rico got mad and shoved her and she fell and skinned her knee."

"And she cried," Javier said.

Conway was losing track of the conversation. "So who did you get into a fight with?"

"Rico," Miguel said. "Javi pushed Rico 'cause he pushed Katie and you told me I had to stick up for Javi so I pushed Rico, too."

"And let me guess," Conway said. "The recess monitor only saw you and Javi push Rico."

Both boys nodded.

"So did Rico get in trouble for pushing Katie?" Conway asked.

"Katie told our teacher that Rico started it, but we still got in trouble," Javier said.

"I'm glad you stuck up for Katie. Boys should never ever hurt girls," Conway said.

"We know. Our mom told us that." Javier bumped his brother's shoulder again.

"Is Santa really a fake?" Miguel asked.

Oh, boy. "What do you think?" Conway asked.

"Mom said Santa was real." Miguel looked at his brother.

"But if Santa's real then how come we only get one toy from our wish list and other kids get lots more?" Javier blinked his innocent brown eyes at Conway.

"Is it 'cause our mom doesn't have a lot of money?" Miguel asked.

"Money has nothing to do with Santa Claus."

"Katie said that Santa's elves aren't real and they don't make toys. She said moms and dads go to the store and buy the toys." Miguel sucked in a breath. "Is it 'cause we don't got a dad to buy us presents?"

The kid sure knew how to twist the knife in Conway's chest. He opened his mouth to contradict Katie's claim, but Javier interrupted him.

"Can you give our mom money? Then she can buy us lots of toys at the store."

"Or you can buy us a Christmas tree," Miguel said.

They weren't getting a tree—Christmas wasn't Christmas without a tree. Before he had a chance to answer the boys, Isi's car turned into the trailer park. Saved by the bell. "Time to face the music, guys."

"Another fight?" Isi glanced between her sons.

The twins studied their shoes and avoided eye contact with their mother. Conway sympathized with the boys but refrained from intervening. He'd meddled enough in their lives.

Isi shifted her attention to Conway. "I wasn't able to check my phone messages until after class, or I would have been here sooner. I'm sorry you had to drive all the way into Yuma to pick them up from school."

"I was happy to help out." That was the truth. Conway couldn't deny that he'd missed the boys and Isi. A whole lot more than he'd expected to.

"Go to your room right now. We'll discuss your behavior in a minute." Hands on her hips she glared until the twins trudged inside the trailer. Once the door closed behind them, she said, "I owe you an apology. I forgot to ask the school to remove your name as an emergency contact."

Conway stared at Isi, thinking something seemed different about her. "Seriously, Isi, it was no trouble—"

"Yes, it was trouble," she said.

"That's what's different about you." He snapped his fingers. "You're wearing your hair down." Isi usually put her long hair in a ponytail. His mind flashed back to the night he'd spent in her bed, running his hands through the silky strands. "You should leave your hair loose more often. It's beautiful."

Blushing, she changed the subject. "Why couldn't Mrs. Sneed get the boys?"

"She said she doesn't answer the phone when her game shows are on."

"Great." Isi's shoulders sagged, as if she carried the weight of the world on them. The urge to hug her was strong, but he doubted his sympathy would be welcome.

"Did the boys tell you what the fight was about?" she asked.

"Santa Claus."

"What?"

He patted the step and she sat next to him. The faint scent of her perfume triggered an image of her naked body in his mind. He shifted on the step, hoping to hide his growing arousal. Making love to Isi had released two years of pent-up desire for her and reining it back in was damn near impossible.

"What about Santa Claus?" she asked.

"A kid at school said there wasn't a Santa Claus and that moms and dads bought the toys."

Isi blinked hard.

He grasped her hand—not to offer comfort but because he had to touch her—he'd missed that intimate connection with her.

"They figured it out, didn't they?" she whispered.

"Figured what out?"

"That they get one gift at Christmas, because I don't make enough money to buy more."

"The boys have plenty of toys." He gestured to the box by the shed.

"But they're second-hand toys. Cast-offs from other kids."

He snuggled her against his side. This felt so right—him and Isi. Why couldn't he find the courage to take a leap of faith and commit to her? "You're doing the best you can for the boys. When they grow up and understand the sacrifices you've made, they'll love you even more."

"Or they'll resent me for making bad choices."

"What bad choices?"

"I made the decision to come to America with nothing but a suitcase full of clothes. Then I slept with a married man and got pregnant."

"Cut yourself some slack, Isi. You were vulnerable and scared."

"Stop being nice. I was stupid to believe Tyler really cared for me."

Conway wasn't used to doling out advice—he was used to seeking Isi's counsel. "I think you'll be happy when you hear the reason the boys got into a fight today."

"You don't have to protect them," she said.

"I'm not. Javier shoved Rico because Rico pushed

Katie to the ground after she told everyone at recess that there was no Santa Claus."

Isi smiled. "Javier stood up for Katie?"

"Yep. And when Rico shoved Javi back, Miguel stepped in and shoved Rico hard enough that the kid fell down and the recess monitor saw them."

"I'm proud of Javi for trying to protect Katie," Isi said.

"And I'm the one who told Miguel that he should always have his brother's back on the playground."

She shook her head. "So you encouraged the boys to fight rather than talk out their disagreements with other kids?"

"Kids this age don't talk, Isi. Besides, fighting was the only way I knew how to defend myself when I was in school."

"What do you mean?"

"My grandpa never taught me how to handle the ribbing I got because of my name. Johnny was the one who looked out for us."

"Johnny taught you to fight?"

"He didn't exactly teach me. I picked it up from watching him defend my brothers against bullies."

"You never told me you were teased."

"With a name like Conway Twitty Cash I've had my share of fights. Though I count myself lucky I wasn't the one named Merle. It's no wonder my brother goes by Mack."

"Why in the world did your mother name you all after country and western singers?"

"Grandma claimed that when our mom was a teenager, she'd lock herself in her bedroom and listen to the music of all the country-western greats."

"She must have known saddling you with those old-fashioned names would cause trouble."

"Our mom was never there when one of us came home from school with a black eye." And when his mother had been at the farm, she hadn't asked her children about their friends or problems they were having in school.

"Defending my name with my fists became second nature. My brothers and I were all suspended from school for fighting at least once. Johnny spent the most time in the principal's office, because he fought our battles for us until we became old enough to hold our own."

"Do people still mock your name?"

"Once in a while, but now I disarm the big-boy bullies with my smile and charm." He sobered. "I'm sorry if I overstepped my bounds, but the twins need to learn to stand up for themselves. If they don't, the bullying might snowball until one of them really gets hurt."

"I'll talk to the supervisor at the school and figure out where we go from here." She motioned to his truck. "I don't want to keep you any longer."

"I'm not in any hurry to leave." There was nothing waiting for him at the farm except an orchard full of nut trees.

She smiled. "I landed a job interview."

"When?"

"Next Thursday after my final exam. A stationery store in Yuma needs an office manager."

"Manager? That sounds impressive."

"Not really. I'd be sitting in a back room on the computer all day, but the position comes with benefits."

"Will Mrs. Sneed watch the boys while you go to the interview?"

"She's supposed to. The interview is at four-thirty then afterward, I have to work at the bar until midnight."

"I hope the interview goes well."

"Thanks. This could be a new beginning for me and the boys."

Conway forced a smile, but the future appeared anything but promising—at least for him. Isi would nail the job interview. She'd quit waitressing for Red. He'd no longer drop by the bar, because she wouldn't be there to talk to. And their friendship would fade into a fond memory.

Exactly what you want, right?

"I better get going," he said.

Isi walked him to his truck. "Thank you for being there for the boys."

He *had* been there for the boys, hadn't he? "Keep me as an emergency contact."

"You sure?"

"Positive." He toyed with his keys. "Maybe I could take the boys next Thursday, while you're at school and the interview. We could do guy stuff at the farm." Conway expected Isi to jump at the offer—her hesitation felt like a punch in the gut.

"I don't know if that's a good idea, Conway. They took it pretty hard when I told them you wouldn't be babysitting anymore."

He understood Isi's concern. He'd hurt the boys when he'd backed away, but he wasn't ready to say goodbye—not yet. "I'd like to make it up to them."

"I suppose the boys can skip school that day. Their class Christmas party is on Monday then most of the kids will be no-shows the rest of the week, because their parents are on vacation."

"What time should I pick them up?"

"Nine-thirty would be great then I can get to school early and study before my test."

"See you at nine-thirty." Conway hopped into his truck and drove off. When he adjusted his side mirror and saw Isi standing by the carport, a sharp pain struck his chest.

Leaving her didn't feel right.

"What's Conway gonna do with us, Mom?" Javier asked as Isi tied his shoes.

"I'm not sure, honey." The second Thursday in December had arrived and she'd almost phoned Conway and canceled his plans with the boys. She was torn between wanting them to have this last memory with their favorite sitter and wanting to protect them from feeling abandoned when Conway didn't come by again after today.

And she admitted she was being selfish—she wanted to see Conway one more time, too.

"How come you're not going with us?" Miguel asked.

"My final exam is this afternoon."

"Are you gonna get an A?" Javier asked.

"I hope so." Isi had lectured the boys until she was blue in the face about the importance of getting a good education, and she had proudly shared her grades with them—As, Bs and the few Cs she'd earned.

"Conway's here!" Miguel shouted from his post at the front window. He raced outside, Javier following him.

Isi ducked into the bathroom to touch up her makeup and hair. She wore black dress pants and a silky blouse with a blazer for her interview after class. She'd secured her hair in a clip on top of her head, the style making her appear older and more confident than she felt. When she emerged from the bathroom, Conway stood in the living room answering a barrage of questions from the boys.

"Where are we going?" Javier asked.

Miguel tugged on Conway's pant leg. "Can we drive the tractor?"

"Stop harassing Conway." Isi smiled.

Conway did a double-take when he saw her. "Wow. You look nice."

"Thanks. I won't have time to change clothes before the interview, so I'm stuck wearing this to school."

"Good luck with the test and the interview," he said.

She gathered her backpack and purse. "Be good for Conway and use your manners." She hugged the boys.

Conway grinned. "Don't I get one?"

"I suppose." Playing along, she stood on tiptoe and hugged Conway only he turned his head toward her and their lips bumped. She stepped back quickly but the boys caught the kiss.

"Hey, I want a kiss," Javier said.

"Me, too." Miguel stuck out his face.

Isi made a big production out of kissing the boys' cheeks then beat a hasty retreat, closing the door behind her.

"We have a lot to do," Conway said.

"You got lipstick on your face." Miguel smiled.

He rubbed his fingers over the sticky gloss on his mouth. "Is it gone?"

Javier nodded then said, "Is mine gone?" He rubbed his cheek.

"Yep. Now, here's the plan. We're throwing a graduation party for your mom."

The boys' eyes rounded. "What's a graduation party?" Miguel asked.

"It's a party to celebrate when a person finishes high school or college."

Javier clapped his hands. "I like parties."

"I talked to Red, and he said we can have the party at the bar. When your mom goes to work after her job interview, we'll all be there to surprise her. First, we need to shop for decorations."

"Do we gotta get a cake, too?" Miguel asked.

"Good thinking. We'll stop at the grocery store and pick one out."

"She likes flowers on cakes," Javier said then in the same breath asked, "Does she get presents?"

Conway hadn't thought about gifts. "Do you want to buy your mom a gift?"

Both boys shouted, "Yes!"

"What should we buy her?" Conway asked.

"A new vacuum," Javier said.

"She yells at ours 'cause it doesn't work," Miguel said.

A vacuum wasn't an exciting graduation gift. "We'll see." Maybe he'd think of the perfect present while they were shopping. "Get your jackets. We've got lots of errands to run before the big party."

Chapter 13

Isi sat across from Mr. Buford's desk in a windowless room at the back of Buford's Stationery and Office Supply and waited patiently for him to read her résumé.

"The school courses you've taken are impressive." He set the paper aside. "But you have no work experience in an office environment."

"No, sir, I don't."

"And your current employer is the Border Town Bar & Grill."

"I waitress there at night. Taking classes during the day didn't leave me with many options for evening jobs that paid well."

"I don't know if you intend to keep your waitressing position on the weekends, but all of my employees work at least one Saturday a month."

"I plan to quit my current job and I'd make child-care arrangements for any Saturday I'm scheduled to work."

Mr. Buford's gaze shifted to her left hand. "Are you married, Ms. Lopez?"

Isi swallowed a sigh. Why had she brought up the boys? "No, sir."

"I was raised by a single mother."

His confession released the tension from Isi's body.

"Making ends meet was a daily struggle for her," he said.

"The difficult times are worth it. I wouldn't trade my life for the world. Everything I do is for my sons."

"Sons?"

She smiled. "Twin four-year-olds."

"What do you do with the boys when you're in school or working at the bar?"

This wasn't a typical interview. She worried Mr. Buford was judging her character and not her job skills. "The boys are in preschool during the afternoon and a neighbor watches them until I get home from the bar."

"No family?"

She shook her head.

"My mother was all alone, too." His attention shifted to the wall across the room. "I was a latch-key kid."

Isi wasn't sure what to say.

"I'm willing to hire you on a trial basis—three months. After that time, I'll evaluate your job performance and if all goes well, I'll make you a permanent employee and you'll be eligible for benefits."

Relief made Isi light-headed. "That sounds more than fair. What hours will I be working?"

"I'm going to leave that up to you. The store hours are Monday through Saturday eight to six. As long as you handle your responsibilities, you're free to work with your sons' schedules."

Isi reminded herself to be firm and confident when she stated her salary requirements. "I'd need at least twelve dollars an hour."

"I'll start you at fourteen dollars and if you stay on after three months, I'll pay you sixteen."

Never in her wildest dreams had she believed she'd make sixteen dollars an hour.

"I give all my employees a Christmas bonus and the amount depends on the total store sales for the year." He smiled. "Incentive for everyone to work hard."

For the first time in years an exciting future awaited her. All her sacrifices might finally pay off.

"You'll begin January second." Mr. Buford scribbled on a piece of paper and handed it to Isi. "My office phone number if you need to get in touch with me or leave a message."

"Thank you for this opportunity, Mr. Buford." She shook his hand. "You won't be sorry you hired me."

"It's a pleasure to have you as part of our team, Ms. Lopez."

As soon as Isi left the stationery store, she whooped for joy, but her excitement fizzled as she drove to work. Her life was taking a turn for the better, but this new path didn't include Conway. When she arrived at the bar, she noticed only a few cars parked in the lot, which was unusual for this time of day.

She grabbed her purse and Border Town Bar & Grill T-shirt then walked to the entrance, where she found the front door locked. Had Red scheduled an employee meeting that she'd forgotten about? She went behind the building and entered through the back door. The kitchen was dark.

"Anybody in here?" She pushed through the swinging door to the barroom.

"Surprise!"

Isi jumped inside her skin.

The lights popped on, and she gaped in shock at her coworkers who blew paper horns and threw streamers and confetti into the air. Then she spotted Conway and her sons standing in front of a banner that read Congratulations Graduate! Her eyes flooded with tears.

"Yeah, Mom!" Miguel yelled. Javier mimicked his brother and the rest of the room echoed "congratulations," "good job" and "way to go, Isi."

"I don't know what to say." She wiped at her tears.

"A toast to the new graduate." Conway raised his beer bottle and several cheers followed.

She smiled through her tears. "No one's ever thrown me a party."

More horns blew. Sasha fed quarters into the jukebox and Red waved her over to see her cake.

"The boys picked it out." Conway chuckled. "They asked the lady in the bakery to put lots of flowers on it."

Isi hugged her sons then Conway. "Thank you. This is turning out to be a great day." She smiled. "I got the job."

"That's awesome, Isi." Conway whistled and a hush fell over the bar. "Hey, everyone, listen up. Isi nailed the job interview and they hired her!"

More cheers and congratulations.

"We got you a present, Mom." Javier handed her a small jeweler's box.

Isi glanced at Conway, wondering if…

Don't be stupid. It's not an engagement ring.

She held her breath as she lifted the lid on the velvet case. A silver necklace with a star pendant. The air in her lungs leaked out and she widened her smile to hide her disappointment.

"It's beautiful, boys."

"Conway said if you wear it, you can reach the stars," Javier said.

"And the necklace will remind your mom that dreams only come true if you never stop dreaming."

Isi swallowed the lump in her throat. She couldn't very well tell Conway that the star wouldn't work, because her dream-come-true stood right in front of her yet remained out of reach.

"The necklace is lovely." The star would always remind her of what she yearned for but could never have. "Let's dance." She twirled the boys and others in the crowd joined them.

Time passed in a blur. Before Isi knew it seven o'clock had rolled around and Red opened the bar to the public after he'd told her to take the night off. She thanked her coworkers for coming to her graduation party and Conway carried the leftover cake to the car for her then retrieved the boys' booster seats from his truck.

"I think we surprised your mom tonight, didn't we, guys?"

"Were you surprised, Mom?" Javier asked.

"I was. This has been the best night ever."

Conway leaned his head inside the car after the boys crawled into their seats. "Be good for your mom."

"Are you gonna come to our house tomorrow?" Miguel asked.

"No, buddy. Now that your mom is finished with school, I won't be hanging out with you guys any longer. Don't worry, though, we'll see each from time to time."

It occurred to Isi that this was her and Conway's final goodbye.

Conway stepped away from the car but didn't make eye contact with her. "Put your belts on, guys." Isi shut the door, cutting off their protests.

"Thank you, Conway. I couldn't have made it through these past couple of months without your help." *Without you*.

"I enjoyed hanging out with the boys."

"Good luck finding 'the one.'" She forced a smile. "I'll miss hearing about your trials and tribulations."

"I'll stop by the stationery store and keep you updated."

"Don't you dare." She laughed. "I don't want to lose my job." Keeping her smile in place she said, "When you do find 'the one,' it would be nice to know who she is."

"You'll be the first person I tell."

Isi couldn't stand it any longer. She hugged Conway hard then walked to the driver's side of the car.

"Isi?"

"What?"

"Take care of yourself and the boys."

"I will." She slid behind the wheel and drove off grateful their goodbye had been short. Tonight after she put the boys to bed and it sunk in that she'd not only lost the man she'd fallen in love with but also a good friend, she'd cry her eyes out.

"How come we gotta stay with Mrs. Sneed if you don't have to go to school?" Javier stood in the bathroom doorway Monday morning, watching Isi put on her makeup.

"Because you're on Christmas break and your school

is closed this week." Red had switched Isi to the day shift at the bar and she planned to use her lunch hour to shop for Christmas toys.

"I don't want to go to Mrs. Sneed's, either." Miguel joined his brother in the doorway.

"She said she'd bake cookies with you."

"I don't like cookies." Miguel's petulant expression tested Isi's patience.

"Cheer up. Christmas Eve is three days away. Aren't you excited?"

"No." Miguel stomped off.

"What's wrong with Mig, Javi?"

"He's sad."

"Why?"

"'Cause Conway's gone."

The boys had already forgotten and forgiven Conway after he'd turned down their invitation to be their dad. She wished she could rebound so quickly from life's disappointments. "You two had a lot of fun with Conway, but he's got his own life to live and…" *He doesn't want us to be a part of it.* "We have our lives to live."

"Mom."

"What, Javi?"

"Can I change my Christmas wish list?"

She stopped applying her lipstick. "We already mailed your letter to Santa."

"I don't want a black Furby."

Good thing she hadn't bought the toy yet. "What do you want?"

"I want Conway to come back."

She finished putting on her lipstick then knelt in front of her son. "Conway can't watch you anymore."

Javier leaned against her and she hugged him. If there

truly was a Santa Claus, then she'd have put Conway on her wish list, too. Javier touched the star pendant she wore. "Can we wish for Santa to bring Conway back?"

"I'm afraid Santa only delivers toys to children, not wishes."

"Conway said if we wished hard enough our wishes will come true," he said.

Isi wasn't a big fan of wish-making. After her father had disappeared, her mother had told her that if she wished hard enough for his return, one day he would come home. All those years of wishing had been for nothing. "Go play with Miguel. I'll walk you over to Mrs. Sneed's in a minute."

After Javier left the bathroom, she closed her eyes and willed the tears not to fall. How long would it be, before her and the boys' hearts finally let go of Conway?

"Who died?"

Conway shifted his gaze to the barn doorway where his brother Johnny stood.

"No one died. Why?"

"You don't normally grimace like that." Johnny walked farther into the barn and stopped next to the tractor. "What are you doing?"

"Testing the fluids."

"Did Dixie tell you that we're all gathering at the Triple D for Christmas this year?"

"Nope." His sister had left him a voicemail message last night, but he hadn't listened to it, because he hadn't been in the mood to talk to anyone.

"Shannon's brothers will be there and Clive's bringing Fiona Wilson."

"Your father-in-law is still dating the town spinster?"

"He doesn't talk about her and I don't ask questions." Johnny picked up a wrench from the toolbox and examined it.

"Shouldn't you be out punching cows or training horses?" Conway asked.

"I needed a break."

"Trouble in paradise?"

"Shannon's been cranky lately."

"Why?"

"I don't have any idea. When I mention her mood, she bites my head off."

Before he met Isi, Conway had believed himself an expert on women. Now, he didn't have a clue.

"Speaking of women, why aren't you watching Isi's boys?"

"She graduated from the community college and starts a new job next month." For a man who'd been dead set against having kids, not an hour in the day passed by when Javier and Miguel didn't cross his mind. The boys had weaseled their way into his heart and the thought of never hanging out with them again left a hollow feeling in his chest.

"Good for Isi," Johnny said. "I hope things work out for her."

So did Conway.

Johnny turned to leave then stopped. "I almost forgot to tell you. Dixie and Gavin bought a house in Yuma. The closing is in January and she wants our help moving."

"I'll be here." Where else did he have to go? After Johnny left, Conway sat in the barn a while longer and reflected on his life. He'd taken over the farm, and with the added responsibility he'd discovered that he enjoyed being the caretaker of his grandfather's orchards. This year's harvest had been a lot of work, but the bond he'd developed with the land fulfilled him in a way nothing else had—not even rodeo. He thought he'd miss riding the circuit, but the time he'd spent on the farm with Javier and Miguel had been his best days.

Maybe he should resume his mission to find "the one." He waited for the rush of adrenaline that usually hit him when he made plans to prowl the honky tonks, but the blood pumping through his veins felt sluggish.

Calling it quits for the day he returned to the bunkhouse to shower and change. He decided to drive into town and shop. He didn't exchange holiday gifts with his siblings, but he wanted to buy a toy for his nephew's first Christmas.

An image of Javier and Miguel flashed through Conway's mind. The boys were the perfect age to enjoy Christmas. They still believed in Santa Claus and he envisioned them tearing the wrapping paper from their gifts with lightning speed.

Not an hour of the day passed by when Conway didn't regret how he'd handled the situation with Javier and Miguel when they'd asked him to be their father. He'd hurt them deeply and he wanted to make it up to the boys so they wouldn't remember him in a bad light. There was no reason why he couldn't buy them a couple of Christmas gifts, too.

An hour later, Conway had showered and left the farm. As he mulled over options for gifts, his truck sped past a parked van that had pulled off the road ten miles outside of Yuma. A sign next to the vehicle read Black Labs 4-Sale.

The boys would love a dog.

Giving no thought to how Isi might feel about owning a dog, Conway made a U-turn and drove back to the van.

"How much?" he asked, studying the five puppies inside a makeshift pen.

"A hundred dollars. They're American labs, not English," the woman said.

"What's the difference?" Conway didn't know a thing about the breed.

"American labs have a longer nose and thinner body but they're more energetic."

Energetic was good. The dog would be able to keep up with the boys. Conway watched the puppies interact—four of them attempted to climb out of the pen and one hung back, watching the others. The shy puppy made Conway think of Javier. He pulled his wallet from his pocket and shelled out the money. "I'll take the one in the corner."

"That's a male."

The woman set the puppy inside a cardboard box with an old towel at the bottom before taking Conway's cash. "Be sure he sees a vet soon for a physical and his vaccinations."

"Thanks." Back on the road, Conway pushed the speed limit into Yuma—he couldn't wait to see the expressions on the boys' faces when he handed them their Christmas present.

"How come you came to get us?" Miguel followed Conway across Mrs. Sneed's yard, Javier trailing him.

"I have an early Christmas present for you." Mrs. Sneed had gladly handed over the boys and their booster seats for the afternoon after Conway promised to return them to her before Isi got off work at six.

"What kind of surprise?" Javier grasped Conway's hand. His small fingers felt fragile and Conway's chest tightened with an unexpected need to protect the kid.

"This kind of surprise." He stopped at the truck and opened the door. The boys gasped when they saw the puppy's face peeking over the edge of the box.

"Is he ours?" Miguel asked.

"Yep." Conway carried the box to the middle of the yard and sat on the ground. When he set the puppy free, the lab tried to climb the boys' legs. The twins took turns holding the dog and giggling when it licked their faces.

"What's his name?" Javier asked.

"He doesn't have one. You two need to come up with a name for him."

"How come you gave us a dog?" Miguel squealed when the puppy pawed at his hair.

"Because all little boys should grow up with a dog." And because the dog would be there for the boys for the rest of its life—unlike Conway.

"Missy has a dog named Pringles," Miguel said.

"Who's Missy?"

"She lives with her grandma across the street," Javi said.

Miguel petted the dog. "We can call him Captain America."

"That's dumb." Javier shoved his brother's shoulder.

Miguel shoved back. "You're dumb."

"No fighting. You can think of names while we run errands." Conway put the dog in the box.

"Where are we going?" Miguel asked.

"The puppy needs to see a doctor to make sure he's healthy." Conway knew of one pet store that had a veterinary clinic inside it. He'd gone there once with a girl-friend whose cat had become sick.

After the boys were belted in, Conway drove across town. The vet appointment took an hour and the puppy passed inspection. A vet tech talked Conway into purchasing pet insurance to cover neutering, yearly vaccinations and dental care.

Puppy supplies were next on the list. The boys selected a red collar and leash. Conway tossed an extra collar into the basket, warning the boys that the dog would outgrow the smaller one in a few months. The boys asked how big the dog would get and Conway found a book with pictures of full-grown labs.

"He's gonna be big," Javier said.

"Big enough to handle you two." Conway put the book into the cart, in case Isi had questions on training the dog. "Next, we need food and chew toys."

By the time he rolled the shopping cart up to the counter, the basket was overflowing. He'd purchased enough food to last three months, because he didn't want the dog to be a financial burden on Isi.

He and the boys hauled their stash to the truck then returned to the trailer where Conway laid Isi's ironing board across the floor in front of the bathroom and told the boys that the puppy would have to remain in the room until he was trained to do his business outside. Javier spread the piddle pads across the floor and Miguel filled the water bowl, then Conway set the puppy on his towel and he curled into a ball and went to sleep.

"Make sure you tell your mom that the vet said to feed the dog twice a day—once in the morning and once at suppertime. And you need to take him outside to do his job right after he eats, okay?"

"What's his job?" Javier asked.

"Poop. You don't want the dog to do that on the floor or on top of your bed."

"Eew!" Javier pinched his nose. "Yuck!"

"C'mon. Time to go to Mrs. Sneed's."

The boys didn't want to leave the puppy and spent ten more minutes saying goodbye before they followed Conway outside. After placing the house key in the potted plant on the porch, both Miguel and Javier hugged Conway's leg and thanked him for the puppy.

"Be good to your new best friend, okay?" Conway crouched in front of the boys. "Never hit the dog and never throw anything at him or tug on his legs or ears, okay?"

"We won't."

"You treat him kindly, and he'll be your friend for life." Conway stood.

"Are you gonna come back and see the puppy?" Javier asked.

"Probably not for a while." They walked in silence to the neighbor's trailer.

When Mrs. Sneed opened the door, Javier said, "Conway bought us a new puppy for Christmas."

After the boys went inside, Conway said, "The puppy's penned in the bathroom right now."

"Okay." Mrs. Sneed smiled and shut the door in his face, no doubt eager to get back to whatever TV program she was watching.

Conway considered waiting for Isi to return to warn her about the dog but he chickened out. After letting her and the boys down, there was no telling what he'd do or how far he'd go to make amends.

Chapter 14

"Mom, you're gonna be excited about the present Conway got us for Christmas," Miguel said as he and his brother followed Isi to their trailer.

When she'd arrived at Mrs. Sneed's to pick up her sons, her neighbor informed her that Conway had spent the afternoon with the boys. Isi didn't know what to make of his visit or his buying her sons Christmas gifts.

As soon as she opened the door and stepped into the trailer, a tiny bark stopped her in her tracks.

Oh, no.

The boys raced down the hallway to the bathroom.

"It's a black lab," Javier said.

"I see." The puppy's tail wagged so hard his back end danced.

"Conway bought us a dog for Christmas and food and toys and bones." Javier went into the kitchen and returned with a folder of paperwork. "Our dog gets to go to the vet for free."

Conway had thought of everything, except who would take the dog outside during the middle of the day when she was at work and the boys were in school.

Miguel cuddled the puppy against his chest. The poignant picture tugged at her heart. The dog would go a long way in helping her sons cope with Conway's absence, but like her graduation necklace, the dog would always remind her of Conway. Emotions aside, this wasn't the right time in their lives to own a pet, not with her starting a new job.

"Maybe you should take him outside and see if he has to go to the bathroom."

"Conway said we have to feed him dinner first," Miguel said. "Then we take him outside so he doesn't poop in the house."

"Does he have a name?" she asked.

Javier spoke up. "We wanna name him Bandit."

"Why Bandit?"

"'Cause that's the name of Mr. Mighty's dog."

Mr. Mighty was a cartoon show the boys watched on Saturday mornings. Isi scratched the puppy behind his ears. "I guess you do look like a Bandit."

A half hour later the puppy had eaten and done his job and now slept between the boys on the floor while they played with their building blocks. Isi got out the camera and snapped a few photos for the infamous scrapbooks then paced the kitchen floor, debating how to handle the situation. They couldn't keep the dog. She didn't have the money to pay for food and treats and bones and then after a year she'd have to pay for vet bills. If she had to spend her savings on a dog, how was she supposed to buy a new car or move her and the boys into a nice apartment?

A lump formed in her throat as she watched the boys cuddle Bandit. She didn't want to be the bad guy and tell her sons that they couldn't keep the dog. Tomorrow, after she dropped them off at Mrs. Sneed's, she'd ask Conway to come get the dog.

Conway pulled up to Isi's trailer at three-thirty. She'd asked him to meet her at four. He got out of the truck and sat on the stoop to wait. He knew what this was about—the dog.

The strain in her voice when she'd left a message telling him she couldn't keep Bandit had been obvious. He'd overstepped his bounds. If he was honest, he'd admit that he'd only been thinking of himself when he'd gotten the dog for the boys. He'd felt bad that he'd walked out on the twins and had wanted to appease his guilt.

He worried about Javier and Miguel's reaction when they found out their mother wasn't going to let them keep Bandit. Everything he did only seemed to make things worse. He heard the clunking sound of Isi's car engine before she pulled beneath the carport. The boys hopped out of the backseat, wearing huge grins.

"Conway's here!" Javier scrambled up the porch steps and sat next to him.

"Did you come to see Bandit?" Miguel sat on the other side of Conway.

"We named him Bandit," Javier said.

Isi's brown eyes clouded with concern. She didn't say a word as she stepped past Javier and went into the trailer. He deserved her silence.

"He's getting bigger?" Miguel said.

Right then Isi opened the door and handed over the puppy then returned inside the trailer as if she couldn't stand to see her sons' faces when Conway broke the bad news.

The boys played with Bandit in the yard, their love for the dog obvious. Conway felt worse by the second. "Hey, guys. Bring Bandit over here and sit down."

Once they were settled on the steps and Bandit happily chewed on a bone, Conway said, "I have bad news."

The twins frowned.

"Bandit can't live at the trailer."

"Why not?" Miguel asked.

"It's my fault. I should have asked your mother if it was okay to give you guys a dog."

"But our mom likes Bandit," Javier said.

"Of course she does, but she works long hours and you two are in school during the day. Bandit's going to grow into a big dog and he needs more space to run around than this small yard."

Javier picked up the puppy and hugged him to his chest. "But he's ours. We don't want you to take him back."

Conway struggled to draw air into his lungs. "I'm not going to take him back."

"Where's he gonna go?" Miguel asked.

"He's going to live at the pecan farm. You guys can visit him anytime you want." For a man who was trying to break ties with this small family, he was failing miserably.

"But the farm is far away," Javier said.

"Bandit will have plenty of room to run at the farm. When you and your mom visit him, you can spend all day there, if you want."

"What if our mom won't take us to see Bandit?" Miguel asked.

"Then I'll bring him over to your house." Right now he'd do just about anything to erase the sad expressions on the boys' faces. "I promise I'll take good care of Bandit for you."

The trailer door opened and Isi stepped outside, her eyes darting between her sons. Javier hugged Bandit then set the puppy down and went inside. Miguel did the same, but as he passed his mother he glared and said, "You're mean."

"Isi, I'm sorry. I never meant for this to—"

She motioned to the storage shed. "Don't forget the bags of dog food and other supplies you bought."

So much for trying to make the boys' Christmas special—he'd ruined it instead.

"Is Nate having trouble sleeping again?" Conway asked Dixie as he climbed the porch steps.

"Yes." His sister patted the empty spot next to her on the swing.

"Kind of chilly out here to be rocking him, isn't it?"

"Nate's plenty warm in his blanket, besides, the cooler air soothes him."

They rocked in silence, until she said, "What's troubling you?"

He didn't know where to begin. When it came to spilling his guts…she was his baby sister and he didn't share his problems with her.

"You're in love with Isi," she said.

"How did you—"

"I guessed you were in love with her at Thanksgiving. You couldn't take your eyes off of her during dinner then you did everything possible to avoid her afterward. And when Will made a move on her playing football your skin actually turned green with jealousy."

"It did not," he said.

Dixie snorted. "You and Will had a tug-of-war match over Isi."

"You noticed, huh?"

"Noticed? You guys almost yanked the poor woman's arm off her body." Dixie smiled. "I was beginning to think she and Will had feelings for each other then she went off with you on a walk." She shifted Nate in her arms. "Is there some sort of love triangle going on between the three of you?"

"Isi told me she wanted to start dating and a coworker set her up with a guy who turned out to be a jerk so I said I'd find her a date."

"So you asked Will to take her out." Dixie chuckled.

"What's so funny?"

"You thought Will would be a safe date, didn't you?"

"Heck, yeah." Conway crossed his arms over his chest, not sure he liked opening up to his sister. "Will's older. Mature. He's not like younger guys who want jump into bed with—"

"Are you sure we're talking about the same brother?"

"What do you mean?"

"Will is all those things you said, but don't you remember he had a reputation in high school of being a bad boy?"

Conway thought back to those days and recalled his brother working three part-time jobs to save up enough money to buy a used Harley. The bike had been a babe magnet. "I forgot about the motorcycle."

"I can tell you from my observations on Thanksgiving that Isi only has eyes for you."

"She couldn't escape fast enough after dinner when she went into the house to help you with the dishes," Conway said.

"Men don't get it. If a woman loves a man that she knows she'll never have, she's not going to torment herself and allow the guy to keep coming around."

Was that why Isi told him to take the dog—because she'd been worried that he'd drop by the trailer to check on it?

"Isi's a nice girl, Conway, and her boys are cute." Dixie sighed. "But you're not going to propose to her, are you?"

He shook his head.

"What are you afraid of?"

He'd never shared this story with any of his siblings—that he was willing to now, caught him off guard. "I think you were about fourteen when I found my father working as a ranch hand in northern Arizona."

"What's his name?"

"Zachary Johnson."

"I'm guessing your visit didn't go well, since you never mentioned it before now."

Conway shook his head. "He said he'd tried to do right by me and Mom but after six months he cut out on us, because he'd felt trapped by the responsibility of raising all of us."

"Did you ask him why he never visited you through the years?"

"He said he didn't know anything about being a father. His old man had cut out on him and his mother, too. And his grandfather had done the same to his wife and child."

"And you're afraid if you make a commitment to Isi, you'll end up running, too?"

That's exactly what he thought, but hearing Dixie say it out loud twisted his stomach into knots.

"What if you're nothing at all like your father?" she asked.

"Isi's sons have already been ditched by one father. It would be cruel if I married Isi then discovered I wasn't cut out to be a father and left her and the boys high and dry."

"Do you love Isi?" she asked.

"Yes."

"Then don't *try*—make it work."

"You're not listening to what I said."

"I heard you. Did your father say he loved Mom?"

Conway thought back on their conversation. "I don't think so." He doubted his father had loved anyone.

"When you love a person with all your heart, everything's on the table and everything's possible."

"What if I can't stick it out?"

"What if you can? What if you stay, and you turn out to be the best husband and father any wife and children could ask for? Are you willing to sacrifice your love for Isi, because you're afraid?"

Conway got up from the swing and walked to the end of the porch. "You make it sound simple."

"Give yourself credit, Conway. You're still here with the family."

"What do you mean?"

"If you were a cut-and-run guy, you would have left us long ago. But you stayed."

He'd never thought of it like that, but maybe his sister had a point.

"And you know why you didn't leave?"

"I'm sure you're dying to tell me," he said, flashing a smile.

"Because you love us and we love you."

Love. Was it possible that the four-letter word held more power over him than fear? "Miguel and Javier deserve a man who knows how to be a father. I've got no experience raising kids." Shoot, he'd already made the mistake of buying the boys a dog and then taking it away from them. And look at the trouble he'd caused when he'd given Javier advice about fighting—the kid had gotten suspended from school.

"You may share your father's genetics, but you also share genes with your brothers and Grandpa Ely. All of them have taught you dedication, caring and responsibility."

What Dixie said made sense. Maybe the two genes would cancel each other out and Conway could start fresh and determine his own destiny.

"None of us had the best parents in the world, but I intend to love my son with everything inside me and hopefully my love will make up for my parenting mistakes."

"I want to believe love is enough." But he had an unproven track record.

"If your father would have apologized for abandoning you and asked for your forgiveness and an opportunity to be a part of your life, would you have given him a second chance?" Dixie asked.

Conway didn't have to think about his answer. "Yes." Having a father, no matter when he came along in his life, was something he'd always wished for.

"There's your answer, Conway. All a child really wants is to know they're loved and that their parents care what happens to them." Dixie smiled. "And you know what else?"

"What?"

"You already said you love Isi. Her sons are a part of her, so I know you love the boys, too."

He swallowed hard. Yes, he cared about Javier and Miguel. Cared about their feelings. Worried over them being bullied at school and wanted to keep them safe from harm. All that caring added up to love.

"The boys don't need a perfect father, Conway. They need a father to love them, faults and all, and not expect them to be *perfect*." She stroked the top of Nate's fuzzy head.

"I guess I have a lot to think about," he said.

"Where's Bandit?"

"Sleeping in the bunkhouse."

Dixie smiled as she shook her head.

"What now?"

"You determined your own destiny when you bought the dog."

"I'm not following."

"Whether you realized it or not, you bought that dog to tie Isi and the boys to you."

"You're crazy." His protest lacked conviction. He had been searching for a way to keep Isi in his life after he stopped babysitting the boys.

"Thanks for letting me bend your ear, Dix." His sister had given him much to ponder.

"I don't know if this will help you decide what to do about Isi, but now that Gavin and I are moving into

Yuma, the farmhouse will be empty. Grandma Ada would want it to be filled with children again."

"Are you saying what I think you're saying?"

"I'm giving you first dibs on the house, but don't take long to decide. After watching one of those HGTV design shows, Porter's talking about making one of the bedrooms upstairs into a man cave."

"Porter needs to get a life."

Dixie laughed. "Conway."

"What?"

"Don't forget we're spending Christmas at the Triple D. We're supposed to be there by noon."

"I won't forget."

"The lights on that store are pretty," Isi said as she drove down a residential street Christmas Eve. The boys remained silent.

She felt like the Grinch. Her idea to drive through town and view holiday lights was a bust, and neither of her sons cared that Santa was coming tonight after they went to bed. The spirit had been sucked out of the holiday the moment she'd forced Conway to take Bandit home with him. Her life had been going along fine until that darn Bridget had broken her nose, then Isi's carefully controlled world had turned into... *fun*.

Conway had brought joy and laughter and good times into her and the boys' lives. Since the twins had been born, she'd worked hard to shelter them from the pain of their father's abandonment. Then Conway had crashed into their lives, showing her that she wasn't enough for her sons—they needed a father. A male role model. But before she'd had a chance to find that man her sons had formed an attachment to Conway and then he'd left them all with broken hearts.

Isi had allowed herself to get lost in the fantasy of being Conway's "the one" and she'd fallen in love with him, even knowing that he didn't want children. Her heart ached for the pouting boys in the backseat. She'd gladly sacrifice her own happiness to put smiles on their faces. Maybe she and Conway could share custody of Bandit. He could keep the dog during the week, and on weekends the puppy could live at the trailer.

Conway had made it clear he didn't want kids, but sharing a dog would keep him involved in the boys' lives. He wouldn't have any responsibility for them, but the twins could turn to him for advice about girls or guy troubles as they grew older.

What about you? How will you ever move on and find a man to love if Conway is always around reminding you that no other man will ever live up to him? She'd have to cross that bridge when she came to it.

"I was thinking," she said. "What if I talked to Conway about the possibility of sharing Bandit."

"How are we gonna share Bandit?" Miguel asked.

"After I begin my new job in January, I won't be working most weekends. Bandit could live with us on Saturday and Sunday and then stay at the farm during the week."

"I want Bandit to live with us all the time," Javier said.

"I know you do, honey, but both Conway and I told you that it wouldn't be fair to leave a dog like Bandit inside a trailer all day."

"What if Bandit wants to stay in our trailer?" Miguel asked.

If dogs could talk… "If you had a choice of running loose at the farm or being cooped up inside the trailer what would you choose?"

"The farm," Miguel said glumly.

"Should we ask Conway if Bandit could stay with us on the weekends?" She held her breath.

"Okay," Miguel said.

"What do you think, Javier?"

"Me, too. I want Bandit to stay with us."

"I'll call Conway after the holidays and discuss the idea with him." Isi turned into the trailer park.

"Mom, Conway's here!" Miguel unlocked his seat belt as she pulled beneath the carport. "Can we ask him now?"

Isi's heart pounded in her chest. What was Conway doing here on Christmas Eve?

"He brought Bandit, Mom!" Javier opened his door and the boys raced over to the porch where Conway sat with the dog. The puppy recognized the boys and barked a greeting.

"Hello, Conway." She stared at him, afraid if she blinked he'd vanish.

"I didn't know if you had plans Christmas Eve," he said.

"We were out looking at the holiday lights." Lord, he looked good tonight. She could smell his aftershave from five feet away and he'd pressed his jeans and Western shirt. She wondered what the special occasion was.

"I thought maybe you and the boys would like to spend Christmas Eve and Christmas Day at the farm with me and Bandit," he said.

Isi's first thought was the camera sitting on the

kitchen counter. One more memory for the boys' scrap-books—Christmas with Conway.

"Can we go, Mom?" Miguel begged.

"What about Santa?" She nibbled her lower lip. Even if the boys were on the fence about whether Santa Claus was real or not, she wanted to pretend at least for one more year.

"Santa stops at our farm," Conway said.

"Is there a place for the boys and me to sleep?" She'd like nothing more than to sleep in Conway's bed but that wasn't going to happen with all the Cash brothers sleeping in the bunkhouse.

"Dixie changed the sheets on the queen-size bed in the guest room and the boys and I can camp out in the yard." He grinned at the twins. "You guys ever sleep in a tent?"

Javier's eyes grew round. "What's a tent?"

"I guess that answers my question." Conway turned his brown eyes on Isi. "What do you say, Isi? Will you let us camp out tonight?"

Miguel and Javier tugged her hands and Bandit jumped on her leg as if he was begging her to allow the boys to spend the night at the farm.

She had no idea what Conway's invitation meant, but she seized the opportunity to salvage the holiday for her sons. "Okay, we'll camp out at the farm."

The boys shouted and jumped for joy.

"I'll need to bring warm clothes and blankets," she said.

"We've got sleeping bags in the tent and extra pillows," Conway said. "The boys and I will stay out here and play with Bandit while you get their things together."

Taking her cue, Isi went inside and packed the boys'

Christmas presents in a duffel bag then covered them with clothes. She threw in their teddy bears in case they got scared in the tent then added her makeup bag, toiletries and tooth brushes.

"All set?" Conway asked when she stepped outside.

"I think so. Boys, go use the bathroom before we head to the farm." Once the twins went inside, Isi said, "I'm sorry."

"For what?"

"For being such a grump about the dog." She smiled at Bandit who chewed on the tip of Conway's boot. "I told the boys that maybe you and I can work out a visitation schedule for Bandit so he can stay at the trailer on weekends."

Conway didn't make eye contact with her, and Isi sensed something troubled him. If they'd been at the bar, she would have asked him what was the matter, but after they'd slept together it wasn't the same between them. "If sharing Bandit is a hassle, I understand."

"We'll work it out." He stood when Miguel and Javier returned.

Isi smiled as she watched the boys play with the dog. Conway had been right to get them a companion—an animal that would love them unconditionally. If only she could find a man who loved her no matter what, too.

Five minutes later, Conway installed the booster seats in his truck and they piled in. The twins chatted the whole way to the farm with Bandit sleeping between them on the backseat.

Conway clenched the wheel tighter as he turned onto the road leading to the farmhouse. He was excited for the twins to see the Christmas tree he'd bought and strung lights on. Every kid deserved to find his presents from Santa beneath a real Christmas tree.

When he pulled into the yard, Javier shouted, "A Christmas tree!"

Standing in the middle of the yard was a twelve-foot spruce with twenty strings of colored lights wrapped around it. Conway had purchased extra extension cords and had plugged them into the outlets on the side of the bunkhouse. Right behind the tree was the tent he'd pitched earlier in the day.

As soon as he parked, the boys hopped out and raced to the tree, Bandit barking as he ran after them. Isi joined her sons and admired the spruce. "This is the most beautiful tree I've ever seen," she said.

The farmhouse door opened and Dixie and Gavin stepped outside. "Merry Christmas, everyone!" Dixie called.

Gavin and Dixie joined Conway and Isi in front of the tree. "Conway was out here all day stringing those lights," Gavin said.

"I've never seen a tree with so many lights." She smiled at Conway. "The branches are hardly visible."

The bunkhouse door banged open. Buck, Porter, Mack and Will walked out wearing Santa hats, Mack strumming his guitar. Bandit ran toward the Cash brothers and Miguel and Javier chased after the dog.

"Where's the hot chocolate?" Mack asked.

"I'll make it right now." Dixie took Isi's hand. "Would you help me inside? I've got cookies in the oven."

After Isi and Dixie went into the house, Miguel tugged on Conway's hand. "Can Javi and I take Bandit into the tent?"

"Sure, but don't let Bandit do his job in there," Conway said.

As soon as the boys were out of earshot, Will spoke. "Are you getting cold feet?"

"No way. I'm ready." Nothing had ever felt as right as wanting to ask Isi to marry him.

Porter jabbed his elbow in Mack's side and whispered. "I told you Conway was serious about proposing to her."

With Dixie's help, Conway had set the scene for his wedding proposal. He wanted his siblings to be present when he asked the most important question of his life. Conway had hoped if Isi had any doubts, his brothers would vouch for him. "Where's Johnny?" he asked his brothers.

"Looks like he's coming right now." Porter pointed to the lights cutting through the trees on the road leading to the farmhouse.

Johnny parked his pickup next to the other vehicles in the yard. He and Shannon got out and joined them in front of the tree.

"Conway, the tree is beautiful." Shannon slipped her arm through Johnny's and said, "Next year we should use colored lights instead of white ones on our tree."

"Colored lights are more for kids than adults," Johnny said.

"Exactly." Shannon ignored Johnny's perplexed frown and moved closer to the tree.

"You have the ring?" Buck asked.

Conway patted his pants pocket. "Right here." He could only afford a small diamond and he hoped Isi wouldn't mind that she wasn't getting a rock like the diamond Gavin had picked out for Dixie.

A few minutes later, Dixie and Isi came outside with

a pitcher of hot chocolate, plastic cups and a plate of cookies.

The boys came out of the tent and joined the adults. While everyone drank cocoa and ate cookies, Conway rehearsed in his mind what he wanted to say but he kept getting confused and mixing up his sentences. In the end, he gave up because there were no words to convey his love for Isi. After a few minutes, conversation died down and Dixie looked expectantly at him.

Porter cleared his throat.

Mack strummed a chord on his guitar.

Buck grinned.

Will winked at Isi.

And when Johnny made eye contact with him and nodded, Conway knew he was ready.

"What's going on?" Isi glanced between Conway and his siblings.

Dixie handed the pitcher to Gavin then herded the twins closer to Isi.

Conway dropped to one knee in front of them and took Isi's left hand in his. Her eyes grew round.

Keep it short and simple and don't screw up.

"Isi, I know you can do better than me, but you're 'the one' and you've been right in front of me for two years. I love you and—" he smiled at the boys "—I love Javi and Mig. Will the three of you marry me?"

Tears leaked from Isi's eyes. "Are you sure, Conway?"

He dug the ring out of his pants' pocket. "This is how sure I am." He slid the diamond over her finger then stood.

Isi flung herself at Conway. "Yes, I'll marry you." After a heated kiss she said, "I fell in love with you a long time ago when you first walked into the bar and swept me off my feet."

Conway turned to the twins. "Boys, I'd sure like to be your dad. Will you let me?"

Javier stepped forward and buried his face against Conway's thigh. Miguel offered Conway a high five then chased Bandit, shouting, "Conway Twitty Cash is gonna be my dad! Conway Twitty Cash is gonna be my dad!"

The adults laughed and offered their congratulations. Then Conway pulled Isi close and whispered, "I've been dying to kiss you forever." The kiss was slow and sweet and everything Conway had dreamed it would be.

When the kiss ended, Isi whispered in his ear, "I promise I'll love you so much and so hard for the rest of my life that you'll never want to leave me or the boys."

Conway closed his eyes, his throat thickening with emotion. "I'm going to hold you to that promise, Isi, because there's nowhere else I'd rather be than with the three of you."

Mack strummed his guitar. "I'm taking requests."

Isi smiled at Conway and said, "I've Already Loved You In My Mind."

Conway was familiar with the song about a guy who meets a girl in a bar. He pulled Isi into his arms and they slowed danced in front of the Christmas tree while Mack's baritone voice serenaded them. Dixie and Gavin joined the dancing couple then Johnny and Shannon. Porter grabbed Miguel and danced with him and Buck twirled Javier.

"How did I get stuck dancing with the dog?" Will laughed and picked up Bandit.

"I'll never forget this Christmas, Conway." Isi snuggled closer.

Neither would he, because tonight marked the end of the long line of cut-and-run cowboys he'd descended from.

Christmas Day at the Triple D was unlike anything Isi had ever experienced. The scent of fresh-cut evergreen, cinnamon and roasting turkey filled the ranch house. An eight-foot evergreen with twinkling white lights stood in the corner of the living room and presents wrapped in shiny red paper rested beneath its branches—mostly gifts for Javier and Miguel and Dixie's son, Nathan. Isi was overwhelmed by the Cash family's generosity toward her and her sons.

Her heart burst with joy and happiness as she watched Javi and Mig open their gifts from Johnny and Shannon. A squawk drew her attention to Nate. Drool hanging from his mouth, the baby sat on his uncle Mack's knee, watching the twins tear at the wrapping paper. Out of the corner of her eye, Isi saw Dixie maneuver Gavin beneath a sprig of mistletoe and kiss him. Fiona Wilson slipped her hand through Clive Douglas's as they stood in front of the fireplace and watched the group. Shannon's brothers Luke and Matt regaled Porter, Buck and Will with humorous stories of their latest court trial, while Shannon snuggled in Johnny's arms next to the tree.

"The family can be overwhelming until you get used to them." Conway wrapped his arm around her waist.

"I love your family." She wiped at a tear.

"Why are you crying?"

"I wish my parents and brothers could see how happy you've made me and the boys."

"I'd like to believe they know how happy we are," he said.

She hugged Conway then pulled away when Dixie approached and handed her a gift.

Embarrassed, Isi said, "I didn't know we were exchanging gifts."

"We're not," Dixie said. "It's a welcome-to-the-family present. Open it."

Isi peeled off the candy-cane paper and removed the lid on the box. A set of shiny keys rested on a bed of cotton. "Do you know what these are for?" Isi asked Conway.

He nodded but Dixie explained. "Gavin and I closed on our new house in Yuma and we're moving in two weeks. I want you, Conway and the boys to live in the farmhouse."

Isi pressed a hand to her thumping heart. "Shouldn't your brothers have first dibs on the house?"

"Grandma Ada always said that a farmhouse was meant to be filled with children and I could tell how much you loved the place when you came for Thanksgiving." Dixie squeezed Isi's hand. "My grandmother would be thrilled to know the house is in your loving hands and that Javier and Miguel's laughter will fill the rooms."

"I don't know what to say." Isi forced the words past the lump in her throat.

"Say yes to the house, Isi," Conway said.

"Yes!" Isi hugged Dixie.

"I'd like to make an announcement," Shannon said.

The chatter stopped and everyone's attention turned to Shannon. "First, I'd like to apologize to my husband for being in such a bad mood the past few weeks. I'm afraid my emotions have been off-kilter since…" Shannon smiled at Johnny. "I found out I'm pregnant."

Johnny's mouth sagged.

"Well hot dang, we got ourselves another baby coming in the family," Porter said.

"Who's having a baby?" Miguel asked.

"Aunt Shannon." Dixie crossed the room to hug her best friend.

"Is it a girl baby or a boy baby?" Javier asked.

"I don't know, Javi." Shannon smiled at her stunned husband. "We won't find out until next June."

Shannon's father hugged her. "Congratulations, daughter. Regardless if it's a girl or a boy, I suspect we'll have another bull rider in the family."

"That'll give Johnny more gray hair," Porter said.

Conway laughed. "Hey, big brother. You gonna just stand there with your jaw scraping the floor or are you going to kiss your wife?"

Johnny took Shannon in his arms and kissed her while the rest of the Cash clan hollered encouragement.

"I'd like to propose a toast." Will held up his beer bottle. "To Conway and Isi—may you always find happiness in each other's arms and to Shannon—thank you for giving our brother his own kid to worry about, so he'll stop sticking his nose in our business."

Laughter and ribbing followed Will's statement. Isi tapped her wineglass against Conway's beer bottle. In the future, maybe they'd add a second set of twins to their little family, but if not, she'd still be the happiest woman alive, because Conway had given her a dream come true—a father for her sons and her very own happy ever after.

* * * * *

WE HOPE YOU ENJOYED
THIS BOOK FROM

Believe in love. Overcome obstacles. Find happiness.

Relate to finding comfort and strength in the
support of loved ones and enjoy the journey
no matter what life throws your way.

6 NEW BOOKS AVAILABLE EVERY MONTH!

**IF YOU ENJOYED THIS BOOK
WE THINK YOU WILL ALSO LOVE**

LOVE INSPIRED

INSPIRATIONAL ROMANCE

Uplifting stories of faith, forgiveness and hope.

Fall in love with stories where faith helps
guide you through life's challenges, and discover
the promise of a new beginning.

6 NEW BOOKS AVAILABLE EVERY MONTH!

"I am so sorry," Daisy told Joe as they walked down the sidewalk together.

The sun had come out and it was warm. The kind of day that made her long for spring.

"I don't know that I need an apology," Joe told her. "But an explanation would be a good start."

She shook her head. "I saw you sitting with your family, and I knew how I'd feel. Ambushed."

"I could have handled it. Now I'm engaged." He tossed her a dimpled grin. "What am I supposed to tell them when I don't have a wedding?"

"I got tired of your smug attitude and left you at the altar?" she asked, half teasing. "Where are we walking to?"

"I'm not sure. I guess the park."

"The park it is," she told him.

Daisy smiled down at the stroller. Myra and Miriam belonged with their mother, Lindsey. Daisy got to love them for a short time and hoped that she'd made a difference.

"It'll be hard to let them go," Joe said.

"It will be," Daisy admitted. "I think they'll go home after New Year's."

"That's pretty soon."

"It is. We have a court date next week."

"I'm sorry," Joe said, reaching for her hand and giving it a light squeeze.

"None of that has anything to do with what I've done to your life. I've complicated things. I'm sorry. You can tell your parents I lost my mind for a few minutes. Tell them I have a horrible sense of humor and that we aren't even friends. Tell them I wanted to make your life difficult."

"Which one is true?" he asked.

"Maybe a combination," she answered. "I *do* have a horrible sense of humor. I *did* want to mess with you."

"And the part about us not being friends?"

"Honestly, I don't know what we are."

"I'll take friendship," he told her. "Don't worry, Daisy, I'm not holding you to this proposal."

She laughed and so did he.

"Good thing. The last thing I want is a real fiancé."

"I know I'm not the most handsome guy, but I'm a decent catch," he said.

She ignored the comment about his looks. The last thing she wanted to admit was that when he smiled, she forgot herself just a little.

Don't miss
The Rancher's Holiday Arrangement *by Brenda Minton,*
available November 2020 wherever
Love Inspired books and ebooks are sold.

LoveInspired.com

HARLEQUIN

*Heartfelt or suspenseful,
inspiring or passionate, Harlequin
has your happily-ever-after.*

With new books published
every month, you are sure to find the
satisfying escape you know you deserve.

SIGN UP FOR THE HARLEQUIN NEWSLETTER

Be the first to hear about great new
reads and exciting offers!

Harlequin.com/newsletters

Love Harlequin romance?

DISCOVER.

Be the first to find out about promotions, news and exclusive content!

f Facebook.com/HarlequinBooks

🐦 Twitter.com/HarlequinBooks

📷 Instagram.com/HarlequinBooks

📌 Pinterest.com/HarlequinBooks

ReaderService.com

EXPLORE.

Sign up for the Harlequin e-newsletter and download a free book from any series at **TryHarlequin.com**

CONNECT.

Join our Harlequin community to share your thoughts and connect with other romance readers!
Facebook.com/groups/HarlequinConnection

◆HARLEQUIN

HSOCIAL2020